A Good Man?

A Good Man?

FARRAN V. HANK HELMICK

iUniverse, Inc.
Bloomington

A Good Man?

iUniverse books may be ordered through booksellers or by contacting:

iUniverse
1663 Liberty Drive
Bloomington, IN 47403
www.iuniverse.com
1-800-Authors (1-800-288-4677)

ISBN: 978-1-4620-6060-3 (sc)
ISBN: 978-1-4620-6061-0 (ebk)

Printed in the United States of America

iUniverse rev. date: 12/14/2011

EDICATION

I dedicate this book to my very first critic and
fan, the mother of my children
Barbara Lee [Spillane] Helmick
On the anniversary of her birthday, and the
anniversary of the completion of my western novel.
September 13, 1924—2010

I also dedicate my first effort to write a western novel to
Theresa Pogue and Heidi Pogue and Jeanne Lobel
My first critics.

SYNOPSIS

In 1877 young horse breeder Matt O'Shannon and his Cherokee blood brother Jon Ridge are caught up in a bloody feud on Buffalo Creek, W. VA. Matt's Grandpa and both his parents are murdered. After the death of his mother and his promise to her to go west to avoid a feud, Byron, Matt's brother returns from the Wild West; he notifies Matt that in much of the West, "It is kill or be killed." Many of his neighbors in Buffalo Creek now shun him as a killer. Consequently, Matt is torn by his vow to his dying Mother that he would go west to avoid any more killing.

The two brothers, Jon Ridge, and three of Jon's Cherokee Indian relatives leave by train looking for a new home in New Mexico Territory. On their way they must play nurse maid to forty temperamental, prime breeding horses. The story picks up in Leavenworth, Kansas where four of their breeding horses have been stolen. They quickly find themselves embroiled in one harrowing experience after another in defending themselves from the large Cotton Brand family of thieves, gunrunners, killers, and claim jumpers.

Sheriff D. I. Smith of Huntington, W.Va., Marshall Pat Desmond of Pueblo, and General David Cook, Sheriff of Arapahoe County and owner of The Rocky Mountain Detective Association of Denver, are drawn into the plots and add authenticity to the history of the era. [Note: The historical records as to who was Sheriff of Wayne County in 1877were destroyed by fire]

ORWARD

A GOOD MAN ?

Just call me Matt. Everybody does with the exception of my parents. If I am to relate to you the story of my life, I feel I must fill you in just a mite as to who I am and how I became so naïve as I was when my life took a drastic turn. As I reminisce, it seems as though everything that I had learned up to my tender age of nineteen, had been to prepare myself from the cradle to the grave for the hell that was to come. My closest friend and blood brother Jon Ridge and I had itchy feet. Whenever we had the chance, we were like Ma's Wandering Jew plant that seemed to have tentacles that poked and pried into every nook and cranny of Ma's kitchen. Yet, for all our adventurousness, we had never been further South from home than Pikeville, Kentucky and Logan, West Virginia, which was a far piece in those days.

Yep—I'm a Ridge Runner and nothing but a simple farmer, but I was a natural born carpenter, and I had been weaned on helping my Grandpa Dillon raise horses on his breeding farm. I might add that boys in my era grew up teething on a pitchfork and a .44 cal. revolver. Except for the Civil War, my family had led an idyllic pastoral life. That is—until the McCoy Clan moved onto Buffalo Creek. However, even before then, our pastoral life had began to crumble after my big brother Michael was killed by the Rebs at Rich Mountain, West Virginia, and in 1876 our beautiful Victorian

farmhouse burned to the ground in the middle of winter, and Pa
and I had to rebuild our home with a log cabin.

Our nearest neighbor was Oral Ferguson. He boarded Pa and
me while we rebuilt our home. Ma stayed with her father, Grandpa
Mathew Michael Dillon, who lived six miles away near the mouth
of Buffalo Creek. It was not practical for us men to commute daily
to Grandpa's home during the short winter days. Pa's friend Noah
Petit, a contract-carpenter in the relatively new town of Huntington,
came to Pa's aid and helped plan the house and lay out the ground
floor before his own work called him back to Huntington. He also
helped Pa design our huge open fireplace so that it would heat the
entire house.

In the spring, after the logs had time to cure, Pa planned to buy
lumber and finish off the inside of the house. During the winter, the
green logs began shrinking as they cured. Upstairs, where I slept, the
chinking began to fall out from between the saplings we had used
to form the gables. I awoke many a morning to find my blankets
covered with a fine film of snow. As usual, I bounded out of bed,
drew on my ice-cold trousers and woolen shirt, and sped down
the stairs in my stocking feet to build a fire in the open fireplace.
Brushing the ashes aside, I found some live coals from where Pa had
banked the fire the night before. From a pile of shavings I had a
cheerful fire roaring in no time; however, it seemed to take forever to
dispel the zero temperatures. My fingers often turned blue from the
cold, which gave me cause to rue the burning of our former home.
Although it had also been cold during the frigid, winter nights, it
was never as bitter cold as the log cabin had been that winter.

When I was a kid our closest population center was Brownsville
originally located in the state of Virginia, the western part of which,
during the Civil War, was to become the state of West Virginia.
Brownsville later became the city of Huntington. Among the very
first settlers, Richard and Benjamin Brown in the early 1800s
established a river landing on the Ohio River. Before long people
were calling it Brownsville. In 1837 Marshall Academy was formed.
One of the founders, John Laidly recommended that the school be
named in honor of the late Chief Justice of the U.S. Supreme Court,

John Marshall. It was a subscription school; and the Virginia State Legislature had incorporated the school in 1837. In 1867 the new state of West Virginia created the State Normal School of Marshall College to train teachers. The settlement soon became the second most populated area in Cabell County and the State.

The Ohio River, Marshall College, and the C. & O. Railroad all added to the success of the settlement. The Ohio River was the primary highway from the earliest settler Thomas Hannon, to the present day. The riverfront had its seedier sections, and we young men sometimes went there just to raise a little old "Billy Hell". No one was surprised when the settlement was selected to be the terminus of the C. & O. Railroad.

Our most noted gossips claimed that Collis Huntington had been interested in making Guyandotte the end-point for his railroad, which was to be connected due west with Louisville, Ky. It was said that Collis tied his horse to a hitching post in front of the local hotel in Guyandotte, and somehow, as horses will, the horse skittered around and ended up on the sidewalk. The town's mayor upon seeing the law breaking horse entered the hotel and demanded to know who owned the animal. When Mr. Huntington identified himself, the mayor promptly fined him. The next day the irate railroad magnate announced that he would not locate his railroad in Guyandotte. Instead he would build a new town in an area that was only a settlement just south of Guyandotte and make it the western terminus for the railroad he represented.

Our closest towns had been Guyandotte and Ceredo, also located on the Ohio River, and inland the city of Fairview, which was the Wayne County Seat. The closest town to our home on Buffalo Creek was the new city of Huntington, W.Va. founded in 1870 by Collis P. Huntington, president of the Chesapeake and Ohio Railroad. Huntington's engineers laid out the town in 1870 on a grid pattern with broad streets and avenues. Magnificent, ancient trees lined many streets, which belied its recent creation. On Feb. 27, 1871, the West Virginia Legislature approved an act incorporating Huntington as a city in the new state of West Virginia. The State Legislature named the town after its founder, Collis P.

Huntington. Its citizens on Dec.31st, elected Peter Cline Buffington as Huntington's first mayor.

Guyandotte had grown its roots downriver from Huntington on the banks of the Ohio River. It had been a hotbed of the rebellion that had erupted into the Civil War in 1861. The first battle of the Civil War in Cabell County was fought in 1861 on Fortification Hill in Barboursville, the County Seat for Cabell County. Guyandotte had been one of Cabell County's busiest growing population centers until the Union Army burned down two-thirds of the city in retaliation against a Confederate Force that had attacked and destroyed a Yankee Recruitment station located in their city. The Confederates quickly established Guyandotte as the new County Seat, which office was returned to Barboursville in 1865 at the end of the Civil War. After Guyandotte's near destruction, the Unionist Newspaper, *the Wheeling Intelligencer wrote regarding them "Guyandotte has always had the reputation of being the orneriest place on the Ohio River, the worst secession nest in that whole country. It ought to have been burned two or three years ago."*

After Abe Lincoln was elected President in 1860, most of the state's residents were loyal to the Union. However, Cabell County and Guyandotte were divided in their loyalties even to the point of a farmer, a congressman by the name of Albert Gallatin Jenkins, forming a group of Border Rangers. Jenkins later became a General in the Confederate Army, and was wounded in the battle of Gettysburg. One of our relatives was named for him, Albert Jenkins Mays. However, Cabell County voted to remain loyal and Guyandotte voted to secede. Most of our family remained loyal to the Union.

Downtown Huntington was situated about eight miles from our front porch. Every Sunday and holy day, no matter the weather, Pa packed us all into his four-wheeled surrey, the one with fringes on top, and drove us to Mass at Saint Joseph's Parish Church in Huntington located on 20th street near the site of the C & O Railroad shops. When the snow was deep, he resorted to the use of his quaint old sleigh equipped with metal runners that pa had picked up at an estate sale in Huntington.

The actual building of the railroad was not completed until 1873. The building of railroads not only helped Huntington to prosper, but it also opened up the interior of the state to its natural deposits of forest-covered hills, coal, and natural gas, which helped break the depression of 1870. One could say the rail line was literally blasted through the mountains, which gave birth not only to the rail line, but created legends that we all love. One legend concerned the Big Bend Tunnels near Hinton that were only made possible by the prowess of "John Henry, the Steel Driving Man" made popular by ballads.

Grandpa Dillon's farm was near the mouth of Buffalo Creek, not to be mistaken for the town of Buffalo Creek. Grandma Dillon had died of pneumonia when I was twelve years old. It had been my first experience with a death in the family, and it had made a deep impression on me. Grandma was a loving, rough-hewn, frontier woman. She smoked a corncob pipe; and from time to time she wasn't above tucking a pinch of snuff under her lower lip. Grandma had a seamed face with high, prominent cheekbones. The seams were like a topographical map, a map from which one could imagine the rugged peaks and serene valleys of her rough frontier life. Unlike Grandpa, who was always laughing and joking, Grandma just smiled her serene smile; however, she would laugh heartily at a good Irish joke. I remember a joke my grandmother loved to tell whether she had a new audience or not.

Pat and Mike were bosom buddies. When Pat died Mike threw a huge wake for him; and that night he personally sat up with Pat's body. The libations had flowed freely, and some wags decided to pull a joke on Mike. They tied a wire to Pat's body and ran it up through the roof. Just as the old clock boomed out its midnight message, one man tossed a black cat through the open window on top of the body and a man in the attic began pulling up the body. Mike jumped up—pushed the body back down and said, "Lay down, Pat. I'll put the cat out."

Grandma always laughed heartily at her own jokes, and everyone joined in just as heartily. My grandparents and parents were old fashioned and very set in their ways. I reckon my family will be saying that about me some day all too soon.

Grandma Dillon filled me with wild Irish tales. In addition, based on her lessons learned on the frontier, she advised me, "Wealth is measured by the amount of butter one can put on one's bread." Another time she would say," The Gypsies will steal you, Matthew, if you're not good." If that didn't impress me, she warned me that bad little boys were sent to the borstal, a prison for children. Of course these admonitions were usually accompanied with a cold glass of buttermilk and some of her coveted cookies. Grandma often talked about fairies and leprechauns, which as youngsters, sometimes had Jon and I searching for the pot of gold, which she said was to be found at the end of each rainbow.

Every time someone died, Grandma was a fountain of advice on the dos and don'ts of *wakes*. She warned me quite seriously, "When I die, Matthew, don't weep for me. Weeping will encourage the fairies that surround the house to pounce on and take my soul." At a wake, Grandma would go through the house and make sure that the doors and windows were open to let the evil spirits out. She draped sheets over any mirrors not covered to hide a person's image in fear the fairies would steal them out of the mirror. In all seriousness Grandma would tell me, "When I'm gone, Matthew, take care that you go to the byre [barn] and the beehives. Let the cattle and the bees know that I'm gone, or the fairies will take my soul."

Grandpa wasn't nearly as superstitious as Grandma was. However, more than once, I saw him sneak a pinch of salt, which he dropped into his vest pocket to ward off evil spirits. Once he saw me watching, and with a wink, he put his finger to his lips and I knew that it was to be our secret.

Every Sunday after Grandma's passing; Grandpa would ride out and join us on our way to Church. He cut a fine figure astride his deep-chested Morgan horse. At sixty-five, grandpa's back was straight as a ramrod; he rode with the easy grace of a man born to and who lived in the saddle. Gramps had a mop of wavy black hair, complimented by a pair of piercing blue eyes. Folks often said I favored Grandpa about the hair and eyes, but Ma insisted that my eyes were a smoky blue; and that I was the spitten image of my Grandpa Matthew John O'Shannon of County Cavan, Ireland.

This flattered me no end, for both were said to be most handsome. Folks also said that I had fallen heir to Grandpa O'Shannon's black Irish temper. Unfortunately, this fighting heritage inherited from both sides of our family, heaped fuel on the conflagrations that later became my cross to bear.

I must admit, I do have a black Irish temper. However, thanks to Ma's patient hand, and Pa's firm direction, my temper was well controlled. As a young child, Ma often said I would walk a mile to get into a fight while my brother Byron would walk a mile to keep out of one. As I grew older, any fighting I did was done on a competitive basis at our various social gatherings, especially at election time. No one from Wayne or Cabell County had bested me in either wrestling, boxing, or shooting. I have to admit that I had the advantage over most of my competitors. I was a strapping six foot four inches tall and weighed in at about one hundred and ninety pounds. I had been raised near a Cherokee family by the name of Ridge, and my best friend was Jonathon, a boy my own age. I was raised with Jon on Indian lore and methods of fighting and coupled with our way of fighting gave me a decided advantage.

After Grandpa's confrontation with the McCoys, I wanted desperately to challenge the McCoy boys at our contests, especially the big one named Gabe. But as a family, they held themselves aloof and never participated in any competitions. But, via the gossip route, we learned that Gabe had a bad reputation in Pikeville as a fighter and spoiler. It was said that he delighted in hurting people, and had left behind him a trail of broken bones, gouged-out-eyes and several dead men. So far none of these dire traits of character had been demonstrated, evidently Parson J.D. McCoy had Gabriel on a tight rein and did not intend for him to openly repeat the mistakes they had made in Pikeville. But again, as far as we knew, Gabe's bad reputation was nothing but cheap gossip.

I had promised Ma and Pa that I would not retaliate against the McCoys. In spite of my promise, every time I saw Gabe and Parson J.D. McCoy, a pulse at my temple would begin to pound, and it took all my willpower to dam the flood of rage that I had inherited from the Shannach genes. I began to have nightmares and they all centered on the McCoys, and I would awake with a start. Before I could get back to sleep, I had to pray the rosary to douse the flames of my passion to challenge the McCoys head on.

Hill kids teethed with a hayfork in one hand and a gun in the other. Most men could cut down a running coyote at a hundred yards with a rifle. Some could draw a pistol, hit a fifty-cent-piece thrown in the air twice, and re-holster their pistol so fast that bystanders would swear the shooter never moved. We young men loved contests and pitted ourselves against all comers in shooting, boxing and wrestling bouts. I had never been bested in any of the contests. We all loved contact sports, but our newest love was a new game called baseball, which, by the way we played the game, made it a mighty-rough contact sport.

After Huntington became a city, we began to receive mail more regularly. Certain country roads were designated as Post Roads. At best, most Post Roads were crude trails or faint paths. They followed the flow of the land and often the bed of small streams was the only trail. When it rained, the Postman faced quagmires of mud and streambeds that often became raging torrents.

Now, confusion, despair and fear gripped my vitals. My family was disintegrating from around me. My sisters were married, and while we still saw them from time to time, I missed the closeness of having a large family at home. Byron, who was two years older than me, had been gone for three years to the western lands hoping to make his fortune. Michael, my oldest brother, had joined McClellan's Army of the Potomac at the beginning of the Civil War. General McClellan achieved the first Union victory at Rich Mountain in western Virginia. His army drove a force of forty five hundred rebels into the Shenandoah Valley, which the destruction of two years later, paved the way for our admission to the Union as the new state of West Virginia. The road to freedom from slavery was paved with the blood of thousands of men from both sides of the controversy including my brother Michael.

Ma and Pa believed that Michael's loss at Rich Mountain was not in vain, for his death had helped to establish the state of West Virginia, preserve our Union, and also freed the black man from bondage. There were nearly four hundred thousand people in western Virginia when the war started. There were a lot less when the war ended. The votes from the western counties were overwhelmingly for the Union. However, many residents of Huntington and especially Guyandotte, W.Va. were staunch secessionists. We lived near the dividing lines between Ohio, Kentucky and Virginia, and loyalties to the Union along the border were tenuous to say the least.

My Great, Great, Grandpa Dillon migrated from Ireland in 1776 and for his services in the rebellion, the new nation granted him land in Virginia. Great Grandpa Dillon later moved his family to Western Virginia when, at the advice of George Washington, the James River and Kanawha Turnpike was constructed. Like his Grand fathers, Grandpa Dillon didn't hold with slavery and he was proud of the new West Virginia State motto, "Mountaineers Always Freemen". Buffalo Creek was divided in their loyalties and it took a few years after the war before most of us became neighborly again.

My three sisters, Theresa Anne, Kristine Mary, and Kathleen Lee were all happily married. Terry had married Richard Tyson, a young attorney in Huntington, whose father at that time was our family attorney. Dick assumed the practice when his father retired. Influenced by my devout sister Terry, Dick had recently converted to Catholicism. Kristine and Kate had married well and were living in Ohio.

As I said, all was going well until the McCoys moved in and it just seemed like the Devil himself had lit a match under the McCoy's rear ends, and all hell broke loose on Buffalo Creek. My extra sensory perception told me that future generations would find their families scattered much worse than just a few miles away, as my sisters were. These thoughts did not help my sense of impending disaster that enveloped me at the moment. But I must not dwell on my fears; let me tell you what really happened beginning in the spring of 1873.

7HE McCOYS

CHAPTER ONE

Mother's mother, Wilhelmina Lee Dillon had foretold mother that she had "dreamt" of the banshees, a ghostly warning of her own death. Ma was not surprised—she already knew. Just before Grandpa's death, Ma told Pa that her father did not have much time left. What she did not know was that Grandpa Dillon was destined to become the first victim of the McCoy malice that had moved amongst us on that dark October eve in 1873.

Just the week before, Tom Vance and his wife Phoebe had come calling unannounced, which in itself was not unusual. However, by their somber visage, I could tell that this was not just a social call. Alerted by the clamor of our geese and guinea hens and by our dogs, Pa and I intercepted them at the barn, and while I took care of their horse and buggy, Pa walked them to the house. Ma met them at the door with her beautiful smile of welcome and in just a few minutes, we all sat down to coffee and lemon meringue pie. Phoebe Vance was busting at the seams.

"Lois Jean," she gushed, "You always look so cool and so nice, how ever do you do it with all the hard work you do?"

Mother smiled and replied, "How you carry on, Phoebe. You, who are the fashion plate of the big city of Huntington."

I left as soon as the pie was gone with the excuse, I had chores to do. I had to leave while I could keep a straight face. Ma had a thin bead of sweat on her hard working brow, but of course women don't sweat. Phoebe had on her Sunday best, and she looked every bit the farmer's wife that she was. I had to get outside—all those exaggerations were just too much for any young man. But I still wanted to hear what Phoebe had to say, she obviously had something on her mind.

Phoebe had received a letter from her kin in Pikeville, Kentucky. It seemed a family by the name of McCoy would soon arrive and they did not have a savory reputation. Phoebe was prone to gossip, so I knew that Ma and Pa would not put too much stock in her story.

But Tom spoke up and explained, "We didn't come here, John, just to be the bearers of the latest gossip, but you folks are Catholics and our best friends. The McCoys are a huge redneck clan, and they hate Catholics and Blacks with a passion. The McCoys have the reputation of having burned crosses in the yards of Negro families, and when a black man was lynched, everyone figured they done it. The Town Fathers were fed up and ran them out of Kentucky. We came to warn you—so you can be on your guard."

A week later, the Reverend Jeremiah Denver McCoy, who had purchased a huge hardscrabble farm not far from Grandpa's farm at the mouth of Buffalo Creek, moved in with his huge family. J.D. McCoy was a renegade, hard-shell Baptist minister, and we later learned the hard way that he did indeed hate Roman Catholics, Jews, Blacks and Indians in that order. There were twenty or so grown men in their clan and with the help of our good will committee, they quickly erected seven rough-hewn log cabins positioned evenly on the slopes of a large sandy basin that reminded me of an amphitheater. The cabins all faced the main house, and when finished formed a sizable community of its own.

As it developed, no one in their immediate neighborhood ever became bosom-friends with any of the McCoys. The Parson did, however, gain a large cult-like following with his electrifying, spellbinding Hell's fire and brimstone preaching. When the McCoys first moved in, the entire community had joined hands, so to speak, and one by one, wagon after wagon, all loaded with tools and building materials, had assembled at the old burned down homestead the McCoys had purchased. Later, the women and children of Buffalo Creek began to arrive with loads of food to feed the hungry men.

Tom Vance acted as spokesman and welcomed the McCoy family. Pa was the natural leader. But Pa was Catholic and even though there wasn't any malice from most of the folks we knew, there was still that natural reluctance ingrained in most Protestants traceable back to the first English Colonists that literally made it impossible for any of their descendants to fully trust any "Papist"

There was no doubt as to who headed up the McCoy Clan. Parson McCoy was a tall slender man of about fifty or so. He had a full, stark-red beard without a single gray hair, cold, cold blue eyes, and a stern visage. He wore common work clothes that were clean and pressed. Tom went up to him and said, "I reckon yo be Parson McCoy, welcome to Buffalo Creek," and he shook hands with the preacher. "I be Tom Vance. We and our neighbors come to lend a hand in getting yo'al settled in."

The parson replied, "The Bible says, we aer all neighbors and to do unto others as we would have them do unto us. Yo aer most welcome." The Parson had a deep mellow voice and he sounded like he was preaching to a congregation each time he spoke. His family flocked behind him and the Parson introduced us to his family.

We were all amazed at the size of the McCoy clan and even more amazed to find that except for the few wives, they were all slim, redheaded men and children, distinguished with heavily freckled, long-lean features. I thought the family resemblance rather eerie, and having seen one McCoy, you couldn't help but recognize a McCoy when you met one. The one exception was the Parson's son Gabriel. He was well over six feet tall and was blessed with a full handsome face crowned with a mop of deep auburn well kept hair. He had inherited the family's chill-blue eyes. When I met and shook his hand, he tried to muscle my hand, but I had little trouble in giving him tit for tat. His face reflected his surprise. My instincts warned me—this man was not to be taken lightly. I had a sudden insight. *One day the McCoy family would bring great grief to our community.*

3

The size of the chore that we had innocently taken on did not deter us from the work we had come to do. We quickly learned that we had not one, but seven cabins and one huge barn to build. We Shannons and Fergusons worked together with Lot McCoy and his family. Lot was nigh on 36 or so and he had a brood of ten children ranging from two to sixteen. Lot was close to his father and it soon became apparent that he and Ezekiel were the ones most privy to Parson McCoy's counsel. The McCoys were cordial, but not overly friendly. Lot was quiet but more likable than most of the McCoys that I met. The clan's personal habits were better than most of our neighbors. They were fastidiously clean to a fault and every McCoy's back was straight as a ramrod. It soon became apparent that the Parson ruled his clan with an iron hand. His word was law and he had a quote from the Bible to back up his every decision. He reminded me of some of the pictures I had seen of an austere Moses [except for the white beard] wrathfully smashing the Ten Commandants when he found his people worshipping a golden calf. The youngest children were the most demonstrative, for the innocence of small children is hard to control. However, any child over the age of six was kept busy with various chores, and they took to their work with a zeal that surprised me.

Lot's 14-year-old son Jeremy was busy skinning bark from a log and I said. "Jeremy, you're doing a fine job. Most kids don't like to work."

He paused, looked up at me surprised, and replied, "Ah don need thanken fer doing ma chores, Mista O'Shannon. The Good Book says, "Honor thy Mother and thy Father.""

Surprised, I murmured, "Well said, young man." During the week I worked with the McCoys, I noted there was very little laughter. The children six and over worked with serious dedication. The word of their parents, and especially the Parson, was Gospel.

Under the direction of Parson McCoy, we cut down trees, dressed them out and erected seven log cabins and one huge barn to get our new neighbors off to a good start. We were all surprised to find the Parson had us erect the cabins like those Jon and I had seen in the backwoods along the Tug River down Kentucky way. The cabins each consisted of two huge rooms. One room was the kitchen and social room, and the other was a bedroom where the entire family slept.

I sometimes speak impulsively and I commented to Jeremy, "With everyone sleeping in one room, it doesn't give a man and his wife much privacy—does it?"

The boy leaned on his adz and looked at me rather surprised and replied, "Ah ain't never give it no thought, Matthew. Now that yo ask, ah reckon it's jes the way we wus raised." Then he became defensive and stated, "Yo ain't putting down the way we live—aer yo?"

I flushed and replied, "Sorry, Jeremy, no offense meant. My friend Jon and I spent some time down on the Tug River. The folks there all live in two room cabins like yours; we slept over with many fine families."

He nodded, wiped the sweat from his forehead and pointed out, "Yo folks sleep in separate bedrooms like yo be shamed of whut the Bible says is natural. We live by whut the Good Book says. Yo come and hear Pa preach, and he kin larn yo about sech things."

I mentally kicked myself and changed the subject; the last thing I wanted to do was hear his pa preach.

We worked from break of day to last light, and by Friday, we had the barn and most of the cabins near finished. During that time, I learned a lot about the McCoy family. Every morning, noon and night Parson McCoy held short prayer services and no one was excused. Out of respect for his beliefs and family, we all stood by and listened to his preaching. I remember well the noon sermon J.D. preached the first day.

He stood up removed his hat, spread wide his arms. Looking up to the heavens he prayed, "Thank yo, Lord God Jehovah fer guiding yo people to the Promised Land. Thank yo fer bringen sech good nabors to do yo work and hep us'uns settle in. We abide by yo word, Lord. My young'ens and grandyoung'ens labor in yo vineyards, cuz they honor their Ma and Pa." He talked for ten minutes until his new neighbors began to fidget, and the Parson finally had the good sense to stop preaching.

Also, at the mouth of Buffalo Creek, just a stone's throw across from Grandpa Dillon's farm, was a small community church. There was no regular parson. The congregation depended on circuit riding preachers, who were an assortment of Baptists, Methodists, Holy Rollers, and whoever came along. When the Reverend McCoy moved near the church, he was given a warm welcome and quickly took over the chore of preaching his own brand of fire, brimstone and bigotry.

Parson J.D. McCoy had a deep sonorous voice and was an exceptionally fine fire and brimstone preacher, which fact held many people mesmerized. The fire and brimstone preaching was common in an era that such sermons was prevalent in both Catholic and Protestant churches. But J. D. McCoy had a special talent, and he held his audiences in a grip of fear of perdition, as he pounded home his sermons of Hell's Fire and Damnation. Before long, he converted many of the flock to his conception of Christianity. When he learned that our family was Catholic, the Minister immediately began his diatribe against Papists, Jews, blacks, and all too soon he learned of our Cherokee Indian friends and they were quickly included. Before long, many of our former friends and acquaintances began to shun us like lepers. Some members, encouraged by their sense of righteousness and the counter preaching by some of the circuit-riding ministers, openly objected to the renegade's bigotry. In retaliation, the Reverend McCoy belittled them publicly, and rode roughshod over their objections. Those members with enough gumption finally chose to walk out. Some formed their own community church and met for weekly services in their homes, while others began attending Protestant Churches in Huntington. Among those who left were some of our closest friends, the Adkins, Fergusons, Harmons, Mays, Vances and Trents.

Three months to the day after his arrival, the parson, accompanied by a dozen of his sons, all armed with rifles and mounted on horses, called on Grandpa Dillon. Grandpa was in his paddock putting one of his horses through its paces. When hailed, he looked up and smiled his welcome. Instead of dismounting and extending a hand of friendship, however, Parson McCoy snarled at him, "I hear tell yer one of them Papist pigs thet werships thet thar Pope feller in It'ly."

Grandpa's eyes frosted over and he eyed the men calmly. Cool as his own springhouse he affirmed, "If you mean am I a member of the Roman Catholic Church whose spiritual leader is Pope Pius IX, I am privileged to say—yes I am."

The renegade minister shook his fist and bellowed, "Yer church's the Whore of Babylon and yo's the Devil's own disciple. We don't want yer kind here. Yo have one week fer to get off Buffalo Creek or suffer the consequences."

Grandpa's Irish temper got the best of him, and flushed with anger he retorted, "Any man who comes to my door in friendship is most welcome. Bigots like you are not. Get out! If any of you set foot on my property again, I'll take a buggy whip to your ornery hides."

The parson's face flamed with fury, he turned to his eldest son Lot and snarled, "Tetch him some manners, Lot." The parson's kin were tall, gangly, and redheaded; each was heavily freckled with high-cheeked, gaunt faces slashed with thin lips that rarely smiled. The group all wore starch-stiff, white collars, black suits and large-brimmed black hats.

The exception was Gabriel. He stood off to one side on his horse, as though to distance himself from his brethren. He stood six feet three or four and his coat seemed unable to contain his broad shoulders, which tapered down to a slim waist. His hair was a deep auburn unlike the common, unmanageable red-mop-of-hair that was his family's distinctive link. He wore a black broadcloth suit with the pant legs tucked into a knee-high pair of spit-shined black boots. A white ruffled shirt with a black string tie set off his suit and his upper lip harbored a thin, closely trimmed mustache. All Gabriel's acquaintances called him Gabe; only his family called him Gabriel. By most standards, Gabe was a handsome man, however, if one looked closely there were the giveaway lines about his eyes and mouth that marked him as a very unhappy man. Unlike his kin, a smile came quickly to Gabe's lips, but I never once saw a smile reflected in his eyes.

At J.D.'s command, Lot slid down from his saddle. However, the audible click of thumbed-back, twin-gun-hammers froze him in his tracks. Startled, Lot looked up into the bore of Gramp's double-barreled, shotgun poking out from the barn loft. I sang out. "Go ahead, Lot, you might get lucky." Suddenly calm, the parson motioned his kin back. Stymied for the moment, he savagely wheeled his horse about and snarled over his shoulder, "Nuther day—nuther time."

Challenged, Grandpa snapped, "Any day—any time."

Luckily I had been there helping Grandpa train his horses. I sensed trouble when the armed men first rode in. By the time Lot started for Grandpa, I was all set with Gramp's Damascus, twisted-steel, double-barreled Parker twelve-gauge-shotgun loaded with deadly double-ought-buckshot [nine balls to the load].

Grandpa scoffed at our fears of reprisal and refused to allow anyone to stay with him. Ma believed that he had sensed that his time on this earth was limited and he did not wish to endanger his family. Ma and I knew intuitively that Grandpa was in great danger. I spent as much time with him as he would allow. A month later, while I was on the way to his farm, ambushers shot Grandpa dead. When Grandpa came out at dawn to feed his horses, his killers made sure he never had a chance. It had just begun snowing and the snow covered his murderer's tracks leaving no clues as to their identity. I counted ten bullet holes and I searched in vein for the spent rounds, but his murderers had been too cunning to leave any sign whatsoever.

Emmet Johnson was the Wayne County sheriff. He had suspects, but no proof of who killed Grandpa Dillon. My parents grew up when the Wayne County Seat was known as the City of Trout Hill. I grew up when it was known as the city of Fairview. However, everyone called the City of Fairview just plain Wayne. Finally, in 1911, the residents had the Fairview name changed to Wayne. The entire Community knew the McCoy Clan was responsible for the deaths of our parents. Proving it—was going to be a challenge. At his graveside, I broke down and swore aloud, "Grandpa, you rest easy. I'll kill every damned McCoy on Buffalo Creek." Ma gave me one of her "Dillon" looks that could freeze a man's soul, and Pa glanced at me sharply and let it rest.

When we got home that evening, Ma went out to the hen house to feed her chickens. The geese and ducks feeding in a small run of spring-fed water clustered about her honking and quacking excitedly.

Ma shrilled loudly, 'Chick . . . eee, Chick . . . eee, Chick . . . eee." In response, a distant, discordant cackling erupted from the top of the high hill overshadowing our home. Mrs. Frankenstein, the Guinea hen leader of the flock, uttered a gobbled cry, sprang into the air followed by a thunderous explosion of wings from our huge flock of Guinea hens, Plymouth Rocks, Rhode Island Reds, Bantam hens with their gaudy Roosters and assorted other poultry. The flock immediately caught the evening updraft of air, and spreading their wings, spiraled down in lazy circles to our chicken yard. When they landed, the birds tumbled and rolled in every direction. Some of the ducks and geese were bowled over emitting outraged honking and quacking. Even in our somber mood, we all broke out laughing.

Every morning Mrs. Frankenstein led the flock up the hill feeding on worms and bugs. By evening they had scratched, clawed and eaten their way to the crest of the hill. There, they awaited ma's evening summons to a cracked-corn dessert. There was one thing about our Guinea hens and geese. They gave our three dogs, a bitch collie named Rex, and a big, raw-boned, floppy-eared, male-hound-dog that answered to Buck, and Jack their offspring, a run for their money as watchdogs. No one could get close to our house without being challenged by the furious uproar of our guinea hens, Geese and dogs.

At milking time, Ma used to send Rex to find the cows, but she brought them in at a trot. When Pa was around, he always sent one of us boys. Running cows, whose sacks were heavy with milk, was not good for their udders. After we got home from the funeral, I called Jack, and we brought the cows in. By the time we took the milk in for Ma to handle, we were all noticeably relaxed. It was an unusually warm spring day. Yesterday we had had snow flurries—today the sun had come out flaming hot, as though seeking revenge. As dusk approached, the frogs began croaking and the crickets joined in chirping their love songs. Pa gestured, and together he and I strolled down to the creek deftly avoiding the black splotches dropped by the cows. Dusk began to settle and from the hillside, a rabbit whinnied plaintively and competing crickets abruptly fell silent upon our approach. They quickly resumed their courtship after we passed.

Pa kindly but firmly admonished me, "Son, I know how you feel about Grandpa. But, it's my chore to take care of the McCoys, not yours. If you call Parson McCoy out and kill him, the law will arrest and hang you for murder. God's Commandments forbids vengeance. The Church allows that we can only kill in self-defense." Pa put his arm around my shoulder and added, "Christian to Christian, I know I can depend on your prudence."

As we neared the creek, the soft cadence of frog's croaking soothed my ruptured feelings. How could I argue against everything in which I had been taught and had come to fervently believe? However, the hate in my heart had slowly evaporated as Pa spoke his piece. I had never been one to hold a grudge. I had a quick flash point, but in most matters my anger evaporated within a few minutes. "Don't worry, Pa, I know you're right. But" I added with a grimace "if I ever get a chance to whomp a few of them McCoys, I most surely will."

The Sunday morning following Grandpa's murder, Pa walked into McCoy's church during services. He walked up to the pulpit, and braced the cadaverous, ferret-faced, redheaded preacher and read him some O'Shannon gospel.

"You, Sir, are an unmitigated bigot, a liar, and a murderer. I am posting notice on you. If you ever besmirch my family name again, I will take a blacksnake whip and drive you from this community. If any of my family or friends is killed, I will hold you personally responsible and I will hunt you down like a mad dog." He turned, faced the congregation and said sadly, "You, who call yourselves Christians, and who once called me friend, all I can say is—shame". There was a stunned silence as Pa strode down the aisle and out the door. True to his word, Pa posted a big notice on the ancient oak that shaded the front of the church. The bold notice proclaimed that Parson Jeremiah Denver McCoy was a murderer, coward, bigot, liar and hypocrite.

After Pa's declaration, an uneasy pall fell over the community. I guess this was about the time that I began to have doubts about myself, and consequently about my faith. I was Grandpa Dillon's heir. I was only seventeen, and suddenly the responsibility of running a thriving business of breeding saddle horses fell upon my young shoulders. I had no trouble in running the stable, especially with Jon Ridge at my side. The reality of running the business myself, the anguish of losing my Grandpa, and facing the mounting tension of a community that fully expected our men-folk to retaliate, soon led to a nagging doubt as to why a good man like Grandpa should be killed, and why I, so to speak, a snot-nosed kid, should presume to take his place? How could I take the place of a good man like Grandpa? I was plagued with guilt. Why hadn't I been there for Grandpa, and why wasn't anyone exacting revenge for such a dastardly deed? Ma saw the anger in my eyes and heart and she made it perfectly clear that the Bible forbade revenge, and for my parents, the matter was ended. However, two years later, in the spring of 1877—disaster struck again.

A GOOD MAN ?

CHAPTER TWO

My name is Matthew Michael O'Shannon, son of John Patrick and Lois Jean O'Shannon, direct descendents of the fierce Shannach Clan of Ireland. Everyone used to say that I was A GOOD MAN! Am I a good man? I ask you, can any person render a fair and unbiased analysis of his own character, or should that be left to one's peers and in the final examination, to one's Maker? To the best of my ability, I have inscribed in this journal the highlights of my life as best I remember them. For those of you who read this journal, I'll leave it to you—am I—A Good Man?

Ma always said I was a good man. Actually she began by telling me, "You're a good boy." The youngest of six, I was her baby. As I grew older, I became reconciled to the fact that she would still be calling me a good boy when I became a senile old man. At the moment, I felt anything but good. Looking down at Ma's pallid face cradled on her pillow, a great lump gathered in my throat. Old Doc McDermott looked up from her side and shook his head negatively. Rising, he took me by the arm nudging me toward the kitchen.

The newly-finished log walls of the kitchen reminded me of our beautiful Victorian farmhouse that had burned down the previous fall. It had happened some time after the McCoy clan moved to Buffalo Creek, however, up to then, we had lived in a peaceful community; we had no reason to be suspicious of any skullduggery.

Doc and I entered the kitchen, and he walked directly to our chromed, high-backed, cast-iron kitchen stove. We had managed to save it from the fire as well as our kitchen oak table; its eight chairs, and Ma's horsehair stuffed sofa. Ma had put up cheerful chintz curtains in the kitchen; a sampler embroidered with the Ten Commandants hung on the wall between the two windows. Pa and I had already finished off the downstairs rooms of the log cabin we had built. I had put in a birds-eye maple wainscoting around the kitchen walls and Ma decorated the upper walls with cheerful, daisy-design wallpaper. In spite of the friendly aura and welcome heat from the stove, everything seemed strangely drab and alien.

Doc, using an iron handle, removed a cast-iron lid from the stove. Taking an old corncob pipe from his vest pocket, he opened his penknife and scraped the dottle from his pipe into the fire. Fingers of fire leapt up eagerly, as though licking the source. Replacing the lid, he crumpled and tamped some fresh tobacco leaf into the pipe bowl. The pleasant odor of fresh tobacco teased my nostrils. Taking a sulfur match from its snake-scrolled, cast-iron-holder mounted by the stove, Doc lit his pipe, cleared his throat, peered at me and gruffly and said, "I've done all I can, Matt, I'm sorry."

My legs turned to jelly and I sank weakly to a chair. In the distance thunder rumbled, a gust of cool air ran frantically through the house and a shiver trickled down my spine, as if the approaching thunderstorm was a portent of doom. I looked up only to see my grief reflected in Doc McDermott's eyes. My voice broke, "There's nothing you can do, Doc?"

He just shook his head wearily and sat back down. He looked away, puffed on his pipe and added, "She's bleeding internally, Matt. I'm amazed she's still alive. Perhaps her desire to receive the Last Rites of the Church is feeding the flame of her spirit. Those damned McCoy hypocrites broke something inside her; and I doubt if she can last much longer."

With sudden concern, I jumped up and strode to the window. In the distance, jagged lightening split the sky and I knew if the storm hit before Jon and the priest arrived, the road might become impassable from high water rushing down normally dry washes and small creeks.

Numb with shock, I returned alone to Ma's side. Knelling, I clasped her hand and prayed as I had never prayed before. Yet, even as I prayed, I sensed that my efforts were futile. Ma often said that I had inherited the sixth sense that ran in her family. For the past month, I had a presentiment of something horrible that was about to happen, and I had also, noticed that Ma was not her usual, cheerful self. I was sure she had had her own premonition. My foreboding had come home to roost.

Looking down on Ma's battered face; a black, unreasoning rage welled up nearly overcoming my reason. Forgotten was my pledge to my father. Only the death of so called Parson, J.D. McCoy could satisfy my anguish. Through a red haze, I knew that never again would I be able to hear mother call me a good boy. Never again would she be there to spoil me with her cooking, sooth my rankled feelings, encourage me in my endeavors, nor would I ever again hear her fine alto voice singing Annie Laurie and her myriad of Irish ballads.

Just the night before tears had coursed unashamedly down my cheeks as I knelt by my mother's bed. I had just finished laying out Pa's body on the horsehair stuffed couch in the front room. Like most country folks, we seldom used our parlor except for special guests. Ma woke up and I could tell by the look on her face that she knew Pa had passed over. In spite of her injuries, she reached out, wiped away my tears and said, "Take me to your father, Matthew."

I started to protest; however, Lois Jean O'Shannon held up her hand in that imperious manner that brooked no argument and I carried her to him. Ma stifled her pain through pursed lips and knelt at Pa's side. She riffled her fingers through his hair and ran her hand lovingly along his strong jaw-line. "Pray with me my, Son" and numb with grief, I knelt and supported her. Ma wrapped father's worn rosary around his wrist and placed the cross in his fingers. She took my hand and laid it with hers on his still warm, work-roughened hands. Then Ma, in a firm voice, led me in reciting the fifteen decades of the Rosary. After we said the Act of Contrition, Ma asked me to bring her the small vial of earth taken by our ancestors from the unmarked grave of Saint Patrick at Down Patrick in the County of Down, Ireland. Family tradition dictated that each member of our kin be buried with a bit of the old sod in their hand. She sprinkled a bit of the earth from the small bottle into the hand of her husband of thirty-five years. Then I carried her back to her bed.

Jonathon Ridge, my Cherokee Indian friend had gone to fetch Doc McDermott and Father Thomas A. Quirk the pastor of Saint Joseph's Parish in Huntington. Doc had arrived half an hour before and was in the kitchen drinking coffee. I expected the priest any minute and I prayed he would arrive in time to give mother the Last Rites of the Church. At last, there came the sound of horses and a buggy as they came galloping into our yard. I met Father Tom at the door with a crucifix and lighted candles, as was the custom. I knelt for the priest's blessing, and then led him to the parlor. There he conditionally gave Pa the Last Rites of the Church.

Just as he finished, the thunderstorm lashed out in all its fury amidst fearsome bolts of lightening and deafening claps of thunder. Jon had put the horses in the barn. He rushed in and we ran to shut the doors and we dashed throughout the house closing windows. Savage gusts of wind and torrents of rain often accompanied our thunderstorms. Breathing hard, I then led Father Quirk to mother's bedside. Ma had been dozing, but awakened by the storm, she greeted the priest with a generous smile. Ma affectionately and warmly greeted the priest by his first name.

"Father Tom, thank you for coming at such an unseemly hour. I'm afraid that birth and death are no respecters of doctors' and priests' sleep."

Father Tom smiled his reply and said to me, "Give me a few minutes alone with your mother, Mathew," and he unfolded his stole and placed it about his neck in preparation to hear mother's last confession. When he called us back in, Doc also came along. The Priest led us in prayer, followed by an act of contrition, and then distributed Holy Communion to the four of us. Jon, Doc, and I remained knelling while Father Tom administered the Last Rites and anointed mother's forehead and palms with Holy Chrism Oil. With his final words Ma's face glowed with the peace of the innocent, reflecting her complete acceptance of God's will.

Ma took Jon's hand and placed it in mine; holding them tight she said to him, "In the Cherokee ritual Jon, you and my son are blood brothers, so I speak to both of you as your mother. Jon, you are too sweet and trusting for your own good, and I pray it will never be necessary for you to change. You, Matthew, have inherited the black blood of the Irish Shannachs. The *Shannack* name was so feared by the British that any man, woman or child bearing that name were shown no mercy and were hanged without trial. The survivors took the name of O'Shannon and the O'Shannons likes to believe that the Shannon River in Ireland derives its name from their ancestors. You, Mathew, are their direct descendent."

"I see the black rage boiling in your eyes, and I fear for your immortal soul. Matthew, the Bible says that we are all brethren. However, Roman Catholics will never be safe on Buffalo Creek with that fanatic McCoy riling up the very people that have been our friends and neighbors for generations. I want you both to leave, and thus, avoid the Curse of Cain. If you remain, a feud may ensue that can only end with the death and ruin of many good families and people we love. Byron has written me of the wonderful opportunities in the West. He says that it is a land relatively free of bigotry and intolerance. Promise me that you will move there so that I may die in peace knowing that the rage I see will never bear fruit." Soothed by Ma's concern, I found that my anger had thawed. I looked expectantly at Jon and at his nod of assent, my eyes misted and I replied. "We've never said no to you before, Ma, Jon and I will do as you ask." I never dreamed then how impossible it would be for me to keep that promise.

Ma's face voiced her pleasure and taking her rosary, she wrapped it around her hand with the cross in her fingers. She held it up and said in simple faith, "This is my passport to Heaven. I have prayed the rosary to Jesus every day and I know Mother Mary will lead me to the feet of her Divine Son when I pass over." Mother smiled and held out her arms to me and I buried my head on her shoulder.

The storm had spent its fury and there was the soft spatter of rain drumming on the roof. Ma's voice was barely audible, "Lord, in your Infinite Mercy." With a little sigh and a smile on her lips,

Lois Jean O'Shannon passed on peacefully to a far better place. Then, true to tradition, from her little bottle, I sprinkled a bit of St. Patrick's earth into her hand.

Doc checked Ma for a pulse, he took out his watch and stated the time of her death, as was required by law and filled out her death certificate.

Father Quirk and Doc MacDermott returned to Huntington together. Father Tom had to prepare for the Black Mass, the name commonly applied to the Requiem Mass said for the dead. The superstitious had labeled the Requiem Mass, the Black Mass. Some said it was because the priests that celebrated Mass were dressed in their black robes and others because of the finality of the ceremony. I asked Jon to notify our friends and family, and I set about building one large coffin for my parents. I hoped Doc would be able to get some much-needed rest. Neither of my parents had wished to be embalmed and that meant a quick burial. My parents had been inseparable during life, and I was determined that they would not be separated in death.

I was good at carpentry and could manufacture anything from beautifully finished furniture to a complete house. I had no use for nails; all my work was done using mortise and tenon and tongue and groove. But woodworking was only a hobby to me, and, while I had a lucrative offer from Noah Petit to join him in his contracting business in Huntington, my first and only love was the raising of horses. When Grandpa Dillon was murdered, I lost more than a beloved grandparent and friend; I had lost my mentor.

Jon sent two of his brothers to inform my sisters in Ohio. Theresa and her entire family came that night, which was a great comfort to me. I rose early in the morning and finished the coffin by mid-morning. I lined it with one of Ma's beautifully hand-quilted comforters. Friends arrived all day; they came in farm wagons, carriages, walking, and on horseback. The women had been busy before they came and had cooked up enough vittles for an army, which included heaping plates of biscuits, cornbread, fried chicken, potatoes, green beans, peas, pies, cakes, cookies, and countless other dishes. The parlor was soon filled with fresh, beautiful arrangements of flowers gathered from their gardens and spring's wild flowers picked by children from lush meadows and hillsides.

The women kept the younger children outside; the muted, happy sound of their playing was a welcome respite to the despair I felt in my heart and soul. My sister Theresa and our cousins Delores Harmon, Barbara Spillane, and Wilma Mays had prepared Ma for burial. When I finished the casket, the men helped me place my parents in one another's arms in the extra wide casket. Ma and Pa looked so natural that I expected them to wake up any moment.

That afternoon, we drove in funeral procession bouncing along the deeply rutted, road that followed the contours of the hills to Westmoreland, and then on into Huntington to Saint Joseph's Parish on Twentieth Street. We passed the homes of our former friends and neighbors, however, nothing stirred except an occasional window curtain. Their dogs; however, ran out barking furiously as we passed, but the crack of my whip kept them from spooking our horses.

As though through a haze, for it was an unusually hot Spring day, I noted little green frogs as they plopped into the road creating little plumes of dust, and my eye caught sight of a delicate green snake, the first of the season, as it flowed fluidly through the branches of the budding hazelnut bushes that hedged the road. Farther along, ubiquitous finches flitted like flashing yellow lights amidst the dust-covered undergrowth. The ride, however, was like a nightmare in slow motion.

My sister Theresa; however, was very much like Ma. After the initial shock, she handled the situation with great dignity, and had arrived the night before with her entire family. There was no way to notify Kristine, or her sister Kate in time for them to attend the funeral, Terry, Richard, their three young sons, and Jon and I gathered together that evening with our friends at the Church. For the past six months, I had been dating a pretty girl, Juliette Renaud. She and her parents came up to me and her mother placed her hand on mine and said, "We are so sorry, Matthew," echoed by Juliette and her father. Somehow, their words rang hollow to me, and I looked at Juliette rather vacantly, as she and her parents mingled and murmured their condolences to the rest of the family.

Suddenly it hit me. I hadn't even thought of Juliette since Ma and Pa had been killed. Common gossip had the two of us engaged and as good as married. However, while Juliet was lovely to look at, she had some fancy notions about her own importance. She was prone to be a bit of a prude. Julie had no use for Indians, no matter how well educated or decent they were. Jon and his family dressed and acted just like everyone else. He was six-foot-one-inch tall; with a beautiful head full of jet black hair His features were very slim, like many of his race. Some of the girls I knew told me they thought he was a doll. Just a few days before, when Jon and I were in town on business, we ran across Julie and her mother while they were shopping. She offered me her hand, and I thought wryly, Juliette Marie Renaud of the old distinguished family of Renauds from Virginia, wouldn't have given me so much as a kiss on the cheek in public even if I had been married to her. While I was putting her shopping bags in their carriage, I heard her make one of her cutting remarks to Jon. On our way home, Jon was unusually silent. Sensing his hurt feelings, I tried to smooth things over and asked, "Okay, Chief Thundercloud, what did Julie say to puncture your ego?"

In an off-handed manner Jon remarked, "Nothing much, Matt, Julie was just being Juliette."

I did not press the issue, Jon had said all there was to say as far as he was concerned; for me that was enough.

Upon entering St. Joseph's Church, the first thing I noticed still hanging on the small narthex wall after two years was an old page-size placard announcing 1875 as a Catholic Jubilee Year. I swallowed hard; there was nothing jubilant in 1877 for the O'Shannon family. Then, per Catholic custom in our Parish, Father Quirk led us in the Rosary prayers for the repose of the souls of our parents.

The next morning at 10:00 AM, Father Thomas Quirk celebrated the solemn Requiem Mass for the dead He blessed the coffin with holy water; Father Tom delivered a most eloquent sermon of which I remember very little. My mind was numb and refused to accept the finality of their passing. Many of our friends eulogized Ma and Pa. Each had their own touching story of their friendship and the help my parents had given them throughout the years.

Strange as it may have seemed to the mourners, Mary Perkins was the first to get up to eulogize my parents. Many folks had referred to her as crazy Mary, and the town's children had seized upon the term and began making her life a living hell. They played pranks on her, and teased and threw rocks at her, as she passed by muttering and talking to herself. For several years, sick and pathetic, Mary had pushed her little, vegetable-laden cart through the streets of Huntington on the way to the small market that had been established on the riverbank of the Ohio River in old Brownsville.

Today, everyone was shocked, for Mary Perkins stepped into the aisle from the back of the Church and walked up to the lector's ambo. Mary's sun-tanned face shone with a warm wholesomeness. She wore a sophisticated black dress with a high ruffled neck. It had to be twenty years old and her dignified black bonnet and veil declared this woman had known better times. I knew that Ma had been the only person in the Huntington area to learn anything about her background. In a refined, Richmond, Va. accent Mary spoke,

"I have come to pay my respects to my friends and benefactors John Patrick O'Shannon and Lois Jean O'Shannon. While good people stood idly by, evil has wreaked its havoc amongst us and struck down two of our most respected citizens. Today our community loses a most saintly man and woman. Ten years ago, a few years after my brother Mercer and I purchased a small farm near here; we both fell ill and were quarantined with typhoid fever. We developed severe temperatures, and soon became so delirious and weak we could not function. Doctor MacDermott called on Lois Jean and John O'Shannon for help and like guardian angels they came and tended to our every need for over three months. The word typhoid fills most of us with fear and few persons are willing to expose themselves, or their children, to such a debilitating disease.

"Once exposed, Lois and John were quarantined with us. Mercer developed complications, and he bled to death in spite of all that Doctor MacDermott and the O'Shannons could do. I went into a state of shock and was mentally depressed for several years. Again, Lois and John stood by me. Misguided children often ran after me and called me crazy Mary, but Byron and Mathew O'Shannon soon put a stop to that." Her eyes clouded up and she added with a sob, "May God bless and keep them all in the palm of His Hand. I am not a Catholic, but I am a believer, and my family and I will pray for them as long as I live."

As Mary Perkins stepped down from the Ambo, for the first time in their lives, the parishioners realized that this woman was more than just "Old Crazy Mary." She was a woman with character and every bit a Lady of breeding.

Jon Ridge's family was well represented by Thaddeus Ridge, Jon's father. Mr. Ridge was a handsome man with long, black wavy hair pooled in front and combed back on both sides of his head. His black, single-breasted, swallow-tailed coat fell to his knees. He wore stovepipe, uncreased trousers that were tucked into his black, high-topped boots that shone with a dull luster. The black suit was accentuated with a white linen frilled shirt, and a high-necked, starched collar that was accented with a black, silken, voluminous cravat that filled the entire front of his shirt. Men eyed his handsome physique with envy and there wasn't a woman present that did not look at him with interest.

Jon's father stepped up to the ambo and spoke for the Cherokee people. I can only hope that someone will speak as well of me when my turn comes to face my maker. In a mellow baritone Mr. Ridge said, "The Ridge and O'Shannon families have been friends for over a hundred years. Our Great Grandfather's, Grandfathers, Matthew O'Shannon and I, and our sons Jonathon and Matthew O'Shannon by our ancient Indian rites are blood brothers. When the O'Shannons were happy, we were happy, and when they were sad we were sad." As he spoke, Thaddeus Ridge also told the story eloquently with his hands using the Indian Sign Language. I was surprised at his revelation of our fathers and ancestor's blood-brother kinship. I learned later that it was not common knowledge lest impressionable young men would choose to become blood brothers for the wrong reasons.

Mr. Ridge added, "When we were sick, the O'Shannons nursed us, and when they were sick, we were there. Lois Jean was midwife to many of our Cherokee women. Our family members, to this day, fondly refer to her as Little Mother. Lois Jean O'Shannon was to us a guardian angel and medicine woman. As families, we shared bountiful harvests and nurtured one another during bleak droughts, insect incursions and savage winters. Together, we celebrated the births of our children and the passing over of our loved ones. Today, the angels and saints in heaven are celebrating and welcoming Lois Jean O'Shannon and John Patrick O'Shannon to their just reward. Heaven's good fortune is also our good fortune for now we will have two more guardian angels looking down upon us and bringing us many blessings. We will miss them for their presence was like a ray of sunshine. We will mourn them, for they will no longer be here to console and enlighten us. But, we are happy for both of them, because there are no tears or unhappiness where they are. We believe that the bliss and the eternal vision of God will be their just reward forever and ever. May the Great Spirit of our ancestors, the one we all recognize as our God and Savior console us, Amen."

Jeannie Dagget, with a newly born baby in her arms, rose and mounted the steps to the ambo as Thaddeus Ridge, his back as straight as a board, returned to his seat. Jon coughed and wiped his eyes and when the beautiful white, cathedral-like altar blurred in my vision, I dabbed at mine with my knuckles.

Jeannie spoke hesitantly, "Yo'al ain't got no ideer who I be. I be Jeanne Dagget. My man Paul and me be river folk. We work on the docks and got a shack nigh the river. Doc MacDermott asked Missus O'Shannon ta midwife my baby. I war haven plumb bad pains. My baby warn't turned jes right and Doc was afeered fer me. But, Missus O'Shannon, she knew jes what ter do. She moved the baby with her hands and when my time came I hed no frets." Tears were running down her cheeks and holding up her baby she added, "Thank yo, Missus O'Shannon. She dun got killed on her way home frum heppen me." Paul jumped up from his seat and helped his sobbing wife down from the ambo.

I marveled at her fortitude. But, it was not unusual in those days for a country woman to have a baby all alone in the fields, wrap the baby in a blanket and finish her day's work before returning to her home to prepare supper for her family.

For two hours, people rose to bid their farewells to my father and mother. My parents had been the first to help their neighbors when troubles had beset them. I was humbled by their devotion. Some of those to speak were Dr. Peter Cline Buffington, the first mayor of Huntington, who was accompanied by his family. He looked very distinguished with his long white beard. Huntington's current mayor T. J. Burke and his family and D.I. Smith, the sheriff of Cabell County, also spoke their praises. Several professors from Marshall College eulogized them and of course, Pa's good friend Noah Petit had words of praise. Afterwards, he came over and embraced Terry and I, but he was too choked up to say anything. The list of former Confederate soldiers that paid their respects sounded like a roll call of the CSA.

My parents had been very popular and the entire parish had turned out for the services. After Mass, my family led the way to the Catholic Cemetery. Ma had asked me to bury her and Pa beside Michael. My older brother had lost a leg in the battle of Rich Mountain during the Civil War, and had lingered in a military hospital for several weeks. Ma and Pa had made the long journey to care for him, but mortification of the flesh set in. Michael died in Ma's arms holding his rosary in one hand, and Pa's hand in the other. Father Tom had just started the graveside services when a horse and rider came thundering up to the cemetery gate. I looked up in sudden irritation, and then my anger melted in shocked surprise. It was Byron. His eyes took in the somber scene confirming his worst fears. Byron's mouth was set and ridges of muscle bulged along his jaw line. Swinging down, he came up to me; his face pasty white, and I saw the anguish in his eyes. He gripped me by the shoulders, and his fingers dug cruelly into my flesh.

"It's true then. They're gone, both of them." I could only nod and he clasped me in his arms and I could feel his entire body shudder with grief. A few seconds later, his eyes brimming, he stepped back and exclaimed, "I must see them one last time."

"Of course," I replied. Jon Ridge and Clarence Ferguson reopened the casket. Byron gasped when he saw the bruises on Ma's face and the deep lacerations on Pa's head. The women and I had done our best. But the severity of my parent's wounds made them impossible to erase. Byron was always of a good disposition and seldom became angry. However, Ma always said, "Still water runs deep. The quiet ones are the men of which to be wary." Ma was right, as always. Byron's jaw set and the controlled fury in his eyes did not bode well for our parent's murderers.

I had a flash temper governed more by impulse than restraint, but Byron had always been the calm one. His anger was such that I feared for his sanity, and that for which he might do. Byron dropped to his knees; the tears flowed down his face, but he never let out a sob. He lovingly touched their faces, bent over and kissed them, then turned to Jon and said. "Thank you, Jon. Please replace the top." Terry and her family engulfed Byron with a mixture of tears, grief and love. Rather dazed, I was still aware that their reception seemed to appease Byron's wrath for the moment.

When we got home that evening, we all pitched in, fed the stock, and performed the necessary chores before we could rest. Terry prepared supper, while Byron, Jon, Dick, and I worked outside. On the road home from the funeral, none of us felt like talking. My mind roamed unchecked; as I tried to accept the hand that fate had dealt. I thought of my childhood and of how close knit our family had been. First, we had lost Michael to the war. Then one by one my sisters had married and moved on to live their own lives. Theresa married for love and made sure she was reasonably close to her mother. Kristine married for what she thought would do her the most good, but ever practical she married a man that loved her; from all appearances she loved him as well. Kathleen Lee, ever dependable, loved farm life, but turned down half-a-dozen proposals until she could marry into a staunch Catholic family in Ohio.

Stacey, one of the Ferguson boys had gone to California to get rich. He returned with little gold, but he kept us on the edges of our chairs listening to his hair-raising stories of gold strikes, Indian raids, outlaws, and fast guns. Before long, I noticed a yondering look in Byron's eye; I was not surprised when he announced that he had a yen to see the Wild Wild West. Shortly after he left, Grandpa was murdered, and now Ma and Pa were gone. Although Byron was home again, my cozy little world was rent all to Hell.

Our neighbors had given us so much food that Byron and I loaded up a wagon for Jon to take to his prodigious family. Jon had been a bastion of strength in my time of need. Byron was blood, but Jon and I had become so closely knit that sometimes I felt lost when he rode off. I drifted off to sleep that night thinking of my relationship with the Indians, but with Jon in particular. Jon Ridge was a full-blooded Cherokee Indian. The Cherokee men were handsome and the women strikingly beautiful. Jon's grandparents, in the early part of the century, had moved peacefully from their lands in the East and relocated in Arkansas at the Governments direction. They prospered, became quite civilized, and many became Christians and took baptismal names common to white men.

Jon's family claimed relationship to John Ridge who had been murdered by his own people in the Indian Territory over politics. Ridge gained political prominence after the forcible removal of his people to Oklahoma in 1830. In 1828, bowing to greedy political pressure, the Federal Government asked the Cherokee Nation to relocate to the Oklahoma Territory. Some of the Ridge family, among others, complied, sold their property, and moved, to the new reservation. Consequently, they did quite well, and later became known politically as the Old Settlers.

Jon's Great Grandfather, however even before the first move, did not trust the Federal government and chose to move back to Western Virginia. In the Eighteenth Century most of the area had belonged to the Cherokee Nation. In a general uprising twelve Indian tribes, including the Cherokee Nation, who lived along the Ohio River made a stand to keep their lands from the clutches of the ever greedy white man's lust for land and more land. The Ohio River was the frontier at that time in history. President George Washington called General Anthony Wayne out of retirement in 1792 to command an American Military Force of three-thousand men to put down this general Indian uprising. General Wayne defeated nearly two-thousand Indian warriors at the Battle of Fallen Timbers on August 20, 1794, near what is now Toledo, Ohio. The twelve Chiefs signed the Wayne Treaty "to bury the hatchet forever" on August 3, 1795.

The Ridge family, through their friendship with Great Grandpa O'Shannon, purchased extensive acreage. Afraid of white men's greed; they wisely purchased the land in Grandpa's name. He in turn, leased it back to the Ridge family for ninety-nine years with an option to renew the lease into perpetuity for the price of the annual taxes. The family attorney, Richard Tyson Sr., had handled the legal papers.

Many Cherokees refused to move in 1828. Consequently, Congress passed the Indian Removable bill in 1830. Federal troops rounded up the Indians at bayonet point and herded them into prison camps. Many Indians died from the rigors of their incarceration, and others starved because they did not know how to prepare the strange rations issued by their captors. The government moved a few Indians to Oklahoma by steamboat. To their discredit the soldiers moved over thirteen thousand men, women and children by foot in thirteen groups. The elements and starvation killed thousands of Cherokees; the Indian's overland route became known as the Trail of Tears.

The government had confiscated the Cherokee's lands, homes, horses and farm implements and only a few managed to retain any of their possessions. During the trips the conductors of the journey pressed the few wagons the Indians had managed to salvage into service for those who were too weak or ill to travel. To make more room, the soldiers dumped the owner's possessions by the wayside. Few indeed were the Indians who arrived in Oklahoma with even an axe to prepare themselves new homes. Over four thousand Indians died on these heartless journeys. It became politically expedient for the bureaucrats to handle the Indian problem by allowing the Buffalo herds to be destroyed, and if that wasn't sufficient, to eliminate the Indians by any means fair or fowl.

Because of my Great Great Grandpa O'Shannon, the Ridges became my second family. In my early youth, Ma said I spent more time with the Cherokees than I did at home. This was not true of course. The Ridge family led a wonderfully uncomplicated life. They had adopted most of white man's ways, but studiously maintained many of their old traditions. The Ridge family was

non-denominational more by chance than by choice. Indians acted
as responsible parents too all children within their tribe. In many
tribes, twelve different women might suckle the same baby, although
this custom was gradually dying out. Never once, however, did I
see an Indian adult strike a child. In their own quiet manner they
dished out their own discipline.

Jon's family lived in a well-constructed, one-story log cabin.
It was much bigger than ours. In the center was a large atrium.
Weather permitting, the family cooked, ate and used the area as a
communal room. When an Indian girl was married, it was common
for her and her husband to live with her parents. With Jon as my
constant companion, I learned to speak Cherokee and the Indian
sign language became second nature. I also learned how to track
man or beast, how to fashion snares and how to make weapons.
In time, I became as proficient with the knife, bow, and wrestling,
as any Indian boy. My training stood me in good stead when I
wrestled with the white children, for I had acquired the wrestling
skills of both races. We both became especially proficient in the use
of firearms. The Ridge family lived in their own private world, and
while the family was known and well liked, they made no show of
their Indian heritage to the outside world.

Together, Jon and I learned to subsist from the bountiful forests
that covered the West Virginia and Kentucky hills. We learned
to distinguish plants that were suitable to eat and those used for
medicines. I learned how to make the seven prismatic colors; the
primary one was indigo. The Cherokee raised their own indigos and
I learned to cut it in the early morning while the dew was still on it,
then we put it in a tub and soaked it over night. The next day we
foamed it up by beating it with a gourd; we let it stand overnight
again and rubbed tallow on our hands to kill the foam, afterwards
we poured the water off and the sediment left in the bottom was
poured into a crock to let it dry. The dry product was stored in a
cloth poke and was ready for use. It made the most beautiful deep
violet-blue. I learned to use walnut bark to make black dye. For
purple dye, I learned to use maple bark. If I mixed maple bark with
hickory bark it made yellow. Hickory bark by itself made green

dye and to make red dye, I learned to mix madder and alum. We found alum in caves and we also used sumac berries to make red dye. When the family ran low on salt, Jon and I eagerly took off for the known salt licks.

Hickory trees were everywhere, as were sassafras bushes. I liked to dig up their roots to make sassafras tea. We learned that elm trees [slippery elm} was used for headaches and for stomach problems and fever. Blackberry bushes and blueberry and papaw plants, hazelnut bushes, chestnuts, walnuts, hickory, apple, and persimmon trees were all most common. Wild grapes, raspberries, and strawberries grew in vast clusters on many hillsides. Ma had her own tansy bush that she had planted and grown from a shoot from Grandma Dillon's bush. For infections, we mixed lye soap with brown sugar and made a poultice that I guarantee would suck everything alien from your body, except your soul. When we got sick, our parents had castor oil, sulfur and molasses, and of course tansy tea that served to heal everything from warts to bellyache, and was guaranteed to cause even the most docile boy in W. Va. to contemplate running away from home. In addition, Ma had a list of herbs that she picked that were good for everything from childbirth to old age. I picked batches of doc weed and young dandelion; leaves of which the flowers were used as flowers, and they also made good dandelion wine, and they all made good greens.

It was a wonderful experience. When Jon and I reached puberty we pledged undying friendship, and in the Indian tradition we became blood brothers. In a ritualistic ceremony, we gathered at their Medicine Teepee. Jon's father, Thaddeus Ridge, cut the palms of our hands, bound them together, and then pronounced us blood brothers. Ma and Pa were present and it was a most solemn occasion.

Even I never knew the exact size of the Ridge family. However, there was a sight more Indians than McCoys. The Ridge's were good neighbors and always quick to lend a neighborly hand when needed. They were a friendly people, but a mite distrustful of the fork-tongued white men and his greed for land. The family tended to keep to themselves, although some, as I stated before did marry and left the homestead. They often intermarried with the remnants of the collection of Mingo Indians and a few trusted white families. They only had one Indian Lodge and that was hidden deep in the middle of their property. It was used to keep alive the ceremonies of their rich Indian Heritage.

In his teen years, Jon, influenced by my family's devotion to God, elected to become a Catholic. Later, when the McCoys learned of this fact, they were doubly incensed and vocally gave vent to their wrath, but were unable to locate the Ridge homestead. If the McCoys ever tried to ambush the Ridge family, they were in for a big surprise. The Ridge family, from the first day they moved to Western Virginia, maintained a constant vigil. There was no road leading to the Ridge home. In spite of their isolation, most of their young men had fought to preserve the Union. Seven of them had paid with their lives for the privilege, and one man of their family was awarded the newly created Medal of Honor for bravery.

The Ridge children all enrolled in the local schools. The children chose to walk the faint deer trails that laced the heavily wooded mountains. The family knew well the disadvantages of illiteracy in a white man's world. The Cherokee Nation was the first Indian tribe to develop its own alphabet. Later, towns sprang up in Oklahoma Territory like Tahlequah and beautiful mansions were built such as the one at Park Hill. The Indians printed their own Cherokee language newspaper named the Cherokee Advocate.

We O'Shannons, in addition to eight grades of elementary school, were reasonably well educated. Ma taught us to read from McGuffey's Reader at an early age and by age four; I could read from the Bible. We had our own spelling bees, and history and geography and mathematic contests. On slates we had contests and drew maps of the USA and placed all the States in their correct places and then went back and put in all their capital cities. We did the same with the known foreign countries. For entertainment on long winter evenings, we memorized entire poems, and recited and acted them out with dramatic expressions and gestures. My favorites were The Raven by Edgar Allen Poe, Jules Verne's books and the Travels of Marco Polo. Ma's taste ran to Sir Walter Scott's Ivanhoe and Waverly. Pa was more technical and he liked Tactics by Vegetius and the Bulwer-Lytton novels. In addition, pa purchased a copy of Blackstone's Basic Law, which, as a family, we all studied and discussed. Pa jokingly said Byron took to law like a pig does to slop. Byron had always been the studious and devoted farmer's son. While I had always been the tumbleweed, and seldom took life too serious, except for my horses and my woodwork. I spent so much time with the Indians that a few times Pa had to preach the word to me.

Ma was constantly correcting our English. We were exposed daily to the common vernacular of the hills. Consequently, we often picked up words such as *fer, us'uns, them'uns, yo, them thar, and thet,* all of which was accentuated by *the Ridge Runner nasal twang.* When we slipped up in front of Ma, she shot us down. Behind our backs, a few gossipy neighbors complained that we were putting on airs; some referred to us as *them city folks.* Others, not so fortunate or hardworking, were just jealous of our success.

Pa owned two hundred acres of prime bottomland as well as four hundred and forty acres of hills covered with prime trees and cleared land, some of which we had cleared ourselves. The bottomland was enriched each spring when Buffalo Creek overflowed and left a rich deposit of fresh soil. We had much for which to be grateful, and we never ceased giving thanks for God's providence.

The evening of the funeral, none of us had much to say. We were all too grief stricken to do more than try to console one another. After chores and breakfast the next morning, we just naturally gravitated to the kitchen. Terry poured coffee for us and as she walked by, a lump gathered in my throat. She was the picture of Ma. Dick Tyson was busy fussing over some papers, when Byron and Jon came in. Terry asked, "Coffee?" At their nod, she filled two cups. Byron sat, blew cautiously and took a hesitant sip.

It was the first time I really had a chance to make comparisons. I never remember calling Byron anything except Barney. He was two years older than I was, and to me he had always personified the Rock of Gibraltar. In contrast, I was the one that had always had an itchy foot. I often teased him calling him Lord Byron, for he had the bearing of an Earl, and his favorite poet was Lord Byron, Barney loved Byron's satirical poem Don Juan, which complimented his own love of satire. I remember how shocked my parents were, when, on his nineteenth birthday, Barney calmly announced, "Pa, if you can spare me, I think I'll take a gander at the Wild West everyone is talking about."

Ma said, gander indeed!"

Byron had left a boy, and there was no doubt he had returned all man and then some. He wore a short buckskin-fringed coat, cut more like a coat than a jacket, a sun-faded, gray-flannel shirt, and black broadcloth trousers tucked into high-heeled, black-leather boots. When not wearing a coat, he wore a buckskin vest. It adequately concealed his Russian, single-action .44-caliber revolver that he had when he left home. As a family, we were partial to Smith and Wesson Russian revolvers and the Henry .44 cal. repeating rifle. I smiled to myself, for nestled inside my own jacket, in a special belly gun holster that I had designed, was the mate to his pistol. With the McCoys so hostile, I wasn't about to go unarmed.

I asked him, "What about those high-heeled boots and that horn on your saddle, Barney?"

He laughed, "No self respecting cowboy would be caught dead without them, Matt. When you rope a 1000 lb. steer, you better have something with which to brace yourself and something to wrap the rope around."

"Where were you when General Custer was wiped out last year?" That news had shocked the Nation and I was really curious.

"I was in Denver. We were all shocked; the newspapers had a field day. It was a bad day for everyone. Col. Custer was too reckless. He acted impulsively and lost the lives of all the men with him."

I raised my eyebrows at that statement and replied, "That's not the way the Independent in Huntington and the Herald in Guyandotte wrote the story. They called it a massacre."

"Most papers did, Matt, but there're always two sides to every story."

"Did you know that the James-Younger Gang was blamed for robbing the Bank of Huntington on Sept. 5, 1875? They got away with ten-thousand dollars, a short time after you left for the west? I don't know him, but R. T. Orey and a friend were in the bank at the time. One of the gang, Thomas McDaniel, was shot and killed, and Jack Keene was arrested in Tennessee a short time later.

Barney laughed, "That doesn't sound like the Jame's gang. With only two men unaccounted for, it appears to me that it's just another robbery blamed on the Jame's boys.

"I grinned, "You have to agree, it sounds a lot more exciting if Cole Younger or Jesse James did the robbing.

Byron's shoulders, I noted, were broader, his waist thicker, his face more full, and his once soft, blue-green eyes had developed a steely glint. Everyone liked Barney's nickname except Ma and Pa. They always called me Matthew, and Byron was always Byron, and so it was the same with our sisters. At twenty-one, my brother was five foot ten or eleven and weighed, I reckoned a hard, two-hundred and twenty-five pounds having put on twenty or so pounds while he was gone. Yet, although he was definitely bigger in weight and height, he somehow looked more solid, more competent, and much worldlier than when he had left. In essence, I concluded, he was not just a man of the West—but all man—wherever or whatever he might choose to go or do.

Before he left for the west, Barney had earned the reputation as the strongest man in two counties. In the summer, the young men from miles about met at our house on Sunday afternoons. Besides playing horseshoes, baseball, wrestling and boxing, we all tried to outdo one another in contests of strength. We used fifty, seventy-five and one-hundred-pound anvils to prove ourselves. Byron could throw the large anvil further than anyone else could throw the small anvil. However, he now had to look up to me, for, while he favored Ma's people, I was all O'Shannon, and even taller than Pa was. I stood six foot four and weighed one hundred and ninety-five pounds, but somehow I doubted if I was ever going to beat Barney at throwing that 100-pound anvil.

We were all sipping our coffee; I was standing near Barney. He looked up at me and said with his little lop-sided grin, "You grew some." Everyone laughed and then deadly serious, he asked, "Tell me what happened."

I remained standing, pacing back and forth from time to time and related all that had transpired since the McCoys moved to Buffalo Creek. I paused a moment, then added, "After the McCoys killed Grandpa Dillon, Pa and I became suspicious about the house burning down. We checked the ruins of the burned out house. We had cleaned it up pretty well, but I found the remains of a torch made of kerosene soaked rags hidden by the weeds. The arsonists had thrown flaming torches on the roof. They thought the fire would destroy any evidence of wrongdoing. The torch I found had evidently rolled off the roof as they fled."

Barney's face was like marble. His eyes were grim, and he demanded with marked impatience, "What happened to Ma and Pa?"

I dreaded the telling. I sat down on the edge of my chair facing him and carefully related the facts. "Jon and I got home late one evening. We had been gone two days and we hoped to find Ma and Pa in bed. Jon's brother Chick was taking care of the stock and he was some worried. Ma had left a note in the kitchen telling me they had gone to help Doc MacDermott deliver a baby. Pa never allowed Ma to travel alone, especially after all the trouble with the McCoys. The note said they would be back soon as the baby was born. Of course no one ever knew when a baby was going to hold up the works.

The moon rose full that night and as you all know our parents had a bit of the romanticist in their souls. They loved to drive along the beautifully illumined country roads, and I could just envision them taking their time enjoying the trip. It was a bit chilly yet, but they always had blankets in the buggy. Yet, with all the trouble we had had, I couldn't help but worry. Jon and I were debating whether we should go looking for them, when we heard a horse whinny. We hurried to the barn and found Pa's horse impatiently nudging the barn door. Ma and Pa were in the buggy unconscious and both were covered with blood. Pa was holding Ma protectively. We carried them in the house and put Pa on the couch and laid Ma on the bed. Ma seemed to be in a deep sleep; she had no serious bleeding, so we tended to Pa's needs first."

"How is he," Jon asked me anxiously?

"I was scared for the first time in my life. I glanced up at Jon and with a sob exclaimed, "He's God-awful bad, Jon. You better get Doc McDermott and Father Quirk. "A few moments later, I heard the thunder of hooves as Jon departed as though the Devil was snapping at his heels.

Pa's right arm was broken, and a broken rib had evidently punctured his lungs, for he was bleeding from the mouth and his breath was coming in gasps. In addition, he had three major lacerations on his head, any one of which might have killed him. Most of the blood on their persons and in the buggy belonged to Pa. I was sick when I first saw the bloody mess in the buggy. No one could lose that much blood and hope to survive. Chick, Jon's brother took care of the horse and buggy. He came in and went to work building up the kitchen fire and making fresh coffee. He knew we were in for a long night. Using compresses I got the bleeding stopped and bound two sticks on Pa's broken arm for temporary support. I looked up and Pa's eyes were studying me gravely.

He started to speak, and I shushed him and said, "Save your strength, Pa, you've lost a lot of blood." He shook his head and blood trickled from his mouth. Pa was broke up inside something fierce. He knew his time was short. Chick started to leave, but Pa motioned him to stay.

Speaking in a shallow, pain-racked voice Pa rasped, "After the baby was born, your Ma and I went into town to see Richard and Theresa, Ma had had one of her intuitions and insisted that we make out our last will and testament. You know Ma when her mind is set. We knew you were at the Ridge farm helping out, so after the will was made out and signed, we visited with Theresa and her family and waited until after supper to set out for home." With an attempt at levity he added, "You know how Ma loves her moonlight rides." With a wry grimace he exclaimed, "Reckon she was right about the will, Matthew." A spasm erased Pa's sickly grin. I wiped the blood from his mouth and sponged his face with a wet cloth. For a moment, I thought he was gone.

He rallied once again and said with a touch of awe, "Strange, isn't it, Son. This morning God brought a life into the world and tonight he takes one away." He gasped with pain and grabbed my hand as though suddenly aware that his time was short. His voice barely audible, he grunted words in short gasps, "Twenty mounted men—McCoys—wore white robes and flour-sack masks." Two men grabbed the horse's reins, and J.D. McCoy yelled, 'Yo O'Shannons hev been tried by God and found want'en.' "I recognized McCoy's voice—their horses. Tried to protect Ma—too many—beat us—pick handles.'

I got all choked up. He cleared his throat and tried to speak. Pa lapsed into a coma again. I thought he was dead. A few minutes later, he woke, tried to rise and fell back with a despairing groan. His eyes cleared and his voice firmed up and he asked, "How's Ma, Matthew?"

To sooth him, I replied, "Ma will be fine, Pa. She's sleeping now."

His face relaxed and he became more lucid and said with a wry smile, "The Angels will be disappointed when I arrive without my Lois, Matthew. Tell Ma my last thoughts were of her and our family. You're a good man, Matthew. I'm proud you're my son. I wish Byron was here—tell him and the girls, and my grandchildren that I love them." He laid his hand on my head, blessed me and added, "Remember your priorities, Matthew. Always be true to God, family, and country in that order." Suddenly, Pa retched and blood spewed from his mouth as a contraction of pain racked his body. He wheezed, "Say an Act of Contrition with me, Matthew."

"We began the Act of Contrition, but Pa's Guardian Angel and I had to finish it for him. After checking on Ma, I prepared Pa for burial. Chick got all choked up and went out to check on the horses and I found out later that he had cleaned up the mess in the buggy. I cut off Pa's blood-soaked clothes, bathed his body, and dressed him in his best suit. I sewed the gashes together, and combed his hair over them the best I could. I kept checking on Ma, but she seemed to be asleep. I folded Pa's hands on his chest and placed pennies in his eyes. Chick kept coming in, maintaining the kitchen fire, and kept checking with me to see if he could help."

I then related to the family how Ma had died. When I finished, I told them, "Ma pleaded with me to promise her that Jon and

I would move to the Western Lands and not retaliate against the McCoys. She had a dread of us killing anyone." I sat down and began sipping my cup of coffee.

Byron snorted, 'You mean that you promised Ma to move out west and not kill anyone?'

"Exactly right," I responded. "Ma quoted your letters. To her, the West sounded like the Promised Land."

Byron shook his head in disbelief. He stood up and began pacing up and down with his hands clasped behind his back, a trait inherited from Grandpa Dillon. He stopped in front of me, placed his hands on his hips and asked hopefully, "You're not going—are you?"

I looked up at him—rather surprised, thought for a moment, and replied. "Barney, I haven't had time to think. I glanced at Jon for support and said defensively, "Now that you bring it up, I promised Ma, and I don't reckon I can break a deathbed promise." Even as the words spilled from my mouth, my heart did a flip-flop. Everyone had heard about the Wild West, and the shootouts and mayhem that went on. Jon and I had read the Penny Dreadful Magazines that depicted the daring exploits of Wild Bill Hickok, Buffalo Bill Cody, and Clay Allison. The stories had made our blood course with excitement. I don't believe many pioneers went west with the thought of killing anyone, but to go into such an environment, and not face such a possibility would be downright stupid.

Byron looked at me thoughtfully and admitted, "I guess I'm to blame, Matt. I didn't want Ma to worry, so I glossed over the hardness of Western life. If I had told her the facts, she would never have asked you to go."

Dick Tyson rubbed his jaw reflectively and interrupted him, "I think she would have, Barney. After the will was completed, Ma spoke to Terry and me of her fears. It seems her neighbor, Phoebe Vance, confided in her about a feud brewing along the W.Va. and Kentucky border, southwest of Huntington down to Pikeville. Most hill people are honest, proud and law-abiding, except when the Federal Govt. thinks they can tell them what they can do with their corn squeezins." he added with wry smile.

But near Pikeville it seems the unwelcome amorous intentions of those trying to sow their seed in their neighbor's womenfolk has led to murder. Abner Vance, Phoebe's cousin, was a staunch hard-shell Baptist. He was an Elder of the Clinch Mountain River Valley Church. He shot and killed a Dr. Horton, who had seduced his daughter. Today, Abner Vance is hidden deep in the hills to avoid arrest. In addition, last year the McCoys and Hatfields got into a silly argument over the ownership of some pigs, which created much bad will. By the way, these McCoys are not related to J. D. McCoy's family. Ma said she had had a premonition that a full-blown feud was developing down there. She was concerned that the same would happen here."

Dick asked, "Jon, you and Matt have explored every hill and dell of that part of the State. "The hills of West Virginia and Kentucky have been populated for generations with very little feuding. Do you think a feud is possible?"

"Yep," Jon replied, "we know that area very well, Richard. "The Tug River is the boundary between West Virginia and Kentucky where all the trouble has been. However, the hill homes are more widely disbursed than those around here. The hills go straight up and down like they are in Logan and you can get lost by just turning around. As you know my family has intermarried with some Mingo Indians who live down that way so my people are rather knowledgeable about the area.

Jon said with some pride, "The town of Logan, W. Va. was named in honor of Captain John Logan, the chief of the Mingo Indian Tribe; they are actually a loose conglomeration of any number of tribes. My sister is married to a kin of Captain Logan, and as you know the town of Logan is the County Seat. Some of our kin moved down on the Tug River right in the middle of that bunch of Hatfields and McCoys. The Tug River is nearly synonymous with Pikeville. That whole area is dissected by a maze of narrow gorges and hills so steep that only a mountain goat or a razor back hog can climb them. It's heavy timber country on the ridges, and there's even a Buffalo Creek down there. It's a wilderness, wild and rambunctious, and the people are a proud, honest, backwoods folk that could certainly be riled to killing to protect their own."

"If I remember correctly," I interjected, "Pikeville, Kentucky was named for Zebulon M. Pike an explorer in the Lewis and Clark era. Pike's Peak was named for him and Pikeville is the County Seat. Jon and I traveled over a lot of Eastern Kentucky. Once the people learned we were neighbors and friends of the Vances, they treated us royally. We shared many a meal with various families. Many of their homes are twenty miles apart, and we found them built on ridges, or down in snug valleys, and some were built clinging precariously to the side of hills that go straight up and down. The mountains are so steep, rugged, and thick with growth that they are nearly impassible. The joke down there is for folks not to walk one way around a mountain more than a month at a time unless they make sure to reverse their path and walk the other direction for a month. It seems one leg will get shorter unless they do." I got hooted down with that pun, but continued,

"Most folks there live in rough log cabins made with two large rooms, one for sleeping and one for eating. They look just like the ones we all helped the McCoys to build when they first moved here. Kentuckians have lived like that for generations. The Vances, Hatfields, Chafins, Mahons, and Ferrells, as well as the McCoys, Sowards, Normans, Stuarts, and Rutherfords have lived as peaceful neighbors for years. They eke out a living from the hogs they turn loose in the hills, and from hunting, fishing, logging, growing corn, and distilling moonshine. The women dig ginseng, pluck feathers, make beeswax, can honey, beans and corn, and make sorghum from sweet cane. To this day Johnse Hatfield sells the white lightning his family distills near Pikeville, Kentucky. When we called on any family, they fed us and gave us the best bed in the common sleeping room. Usually, we got a fine down-feather-bed, while the rest of the family slept on corn-husk-filled mattresses. I have to agree with Jon, if those folk's pride got hurt, there would be all hell to pay."

When I paused, Dick Tyson stated, "As I told you, Ma had one of her visions after her talk with Mrs. Vance. She sees nothing but bloodshed and violence for those people for years to come. She also said that our current situation here is more explosive than that of the McCoys and Hatfields. Ma pointed out that a feud blossoms from pride, ignorance, bigotry and the breakdown of basic Christian principles. She simply did not wish to see her family destroy itself through vengeance."

"That's well as it might be," Byron said grimly. "I can tell you boys point blank, if you go out west with a pacifist philosophy, you'll win a free trip to boot hill. I reckon it's my fault for not telling Ma the bad as well as the good. Like the Promised Land in the Old Testament, the West is truly a land of milk and honey. The Hebrews, however, had to learn first how to survive in a hostile environment, and then they had to take by force the Canaanite's land promised them by God.

I encountered three major obstacles during my tour of the West. First, the West's "Canaanites" are hostile Indians from a hundred different tribes. Many of them are the remnants of tribes driven from their homes in the East by the westward expansion of the United States. During the last three Centuries, they have carved new homes for themselves throughout the Western Territories. The territories they occupy belong to them by right of conquest. They don't lay claim to individual plots of land the way white men do, to them a vast tract of land is considered their back yard and they will fight other tribes, or the white man to keep it.

The Indian warrior gains prestige by how great a hunter he is and the number of horses he steals, how often he counts coup, and how many scalps he takes in battle. Second, the West is full of human parasites. Like vultures, they prey on the hard work and sweat of honest men. Killing is all too common. Third, your worst enemy is the land itself. You are either in tune with the elements, or the land will bury you. If you want proof, the wagon train trails are paved with the graves of hundreds of pioneers.

Most settlers never took into consideration the fact that they would be hundreds of miles from apothecaries, stores, and doctors. The law is even more remote. The only law west of St. Louis is the law you tote in your holster." Byron stood up, came over, dropped his hand on my shoulder and said; "If you two sprouts naively go west and won't kill—even to protect yourselves—your promise to Ma will become your epitaph."

I bristled a bit at the word 'sprouts' and replied tartly, "You been there three years, Barney, and I don't see any notches on your pistol."

Byron's jaw tensed, "Notches are for tinhorns and four-flushers." His eyes flashing steel, he added, "Somehow, I expected better from you." I bit my lip, and had the grace to blush.

Dick spoke up and in his best professional voice declared, "Perhaps now would be a good time to read the will?"

Dick had all the where-as and where-fores in the correct places. The gist was; as the eldest male, Byron inherited the farm. I had already taken control of Grandpa's horse farm, which, I had been running for two years under Pa's supervision. My three sisters inherited the rest of the estate, which, when split three ways was a nominal amount. Jon was also included and fell heir to a pair of Pa's best Arabian breeding horses that Grandpa had trained. Grandpa had named the stud for Chief Logan, and the mare's name was Pocahontas. After Grandpa's murder, my mother and father told Jon of his future inheritance, they insisted that Jon start handling the horses as his own. Jon had been riding Pocahontas for three years, and had bred her twice with Chief Logan.

The will contained no surprises, for Ma and Pa had made their intentions clear over the years.

Afterwards, I made my peace with Byron. I asked, "Forgive me, Barney for my big mouth. I think I've been reading too many Penny Dreadfuls?"

He was pleased, evidenced by his warm eyes and lop-sided grin. The concept of actually killing people was a new experience for me. True, I had vowed vengeance after Grandpa was murdered, and had done the same when Ma and Pa lay dying. Pa had had a talk with me after Grandpa was murdered. He read the black mood I was in and suspected that I would seek to revenge Grandpa Dillon. Because of Pa's guidance, there had been no gun justice for Grandpa, and now there would be no gun justice for Ma and Pa. I had, in effect promised Ma; I would—like a coward—runaway.

*B*ITTERSWEET VENGEANCE

CHAPTER THREE

Byron was the patient type; for the next day or two the subject of my going west never came up. We both had farms to work. Yet, I knew we had to talk—and soon. Farming wise, I had less of a problem than my brother did. Actually, Grandpa's place had been mine since his murder. For two years, I had been learning the pleasures as well as the grief of owning and running one's own farm. Grandpa had written his will after Grandma died. He and Pa agreed that Byron, as the eldest son, would inherit Pa's farm, and I was to inherit Grandpa's farm upon his death. Dick Tyson, as the administrator of the estate, was holding the farm in trust for me until I was twenty-one. However, before Byron and I could get started, the arrival of grieving family and friends made our agendas for us. The Ridge families, once again, God bless them, came to our rescue and took over our chores.

Kristine Mary, her husband Dallas Pinckard and their two children arrived the day after the funeral. Mary Kathleen, her husband Thomas Jackson Helmick and their four children arrived shortly after the Helmicks. Upon each arrival, I had to retell and relive the nightmarish details of our parent's violent deaths, although, I had learned to mitigate the more severe aspects of their murders. Of course Terry and her family came immediately amidst a flood of friends and sympathizers, who beat a path to our door bearing gifts of food, love and empathy, and in spite of our mourning, we counted our blessings.

A week later, Byron and I stood in the barnyard waving and shouting final good byes to our sisters and their excited children as they drove off at a spanking trot in their fancy, fringed surreys. Heavily armed, Jon and five of his relatives escorted them into Huntington to see them safely ferried across the Ohio River. As the rigs faded from sight, Barney and I instinctively locked eyes, as though seeking some redress for our misery. In his eyes, I saw the same bewilderment and gnawing grief that had kneaded my gut into knots for days. We turned and walked inside.

The empty kitchen and the sudden silence accentuated our misery. Byron poured two cups of coffee, looked at me speculatively and quipped; "Now we know how a duck feels in a shooting gallery."

"Yeah," I responded, "every time I step out the door I feel naked as a plucked chicken. A bushwhacker can pick us off anytime. I can't carry a rifle and get any work done; while a six-gun is comforting, for distance, it's useless as the teats on a boar hog. I send Stonewall Jackson out every morning to scout, or I would be jumping at every shadow." Hearing his name, Stone Wall's tail thumped a happy beat on the front porch where he lay sprawled without a care in the world. Half collie and half hound, he had inherited all the aggressive and defensive traits of Rex our bitch collie, as well as her beauty. He had all the hunting talents, and good disposition of Buck, his sire. Rex jumped up and trotted to the door looking hopefully for a handout, while Buck slept fitfully, his muscles quivered and jumped, as in his dreams, he reveled in his latest rabbit chase.

Jon and I, when we were hunting, had taught Stonewall to scout ahead. The first morning I worked grandpa's farm after his murder, I went to the door and spoke, "Jack." His ears twitched with joyful anticipation and when I said, "Scout," he turned casually and strolled off the porch and like a wraith faded off into the early morning mists. Jack never broke his trust by chasing rabbits, coons, or startled deer. He was as serious as any Indian Scout ever was. When he found something note worthy, he came back and assumed a perfect point facing the direction of his find. Now feeling our tension, on his own initiative he began to scout around the house at night.

"Too bad Jackson isn't twins," Barney griped, as he slipped a packet of long cigarillos from his shirt pocket, a habit he had acquired from the Mexicans in the New Mexico Territory. He offered me one of the thin cigars with a quizzical grin.

I declined and said, "Reckon, I'll stick to Grandpa's favorite, and I filled my corncob pipe, which was the twin to Grandpa's old pipe.

I stoked up and Byron asked, "Is this branch of McCoys related to the ones you said Ma dreamt about?"

"Their family lived near Pikeville, Kentucky, Barney, but Tom Vance, whose family still live there, claims they were shirttail kin at best. They're a clannish bunch. If you see one McCoy, chances are there's half-a-dozen close by. Gabriel is the eldest son by J.D.'s second wife. I've never seen him in action, but Vance's kin claims Gabe's streaked lightning with a pistol; a crack shot with a rifle, and has a rep as a bruiser. They said he fancies himself as a ladies' man. Vance's kin claims he was sparking one of the Hatfield gals in Pikeville, but it seems he erred in judgment. She said no! When he tried to force the issue she screamed and papa came running. According to the gossip the McCoy boys had a bad reputation, and Gabe was said to be the worst of the lot. The Community was fed up with the McCoy's shenanigans and the Reverend McCoy's gospel of hate, and when they thought the McCoys had hung another black man, the folks turned ugly and dispensed a little swift justice. So you don't get confused there are McCoys and Hatfields living on both sides of the Tug River. The Hatfields, backed by their friends and city authorities, sent the entire bunch packing. That was Pikeville's good fortune and the beginning of our grief."

Byron stretched, yawned, and complained, "Matt, you know as well as I do, if those bushwhackers want us dead, it's just a matter of time until they succeed." He eyed me and said, "Every time I go to the outhouse, I feel like the bull's eye in a shooting gallery."

I snorted, "I have to admit, I've developed the tightest pucker on Buffalo Creek."

He chuckled, but then added seriously, "Matt, it's time we made a move. If I learned anything out west, it was that a good offense is the best defense. The McCoys have had things going their own way too along. Those bastards have killed three members of our family with impunity. You know damned well buzzards like that won't be satisfied till they've laid us in the ground. What's worse," he emphasized with an out-thrust jaw, "with no witnesses, they'll get away with it. I'll be damned," he added with lethal intent, "if I'll just sit here like a good little lamb and wait to be slaughtered."

I got up, shook down the kitchen stove's ashes, and added a couple of pieces of wood. My brother wasn't one to act rashly—that was usually my trick. I knew he was deadly earnest. I was somewhat surprised with Byron's invective. Before he left home, I had never heard him cuss, and to Ma, the use of "ain't" was like swearing. Of course being alone with Ma and Pa so much, we spoke as they spoke. Off-color jargons were certainly common, and believe you me, we knew all the words, but we had never become accustomed to using them. In our era men of good character seldom relied on vulgarity to express themselves. However, for Byron, all that was three years ago. In his absence, however, Barney had not become course or vulgar. Instead, I noted he seemed to have grown mentally tough and worldly wise in a land that allowed few mistakes.

My conscience left me no recourse. I removed the pipe from my mouth and replied thoughtfully, "Reckon I'll just have to bite the bullet, Barney. For now, discretion is our best bet. Pa warned me, if anything happens to a McCoy, the law would lay the blame on our doorstep. If we need to go into Huntington, we can avoid confrontation by taking the ridge, logging trail we made when we felled trees for the house. The road ends in Westmoreland and we can, go on into Huntington together. Better yet, we could just transfer our business to the County Seat in Wayne."

Byron's jaw tightened and he said bluntly, "The day I take one step to avoid the McCoys will be the day Church Bells ring in hell."

I knew Barney was right, because, I felt the same way, but this attitude could only lead to gunplay. I was some surprised. This wasn't the old Barney that I had known three years ago. He got up, poured himself another cup of coffee, held up the pot and at my nod refilled my cup. Yet, we were both of stubborn stock. When he made up his mind, my brother was like granite.

I hoped to back him off from his determined stance and said, "Barney, I promised Ma I would go west to avoid killing. She would want you to do the same. If it wasn't for my promise, I'd have killed every damned McCoy on Buffalo Creek, or run their asses back to Kentucky. But Ma was right; with time, my desire to exact revenge has cooled. But, I am too much like you, if I see a McCoy; I sure as hell won't run. I think it's time we head west, before all hell busts loose, and I end up breaking my promise to Ma."

Restless and as dangerous as a coiled rattler, I could see Byron fighting for control. He stood up, leaned forward, and resting his knuckles on the table top, he stated flatly, "Why can't you get it through that thick head of yours, if you go west, the odds are you'll end up having to kill someone or you won't last a month. Even if fighting riff raff can be avoided, when Indians attack, you kill or you die." His tone softened and he added gruffly, "Matt, you of all people, know that I'm not a violent person. However, I know what I'm talking about. Two men lay dead by my hand and at least six Indians. Believe me, old Son, killing was my last alternative. I took no pleasure in their deaths."

I was stunned, quiet, good-natured Byron, a killer? At first, my mind refused to accept such a concept. Then, with a sick feeling, I had to acknowledge the fact. My brother had never lied to me. My heart went out to him. My artless statement about notches on his gun must have cut like a knife. Byron wasn't one to share his innermost feelings, but I knew his killing of any man would rest heavy on his conscience. My voice gruff with emotion, I went to him and said, "My God, Barney, forgive me and my big mouth. I can only imagine how you must feel."

He gave me a warm hug and grunted, "Forget it, Matthew. But keep it between the two of us. There's no reason for the rest of the family to know. I only told you to keep you from getting yourself killed."

I sat down, my heart heavy. I was a homebody. I had never really considered going west or anywhere else for that matter. I looked at all the kitchen items, so familiar to my glance. The thought of never seeing any of these familiar items again caused my heart to do a flip-flop. The more we discussed going west, the more I realized that that was exactly what I had to do. What's more, I had to convince my brother that he didn't have any more choice than I did. I pointed out, "Barney, the longer we delay, the greater the risk that we will tangle with the McCoys. You can bet those skunks will have a whole passel of witnesses swearing that we started the trouble."

Rubbing his chin thoughtfully, he sat down. Looking me in the eyes, he stated firmly. "I heard you before, little brother, and I assure you, I'm not dumb enough to play into their hands. Here's what I think we should do. By now, those McCoys think they have an open hunting season on us O'Shannons. I don't think it will be long before they set up another ambush. Why don't we make it easy for them? When Jon comes back tonight, I'm sure we can hire some of his Indian cousins to take over the work on our farms. We need someone to work the fields, take care of the stock, and guard the barns and houses, or sure as hell the McCoys will burn us out when we are working the fields or go into town."

Getting up, Byron stepped over to the small bookrack, took down Pa's copy of Blackstone—slapped it down in front of me—and said, "We've all read this old book again and again. If we hope to put the McCoys in jail, we'll have to prove that they intended to do us great bodily harm. Let's go to Wayne tonight and see Emmet. I'm sure the Sheriff will give us a couple of deputies for a few days. Then we can form a legal posse and beat them at their own game. We both know a dozen men who will help us stake out a reception committee for those back shooting rats."

I jumped up and exclaimed, "I'm sure Emmet will be glad to cooperate. He was sure frustrated when he couldn't bring the McCoys to justice. Pa and the sheriff were close. Right after you left, Pa campaigned for him when he ran for sheriff of Wayne County. Pa's efforts insured him a Catholic majority in Huntington, and his influence with our neighbors swung the Buffalo Creek vote. Another thing you should know. Tom Vance knows quite a bit about the McCoys and their bad habits. It seems they take great delight in intimidating folks and they like to play on the superstitions of their victims. Back in Pikeville, they used to mask themselves by wearing white sheets and sugar-sack masks like those Klansmen we've been hearing about from on down South."

Barney murmured, "Maybe they are Klu Klux Klan members?"

I nodded in agreement and agreed, "Yep—could be. Vance says the McCoys before they left Pikeville burnt crosses in the yards of several colored families, as well as a couple of Catholics and one Jew. They hung two black men, and horsewhipped a few others. The law was helpless because they had no witnesses, although everyone knew it was the McCoys. The raider's habit was to strike during the light of a full moon. Ma and Pa were killed during a full moon. The moon won't be full again for a few weeks. I doubt if the McCoys will make their move now when it's as black at night as the caverns of hell. It should give us plenty of time to prepare them a proper reception committee."

Barney grunted, "There is one big flaw in my plan, if the McCoys fire their weapons, the law will have to call on them to cease and desist. Even if they killed one of us, they may be too smart to resist arrest. If caught, old J. D. McCoy would simply claim that they were out hunting coons and had no idea their shots endangered our lives."

I grinned and said wryly, "I have to agree," and my eyes sparkled with an idea. "How does this thought grab you?"

As I spoke, Byron began nodding his head in agreement. "It's so blessed simple, it just might work." He looked at me as though seeing me for the first time since his return and commented, "You not only grew big as a house while I was gone, but I reckon you picked up a little gray matter." He bobbed his head in approval and asked me, "Just how good are you with that pistol? You were pressing me hard when I went west."

I countered and reminded him, "I remember before you pulled stakes that you and Angus Ferguson were considered the best shots in Wayne County. How much have you improved?"

Byron, with his faint lop-sided grin, replied, "Some, and you?"

I puffed contentedly on my pipe, enjoying the bite on my tongue and remarked, "Reckon I'll let you tell me, when the time comes." He eyed me speculatively for a moment and then let it lay.

The next night we rode up over Harmon Hill, and down through Lavallette country. About ten that evening, we rode into the quaint city square that surrounded the Wayne County Courthouse that reigned majestically from the center of the square. Pressing on past the square, we approached Emmet's comfortable, two-story Victorian house that was loaded with all kinds of frills and fancy scrolls of woodwork that folks referred to as—gingerbread. Like most folks thereabouts, he had gone to bed with the chickens, but his dogs gave us a hearty welcome. The time was nine-fifty and we heard him growling irritably as he thumped down the stairs. When he saw us, he exclaimed "You old, coonhounds," and grabbed us by the hands, "You're pure d lucky I didn't open up with my scatter gun." His grin softened his words. He demanded, "What's you fool kids doing waken a man up in the middle of the night?" His face suddenly flashed concern and he asked, "Yo folks ain't had no more ruckus with them thar McCoys—hev yo"

Before we could answer Emmet's wife Lettie came down the stairs tying her robe about her waist. Seeing us she gushed, "Emmet, whar's yo manners. Yo boys come right on in," and she grabbed us and marched us into the kitchen. "Sheriff, yo jes set them boys right down, and I'll fetch that apple pie I jes baked, and a pitcher of cold buttermilk."

Lettie had taken the death of our parents hard, but like most countrywomen, she was delighted to have company. She whipped out a mouth-watering apple pie from her pie safe; without asking—she cut it into quarters. The four of us dug in and made short work of it. She passed the time of day and when we finished eating; she gathered the dishes into her dry sink and excused herself.

The sheriff patted his stomach and growled as she left, "If I get indigestion, yo boys aer gonna be in big trouble with the law." We laughed and he asked, "Now, jes what in tarnation are yo fellers doing here this time a night?"

Byron smiled, "We apologize for the late hour, Emmet, but we want to keep our business mighty private. Matthew will fill you in, it's his idea."

I leaned back, burped contently, and outlined to the Sheriff what we had cooked up. When I finished, he scratched his belly contentedly, grinned and asked, "Yo say the room will be all lit up and only be a hunnert yards from the tree line?"

I nodded and he rubbed his chin, chuckled and said, "If caught, it sho won't give a man much room ta squirm. Jes to be sure, I'll check with the County Judge and if he agrees, we'll be thar after dusk the night before the full moon. I'll send yo word if we'uns ain't a coming." Rubbing his chin thoughtfully he observed, "Reckon three or four deputies kin kiver all the likely spots."

On our return, when we neared Harmon Hill, we dismounted and from our saddlebags took pads of deer hide and wrapped the horse's hooves. It was no time to get careless. We didn't even want Tom Harmon to know what was going on until the time was ripe. We were beat when we cantered into our barnyard about four in the morning. Out of the shadows, Jon's voice greeted us with "How"

Barney holstered his pistol, grinned and growled, "You still playing that silly game, Jon?"

He laughed and replied, "Call it poetic Indian justice. 'Know-Nothings' expect Indians to be ignorant; it amuses me to play on their bigotry. When you fellows came tippy toeing up the path with muffled hooves, I sure thought I had me a couple of McCoys." He stepped from the shadows, a double-barreled shotgun cradled on his arm. Taking our horse's reins, he asked. "How'd it go? Should I put on my war paint, do my war dance, and sing my death song?"

I chuckled and replied, "I think the McCoys will dance to a different tune this time, Jon."

He grunted his approval and said, "Foods hot in the Dutch oven; there's cold milk in the spring house. You fellows go eat; I'll take care of Pat and Mike. The horses hearing their names nuzzled his arm.

Dismounting, we stomped life back into our legs, and Byron asked Jon, "The Know-Nothing Party, I haven't heard of them in years. How come you're so all blamed smart?"

Jon put on his blandest Indian face and said, "Poor ignorant Injun hear'um white-eyes teacher speak of Samuel F. B. Morse, inventor of singing wires. Teacher say, he heap big man, but also heap big bigot, and rabid hater of Roman Catholics. He start Know-Nothing movement and in the 1850s the American Party elected one hundred members to Congress. Millions of starving Irish immigrants was pouring into American cities and the demagogues claimed, "Irish no appreciate democracy, liberty, or hard work," and they predicted the fall of democracy."

Byron laughed saying, "Save your phony lingo for the bigots. Those same people accused the Irish of sloth, the Italians for distrusting outsiders, and said the Mexicans trusted nobody outside the family. Bigots thrive on hate and I'm afraid immigrants will always have people like the McCoys with which to contend."

Jon came in as we finished eating, and I poured coffee all around. I nodded to the door, "Good idea that blanket."

Jon grunted, "Tain't no reason to give em a good target."

"Any problems," I asked?

"Nope! There's six of my kin on each farm, four sleep and two guard round the clock. Work's all up to snuff. Jack scouts half the night; he 'hain't pinted' once," he added with a grin. The McCoys are lying low." He smiled, "A few of our youngsters volunteered to keep an eye on their comings and goings."

Barney looked up, concerned, "Jon, that's no place for children. The McCoys consider them nothing but varmints."

Jon chuckled; "They are having the time of their lives. There isn't a McCoy that will ever set eyes on them. If they use dogs, the boys have paprika, mustard and rank smelling plants that no dog can handle."

The three of us, accompanied by Jack, were in the saddle before dawn. Just up the hollow, which faced our cabin, was a tall, but shallow, sandstone cave. To the left, up a steep bank, was the lumbermen's ridge road that led to Westmoreland. The cave commanded a natural access to the farm and from there it went up a steep path to our cornfield on top of the hill. I noted, "We'll have to guard our front door. A few riflemen could make it hot for us from up here."

Barney nodded his agreement and suggested, "While we're here let's go on up and check out the cornfield. As the horses labored up the rugged path he commented, "I hate to think of how many times I plowed these forty acres."

"Yeah, I know." I agreed. "Who do you think inherited the job when you left?"

"It couldn't have happened to a nicer kid," he replied with a laugh.

On top of the hill my ancestors had cleared the land of trees, brush and rocks. While plowing the ground I had often thought of the weeks and months of hard back breaking labor it had taken to clear so much land. They certainly didn't do it all at one time. From there, I knew if one turned left—cut down the far side of the hill, and followed the natural water run off one came to the shallow, sandstone bed-rock, Little Sandy River, in which we youngsters had learned to swim and fish. Across the river sat a thriving food, grain, and feed store. When we grew older, however, the Ohio River became our favorite haunt for fishing and family gatherings. We boys loved to go boating and ride the waves made by the paddle wheelers that made regular runs up and down the river. We often saw huge rafts of logs and barges loaded with trade goods heading for the larger markets downstream. We fished near waterlogged piles of logs and caught huge pike catfish and pike garfish. We never ate the ugly garfish but they sure put up one-heck-of-a fight.

As we emerged on top of the hill, Jack froze into a point. At my gesture, Jack flushed the covey. The quail exploded in our faces. My pistol flowed into my hand; I cranked off three rounds. Beside me, a split second later, Jon's six-gun coughed off two rounds and when Barney looked up our guns were holstered.

Barney sat frozen with his hand on his pistol grip. He laughed and said, "You crazy kids, what are you wasting your shells for?" I smiled and Jon ordered, "Fetch, Jack." A few seconds later Jack laid three headless quail at my feet, and dropped the last one at Jon's foot.

Jack sat down, cocked his head with his tongue lolling in his mouth and looked up for approval. "Good dog, Jack," I slid down, picked up a quail, and tossed it to him. While I stuffed the quail in my saddlebags, Jack trotted off into the brush, and we could hear him making a quick breakfast.

Barney gaped a moment and then grunted, "I seen it, but I don't believe it." Looking at me, he asked, "How come Jack gave you three birds and Jon only one?"

Jon grinned and admitted, "I reckon I shot a mite fast my first shot, but Jack always knows the score.

Barney took off his hat, scratched his head, and commented, "I've heard of a few men who shoot that well, but I have never seen it done." He put his hat back on and tipping his hat to us said, "I take my hat off to you, gentlemen, I reckon the McCoys are in for a real surprise." Then his face fell and he growled, "What good does it to shoot so blessed well if you stick to your promise to Ma?"

I looked him in the eye and stated firmly, "Barney, I promised Ma, and I'll do my best to keep my word. However, I never said I wouldn't defend myself. Jon and I've talked it over, and I reckon, to keep alive, we'll just have to shoot any bad men or Indians that want our hides. We shoot just as well with rifles, although I have to admit Jon is by far the best. He can bring down a running buck at four hundred yards."

Jon said, "I told your ma, Barney, that I wouldn't kill McCoys, and I'll do my dad-gummed best to keep my word. If I can't stop a man by winging him, I reckon I'll have to cross that bridge when the time comes." Byron didn't approve our decision, but we did agree as to where we should post the posse men subject to Sheriff' Johnson's approval.

Two weeks later, dusk shielded the arrival of the Sheriff and his four deputies. Among them was Shurley Elkins a well known hunter and trapper, his companion Lesley Adkins, and two regular deputies, John Murdock and Stanley Scarbury, all tough, dependable men. Stanley had lost his right arm during the Civil War, but he could handle himself better with his stump and one arm than most men could with two. Jon had scouts out to warn of any unwanted guests. One by one, twelve of our loyal friends drifted in throughout the night, most of them arriving just before daylight. We bedded them down in the two huge upstairs bedrooms. Emmet swore in the posse and we spent the rest of the day under cover firming up our plans, playing poker, laughing and hurrahing one another.

That night, had I prayed long and hard that there would be no casualties. Then doubts plagued me, and I began to question my own judgment. Had I miscalculated the McCoy's intentions? With a curse, I flopped over and tried to get some sleep, with the men coming and going it was going to be a long night.

Eight of the Indians we hired had also volunteered their services; altogether we totaled twenty-eight men. Opposing us, we had to assume that there were at least twenty McCoys and possibly more if they recruited some of our turncoat neighbors. I didn't believe they would—McCoys trusted McCoys—no one else. They wanted no witnesses to their dastardly deeds. At nine o'clock the eight Indians faded off into the night forming a ring of scouts about the farm.

The full moon was soon climbing the sky, its muted light revealing an enchanted, serene panorama that belied the lethal intent of the scattered groups of our posse. The moon created dark shadows about the forests and farm buildings, which only aggravated our frayed nerves. The sheriff and two sharp-shooting neighbors were entrenched in the house. Its foot-thick, near impenetrable log walls gave them ample protection from all but perhaps a .50 caliber Sharps rifle. A kerosene lamp's flickering light outlined the details of the downstairs bedroom. We had posted men on the road and creek about a quarter of a mile from the farmhouse. None of us believed an attack was likely from the creek beds since they were so rough, pitted with deep pools, and laced with dead trees. Our plan was to allow the McCoys to pass our guard positions; then our men were to quietly close in behind them. After the posse settled down in their various posts—silence filtered like a shroud over the valley floor. Deceived by the calm, a rabbit whinnied from the hillside, and a barn owl hooted inquiringly. The night was filled with the added chorus of crickets and frogs, which could have lulled us into a false feeling of tranquility if our mission had not been so serious.

We had posted Jon and a deputy with a small group of men just off the road between the farm and the McCoy homesteads. We deemed it entirely possible that in their arrogance, the McCoys might come straight down the road leading directly to our farm. Our barn, which bordered the dirt road, was located a hundred yards in front of the house. My post was inside the barn backed up by three men and one deputy. Byron was also with us. The basic plan centered on him, and the timing of the arrival of the McCoys. The remainder of our men lay concealed behind grain-filled sacks placed strategically between the house and the barn. Then came the hard part—waiting.

Sheriff Johnson had agreed to our plan. Jon's assignment was to guard the road along with Deputy John Murdock, Tom Harmon and Les Adkins. He told me later all that happened. As the night dragged on, we all lay back and relaxed enjoying the beauty of the night, and the dog chorus that had erupted the length of the valley. The dogs loved the full moon. Early on, from far down the creek one dog started howling, and one by one, the dogs from the next farm joined in, soon every dog in the valley had picked up the chorus. All up and down Buffalo Creek, the animals began their song that was to last for half the night. Some owners, tiring of their howling, yelled and stoned them to silence, only to have them erupt into song again even before all was quite inside. In full voice, coyote families added their yipping and yowling; and from somewhere far off sounded the wails of a lonely wolf. Many a night, I had drifted off to sleep soothed by this primitive choir of the wild.

I had tied Buck and Rex in the barn. The geese and guinea hens were penned up in their hen house as usual. Before long old Buck's deep baying and Rex and Jack's barking joined in howling in perfect harmony with Harmon's dogs on top of the mountain. We made a game of identifying the dogs by their distinctive baying, which helped pass the time, and before long midnight was closing in on us, and I was beginning to think we had wasted every ones time for nothing.

Jon's group made the first contact. He told me later of their actions. Jon said, "I hid my group deep in the shadows just off the road. We settled in. It was a beautiful, moonlit, tranquil night, and after awhile I began to reminisce about my heritage. My people have proved to be a most patient race. My people, the Cherokee, in the late 1700s and early 1800s had seen the wisdom of the white man's ways, and had adopted to live like white men. However, as Indians, they had their own manner of preparing and the eating of their produce. The Cherokee had simply been much too successful. The white man soon became envious of their rich lands, and beautiful homes; they passed laws to take their homes away from them. Most of our ancestors were uprooted from their comfortable homes in the Southeastern United States, because of white man's avarice for their homes and property. Soldiers forcible marched the Cherokee people to the Territory of Oklahoma, during which many thousands perished, it is remembered by our people, as the "Trail of Tears."

In 1809, prior to these events, my forefathers, fearful of the greed they saw in their white neighbor's eyes, sold their farms and moved to Western Virginia seeking refuge from the Cherokee's fate, which they considered inevitable. The O'Shannons purchased huge holdings for my forefathers. Much of which they did not fully develop, we grazed a few small herds of cattle and horses, and kept our tilled lands small and inconspicuous. We built simple, modest homes away from the known roads and trails, and learned to keep a low profile. In essence, we tried to make ourselves invisible to our white neighbors. We had remained so until the McCoys became our neighbors and focused every one's attention on us, which worried our leaders no end. Most of our people were Christians, but we were careful. We did not support the local church, but went to different churches in the surrounding area. My friends, the O'Shannons and their Catholic Religion impressed me, and when I was sixteen I converted to Catholicism. A few others in my family did likewise.

I read in White Man's books the history of the Indians that had preceded us in W. Va. I often wondered about the mysterious Mound Builders that had settled in West Virginia over 2000 years ago. They had built huge burial mounds, and little was known of their culture. What had happened to them? I was curious what history would say about the Cherokee Nation? We still taught our children the heritage of our people. Deep in the woods we learned the customs and lore of our forefathers. Drums we never used, but the clapping of hands and the slapping of thighs became a good substitute. We found arrows of the Huron Indians, who had preceded us, and we found the relics of the various tribes of the Iroquois Confederacy, including the Seneca that had used West Virginia and Kentucky as hunting grounds. They fought our people over them often, and Kentucky became known as the "Bloody Hunting Ground".

Our people married into the remnants of the Mingo Tribe, which was not really a tribe, but a multi-cultural group of Indians that settled in several points in West Virginia, especially around Logan. We found relics of the Conoy and Canawese people for whom the historians say the Little Kanawha and the Great Kanawha Rivers were named. The Shawnees—what had ever happened to the Shawnees? I had to face the facts—a bigger—more sophisticated enemy—the White Eyes—had conquered all the Red Races—I had to wonder—would they fare any better than we had—or would the white man—like the Indians—be eliminated by some superior race that would, say, in a thousand years—make it difficult to find remnants of their race?

Suddenly Les touched my leg and whispered, "Jon, we got company."

I had heard them long before, but said nothing. I grunted and whispered, "Time to play possum—not a sound now." The bright moon flooded the valley with light, and the Klan boys were riding right into our trap. Matt's hunch had been right, and I chuckled to myself amused by the predictable antics of the arrogant bushwhackers. Then, we saw them. The mounted men created a mottled white blotch that seemed to flow ominously along the contours of the road. The men dressed in their Klu Klux Klan robes rode past my men and me silently; grim specters of death; the shoes of their horses padded with deer hide. The only sounds were the soft clomping of hooves, the rustle of bits and the creaking of saddles. A horse suddenly slobbered with a snort cut short by a muttered curse and a savage yank on the reins. As the McCoys passed, the honest sweat of horses filled the Posse Comitatus men's nostrils, spoiled only by the honest smell of saddle leather and the nervous sweat of the bushwhackers. There were twenty of them, just like we had figured. Silently, we fell in behind them—every man alert with his rifle held ready. We walked in single file hugging the shadows at the side of the road leaving few signs for the McCoys to detect. Meanwhile—back to the barn where Matt was holed up.

Jon's brother, Martel Ridge, one of the scouts, flitted from shadow to shadow like an elusive will-o'-the-wisp, and slipped into the protective blackness of the barn. He declared his presence to us with the distinctive Screech of a hoot owl. As planned, Barney stepped from the barn carrying a lantern and headed for the house. Behind him, a cow lowed plaintively; there was nothing unusual about a farmer tending to a sick cow at any hour of the night or day. The Klansmen, seeing the light, stopped abruptly; then they swung off to one side of the road. After a quick exchange of whispers, two men detached themselves from the group and cut off on foot down into a field of young corn that was sprouting proudly. Strangely, but instinctively, the intruders, obviously farmers, for they crept between the rows and avoided stepping on the new corn. The men moved stealthily toward the house, the soft dirt muffling their footsteps. The breeze favored them carrying away their scent, and any sound they might have made, which ordinarily would have warned the dogs. However, alert to every sound, Jack growled, only to fall silent at my touch. The bushwhackers came to the split-rail fence that separated the house from the cornfield. Knelling, they used the top rail on which to rest their rifles. The lighted bedroom outlined Byron entering the room. He stopped, stretched, and tiredly tossed his hat and coat on a chair. Rosary in hand, he dropped to his knees before a statue of the Blessed Virgin Mary. Barney slowly made a sign of the cross, and began saying the rosary. At that precise moment, the screech of a cougar rent the air. Grandpa always said they sounded like a woman's scream. A shudder went down my spine. Suddenly, the sharp spang of two rifles ripped the beauty of the night into shreds; the two shots nearly blending as one. The sound of breaking glass shattered the night's calm, and abruptly the bedroom was plunged into darkness.

A shrill rebel yell of EE-OOO-EE rang out from the Klansmen—en masse, they thundered down the road, swung around the barn, and pushed on into the yard making enough noise to terrify the Devil himself. Every Klansmen's rifle bellowed its rage as the killers shot into every opening of the house creating a deadly hail of lead. Suddenly, hay soaked with kerosene that we had piled up a hundred feet in front of the house burst into flame outlining the bushwhackers in stark relief. The Sheriff bellowed from the house, "This here be Sheriff Johnson—drop yo weepons."

The Klansmen stopped firing and milled about utterly confused. There was a whispered consultation, and a dispute erupted with voices raised in anger. I recognized the Parson's roar of defiance.

The bushwhackers, some bending low over their horse's necks, wheeled about and at a dead run headed for the road firing their weapons at every shadow. The posse concentrated their rifle fire on the bushwhackers, as the Klansmen ran a gauntlet of fire down the full length of the yard. The sheriff and his men were firing from the house, and the bushwhackers ran into our pointblank fire angled from the barn. We emptied several saddles, and I saw men swaying in their saddles. I shot only once and was gratified to see a rifle go flying. The man's arm flopped with every bounce of his horse. The posse men from the cave wisely withheld their fire lest they shoot into our own people.

Jon told me that he and his men waited for the bushwhackers sheltered by the trees alongside the road. Four of their rifles coughed in unison emptying two saddles as the bunched bushwhackers pounded into view. One man cried out, and another emitted a hoarse gurgle of fear and pain. Jon raised his rifle to fire again, but his finger seemed frozen to the trigger. What was it that gripped his trigger finger? Was it Ma O'Shannon's spirit that stayed his hand, or were his ancestors calling on him to prove his manhood by counting coup? On sudden impulse, in spite of the Klansmen's deadly return fire, Jon jumped into the middle of the road facing the fleeing men and began chanting his Cherokee Challenge. The lead horses swerved slightly at the last second—Jon counted coup by touching the legs of two men with his rifle barrel as they thundered past. A gun muzzle suddenly flashed in his face and knocked him flat on his back. Jon felt pain shoot through his chest, and he was unable to get his breath, with a start, he realized that he had been hit—and hit hard.

Pitiful cries of wounded men rose from the barnyard; evidently Jon wasn't the only one hurt. Dazedly, he sat up panting for breath. He ran an exploratory hand across his chest feeling for the wound. "Damn," Jon exclaimed, and jerked his hand back—a wooden splinter stuck in his finger. With a curse, he yanked it out and began counting his blessings. A bullet had struck the stock of his gun driving the rifle into his chest. The blow had knocked him flat on his back and bashed the wind out of him. He grunted with pain as he got up.

Deputy Murdock ran to him exclaiming, "Yo all right, Jon, yo hurt?"

"Just my dignity, John, just my dignity," he growled rubbing his hind end. "Les, Tom," Jon called out, "you okay?"

"Great," Tom exclaimed excitedly. "Guess we'uns showed them thar bushwhackers a little ridge-runner justice." Les touched Jon and said with genuine awe, "Man, aer yo crazy? I never seed nuthen like that."

"Old Indian custom, White Eyes, but don't expect a repeat performance," Jon answered ruefully—still rubbing his rump.

John exclaimed, "Let's see if them two fellers aer done fer? Keerful now," he cautioned. He yelled, "This be Deputy Sheriff John Murdock, if yo McCoys aer still alive, yo's under arrest."

Jon sang out, "Don't get stupid, we've got four guns pointed at your belly buttons." Cautiously, Jon sidled near and a whiney voice pleaded, "Don't shoot, I'm hard hit."

Jon stepped behind him, removed his pistol, and yanked off his mask. "Well what-cha know," he drawled, "if it ain't little Benjamin McCoy. I was hoping for a bigger fish than the baby of the family." Benjamin was holding his shoulder, rocking back and forth in pain. Jon said cheerfully, "Reckon you must be the one I shot. I aimed for your shoulder, or you'd be dead now."

Gaining courage, Benjamin snarled, "Ain't yo gonna fix my shoulder, I could bleed to death, yo damned heathen?"

Murdock snapped, "Shet yer mouth, boy. Yo's under arrest for tempted murder and resisten arrest. If ary of our men be dead, yo'al be charged with murder."

Les and Tom came over, and Les exclaimed, "John, thet other McCoy was Eli, He's got three slugs in him—all plumb center; he never knew what hit him. Seems like we all picked the same target."

Murdock grunted, "Good riddance. Les, you and Tom lug Ben to the kitchen and bandage thet thar shoulder. Then decorate him with these irons. Jon and I'll tote Eli to the barn and hitch up a team."

The posse rounded up the McCoys downed in the barnyard. Three more raiders were dead, Ezekiel, Daniel, and Meshach. Ezekiel was J.D. McCoy's second eldest. His death would be a bitter blow. Lot, the oldest son, was gut shot, and he died a slow painful death.

His brother Joshua, nearly blinded with blood from a superficial scalp wound, held him in his arms trying to calm him.

Lot writhed in pain, and between spasms of pain complained bitterly to his brother, "I told Pa not to hurrah them folks. He refused to hear me. Said the Lord tol him it wuz right."

He doubled in pain and gasped, "Sheriff, ah tried ta tell J.D. not to fight. Ezekiel called me a yellow-livered coward. He let out a rebel yell, and the rest followed him like blind sheep." He gagged and grabbed Joshua by both arms and ground out. "Take care of Carrie and the kids; keep Jeremy away from Pa and Ezekiel. Joshua, promise me?" He stiffened—the light flamed out of his eyes, and he died without hearing his brother's answer.

I walked up just in time to hear Lot's plea for his oldest son. Evidently there was friction in the family in spite of the big show of family togetherness that they had put on for the community. I felt bad about Lot. He was one of the few that I had really liked. As I walked away his plea for his son Jeremy rang in my ears.

"May God hev mercy on thar sorry souls," Sheriff Emmet prayed—then exclaimed, "My God, Matthew, five dead McCoys, two wounded, and Stan Scarbury captured them thar two bushwhackers thet tried to murder Barney. It wus them twin buggers David and Saul. From what I kin gather, three or four others peared ta be wounded as they rid off. We came off easy, only two men hurt. Ferguson ketched a slug in his arm, and Les Adkins ketched one in the leg. Peers hit's nuthen serious."

Barney walked up grinning and said, "Reckon that silly idea of yours worked like a charm, Matt. Those boys blew Ma's full length mirror all to hell. I got cut with flying glass, but nothing bad."

Sheriff Johnson cut in, "Reckon Barney plugged Daniel, and reckon ah got Lot cuz I shot low. Peers like we done cut the odds in half. What's more, Lot's dying confession named Parson McCoy and Ezekiel as thar leaders. Reckon, ah'll jes call on the McCoys in the mornen. If they don't give up, them thar buggers will have to dig a few more graves."

At daybreak, we moved out twenty-one men strong. A wagon loaded with the dead and wounded followed. The dew had been heavy in the yard and the hocks of the horses were drenched. Vapor was rising from the tops of the fields as we rode along ever on the alert. Once at the McCoy's farm, the Sheriff sent a man into town for old Doc McDermott to go to the jail to tend to the wounded. We pulled into the housing area and the men spread out taking cover from the ominous looking semi-circle of houses. However, our trip proved fruitless. The older children and their mothers were in the fields prepping soil and planting seed.

Mrs. Sadie McCoy, a tall, hawk-faced women, the third wife of J.D. greeted us brazenly from her doorway and asked testily, "Whut kin I do fer yo men? If yo be looken fer Reverend McCoy, he and some a his young'ens left fer Huntington yesterday mornen." Sadie McCoy was half J.D.'s age. According to the Vances, his first two wives, sick and overworked, had died at childbirth.

Sheriff Johnson tipped his hat and replied, "Sorry to bother yo, ma'am. Howsomever, we know yer man was at the O'Shannon's last night. He's wanted fer tempted murder."

Sadie's jaw hardened and she snapped, "'Tain't so! J. Ds a parson, he don't hold with no killen."

Sheriff Johnson swung down from his saddle and declared, "Sorry, Ma'am, we gotta check yo house."

In reply the woman whipped up a shotgun from inside the door and snarled, "'Tain't likely, Sheriff, less yo be tired of liven."

The Sheriff eyed her speculatively and then said over his shoulder, "John, bring up the wagon."

Sadie McCoy stood her ground defiantly until the wagon, with its grisly load of dead men, drew up in front of the porch. Her face sagged, losing its defiance and her shotgun wavered. Johnson said, "Benjamin's yo son. He caught a slug in his shoulder last night. Reckon thar's nough dead and wounded McCoys, less yo want more killen?"

With a wail, half anger, half concern, she dropped the shotgun and ran to the wagon. Gathering her son in her arms, she screamed, "Damn yo all ta Hell. God's wrath will strike yo'al daid."

Sheriff Johnson ignored her ranting and with a nod of his head ordered, "Yo men check the cabins—be jest as polite as yo kin. Yo-all be keerful now, yo hear?" And he stepped down and entered the house. A passel of stiff-faced children and wives made way as we checked each cabin, and finally the barn. As expected, we didn't find one adult male.

It didn't take long to check the bleak, two-room cabins. One cabin had been added since the initial building bee, a class room, and it was obvious Parson McCoy was conducting his own religious school as evidenced by a blackboard and rough benches made by splitting logs and adding legs. McGuffey's Readers were neatly stacked beside a pile of Bibles on the teacher's desk. The children and women I saw were clean and dressed in homespun shirts, and pants, and drab dresses. The entire layout suggested that the Parson was conducting his own cult. I felt sorry for the children; they would be taught a legacy of hate and bigotry that would scar their lives forever.

Leaving the dead McCoy men to be tended by their families, we rode on into town and Sheriff Johnson enlisted the help of Huntington's Sheriff D. I. Smith who agreed to hold Benjamin and Joshua in his jail until they were well enough to be transferred to the Wayne County jail.

Sheriff Smith sent for Dr. Buffington to assist Doc McDermott to tend to the wounded men and with the Sheriff's help, we canvassed the Huntington area looking for the fugitives. We soon learned the McCoys had friends in Ohio. Ferried across to the Ohio side, we ran into a brick wall. The McCoys had split up, and the trail was stone cold. At noon Sheriff Johnson called off the posse; frustrated and irritable we all returned to our homes. The Sheriff with his deputies returned to Wayne with the twins David and Saul in chains.

I had a sick feeling in the pit of my stomach, and I noted that Byron and Jon were just as disjointed as I was. We knew damned good and well that with over half of the McCoy Clan still at large our troubles were far from over.

For two weeks, we buried ourselves in playing catch up to our necessary duties as farmers and stockmen. The work kept me from dwelling on the five dead men and the omnipresent danger that hung over our heads as long as the rest of the McCoys were on the loose. I had a presentiment of trouble that never allowed me to get careless. We were far from being free of the McCoys and each day only added to my apprehension.

I knew we should head west, but Byron was adamant, "No damned McCoy is going to run me off Buffalo Creek."

Jon stuck close to me like a burr under a saddle, but unlike a burr, he was never irritating. I never asked and he never volunteered a reason. I hired two of his brothers to work the fields and when it came time to pay them, I paid Jon as well. He started to protest and then with a nod accepted his pay. Just his being there was a Godsend and in farm work, he was worth both his brother's efforts, and in horse training he was worth all of us put together. Not because they didn't work hard, but simply because Jon had a natural ingrained talent with horses, the proper term was "horse savvy," and just good common sense. I had had the best teacher in the business, my Grandpa Dillon, and while I was an excellent breeder, Jon was on a plain all his own. I readily acknowledged him my superior. We all talked to our horses, but when Jon whispered his Indian lingo into a horse's ears, I'd swear they understood his every word.

Grandpa and Jon never gentled a horse by riding them to a standstill as many white men and Indian horse breeders did. Grandpa told me that horses were like children, they became unruly when subjected to the whip and spur. When the colts were still small, Grandpa began their training by snubbing them to a post and putting a simple halter on them, all the while he talked, soothed and gained the trust of the animal. Before long Grandpa would be leading the animal by the halter, and at the appropriate time, he replaced it with a bridle and repeated the process. To break them to a rope, he snubbed and placed a short rope high up on their neck. He then turned them loose and when they wheeled away grandpa called out 'Whoa". The short rope jerked them to a halt and the colts quickly learned their limitations and to obey the spoken command.

Later, Grandpa began putting blankets on their backs until they were used to the feel. Then he would snub them to a post and place a light saddle on their back. If they fought the saddle, Grandpa tied a rope to their foreleg and pulled it up so they couldn't hurt themselves. When they became accustomed to the saddle,

Grandpa placed a saddle bag across the saddle to which he gradually added weights up to a hundred and fifty pounds. While doing this Grandpa would add some of his own weight by hanging onto the saddle from both sides of the horse. In this way, the horse became used to a person being on or seemed to be on the saddle. When he thought the time was right he would swing up into the saddle. Sometimes Grandpa would again have to tie up one front leg of the horse until they become accustomed to his being in the saddle. The more spirited horses usually had to have their leg tied. The rest of the training consisted of teaching the horses the five gaits, which took knowledge, time, and patience. However, when we sold a saddle horse, we sold them at a premium for Dillon horses were always in demand. The D brand was a recognized, respected brand and I was proud of all that it stood for.

Jon with his special touch could train a horse better and faster than anyone, I knew. We all teased him. I accused him, "Jon, you're hypnotizing those horses like that Mesmeric doctor in Germany."

He just grinned and retorted, "White man no understand. Indians are one with animals, nature, and the Great Spirit."

I snorted, "After that coup you counted last month and all this nature stuff, Jon, I'm thinking your heathen alter-ego is taking over."

"Don't you believe it, Matthew? My Pa just told me the other day that, 'Hell hath no fury like a converted Catholic."

I laughed and replied, "That's probably true, Jon, unless you take into consideration a drunken Irishman."

"By the way," he asked, "are you still having doubts about our faith since we had that ruckus with the McCoys?"

"Why should it, Jon? It doesn't change anything about Grandpa's murder."

"I just thought that the justice we doled out to the McCoys might help a bit.

A voice called out interrupting our conversation, "Hello, the house."

I yelled back, "Come on in if you're a friend, come in with your hands empty if your not."

Tom Vance rode up and jumped off his lathered horse, both were breathing hard. He declared, "You got trouble coming, Mathew. The McCoys done busted Benjamin and Joshua outta jail in Huntington. They kilt a jailer and beat another'un to a pulp. They larned they's a bounty on thar hides and they's fit ta be tied. The jailer heard em say, "They's a hunten O'Shannons and ary man of thet thar posse that kilt thar kinfolk.

"Sheriff Smith thinks they's hid out in Westmoreland, and he's a getten up a posse. He sent me to warn yo and the rest of yer friends."

I swore wrathfully and said, "Damn it all to hell! I knew they would never quit." The horses we were working shifted about nervously—sensing my state of agitation.

"Whoa! Whoa!" Jon cooed to the horses and they nuzzled him, trust shining in their eyes.

The horses and I were both calmed by Jon's reassuring voice, I added more rationally "I knew they'd never quit, Tom. Come in and I'll get you a quick bite to eat. Jon and I will warn my brother," I said to him as I led him into the kitchen.

Jon sent one of the Ridge boys home to get more men to come down and guard both farms. Jon came into the kitchen to talk to me. A moment later, as I walked him back outside, he suggested, "Reckon we better go get Barney and join up with Sheriff Smith's posse. It's not going to be too healthy traveling alone." He gathered in the two horses we had been working with, and headed for the barn and called out over his shoulder, "While I saddle up could you put together a sandwich for us and fill our canteens?"

Far to the south, a black thunderhead began to shape up into a possible thunderstorm and as if to prove the point jagged lightning rent the cloud and a few seconds later we heard the muted thunder as though a higher power was setting the stage for the final curtain. Warned, Jon wrapped slickers around our blanket rolls.

We found Barney working in the barn and he began saddling his horse, as soon as he heard the news. Jon asked his brother Martel to go to Wayne and warn Sheriff Johnson of the jail break, so that he could reinforce his guard on his prisoners, David and Saul. As Martel saddled a horse Barney, without a word, mounted up, wheeled his horse about and grim of face he exclaimed, "I hope you two shoot straighter this time, or we'll be chasing and wounding McCoys the rest of our lives."

Jon chuckled and replied, "Rounding up the McCoys sounds like a mighty puny challenge for a warrior like me, Barney. But, I don't know about you white boys."

Byron snorted his disgust and we set off at a mile-eating trot. I had rode and walked this road thousands of times in my short lifetime and I knew every wagon rut, tree and rock along the way. We passed the big elms that shaded the Ferguson farm house. Surrounding the house was row on row of blooming apple trees that filled the valley for a mile. Birds were flocking and hunting cover from the coming storm. Gusts of colder, moist air struck us from time to time, as the lightning and rolling thunder grew closer announcing its coming like a herald in King Arthur's Court. In spite of the coming storm I rode like a zombie, my mind numb and my eyes unseeing. I was intent on just one thing, the McCoys. Our steady pace soon put us fording the stream into Westmoreland. That's when we met the McCoys head on.

The terrain was relatively flat and across the stream was a Duke's mixture of pristine and second growth timber, including massive red and white oaks, and smaller thickets of hickory, dogwood, Dutch elm and ironwood. There were six McCoys led by that redheaded devil of a parson J. Denver McCoy. The escaped jailbirds—Joshua rode to his left—and Benjamin rode to his right. When J. D. saw us, he drew up, and at his gesture, Sirach, Zechariah, and Jonathan rode to his right forming a skirmish line facing us.

As we rode out of the water, I moved to the right of our group leaving Byron in the middle. The adrenaline began pumping and blood pounded at my temples. I was as finely tuned as a fiddler's fiddle, and I murmured, "I'll take J. D. and Joshua, Barney you take the two in the middle and what's left over is your meat, Jon."

It was no time to argue and with a grunt, Byron led us to within thirty feet of them, pulled rein and said, "Looks like you McCoys been right busy. Benjamin, you and Joshua got off easy the other night. You might not be so lucky this time. Reckon you men better give up now while you still can. We sure don't want to have to haul you in belly first over your saddles."

J. D.'s face turned white with fury. He carried a double-barreled shotgun across his saddle, the barrel resting on his left arm. He screamed, "Yo Papist pigs done kilt my boys. We'uns gonna lay yo killers in yo grave, jes like we'uns done yer Ma, yer Pa, and yer Grandpa."

The gorge rose in my throat. All my self-control was submerged in a deluge of *black Shannach rage.* I was suddenly transformed into an avenging angel from hell. That mouth—that blaspheming McCoy mouth that had shattered the security of my mind, my heart, and my soul was like a magnate that focused all my pent up fury into one blinding passion. I'd close that frigging mouth or die trying. McCoy's mouth was wide open venting his spleen and he screamed, "Kill em all," and he cocked and swung his shotgun to open fire.

My .44 cal. Smith and Wesson flowed into my hand smooth as cream. I thumbed two shots so fast they blended as one. The first slug caught Parson J. D. McCoy in his upper teeth, which threw his head back causing my second slug to catch him in his lower teeth, blowing his teeth and brains out through the back of his skull. Still in the saddle, he fell backwards with his back arched all out of proportion, his head stopped by his horse's rump. J. D.'s horse, crazed with the smell of blood, and the thunder of guns, reared up snorting and slobbering with fear trying to free itself of the grisly burden on its back. Without mercy, I slammed two bullets into Joshua's chest, his six-gun barely clearing leather.

The rage still in me, I wheeled Pat, prepared to kill any McCoy left standing. Grey smoke from our black powder guns formed a barrier; it took a few seconds to clear off before I could see Benjamin's lifeless body sprawled on the ground. Two red holes blossomed over his heart said it all. Zechariah was down holding his stomach with both hands trying to dam the lifeblood that poured from his body. Facing Jon was Sirach still astride his saddle rocking back and forth painfully. His face was chalk white, and he was completely helpless with two broken arms flopping uselessly. His brother Jonathan was sitting on the ground crying pitifully nursing a shattered shoulder. Jon swung down, picked up Jonathan's pistol, and tossed it into the stream. Automatically, the three of us stopped, punched out the spent shells, and reloaded our pistols.

As I looked about at the carnage, my black rage slowly spent itself, and I became aware of the havoc that we had created. Lightning flashed and thunder roared as the storm spent its fury over the Ohio River. Then, like a brick in the face, I remembered. I had broken my promise to Ma. I looked over at Jon, marveling. True to his word to my mother, he had shot only to wound. Remorse suddenly overwhelmed me. I slid from the saddle and walked away—too ashamed to even look at Jon or my brother. Suddenly, my hands began to shake and I steadied myself on the trunk of a stalwart red oak tree. Whether I was a good man made little difference now. I had killed two men. What's more I felt no remorse, and I knew I was marked for life with the *Mark of Cain.*

Barney came over and put his arm about my shoulder and said, "No man knows himself well enough to know how he will react under pressure, Matthew. Your inherited instincts merely asserted themselves and overcame your good intentions, and I might add—with good cause. You have learned a bit about yourself, and you'll be better equipped to deal with any future situations."

What Byron said might be true, but that did not alleviate my ruptured bubble of good intentions. Jon caught up the reins of J. D.'s crazed horse and began talking to him soothingly. The roan quit bucking and stood trembling, nudging Jon for comfort. When Jon freed the dead man's feet from the stirrups, the parson flopped over and fell flat on his ruptured face. With a snort, J.D.'s horse shied away from the corpse.

I took off my hat, and inhaled a gust of cool air from the storm. I wiped my face with my bandana and exclaimed, "There must be something wrong with me, Barney. I feel no remorse for having killed those bastards. The only thing sticking in my craw is my promise to Ma."

Barney replied, "Give it time, Matt, just remember—it was them or us. I would have exterminated J.D. like any other mad dog, if you hadn't killed that son of a bitch. It's not easy to take a human life," Barney added grimly, "but I sure as hell ain't gonna loose any sleep over dead, hate-slobbering McCoys."

We had just finished putting bandages and stick splints on the wounded men and slung the dead men over their saddles, when Sheriff Smith and his posse came roaring up in a thunder of hooves. Smith jumped down and exclaimed, "We heard the shooting and come running. Any of you men hurt?"

With a wry smile Jon replied, "Just our feelings, Sheriff, there just weren't enough McCoys to give us a decent fight."

A man in the posse swore and said, "My God, what did you do, bushwhack them?"

Byron froze in place, stony-faced he turned to the man and said flat out, "We took them on—man to man—the tracks speak for themselves. The McCoys thought they had us cold—outnumbered as we were. The parson started the shindig—we finished it. Now, mister, I suggest you eat those bushwhack words," and he brushed back his coat freeing his gun.

The posse man's face blanched white. Sheriff Smith snapped, "Olson, you stupid idiot, apologize before you get your damned-fool-head shot off."

The man swallowed hard, and stammered, "Sorry, Mister O'Shannon, for running off at the mouth, I meant no harm."

Barney nodded, his face softening, "Reckon it was a bit shocking." He turned and filled the sheriff in. Smith nodded and said, "You boys come in town tomorrow and fill out a report. There will have to be an inquest, of course. You fellows go on home. I'll take care of the McCoys."

We rode home, solemn and subdued. The closer to home we got—the more oppressing the forested hills became. None of us were so callous that we took any joy in what we had done. However, my mind was muddled with a feeling of satisfaction that Parson J. D. McCoy, bigot and murderer of my Grandpa and my Ma and

Pa, was dead and by my hand. Yet, I suffered deep anguish, regret, and chagrin that I had broken my promise to Ma. Yet, I felt no real remorse for the actual deed. I'd be a liar if I said I wasn't glad that bastard was dead. I had shot in self-defense; the killing wasn't a mortal sin. Yet, I knew I could not go to confession to Father Quirk. I felt no pang of conscience; I certainly felt no forgiveness in my heart for the murderers of my parents. I was supposed to forgive my enemies and pray for their souls? Instead, I sincerely hoped J. D. McCoy would burn in hell forever. Finally, we rode into the barnyard at the old homestead, which interrupted my soul searching. I looked up and saw Sheriff Johnson and Martel riding down Harmon Hill leading a sizable posse.

Emmet grinned as he reined in and said, "Looks like yo boys aer fit. Martel here, warned us'uns jes in time. We'uns no sooner barricaded the jail than Gabe McCoy, and his kin, come a riding down the street as calm as all get out. Reckon they thought to take us by surprise. We'd a had em cold, as they rode in, but some drunken tinhorn shot at em from the saloon. Gabe had Samuel, Shadrach, Micah, Isaiah and four youngsters with em. Then, with a shrill rebel yell, they come a shooten, whoopen, and a holleren. When we opened fire on em from the jail, them fellers kept right on ago'en. We followed em until they split up and took to the hills. Half the Posse is still after em. We'uns gonna set up an ambush for em at thar cabins."

When he finished, Barney brought the sheriff up to date. The posse men all looked at us a bit awe-stricken. The sheriff exclaimed, "Man, yo O'Shannons aer a caution. With yo around we'uns don't need no posse. We gotta go, Barney. Yo boy's sho raised merry ole Hell." He turned to his men and warned them, "Keep yo eyes peeled, men, thet Gabriel is kinda slick."

We watched them as they rode off, and I said, "Let's get out of sight; ole Gabe just might come a calling." As we readied for possible trouble, I found myself saying a prayer that Gabe would attack. With any luck, I could avenge my family's murders once and for all. Two days later we attended the inquest. Their ruling was a foregone conclusion. The McCoys were all wanted fugitives and most people were relieved that old "fire and brimstone McCoy" had gone to his Maker.

Father Quirk was there; I found that I could not look his way. He approached me after the inquiry and took me by the arm and said kindly, "If you need to talk to me, Mathew, you know where I'll be." I mumbled my thanks with downcast eyes. It was Friday and the three of us slept over with Dick and Theresa. I finally found myself relaxing from the attention that I received from their children.

The next day Dick pulled me aside and said, "Let's take a little walk." Richard was older than I was, and while he was still a very young man, he had the air and manner of a patriarch. When troubled, I had always been able to talk to Dick, for I had the highest regard for his sagacity and wisdom. It didn't take long before I told him how I felt. I hadn't been able to pray for the men I had killed. I didn't feel worthy to even pray for myself.

After I unloaded my woes, Dick suggested, "Why don't you go over to the Church this afternoon and spend some time in the presence of the Holy Eucharist in the tabernacle? Perhaps God will do for you what you cannot do for yourself?"

I stayed that night with them, and the next afternoon I did as Dick had suggested. I walked to St. Joseph's and entered the familiar surroundings. The stained glass windows, the statues of Mary and Joseph, the cross of the crucified Christ, the ambo, and the holy Altar built up against the back wall of the church always had a soothing effect on me. I knelt at the altar rail, which was set well in front of the altar upon which the Holy Tabernacle reposed and from which the holy mass was said each day. I knelt and tried to pray. Strangely enough, after awhile I found my body and mind beginning to find a peace that I had not felt since I had killed the McCoys. Another hour passed and Father Quirk came in to prepare for hearing the scheduled confessions held at four o'clock each Saturday afternoon.

Seeing me, he came over and asked, "Did you wish to go to confession, Matthew?" I answered with a shake of my head and replied, "Father, I have no remorse whatsoever for having killed those two men. I know you can't give me absolution under such conditions?"

The priest shook his head regretfully and said, "You need a little time to meditate and sort out your priorities. You are suffering a guilt trip right now. There is one thing you can do for me, Matthew. While you are meditating, will you say your Rosary every day? Jesus and Mother Mary have a way of leading their children out of the dark valley."

I got up, looked him in the eye, and replied, "I've said my Rosary every day with my family as far back as I can recollect, Father. I'll do my best to honor your request." I saw Jon come in and join the line of people waiting to have their confessions heard. My heart went out to my friend. He had remained true to his word. I wished with all my heart that I could join him, but my hot Shannach temper had blotted out in blood all that I thought that I stood for. Seeing him, I remembered Ma's last words to Jon. She had said, "Jon, you're too sweet and trusting." I had to smile, Jon Ridge, in spite of his banter and easy-going disposition, was intelligent, discerning and trustworthy. He was more of a man's man than any person I had ever met. In a by-gone day, he would have been a great chief and warrior. I was fortunate to have such a friend, and I knew that I had failed to measure up to his standards. All I could do was hope that someday, I would again feel worthy enough to call him brother.

As I left the Church, Byron came in and joined the long confessional line. My eyes clouded up and my heart overflowed. Byron had suffered a great deal over taking the lives of his fellow men while out west. Now he had killed three of the McCoy clan and I knew how badly this must have affected him. In spite of our anger over the murder of our family, we both had sought only justice, not vengeance. As members of the first posse, he shot to kill, and I, true to my word, shot only to wound. Yet, in a later confrontation with the fugitive McCoys, we again had to face the wrath of the McCoys. Yet, he did so only to save his own life. And I, in spite of my good intentions to only wound to save my own life, had suddenly gone berserk. In a black Shannack rage, my intention had been to kill, and to exterminate the vermin that had killed my beloved grandfather and my parents.

I was happy that Barney could seek relief in the arms of the Church, because I knew how greatly he regretted the taking of human life. He and Jon could go to confession, because they were sincerely sorry for what had been forced on them. Yet I, with rage still burning in my heart, felt no sorrow or compassion for killing J.D. McCoy and his sons. They were the scum of the earth, and I walked away from the Church unrepentant and unshriven.

Absentmindedly I lit my pipe, to do some serious soul searching. I determined that while I could not receive the Sacraments of the Church, I would go to Church when possible, and I would say the Rosary every day as Father Quirk had requested, I had never thought otherwise. I resolved to do my best to honor my mother's request and never shoot to kill again. To do so, I resolved to leave Buffalo Creek within a week. There were still murderous McCoys out there with which to contend. I could not remain in Buffalo Creek and hope to keep my new resolve.

The next day Byron, Jon and I attended Sunday Mass at St. Josephs in the company of Dick and Theresa Tyson, and their children. Parishioners had gathered outside the Church and everyone was gossiping and arguing for all to hear about the O'Shannon and McCoy feud. My heart sank; Ma's worst fears had become a reality. Like it or not, folks now labeled our defensive actions as a feud, which could only end after involving many innocent families. As Ma had pointed out, in feuds there were only victims—not winners. I was shocked to hear people calling us killers, feuding troublemakers, and one big mouth was even talking about the massacre of the McCoys.

With a feeling of relief, I saw the Renaud family was grouped nearby and as usual, since I had began dating Julie, I headed her way to escort her into Church, surely here, I would find a kindly word and a smile of welcome. Julie turned and saw me coming; the lovely smile on her face froze to a grimace. She looked me up and down as though she was seeing some sort of a fiend. Then quite deliberately—Juliette turned her back on me. My ears burning, I rejoined my family; we found our pew, genuflected, and knelt to pray. Protocol dictated that there was to be no talking inside the church out of respect to the presence of the Holy Eucharist, and also out of respect for those wishing to meditate and pray. Yet, that did not stop the viscous gossip that I heard all about me. I felt the black Shannack temper building and I struggled to control my temper. Suddenly, a great calm engulfed me, and my mind was clear as to what I should do. I went into the Sacristy where Father was dressing for mass. I asked Father Tom if I could say a few words before mass started and I explained why. Father agreed and said, "Just one stipulation, Mathew, you must control that Irish temper."

After everyone had trickled into church, I strode up to the ambo and surprised the parishioners, who felt silent. I went right to the point, "You all know me and my family. You are all aware of the trouble we have endured since the McCoy family moved to Buffalo Creek. You know our family has suffered greatly by their persecution of our family for being Roman Catholics. I might add that suffering for the name of Jesus has been a privilege. Parson McCoy's persecution of the Church and the Pope is a persecution of all Catholics. He has called our Church the Whore of Babylon and refers to Catholics as Papist pigs. Their attacks were not just reserved for O'Shannons, for their bigotry was a challenge to the faith of every person here. When the McCoys first moved to Buffalo Creek, Parson McCoy poisoned the minds of many of our Protestant neighbors with his bigotry and hatred of Catholics. Those same families had been our friends for generations. Today many Buffalo Creek families will not even speak to us. I was shocked and saddened when I came to Church today, for I overheard some of my Catholic friends and acquaintances calling my brother and me—killers—murderers—and—feuders." I looked about and said, "I expected better from my fellow Catholics whom I have assumed for years to be my friends. Unfortunately, some of you reacted very much like our hypocrite Protestant neighbors on Buffalo Creek. At first, I was angry—then my feelings were hurt—but when I thought it over, I realized that we are all sinners, and most of us succumb to gossip from time to time when we should be praying for one another. I want you to know that I take no offense, and forgive those of you who need forgiveness. I beg you to pray for the souls of all the individuals involved in these shootings. I know that my brother Byron and Jon Ridge deeply regret the taking of human lives. I take this occasion to bid you all goodbye. Next week I am going west to seek—what—I do not know. I trust my departure may relieve some of the tension that has so recently besieged this community. Good bye—and God Bless you all."

Father Quirk began the Mass immediately. It was a month past Easter and the homily concerned the passage in John 13-31, "Love one another as I have loved you." The message was most appropriate. Perhaps it helped a few persons to repent their careless gossip. For the first time in my life, since my First Communion, I was not in a state of grace. No longer could I receive the body and blood of Christ unless I could learn to forgive Parson J.D. McCoy. I did pray for the souls of the Parson's kin that we had killed. But, for the life of me, I could not pray for J.D. Then my conscience began to belabor me. I squirmed in my seat uncomfortably. Deeply troubled, I mused, who the hell did I think I was to get up in public and criticize my fellow parishioners? Then, again, my Black Irish temper reared up; I sat up, my back straight and defiant. I stared blindly ahead as parishioners rose and filed past me with bowed heads to humbly receive our Lord in Holy Communion. Interiorly, however, my soul was in torment. Mentally I huddled in my seat in abject shame. Before communion was over, I left the Church accompanied only by my stiff-necked-pride. I did not know it then, but it would be a long time before I again entered a Catholic Church.

My eyes flew open as first light filtered through the open window of my bedroom, which looked out over Grandpa's paddock and corral. I jumped up and leaning on the window sill with both hands, I studied the herd of horses that we had corralled the night before. My two Indian hands emerged from the barn and headed for the kitchen and hot coffee. The horses were just beginning to stir and a colt nuzzled its mother's side searching for its breakfast. The sight brought me a brief sense of peace. There was my future; a herd of fifteen magnificent Morgan quarter horses with four colts, twelve

Arabian, Al Rasul thoroughbreds with two colts, two Appaloosas from Montana, and a half dozen of mixed-breed horses. Quartered separately in the barn were the stallions: one Morgan, one Arabian, and an Appaloosa, and of course my beautiful stud and riding horse—Patrick. With a satisfied grunt, I hurried into my clothes. A hundred details had to be attended to before I could head west.

Before I could get to work, Byron and Jon rode in and corralled me in the kitchen. Jon poured three cups of coffee and handed me one. Barney sipped his cautiously and asked, "Knowing you, I reckon you got a plan all laid out. How about enlightening us peons?"

Startled, I snapped, "No need for that. I don't plan on any company."

Barney took out a cigarillo, looked at it pensively and complained, "I've been nursing these for a week now. Getting mighty low, I've been planning on heading west myself to stock up."

Jon tried to sip his coffee and burnt his lip. "Man, this here coffee's hotter than a blacksmith's forge." He poured a little into a saucer and slurped loudly, looked up and stated solemnly, "Had me a dream tother night, Matthew. Dreamt I counted coup on two Sioux, and killed six Apaches. You know it's bad luck for a Cherokee to disregard his Spirit Guide. Besides," he added, "I promised your ma I'd go west with you and keep your butt out of trouble."

Their easy comradery helped dispel my intense mood, and I growled, "Seems like you have it all backwards like you usually do." I turned to Barney; "I've saved this lothario's hide half a dozen times from irate fathers."

Jon countered, "Talking about rakes, "What ya plan to do about the petite Juliette Renaud when you leave?"

Julie, I thought with a pang. She was sure pretty, but Ma had always said, "Petty is as pretty does." Thinking back on the situation, it dawned on me that Ma hadn't been too keen about my dating Juliette. Ma had an intuition about folks that was uncanny. She would never cut a person to pieces, but she had a way of letting the family know that she discerned a serious flaw in a person that everyone else had overlooked. I had to admit to myself; Juliette was certainly a self-centered girl. At Church Sunday, she had turned her back on me. So much for loyalty, I thought. We had never talked marriage, but it had seemed like the next probable step. Strangely enough, I found that I didn't really care. Perhaps it's true that it's an ill wind that doesn't blow some good.

I grinned and replied, "Barney tells me there are lots of black-haired beauties in New Mexico Territory. I'm sure I can find one to console me."

"I hate to break up such an enlightening conversation," Byron said dryly, "but Father Quirk told me last night that Gabe McCoy made a second try to break his brothers out of the Wayne County jail and this time he succeeded. He had dynamite, and blew the entire back end out of the jail. He then began throwing dynamite all over the place. According to the latrine news, 'from the number one hole,' he has sworn vengeance and won't rest till we're all dead. He busted out David and Saul and he has Shadrack, Micah, Isaiah, Samuel and Abraham with him, seems there's also four McCoy young'ens of about fifteen or so riding with him."

"Ma was right," I said. "There will be no end to the killing until all the McCoys are dead, or we are. I don't regret killing J. D. McCoy, but I can't help feeling sorry for his kids. They never had a chance with their daddy filling them with hate and bigotry. I don't choose to be the McCoy's executioner, especially those youngsters Gabe has with him now, but I sure as hell don't want to be their next victim either."

Byron tilted back in his chair and murmured, "You have to admit—It's like the words out of the Old Testament, "An eye for an eye."

Jon put his cup down and said, "Well, they damned well know now that they can't outshoot us—so that only leaves them one choice—bushwhacking."

I looked at Barney and asked, "So where does that leave us now?"

He leisurely blew a blue smoke ring into the air and stated, "I've given it some thought, Mathew. Let's go talk to Jon's pa and if they agree to lease our property, we'll go see Dick Tyson, wrap up the paper work, and be out of here by Saturday."

I looked at him thoughtfully and then grinned, "You son of a gun. You've been planning this all along—haven't you?"

"Yep! Like Ma always said, "Still water runs deep," he admitted with his lopsided smile. "But my plans didn't include you youngsters." A grim look shaded his face and he added, "I left some unfinished business in Denver that needs tending to. Now that I know you two won't be a millstone around my neck, I reckon you two can tag along."

I jumped up laughing, "Tag along, big brother, it seems you're the one that needs a nurse maid?" As I spoke, I hooked the rung of his tilted chair with my booted toe and flipped him flat onto his back. He hit with a crash, and came up with a roar. Jon and I both had the good sense to run.

Sleep didn't come easy that night, for I still had my conscience with which to contend. If revenge was sweet, why did I feel so bitter? In addition, there was the sadness of my leaving behind nearly everything that was near and dear to me. I have to admit, however that my concerns were countered somewhat by the excitement of my leaving for the Wild West. The only things I would take with me, I had decided, were Grandpa's and my beloved horses—not all—just the best breeding stock. I finally found refuge in my Rosary; and fell asleep saying the "Hail Holy Queen". My sleep was distorted with nightmares of J.D. McCoy's blasphemous mouth shredded with bullets—and an ominous feeling about my brother. What had Barney meant when he said—He had unfinished business to attend to in Denver?

7HE WILD WEST

CHAPTER FOUR

Sweat was running down my pits. I pushed my black Stetson back and wiped my forehead. I was surprised to see the size of Leavenworth. It wasn't very large for such a popular frontier-prairie town with a population of only 800. Close by they had Ft. Leavenworth, a large military prison, and a sizable munitions depot. The town provided recreation and services for the fort and for the soldiers. Leavenworth was known as a jumping off town that serviced wagon trains that were headed west, although more and more people were using the new Continental Railroad.

I headed directly for the Marshal's Office. Marshal Clemens was a tall, stern looking, lean man with weather beaten features. He was a good listener, and quickly made out a report on my four stolen Arabian horses; said theft having taken place in nearby Kansas City. Three mares and one stud, all prime breeding stock. He had no new leads for me, but promised to keep his eyes open for my horses.

I set out to check every Livery Stable in town. I appreciated the shaded, wide streets and the neat boardwalks bordering many mud-filled streets. I didn't have far to go—livery stables were noted for locating at the edge of towns. The first thing I did was stable my mule and trail pack. Danny the stable boy was a nice kid and he promised to take good care of my pack. However, it took me a while to check every stable in town. I started on Levee Street and checked Delaware, Olive and Shannon Streets, but no sign of our stolen horses. I had no better luck with the Kansas Pacific Railroad Depot on Olive Street. The Silver Bow, the St. Louis and Omaha Steamship Packet docked, while I was checking the docks and the stockyards. I paused to look at the lethal canon set between the Packet's smoke stacks—placed there to fight off river pirates, but still no horses.

I had stopped and inquired of several expressmen tending their rigs, and I even talked to the Gordon B. Bros. Grocery deliveryman. I was discouraged. I rode back to the livery stable where my mule was stabled and left my stud, Pat with Danny. I intended to eat; then buy some supplies for the trail and head for Denver. I was walking down the street with Jack at my side when he suddenly darted into an alleyway. I instinctively followed, for Jack's dereliction was surprising, without warning my head exploded, and I knew no more.

I woke up lying on a Dr. Elbee's couch. Later, sitting on the edge of the Doctor's treatment table, I watched as his wife and nurse carried a pan of bloody water out the back door and I heard the splash as the water hit the ground.

"Mathew," the Dr. explained, "I had to take fifteen stitches to close the lesion on the back of your head. The fact that you have some memory loss is not surprising. You suffered a severe trauma from the blow to your head. You must take it easy for a day or two, or you could drop dead from the concussion. If you remain in town—come back every day and I will change the bandages. If for some reason I am not here, my wife will change the bandages for you. Do you understand?"

I gave him a weak grin and replied, "Thank you, Doctor, I sure do understand. I've been hit on the head and robbed and I don't really know who I am. I tenderly felt the back of my head." I paid him, but my mind was whirling like a kaleidoscope from which I could only catch a name or a fragment of a name. I couldn't remember my name, but from the form I had filled out at the Marshal's Office, Marshal Clemens told me my name was Matthew O'Shannon; someone had stolen four of my horses from the train in Kansas City. I, and someone named Jon Ridge, was looking for them. Where was I from, or where was I going? The thieves had taken my wallet, and any papers I might have had to identify me. It was a fast professional job. In their haste, they had left my weapons. Luckily, they hadn't taken the change in my pocket—in which I had a purse of gold double eagles. However, they left no clues that would identify them. The report did jog my memory. But—where was Jon, and for that matter—where the hell was Barney and the rest of our men and horses? Barney—who the heck was Barney?

Marshal Clemens told me the theft and assault had been cleverly done in broad daylight. The City Marshal figured that when I was passing an alley someone waylaid me.

He explained, "The thieves had put a bitch in heat in a cage. Jack followed his instincts—and you followed Jack. Just as Jack got to the cage, a blanket was thrown over him. That's when you were savagely slugged from behind. Later a passerby saw you laying there, your head covered with blood. Jack had torn the blanket to pieces and stood over you, and refused to allow anyone near. Another Marshal solved the dilemma by throwing a blanket over the dog, and held him while two other men carried you to the Doctor's house."

My head hurt. I had been struck from behind in Kansas City, or was it Leavenworth? I could feel the place I was hit on the back of my head. I had temporarily lost my memory, and even now I had trouble remembering certain things. I did remember the Marshal in Kansas City—no—it was the Marshall in Leavenworth—my head swirled. No matter—he had been very good to me. Then I remembered. Marshal Clemens had told me the theft and assault had been cleverly done in broad daylight.

When the Marshall and I came out of Doctor Elbee's office, Jack ran to me excitedly and I remembered his name. I dropped to my knees—embraced him and he licked my face. Then he cocked his head at me as though saying, "Where to". When I didn't show any initiative, he started down the street turning his head to see if I was coming.

Marshal Clemens said, "Reckon he knows where to go even if you don't. Let's see where he leads us?"

The dog led us to a livery stable; he went directly inside to a stall that held a beautiful palomino stud. The horse nickered when he saw the dog and Jack jumped up on the side of the stall and licked the stud's nose. Then the horse saw me, and he bobbed his head up and down and nuzzled my shoulder nickering softly. My memory clicked—it was Pat.

The stable boy trotted over and asked, "What happened to ya, Mista Matt? You get conked on the haid, or somethung?"

I gingerly touched the bandage, grinned ruefully and replied, "Or somethung?"

"Hi, Danny, "Marshal Clemens said, "You know this gent?"

"Yep! Sorta? He came in this mornen with that big stud. Ain't he a beaut, Marshal?"

"Never mind that, youngster. What did he say to you?"

Danny looked at me quizzically and replied, "He came in twice; the first time he left his mule and pack. He asked the price and then said ta water, hay and grain the mule. The second time he came in, he left the stud. Said the stud's name was Pat that he wuz gentle, and ta give him the same as the mule. He said he would be back in a few hours. He said his name was O'Shannon when he paid me; then he left."

"Where's his gear, boy?

"Over yonder, Marshal," and he pointed to a long rack loaded with saddles and gear.

My saddle was the only one without a saddle horn, which screamed that I wasn't a cowboy. The butt of a Henry rifle stuck out of the boot of the saddle. My head was reeling. Where the devil had I come from, and who the devil was Barney.

"By the way," Danny added, "he asked me how ta get on the trail to Denver."

Marshal Clemens put his hand on my shoulder. "I guess your handle is Matt, Mr. O'Shannon. There's no doubt the hoss and mule are yours"

I didn't intend to ignore him, but my heart was pounding with anticipation, as I eagerly opened the saddlebags. My anticipation turned to despair. All I found was the usual shaving gear, toothbrush, soap, towel, underwear, and a change of clothes, and of all things—two pair of beautifully beaded Indian moccasins, a frontier shirt with long fringes, and a pair of binoculars. No papers—no name—just more mysteries. The trail pack was no help either, I grabbed my head; pain flashed with each beat of my heart. I was utterly confused. I was right back from where I started, except that at least I now had a name, a horse, a saddle and in the boot a fine Henry rifle, two Russian pistols, a destination, and enough money to grubstake my trip—I also had two pairs of moccasins, an Indian shirt, and a change of clothes. My head reeled—I staggered.

Marshal Clemens grabbed my arm and said, "Steady fella—that was a wicked blow you took on the head. Maybe you better lay up in the hotel for a day or two?"

Danny sidled up to me and said, "I'm sure sorry, Mista O'Shannon."

"So am I, Danny," I replied patting him on the back—my spirit was squelched, but I gave him a two-bit tip. I took the Marshall's suggestion and stayed at the National Hotel for two nights and tried their Turkish bath. It felt so good that I repeated the bath the following day. I ate at Delmonicos both days and enjoyed Marshal Clemen's company at dinner before I left.

I felt some better, but my memory came and went. Marshal Clemens assured me that every effort was being made to find whoever was responsible. But I was worried, I had finally remembered, the papers the thieves were looking for were sewn into a double lining in my boots. I took Clemens into my confidence and told him my plan—he agreed to help me. It was obvious that whoever wanted the papers on my horses would most likely keep on trying. After dark, the Marshal returned; we had a hurried conversation, and I slipped out the back. I made sure I wasn't being followed, and wended my way to the home of the Marshal's leather working friend. When I arrived the back of the house was dark; I tapped on the back door and was admitted. I explained to the man what I needed, and within an hour my papers had been sewn into a heavy, spike studded collar for Jack. I had Jack's name embossed on a brass plate on the collar. If my memory failed me, at least I would know the dog's name. The remainder of the papers were replaced into my boot and neatly re-sewn. I tucked Jack's collar into my shirt and returned to the hotel's stable. I hugged Jack and allowed him to smell the collar before putting it on his neck. I said, "Jack"—he looked at me intently—I held the collar, shook it and said, "Guard." He growled and put his head on my shoulder, as I fastened the collar about his neck. I know Jack didn't understand it all, but I knew he would guard the collar with his life.

While reading the papers, I had been able to fill in some of the missing gaps in my memory, but my mind was still full of missing pieces. I remembered we started from Huntington with forty horses, plus our riding mounts. We were missing four prime horses and there was still no sign of Jon. He was supposed to have met me here at the National Hotel—that much—I remembered. Where the dickens was he? Had something happened to him? If I could find Jon, he would know what to do. At this point, I couldn't even remember how I got to Leavenworth from Kansas City.

I remembered, after reading some of the papers that Byron was my brother and that Jon Ridge was my partner. It wasn't so much as memory, as it was of acceptance of what I read. The papers recorded that Jon and I owned a small herd of breeding horses; and that four of his relatives were partners with him. His cousin Martel had been killed during the theft. Martel would be missed—he had been like a brother to me for nineteen years—he would be avenged—not by me, but by Jon and his brother Chick. I had seen their faces, when we found Martel murdered, and I knew they would never rest until Martel's murderers had been brought to justice.

Winding down after supper, I made sure the animals were fed and given exercise. I had Jack sleep in the same stall with Pat. For extra protection, I wedged a chair under my doorknob each night, and both nights I heard someone trying the door. I complained to the Marshal; the second night the Marshal's men nearly caught the person, whoever "he" was, but he was too clever and avoided capture. I had just fallen asleep for the second time, when a ruckus broke out. Men were shouting, cursing and shooting, and then a woman's ear piercing scream jerked me straight up in bed. When I awoke the next morning—I felt burned out before the day even started.

Marshal Clemens laughed when I asked him about the ruckus the night before; he explained, "You won't forget Leavenworth for awhile will you, Matt? We seldom have trouble. I have to apologize for the town. It's really a good place to live. We get a few loud soldiers from time to time, but that's an exception—not the rule. That row you heard last night was just some cowboys letting off steam. There were six of them. They tried to tree the town and tore up the Star of the West Saloon. All they got for their efforts was sore heads, a week in the hoosegow, and a big fine for the damages."

I had to agree with him. People I met were cautiously friendly—more curious than social. Gossip runs like a prairie fire in a small town, and I reckon no one wanted to get involved with a man that had been hit on the head, and couldn't remember who he was. I talked to the Marshal about Jon. He promised to be on the alert for him, and wired the authorities in Denver and St. Louis of what was going on. The horses had been stolen from the train, while it was sidetracked in Kansas City. I remembered we had made a report to the authorities. I really didn't believe Jon was here, but I knew it's best to leave no stone unturned. Enough of my memory had come back that I felt reasonably secure in traveling to Denver. I was sick of trains, and Marshal Clemens had arranged for me to ride along with a small wagon train. I had to sign their articles, a Train Contract, even then Captain Hutchins, the Wagon Master was reluctant to take me on. From what the Marshal had told him, he was worried that someone might be following me and might cause trouble for the Wagon Train. I couldn't blame him, but I was grateful that he agreed to let me join the train. I thanked Marshal Clemens before leaving, for all his help and support. With my gold coins, I was able to buy enough supplies and another mule for the trip to Denver.

My custom before going to bed, and also the first thing I did when I awoke was to check my weapons. We O'Shannon men were devotees of the Smith and Wesson Russian .44 cal. Pistol, and the .44 cal. Winchester Henry rifle. My weapons might be needed in defense of the wagon train, so I cleaned the weapons thoroughly, before settling in for the night.

Traveling cross country with a wagon train proved to be excruciating hard work for every man, woman and child big enough to drive a wagon, help with the stock, or just the hard work of walking five to fifteen miles every day. Every gulley, every creek, every river, every hill proved to be a challenge for each individual wagon. The first few days I wasn't much help, but I was young and healthy as a horse and my body and mind quickly healed. I was big and strong as a mule and I quickly became everybody's friend. I was in demand everywhere, and I can vouch that I did more than my share to move that wagon train over five hundred miles during the next thirty-four days. Pike's Peak was now only a hundred miles away. It stood out like a beacon; for some reason it was comforting to me. The trail had grown harder, for we were already in the Eastern Colorado Plains, and we had ascended to more than three thousand feet. While riding, I was busy sizing up the land. The obstacles became more frequent, for there were more small streams and hazards. I was fascinated, for off the main trail, the grass and wild flowers stood belly deep to my horse. This was the kind of land a man could learn to love.

That night we camped on the edge of a sizable meadow bordered by a small stream. The only trees that occurred naturally on these plains were on the riverbanks and streams. Captain Hutchins, as darkness fell, pointed the tongue of the lead wagon toward the North Star. The travelers had circled their wagons. After supper they gathered in family groups, and sat relaxing about their buffalo chip fires, or were mending broken gear and sewing tears in their garments. Frequent crosses along the way told the story of the hardships endured by the thousands of people that had preceded us. The multitudes of people traveling this trail had long since used up most of the Buffalo chips, and on the plains there were few trees. There was still a supply of buffalo chips, because the vast herds of Buffalo generously dropped more billets each season as they passed on their way south. Every one picked up anything that would burn and tossed it on the heavy tarps slung under each wagon, especially the buffalo chips. I stopped to pick up chips along the way to help out the Captain's wagon. I imagine everyone would welcome the fallen wood that was becoming a little more evident. Captain Hutchins was always out circulating among the people tending to their needs. He was short and heavy built and he reminded me of Barney, my memory slipped again—who the heck was Barney?

I was sitting in a Captain's chair with my hand trailing on Jack's head when I felt one of his low growls of warning. A minute later the Captain returned, and I heard the soft thud of a horse's hoof and the rustle of reins and the creak of saddles. I said calmly, "Easy now, Captain—we have visitors—get up move about—arm yourselves and take cover. In seconds the word had spread faster than gossip throughout the circled wagons.

A minute later a voice called out, "Hello the camp—there are four of us—may we come in?"

A second later a sentry called out, "I got em covered, Captain Hutchins. It's like they say—thar's four of em—thar arms aer holstered."

Hutchins called out. "Josh, clear a way for the leader to come in." Two men jumped to clear a passage, and a beautiful roan mare picked a dainty route between the two wagons.

The rider was well equipped and he knew his etiquette. He drew up and said with a smile, "May I dismount."

Captain Hutchins stepped out of the shadows, ignored his request and asked, "What may I do for you, sir."

"He leaned forward with a smile on his face and said, "Names Able Brand. We been riding hard, saw your camp, and thought we would like a cup of coffee and some companionship." Brand had a lean, hawkish face with eyes that had the look of a bird of prey. His eyes made me wary. I chided myself—Captain Hutchins himself had a hard look, but his I felt came from the responsibilities of command—of Brand's—I wasn't sure. His eyes were too busy, inquisitive, and prying to suit me. My subconscious was trying to tell me something. My head was splitting again—Brand—where—where—had I heard that name before?

Hutchins eyed him hard and replied, "There's a small stand of trees a hundred yards or so behind us. Its got water. Why don't you make your camp up there? Come by in the morning and have breakfast with me. It's bedtime for us now."

Brand's eyes narrowed a bit, but he smiled and said smoothly, "We didn't mean to disturb anyone. It is some late. Thanks for your invite. See ya in the morning."

As he left Jack growled deep in his throat. He sensed a danger we couldn't see, but one that Hutchins had neatly avoided. After the men left Hutchins yelled, "Let's call it a night" He circled the camp, and put everyone on their alert and immediately doubled the guard. I was beginning to form a new respect for the Captain.

Brand timed it just right in the morning. He waited until people were up and well into their meal before he came calling with just one man. Captain Hutchins invited them in and they both opted for coffee. Both men had bold roving eyes and I felt violated. Something was wrong; Captain Hutchins picked up on it at once. He was a very careful man. Brand—where had I heard that name before? My headache had dissipated overnight, but it seemed the more I tried to remember—the more it hurt. I was standing back from the fire leaning against a wagon wheel nursing a last cup of coffee.

Brand said, "My friend is Justin Trudeau, Captain. And yours?" He added casually, as he turned to me. I ignored him, and just looked at him curiously, shifted my coffee to my left hand, thinking—just what was he up to? He hadn't wasted any time getting to the point—the point—obviously me. His friend Trudeau looked and sounded French—he had a shifty look about him that kept me alert.

Hutchins was eyeing Brand carefully and asked, "You and your friends were traveling late and hard last night. What is it you want?"

"We are looking for two horse thieves, Captain." He looked at me and said, "That's a fine looking bay stud you have there, young man. Do you have the papers on him?"

"That's a rather strange question to ask a man, Mr. Brand," I replied. "It implies that I'm one of your horse thieves. Captain Hutchins, do you have the papers on your horse, and for that matter, Mr. Brand, do you have the papers on those two horses you gentlemen are riding?" I could tell by their faces that none of them did. I set coffee cup on the tailgate of the wagon, and hooked my right thumb in my gun belt and said "I'll tell you what I'll do, Brand. You meet me and Captain Hutchins in Denver. We will all telegraph our home towns for verification of ownership." I looked Brand in the eye and said, "We will let those without papers answer to the law." Brand tried to keep his face bland, but for an instant a flush of anger showed his true feelings.

"Well, Brand?" Captain Hutchins asked impatiently?

"It seems I was mistaken, Captain. Please accept my apologies," he said with a little bow. "Please excuse us—we still have two men to find." As he swung up on his horse, his eyes caught mine for a brief second—for the first time—I knew who had my horses—that sixth sense of mine was working just fine.

I looked Brand in the eye and said, "It has been a pleasure, Brand. Till we meet again," and with my left hand I tipped my hat to him.

He got the message, but it was Trudeau that replied with a grim smile, "Au revoir, Messieurs." Unless I missed my guess, Brand had been recruiting men of French descent living in the St. Louis area, or possibly New Orleans. Trudeau's family line most likely dated back before the Louisiana Purchase. If Brand was a horse breeder, my papers would add prestige to his line.

As they rode away, Captain Hutchins called out, "Break camp." Then he turned to me and said bluntly, "And that, Mathew, is exactly why I did not want you on my Wagon Train. You have been invaluable to everyone, especially me. I want you to know how much I appreciate your work. But," and he spread his hands expressively.

"I understand, Captain Hutchins, and I appreciate your taking me this far. With your permission, sir, I will leave camp immediately after dark tonight."

"You're a good man, Matthew. I wish I could do more for you. You go with my blessings."

Brand was still camped when we pulled out. We were in foothill terrain, and I sometimes rode ahead with the scouts leading my pack mules. Two hours later we came to a shallow, clear running mountain stream wooded on both sides, I held back, watered my animals, and as the scouts passed on over a rise, I lifted Jack to the pad and turned down the middle of the stream and kept right on going, the water taking my trail with me. Some of my memories were coming back to me, but I had not said anything to the Captain. Brand had made a serious blunder. Until he came into the camp I wasn't sure who had stolen our horses. I gathered by his actions that Brand was impatient and impetuous—bad traits that could get a man killed. I knew I was impetuous—a lesson learned—I hoped.

Captain Hutchins had said when I left him that I was a good man. For some reason I seemed to have developed a fixation on that phrase. That one compliment would not alter or make up for my past, but it made me feel better. Now I had two names, two faces—and something tangible to pursue in my quest to find our stolen horses. I sure as hell wasn't going to run, but it was prudent to put some distance between me and four men that no doubt were pursuing me. Why, I did not know. I rode up out of the streambed opposite the side I had entered. If they were following me, I wanted them to think I was an amateur.

I headed for a small stand of trees. We had gone about half way through the grove. Without warning Jack jumped down—froze in place, sniffed the air and looked up at me curiously. I called out, "I would send Jack out to scout, but you would ruin his scent, Jon."

Jon jumped up rifle in hand laughing and exclaimed, "I'm a better woodsman than you, but I can never get you away from Jack long enough to get a fair break." Jack ran to meet him and jumped into his arms and began licking his face.

I slid out of the saddle and gave Jon a bear hug and told him, "The wind gave you away. Jack smelled you first; then I caught your scent."

Jon grunted, "I told Mom not to put so much bear grease on me—it makes me smell just like an Indian." I didn't have time to laugh, Jack growled, a branch cracked and we all hit the ground. A fusillade of shots cracked over our heads.

"Run, Pat—scout, Jack," I snapped, and as Pat wheeled away, I raised an arm up and slid my Henry out of the boot. Jon's horse Pocahontas instantly broke from cover hard on the heels of Pat. She loved my big stud. No one shot at the horses, Indians love a good horse; their wealth was measured in horses—not gold. If the enemy was Brand and his men, they wouldn't risk hitting the horses either. Jack came slithering back to my side. From a crouch, he pointed again, again and again. We were encircled. Jon looked to me; I pointed to my eyes, patted my weapon and pointed to the front. I then pointed to him, patted my rifle and pointed to the rear. We both slid off on our stomachs. A good offense was our best defense; there was no reason to waste time. Catch them when they least expected it.

Within a few minutes, I had Brand and three men in sight. They weren't wasting any time. They were rapidly moving through the trees. Three men? There either were more than four men in his group, or someone else had invited themselves to our party. Jack growled and Jon slid in beside me. "Cheyenne," he breathed in my ear. He flashed his fingers—twenty—maybe more. He slid his fingers down his face—war paint—it was a Cheyenne war party. I had Brand spotted—I called out—"Brand!"

He froze—really startled.

"If I wanted you dead—you would be. There's about thirty Cheyenne right behind us. Together we have a chance. Truce! Yes—or—No!"

A brief pause and Brand hissed—Yes!"

I rose to my knees to move forward and Brand raised his rifle and shot right at me—a Cheyenne warrior grunted behind me and nearly fell on top of me. I started to say, I owe you one, but there was no time for conversation; all hell broke loose. I swung around and shot from the hip and shattered a screaming painted face with a .44 slug. We met a wall of screaming half naked Cheyenne with a hail of our lead that cut down their leading warriors like a scythe welded by the Angel of Death. The screen of smoke from our black powder shells helped camouflage our positions, but now it also hampered accurate shooting. We met the Cheyenne's blood curdling whoops with curses and screams of our own. Above the roar of battle, rose the voice of a Cheyenne singing his death song that ended in a gurgle. I dropped my empty rifle—slid out my Russian .44 and dropped two Cheyenne right on top of me—suddenly the firing ceased.

The war party disappeared as quickly and silently as they had appeared. It was as though they had dissipated with the smoke. Jack rose from where he was crouched at my feet and as I turned I said, "Jack, fetch Pat"

Brand stepped from behind a tree and his rifle was pointed right at my gut. He snapped, "Drop that pistol, Shannon."

The perfidy of the man! Fierce Shannach blood throbbed in my temples—black rage engulfed me—my pistol was hip high; I triggered it and placed two shots an inch apart over his heart. The two .44 slugs knocked him flat on his back. He was dead before he hit the ground.

Jon yelled, "I got your back, Matt."

Two men faced me—their weapons half raised—at Jon's voice they froze in place. A third man was lying face down over a limb of a tree with a big hole in the back of his head. Brand's man Justin Trudeau looked at me—shocked—he gasped and exclaimed, "Mon Dieu! You keel him."

"He named the game, Justin. Remember that boy you hit on the head in St. Louis when you stole our horses—he died the next day. You fellows have a bad habit of hitting people on the head," I reached up and gingerly touched the back of my head with my left hand. "Murder's a hanging offense—and in case you haven't heard—west of the Mississippi, they hang horse thieves."

"Murder!" Trudeau shouted. "We no murder anyone."

Panicked—his partner leveled his rifle. Jon shot him between the eyes—no doubt thinking of his brother Martel.

The distraction gave Trudeau his chance. He was lightning fast—my shot was faster. It struck his rifle stock and tore it from his hands. He recovered like a big cat and crouched. His hand flashed down, but as his pistol came up I shot off his thumb. "Mon Dieu! Mon Dieu!" He screamed. He fell to his knees, his eyes wild with shock; he grabbed his hand, and screamed at me, "Diable! Diable!"

I eyed him coldly. They had stolen our horses, killed Jon's cousin Martel, ambushed me—hit me on the head, stalked me, and after I saved their lives, broke the truce we had just made. I could only guess what they intended for me next. I felt no compassion, but this man knew where my horses were. If I had to kill him to find out—well—we'd see. I called out, "Don't shoot him, Jon. If he talks—he lives. If not—he dies."

I jerked him to his feet and asked, "What's your name?" He just glared at me. I slapped him. "Where are my horses?" He sneered. "Tell me, and I will take care of that thumb and turn you loose."

With a look of cunning he replied, "Non parley English."

I glared at him and growled, "I killed Brand for mispronouncing my name. What makes you think I won't kill you?"

Jon turned his head to keep from laughing. He drew near and the man spat at him. Jon just shook his head sympathetically and commented. "He can't be from Quebec—the French there have manners. Some of these Frenchies are a mite tricky, Matthew. Give me a few minutes and I'll get something that will settle him right down."

I let the man sit there to hurt—to bleed—to sweat.

Ten minutes later Jon came back carrying a sack. He shook it and something threshed about in the bottom; then came an ominous rattling sound. Jon looked at me real serious and said, "Now, as I see it—if he talks—we don't put this rattlesnake down the front of his pants."

I glanced at Jon's Stetson hat. We had purchased them together in St. Louis. Only difference was he had a fancy band around the crown with the rattles from a rattlesnake attached for decoration. The rattles were gone. I smiled grimly; with my left hand I seized the Frenchman by his throat—lifted him from the ground, and slid out my razor sharp knife. He grabbed my hand. I tightened my grip on his throat; instinctively, his hand let go, and grabbed the hand choking him. I slid the knife between his shirt and gun belt, twisted the knife severing the gun belt and pant's belt. I dropped the knife into its scabbard, and held open the front of his pants.

I snarled at the Frenchman, "One last chance, Frenchie. Where are our horses, or he drops the rattlesnake into your britches?"

I loosened my grip on his neck and he rasped, "Non! Non!" and Jon dropped the snake into his pants. The Frenchman screamed and fainted—at the same time his bowels let go.

Jon held his nose—backed away, and said accusingly, "Now look at what you went and did."

I dropped him. The blacksnake slithered out, bit the Frenchman on the hand and indignantly slid out of the befouled pants and disappeared into the brush. I picked Brand's canteen from his belt and poured water on the Frenchman's head. He snorted—and awoke—back into his world of pain. The snakebite hurt! Frenchie looked at his hand—thought the worst—and screamed. I held up my match vial—wiggled it—and said, "I have serum. You don't have much time—talk."

Frenchie was babbling—I slapped his face—"One last time—thief—the horses—where are our horses?"

He broke and sobbed, "The horses are in Gaveston's Stock Yard in Kansas City. Brand left two men to feed and guard them. The serum—please give me the serum." Jon nodded to me. He believed the man, and he was a better judge of when people were telling the truth than I was. But I ignored the Frenchman and let him sweat.

Jack came up to me with Pat's reins in his mouth, and the other two horses were right behind them. Pat shied at the smell of the blood. I praised Jack and comforted Pat, he nuzzled my cheek. I took a piece of jerky out of my saddlebags—tossed it to Jack, and fed each horse and pack mule a sugar cube.

Remembering the fear crazed eyes of the Frenchman, I took out some powdered Tansy Tea from my saddle bags, and put it into my little collapsible container—poured in some water—shook it—and gave it to him. "Drink it all," I ordered . . . He did . . . I fully expected him to complain; it's a dank looking evil green concoction with a few deadly looking air bubbles when shaken. When drank, it tastes like pure d hell. Only castor oil could kill the taste. I wanted him to complain, but we don't always get our druthers. Frenchie didn't complain—he thought it was the elixir of life. I cleaned and dosed the wound with slippery elm powder, put pine-sap on the stump to seal the wound and stop the bleeding, and then bandaged it with one of my clean neckerchiefs.

I got Frenchie's horse, checked his gear, reloaded his weapons, and saw that he had food and water. When he was all set to travel, I told him. "You are one lucky Frenchman; Trudeau You lived through two shoot outs, and a deadly snake bite. Stay away from Denver and Kansas City. If I ever see you again—I'll kneecap both your knees. Count your blessings that I don't kill you right now."

He looked at me, a totally beat man. He dropped his eyes and replied. "No cross! No Cross! C'st viril le Diable."

I still didn't trust him and I said, "My dog Jack will escort you a ways. I've left you your weapons—those Cheyenne are still in the area. I wouldn't send anyone out there naked. Be careful, with your hand messed up—it could get sticky." I saw the look of hate in his eyes and I said, "Don't let your stupidity make you draw on me. I could shut my eyes and still outdraw and kill you."

"Jack, guard. Jack, come back." He wagged his tail. He understood. Jack would come back when the man was gone.

After he rode off, I started checking Pat and my pack mules. Pat kept nuzzling me for sugar—and the one mule nibbled at my hair, I had spoiled them both. Jon joined me. It was the first time I had a chance to talk to him, and I asked, "Where ya been?"

"I got on the trail of Brand and his men. I learned about your problems in Leavenworth, but that Justin was tricky. He ended up on my tail, and I couldn't get close to you until I spotted you through my binoculars the morning you met Brand. When they set out to cut you off, after you left the Wagon Train, I cut around them and ended up in your backyard. How bad are you hurt?" Jon asked.

I bent over and showed him the back of my head. He clucked sympathetically. "He should have known better than to hit you on the head. He could have broken his pistol.

"Serve him right, if he did, Jon. I couldn't remember who the hell I was when I woke up. I stayed two nights at the National Hotel, hoping to see you, but you were out playing Indian. I decided to go on to Denver. I told the livery boy where I was headed, if you showed up. My memory still comes and goes. One thing isn't clear yet—who is Barney?"

Jon chuckled, "He's your big brother. Before we left home, Barney mentioned he had trouble in Denver? After our horses were stolen from the train in Kansas City, he told us he thought that the Brand brothers were the ones that had stolen them. His trouble is our trouble now. The thieves killed Martel and we had to bury him in Kansas City. Damn it all to hell, Matt. Martel was special—he didn't deserve to die that way." Jon regained his self control and continued, "We agreed to take the rest of the horses off the train in Kansas City. Barney and my brothers are driving them to Denver along the southern side of the Oregon Trail. Our job was to find our stolen horses."

"You may not remember, but in Kansas City we learned that Abel Brand was the brother of Cotton Brand, Barney's mysterious enemy in Denver. The Sheriff informed us that Abel had about twelve men with him in Kansas City. The big clan of Brands—from what we learned—had resettled in Denver. They came out of Texas just one jump ahead of the Texas Rangers. The Brand Clan had been the chief cause of a feud in Texas with a prominent family. Texas had the reputation of being the worst State in the Union for feuds and the Texas Rangers were given the job to break them up. The last persons the Brands killed in Texas were Thomas J. Newby and his brother in law Padilla Baca. The Baca family was among the original Mexicans that settled in Texas, and they fought with General Sam Houston against Santa Ana. It's funny—funny peculiar. We were chasing Abel Brand, while he was chasing us. Brand split his men up. He sent six men into Leavenworth where you had gone to buy supplies. It's obvious that they are the ones that slugged you."

"You got that right, Jon. They wanted our bills of sales, and our purebred documentation on the horses."

When I told Jon where I had hidden the papers. He laughed and marveled, "It's the best safety deposit box I ever heard of. Anyway two men came out of Leavenworth and met Brand. They evidently told him you were leaving on the wagon train. He followed you; I followed him, and you know the rest."

"I figured they must have split up, after I was hit on the head, I forgot everything you just told me. Little by little, my memory is coming back to me. If those six men of Brand's are the ones that slugged me in Leavenworth; I bet they are still there. Doesn't it strike you strange, Jon? Why did the Brands put in so much effort just to get some papers? With people like that, it seems to me they could forge any bills of sale they needed." We thought about that for a few minutes and I growled, "It never rains trouble, but what it pours."

"Isn't that the truth," Jon agreed, "The Brands want all of our horses, and like it or not we are the unwilling victims of another feud. Denver has plenty of law, and if any kind of word leaked out that the horses were stolen, they would find themselves guests at a Hanging Bee. They may not be sure what we look like, but for sure—they want us all dead."

"Could be," I agreed, "but they had a chance to kill me in Leavenworth and didn't. You know, those Cheyenne were good fighters," I said, changing the subject, "but they left some of their dead. If they don't run into more trouble, maybe they'll be back? Think we should lay those bucks out a bit more dignified?"

"They'll be back," Jon agreed. "I think that last one you killed was a War Chief." Jon began making a clearing.

We hauled some poles down the slope and made a platform. We laid the Indians out in their natural splendor, and placed their weapons, food, and water skins beside them, but I did take one precaution, I jammed the firing pins of the weapons. "They won't need firing pins in Shadow Land, right, Jon.?"

He laughed. I looked up and sitting on a low bank was Jack. His tongue was hanging out one corner of his jaw. I swear he had a smile on his face. I figured Frenchie must have tried to shoot him, but Jack was too smart for that.

We bundled up all the fallen weapons and tied them to the mule's packsaddle. We found a low spot in the timber and laid Brand, Justin and their comrades beside them and covered them with logs topped off with heavy rocks. Jon said a word over their grave. I figured they got what they deserved. I felt no compassion for them.

As we saddled up Jon said, "I reckon we ride back to Kansas City—obtain a warrant, collect a Marshal and recover our horses. The ride will give you time to recover, and once we retrieve the horses, we can either catch a train, or herd the horses cross country, and meet Barney in Denver."

"The way I feel—that makes good sense. Why don't we make up our minds about the route once we get there," I suggested. My conscience was already bugging me. I was remembering J.D. McCoy and his boys and my broken promise to Ma. Now, I had killed at least three or four Indians and on top of that I had killed another white man. I was tallying up quite a score for a greenhorn. My promise to my mother kept repeating itself in my mind and my head was splitting. It was late afternoon, and I knew we should put some distance between us, and the Cheyenne. We found Brand's horses, unsaddled them and turned three of them and the pack horses loose. I tethered Brand's horse loosely to a bush and placed the reins in the hand of the dead Chief. Jon and I agreed the Chief would need a horse in Shadow Land. Shadow Land was Cherokee, but neither of us knew the Cheyenne word for heaven. I am sure that there were just as many Injuns in heaven—as there were of us tahboy bohs [white man].

The Cheyenne did come back. They had another chief leading them. The Cheyenne were great warriors. They had been the most aggressive fighters during the Indian war with ex-Brevet Major General George Armstrong Custer and the 7th Cavalry. When they found we had honored their dead by laying them out, they were pleased. Chief Lone Wolf said, "A good man and great warrior has honored our dead."

We learned about the Indians later and I was amazed that the Chief had used that phrase again. "He was a good man." We rode for several hours and covered our trail the best we could. Jon found a suitable camp from which we could keep a constant lookout. We had Cheyenne Indians behind us, and in Leavenworth there were six or more of Brand's men to steer clear of. However, we were thirty-four wagon train days from Leavenworth, but we could more than triple that pace going back. Along the way, we debated whether we should bypass the town.

Every dawn we were in the saddle, and the trip was most therapeutic. However, one phrase that kept coming to mind that I found rather up setting, but appropriate, was, "Love one another, as I have loved you." The words of the Scripture that Father Quirk had read at the last Mass I had heard him preach in Huntington. The phrase popped up whenever my mind began to dwell on the McCoy men, the Brand men, and the Indians that I had killed, and while appropriate—it made me do a lot of soul searching.

By the time we reached a rise from which we could see Leavenworth, and the mighty Missouri; my headaches were just a bad memory. We reined in and we studied it carefully with our binoculars. "It looks peaceful enough," Jon said, "but that doesn't mean a blessed thing."

I nodded my agreement and said, "Brand most likely recruited his men from the men of French extraction in Saint Louis, but there were also sections in Texas that were settled by the French. We better be alert to any Frenchmen that we run across."

They dress a little different and have distinct accents that we can hone in on," Jon said thoughtfully. Why don't we call on Marshal Clemens, and see if that bunch is still in town? If they are, maybe we can get a good look at them without being seen?"

"Good idea," I agreed. "We have been real lucky up to now, but sooner or later the law of averages is going to catch up with us." We found a clump of trees and made a comfortable camp on the edge of the Missouri River. At dusk the mosquitoes began eating us alive, so we rode on into Leavenworth. Clemens wasn't there and we headed for Delmonicos Restaurant for a change from range grub. I led Jon to the rear of the restaurant and tied up our horses. I looked at Jon and said, "No sense in advertising where we are."

He grinned, "That's what you get for showing off that stud of yours."

"It's a punishment I can live with, and as far as that goes—what about that lady that you are riding," I growled and we walked into the restaurant.

We got a break. Marshal Clemens was waiting to be seated and he greeted me like a long lost brother. I introduced Jon; the Marshal took his companion's arm and said, "You are in luck. This gent is Texas Ranger Ron McMullen. He has a story you have to hear, but let's eat first, I'm so starved, I could eat the south end out of a North bound boar hog."

Ranger McMullen looked every bit the Texas Ranger. Big boned, lean and rangy with a square set jaw, and a craggy leather bitten face that was topped off with a mop of uncontrollable sandy hair and a sad looking, drooping, handlebar mustache that traveled in every direction but north.

We topped off our steaks with hot, deep-dish, apple pie; I sat back with a sigh. Ranger McMullen slurped on his coffee and said, "Ah reckon yu'all aer plumb curious by now. It seems the fellows you have been playing around with are part of the same bunch I been trying to corral—the feuding Brand clan."

Jon said, "We heard your outfit was after the Brands. It's too bad you didn't start a might earlier."

My heart sank; another family similar to the McCoys. We were embroiled in another feud. My stomach churned. This was the last thing I wanted to hear. McMullen looked at me and said with concern. "You all right, son?"

I swallowed hard and grinned, more of a grimace and answered hollowly. "Yeah, I'm okay, Ron. It's just that we don't need another feud. Sorry I reacted—go on with your story."

"To make it short and sweet, Texan pride and honor has started more feuds than the Rangers can keep up with. The Brands were one of the worst. They were all good shots and they never give a fellow an even break. The two brothers Lance and Cotton Brand are said to be the leaders. Some say Cotton Brand is the one with the brains. All the evidence I have is on Lance and his sons. If he sees he can make money out of a deal; he picks a fight and kills the man. Then we have Lance's sons. The oldest is Abel, then Chauncey, Starr, and Kyle. Abel is a lot like his father; devious and quick to call a man out. He is a pistolero and a real hothead. The rest of the boys are good with weapons; the entire family is arrogant and overbearing. Other than that, they are nice people."

"On the other hand, he added thoughtfully, I have never obtained any evidence on Cotton Brand. Cotton and Vance moved to Denver several years ago. Some said they left to avoid all the trouble that Lance and his sons were cooking up. I did learn that Vance is a real good man, and he has a beautiful daughter. They are the only members of the family that have ever amounted to anything. They are decent, God fearing people."

Jon spoke up, "You can scratch Abel. He held a rifle on Matt and died before he could regret it."

Ron eyed me speculatively. I don't think he had taken me seriously until that moment. "You say Abel had a rifle on him?"

"Yep," Jon replied, "Able was plumb mean; just like you said. He was so arrogant that he never dreamed that Matt would shoot with a rifle trained on him. Matt drilled him—two shots in the heart an inch apart. He was dead before he knew he had made a bad mistake."

I gave Jon a dirty look, but he just glanced away—looking very innocent.

Ron took in Jon at a glance, turned to Clemens and said wryly, "If these boys will have me, I would like to tag along and see what develops."

I scooped up my last piece of apple pie and with my mouth full, I mumbled, "Glad to have you."

Two days later, we caught the Kansas and Pacific Railroad that connected with Kansas City. The three of us rode with Pat and Jack in the stock car. I had no intentions of losing another horse. Jack was pleased and when I sat down on a bed of straw, he lay with his head on my lap and promptly went to sleep. I was more at home with the animals than I was with a cigar, smoke-filled passenger car.

The night that we had returned to Leavenworth, Marshal Clemens had pointed out the cowboys that had been arrested. Starr Brand was the leader and it was obvious they were not cowboys on a spree. Starr was bigger than his brother Abel. He had that same intent, arrogant manner that I had noted in Abel. He was about six-foot two and slimmer than Abel. Starr's forehead caught my attention immediately. Ron said he had been born with a natural star shape on his forehead most likely caused by the Doctor's instrument that had extracted him from his mother's womb. But the star wasn't necessary to identify him as a Brand. They were all cut from the same mold, as were the type of men we had encountered with Abel Brand. No one told Starr that his brother was dead—there would be a proper time for that little bombshell. I was grateful to have a Texas Ranger along. It added authority and legitimacy to our endeavor to recover our horses. In addition, we could now be reasonably informed as to what we were up against.

The next day Jon and I went to see Dr. Elbee. After he checked me, he said, "If you don't stop a bullet first, Matthew, you should live to be a hundred."

"Heaven forbid," I complained with a laugh.

Jon grinned, "I think the only people that want to live to be a hundred is a person that is already ninety nine.

When we entered Kansas City, I was bug eyed, the same as I had been the first time I had seen the big city. It was a bustling town bursting from the seams. The Missouri River traffic and huge railroad center had helped make it a major gateway to the West. We found a large Livery Stable. It was the biggest livery I had ever encountered; the owner took great pride in his establishment. When I explained our concerns to him, and impressed by the Texas Ranger, he assigned one of his men to stand guard over our horses—armed with a rifle. He remembered reading of the theft of our four horses and wished us luck in their recovery.

We looked up Durwood Pruitt, the attorney that Marshal Clemens had recommended. I told him my story; and showed him my papers for the horses. He jumped up and said, "Times wasting." His secretary filled out the proper papers and we all headed for a judge to sign the warrant. We had no problems and when we contacted the Kansas City Chief of Police, he assigned Sgt. Thaddeus Murphy and three officers to assist us. The Sgt. loaded us into a police paddy wagon and we set off at a fast clip for the Stockyards. That's when our luck ran out. We quickly found that there were dozens of small stables and workshops. I figured we had our work cut out for us. However, Murphy knew his way around, and he rounded up the stockyard manager. His name was John Quinn and he listened patiently to the Sgt.

He smiled and said, "I know where the buggers be. Ye be careful with them shooten irons, sonny, there be a passel of valuable animals in yonder, and responsible I be for them all."

"Rest easy, Johnny bye," Sgt Murphy replied. "Tis most careful we'll be."

John led us to the stable; the Sgt. waved us to stand back. He sent one man to guard the rear entrance; and, aided by two men, he opened the double door and charged in. There was some yelling, and two shots; before Sgt. Murphy came out and waved us in. One man lay on his face—dead—the other was sitting up in his bunk, his face ashen and his hands held high—wondering what was going on. In the stalls were three beautiful Arabian mares and one magnificent Arabian stud. We had our horses back.

The stockyards smelled like one huge cow dung heap. I wondered how the city folk put up with the cloying stench of manure, dust, and dirt blown every day from the stockyards into their homes. We were cleared by the Marshal's Office, obtained tickets to Denver, and loaded our horses onto our assigned stock car. We were glad to get away from the stench. Each time the train whistle sounded, or an engine blew off some steam, we three had our hands full of horses scared witless by the noisy contraptions that some call progress.

Jon and I were taking no chances. The horses were going to need attention, and we had no intentions of letting them out of our sight. It had been Martel and Jackson Lee Ridge's turn to tend and guard the horses when they had been attacked and knocked unconscious and four horses were stolen. Martel had been killed, and Jackson Lee stunned, but Jackson regained his wits and shot two of the men and saved the rest of the horses. We had a total of six horses and two mules to tend to that would keep us busy. Some railroads put as many as forty horses on one car. I was relieved when I read the capacity sheet attached to the door. I learned that we had been assigned to a car that only contained twenty horse stalls. We would have plenty of room.

We arrived early and placed our horses in the stalls in the near end of the car. When the bales of hay were delivered we stacked them so our animals were separated from the rest of the animals. Baled hay was a pleasant novelty to us. It gave us a place to sit or lie down on. The last horse stabled was a big gray stallion with cropped, laid back ears, and a wicked eye. I told the stockmen to stable him at the other end of the car. When he saw Pat, he wanted to fight. The men explained that the stud was a bucking horse and that no one had ever been able to ride him. The animal was being shipped to a rodeo in Denver. The four men were well experienced in handling fractious horses, and stabled him with a minimum of trouble. They tied up one foot and tied his head down nearly to the floor.

That didn't set well with me or Ron. I glanced at Jon—he was primed to jump in with both feet. I gave him a negative shake of the head. Now was not the time. Just before they took the loading chute down, a stocky, tow-headed young man came running up the chute, he stopped short surprised when he saw us and said, "I didn't know I was going to have company this trip." Jack was lying in a corner and he didn't bother to get up—but I noted the growl deep in his throat.

Jon grinned and said, "Well, don't just stand there fellow, come on in and make yourself ta home." He stepped forward and said, I'm Jon and this sad bronc," he nodded to me, "answers to Matt. The dog's name is Jack and he is fine if you leave him alone. That ugly brute over there is named Ron. You can't get us mixed up—I'm the handsome one.

"Name's Jerry," he replied curtly and hung up his gear. Without another word, he turned and began checking the horses. That's one tough looking kid, I thought. He had distinct crow's feet about his eyes and his eyebrows were scarred. A livid scar ran from his left ear nearly to his mouth. He wore jeans, a faded blue shirt and a heavy leather vest. He wore a hunting knife on his right hip and a lump suggested he had something heavy inside his vest. He seemed to know what he was doing, but when he got to the stallion, he gave him a shove, moved him over in the stall, and looked in to make sure he was tied down.

The train whistle blew twice, a plume of steam roared from the side of the beast, and with a series of jerks the train pulled out of the station. The horses reared in their stalls; the stallion went wild—kicking and fighting. He fell, but scrambled to his three feet, and yanked free of the rope, Jon was a flash of denim, and with one bound he leaped to the stallion's back. The bucking champion reared up, but Jon leaned forward and grasped the horse's neck and began whispering to him.

Jerry let out an outraged oath and headed for the corner yelling, "You crazy son of a bitch, are you out of your mind?"

I grabbed Jerry by the arm and he came to an abrupt standstill. Jack was on his feet—ready for trouble. Jerry's face flooded with rage; his scar stood out livid against his tanned skin. I gave his arm a little tug and he felt the strength of my grip. "Easy, Jerry, watch and learn!"

Jon was crooning something to the big horse, and you could see the horse losing his tenseness like water shedding off a duck's back. A few minutes later the horse nickered and when Jon slipped off his back, he nuzzled Jon's neck. Jon fastened the horse loosely to the ring and untied his leg. He spent half an hour with the horse. I reckoned the rodeo wasn't going to be pleased with the outcome. Jon untied the horse, backed him out of his stall and walked him up and down.

Jon looked at me and said, "This is one hell of a horse. If I don't miss my guess his ancestors came from the Conquistador's herds. He would make a great stud for the herd we are going to build."

Jerry wrenched his arm loose and snarled. "What the hell do you think you're doing? Mr. Springer, the Rodeo Manager, will turn you inside out for messing with his Champeen bucking hoss."

Jon's eyes sparkled, "Bucker—what on earth are you talking about? Why I could ride that horse right now."

"Not in here you can't, but when we come to the water and fuel stop, I'll get Mr. Springer and I'll bet you a hundred simoleons, he can't be rid."

"You got a bet!" Jon laughed and asked, "No offence, but you do have the hundred—don't you?"

Jerry's face turned deadly white. He snarled and went into a gunman's crouch. "You calling me a welsher?"

Jon laughed, "Of course not. What do you say we put up our money when the train stops, and we will let a disinterested party hold the bets."

Jerry's face set, and I knew he was going to draw. I watched him close and when his hand flashed, I drew! Before his hand cleared his coat, he was looking at the business end of my Russian .44.

"Now, Jerry, I said for you to relax and maybe you might learn something. Instead you tried to throw down on an unarmed man.

Now let's see that hand come out nice and slow with whatever you have—just two fingers. His hand came out gingerly holding a wicked looking throwing knife. "Drop it!" I snapped. "Step back!" Jerry stepped back and with the toe of my boot, I flipped the knife to Jon.

The Texan had slept through most of the incident, but he woke up in time to witness the altercation.

Jon was angry, but it didn't show. He said to Jerry, "You think you're pretty good with a knife?"

Jerry, his jaw set, just glared his reply.

I holstered my Russian .44, and stood back.

"You have a knife on your hip," Jon said, "if you want to teach me a lesson pull it out and start teaching."

Jerry slid the knife out and made a vicious slash at Jon's jugular. Jon slid under the slash to Jerry's left and Jerry suddenly found himself completely vulnerable, he threw himself backward to avoid the oncoming slash, but he was too late. Jon cut a deep x on Jerry's forehead. Blood gushed and ran into his eyes—Jon stepped in and slashed another deep x on his opponent's chest.

Again Jerry leaped back, but immediately stepped forward and slashed for Jon's eyes. Jon was ready for him and slipped under the knife and to his left once again. Jon slashed Jerry's other cheek and countered his opponent's incoming knife with a slashing cut that laid his wrist open to the bone.

With a gasp, the knife fell from Jerry's nerveless fingers. He grasped his wrist with his left hand to stop the gushing blood. "Damn you, you're a blasted magician," Jerry ground out between clinched teeth.

"No! Jon replied, "You're all mouth. I suggest you quit carrying men's weapons before you get yourself killed."

"Damn you to hell," Jerry shouted red with rage. He dropped his wrist and uselessly clawed for his gun—blood flying in every direction.

Ron stepped over and slapped him on the side of his head with the barrel of his pistol rendering him unconscious. "Quick, Jon," I said, "put a tourniquet on his arm. Get a tight bandage on that cut and stop the bleeding or he'll bleed to death." When Jerry came to, we had all his wounds stitched up, and we had covered him up with a blanket.

To be on the safe side, Ron frisked him and relieved him of three knives and a small Bulldog .38 cal. pistol and stowed them in Jerry's pack.

I told him, "You have a bad temper, Jerry. It'll get you killed, unless you change your ways." Jack got up and moved away from the stockman as though he didn't want to be seen in such low company.

Ron said, "You're wasting your breath, Matt. Guys like him never learn."

Jerry glowered at us all—curled up into a ball, and rocked back and forth nursing his pain.

That evening the train chugged to a stop. When I slid open the car door, we could see the train crew taking on water from a large water tower. There were three buildings and off to one side was a big sod house with a log cabin attached on front with a crudely painted sign reading—Saloon. The brakeman came by and said, "We will be here ten minutes. If you want a drink of pure poison—and he pointed to the saloon—you have just enough time." He saw Jerry curled up on a bail of hay and exclaimed, "What the hell happened ta him?"

"My friend had to teach him about the manly art of self defense," I explained with a harmless grin.

He just shook his head. "If I tol him once, I tol him a hunret times that his temper was gonna get him into a lotta grief. Kids never listen." He walked off muttering to himself.

A man wearing a big white Stetson stuck his head in the door, and asked, "How's that ornery stallion of mine riding? Where's Jerry?" He saw Jerry and exclaimed, "Asleep again, huh?" And he climbed into the car. He was a man in his forties and obviously a man used to having his own way. Without waiting for an answer he limped down the car and checked on his horse. He swung toward Jon, who had followed him and demanded, "Why isn't this horse fastened the way I ordered?"

107

Jon leaned up against a stall and replied nonchalantly, "When that whistle blew; the train jerked. I just don't think that horse appreciated having his head tied to the floor and his leg tied up. He went plum crazy—but I want you to know that once I had a little talk with him—he settled right down and I was able to walk him up and down a mite."

The rodeo man snorted, "You cowboys are all alike. You spin one yarn after another. It took four men to put that critter in that stall." He stomped down the car—grabbed Jerry by the shoulder, "Hey, boy, what happened to my horse?"

Jerry came uncoiled like an angry rattler, his eyes glazed with pain. In spite of Ron's efforts, he had another knife in his left hand—he drove it into the man's leg. "Are you crazy? The man snapped. Instinctively his big ham-like hand slapped Jerry across the face stretching him across the floor. He saw the blood and bandages and exclaimed, "What the hells going on here?" He stood there, the picture of outrage, arms akimbo and the knife protruding straight out from his leg.

I pointed at the knife and mimicked him, "I agree! What the hells going on here?"

He looked down—saw the knife—and his face relaxed into a grin. Then he bellowed with laughter. It was contagious, and we all laughed until he gasped, "I have a peg-leg," he explained. "A bronc fell and crushed my leg. I had a leg made with my other boot attached. Most folks don't know I have a peg leg. He pulled the knife out—tossed it to me hilt first—and asked, "What's the story that goes with that?"

Ron explained what had happened, and coming from a Texas Ranger no one ever questioned the story. Jerry had crawled back on his bed of hay and pretended to be asleep. The rodeo man looked at Jon thoughtfully stuck his big paw out and said, "My handle is Rowdy Springer." I finished the introductions and Rowdy said to Jon, "So you think you can ride that hoss of mine?"

"I reckon so," Jon agreed with a smile.

"I bet you five hundred dollars that you can't stay on that hoss ten seconds."

"Mr. Springer, I really don't want to take your money."

"Just another sandy, eh kid?"

Jon just grinned and replied, "Tell you what I'll do. If I stay on the horse ten seconds—I get the horse. If I can't ride him, I'll pay you five hundred dollars."

"Deal," exclaimed Rowdy, by this time a dozen men had been attracted by the conversation and Rowdy yelled, "Boys, get that loading chute up here and let's have a show."

The brakeman and the conductor stood by with their jaws hanging slack. Rowdy went up to them and said a few words and slipped them a twenty each and within minutes Jon was leading the stud down the ramp. Most of the passengers had piled off the train and were standing off to one side to see the show. When they saw the horse being led some laughed and others began clapping with appreciation.

When Rowdy saw the saddled horse coming down the ramp as docile as a lamb, his face flushed and he roared, "What have you gone and done with that there bronc of mine?"

Jon grinned and answered, "Just a little tender loving care, Rowdy; horse and I got us an understanding." Jon stopped and turned—the horse stepped up and nuzzled him. Jon whispered in his ear, then walked around and stepped into the stirrups and swung up onto the hurricane deck of the rogue horse. The rogue tensed—he laid back his cropped ears and a wicked gleam shone from his outlaw eyes. I knew he was ready to explode. Jon leaned forward again and whispered into the horse's ear. I was amazed to see the bucker's ears slowly straighten out—tension flowed out of him like the air dumped out of a fallen cake. Jon sat back casually and began whistling—the stud walked off—then broke into a trot. Jon posted, with a click of his tongue the horse cantered and once past the saloon, the rogue broke into a run.

My eyes gleamed. That gray bucker could run like the wind, Jon returned with a thunder of hooves, and slid to a stop in a whirl of dust. He jumped down and exclaimed, "He's gaited—rides like a dream, and I've never ridden a faster horse."

Rowdy slammed his hat on the ground and yelled, "I'll be double damned. I saw it, but I still don't believe it." He handed Jon a bill of sale and said with a big grin, "You sure as hell got the best of that deal, young man. You go to work for me, Jon, and I'll pay you five-hundred-dollars a month."

Jon slipped the horse a cube of sugar and said seriously, "Thanks, Rowdy, but no thanks. That's quite a compliment, but I'll be raising horses—not managing them."

I glanced up at the horse car and Jerry was leaning up against the side of the entrance. He was trying to train a rifle on Jon with my Henry rifle. I drew and placed a shot right beside his head. My bullet hit the frame of the doorway, and threw splinters into his face. Jerry screamed, dropped the rifle, and fell backwards into the car. I ran up the ramp—Jerry lay there—too scared to open his eyes—his hands touching the splinters trying to figure out what to do. His face looked like a porcupine's hind end.

I ran to him and grabbed his hands and said, "You damned idiot. Keep your hands down and I'll try to get these splinters out." I thought for sure that the splinters had penetrated his eyes.

He was half sobbing with fear saying over and over, "My eyes—my eyes."

I had no patience with this would be back-shooter. I snapped, "Shut up—and lay still. You're damned lucky to be alive." As I picked out the last sliver I said, "Open your eyes."

He cautiously opened his eyes—blinked a few times and said with obvious relief, "I can see."

Jon retorted, "Yeah lucky you. You can see good enough to shoot someone else in the back."

While we were taking care of Jerry, the Texas Ranger led his saddled horse down the ramp and called, "See you boys later. This is as far as I go."

Jerry's face flushed—and I could see the anger in his eyes. The train was ready to depart. I grabbed Jerry by his good arm and tossed him out the door just as the engineer blew his whistle, and the train got underway. I tossed Jerry's bag out. Sitting in the dirt on his prat, he was so surprised he didn't even have time to make a threat.

Jon called out. "Don't forget that hundred you owe me, Jerry."

I called out laughingly, "Sorry to do that to you Ron, better watch your back." Ron laughed and just waved us on good naturedly.

Still laughing Jon said, "Jerry didn't even have time to open his mouth. I don't think you made his day, but you sure did improve mine."

"That's quite a horse you added to our breeding stock," I said. It was the first time I had an opportunity to talk to him since his spectacular ride.

"Someone deliberately turned that stud into a man hater, Matt. He has whip marks and signs where he had been severely beaten. By the way, I've named him "Whip Shy."

"A fitting name," I said "I would hate to be the person that whipped him, if that stud ever picks up his scent when he isn't penned up."

Jon shook his head in agreement; as he took a curry comb to Whip Shy's scarred sides. "You know, when I took that ride on Whip Shy, I saw something that didn't set right." Jon rested his hand on the horse's withers and turned to me. The Stud's head swiveled and seeing Jon's lack of attention, he nudged his hand. Jon laughed and ran his hand up the horse's mane, "It didn't take long to spoil you—did it?"

He went back to currying Dusty and said, "Anyhow, we ran up to the edge of a camp; must have been about ten or twelve men. When I swung around a man stepped out and sized me up. He reminded me of that fellow Abel Brand. I got a glimpse of some of the men and a few of them wore clothes similar to Justin Trudeau's. Two of the men that got off the train to see me ride didn't get back on. I saw them walking toward that campsite. They wore their guns low and tied down."

"I wonder if that is why the Ranger got off here," I mused softly. "He said he was going on to Denver with us.

My heart sank. Was I going to be plagued with gunmen everywhere I went? Maybe this was God's way of punishing me for killing all those McCoys? I certainly didn't want to pass on my negativity to Jon, so I replied lightheartedly, "Jon, I swear the way you worry, you're going to be seeing Brands, or Injuns behind every bush."

Jon laughed and retorted, "Yeah and you'll be seeing McCoys behind every rock."

I stepped over and began currying one of our brood mares. She loved attention and nibbled at my hair to show her appreciation. I said thoughtfully, "You know, with that telegraph so handy back yonder, do you reckon we might get some visitors along the way, or do you think they just might wait until we get to Denver?"

"I think they're out scouting for Barney."

I stopped—shocked—damn!—Jon might be right? Why else would Brand's men be out here? That is—if they were Brand's men? But could I take a chance they weren't? If they were Brand and the men we had seen in Leavenworth, it would mean that they had come out here on yesterdays train."

"Jon," I said—"If you agree—saddle up our horses and the mules. We're going back." He nodded his agreement and grabbed a saddle blanket. I headed for the end of the car and climbed up the ladder—crawled out and worked my way down the ladder outside—and jumped across the car couplings. I found Rowdy Springer in a poker game.

He looked up in surprise, but didn't hesitate when I motioned him to one side. "I have to get off, Rowdy," and I explained briefly. "Will you take care of my horses and stable them in Denver until I show up?"

"Yeah," he answered, "but how are you going to get off?'

I smiled and reached up and pulled the emergency cord. The engineer hit the brakes and money, cards, baggage, and people flew in every direction. A cowpuncher knocked to the floor looked up and complained, "Damn it all to hell—I had a full house."

I handed a wad of money to Rowdy and said, "That should take care of the train people and getting the horses into a stable." As I ducked out, I yelled over my shoulder and said, "Give that cowpoke fifty bucks." I ran to the end of the car and jumped off the train—just in time to see Jon jumping out of the box car with our three horses and my two loaded mules out of the boxcar. Right behind Jon—Jack came sailing through the air. I ran to them and caught Jack up into the saddle and galloped away from the train. The train started up with a puff of indignation; it soon disappeared with a shrill blast from the train's whistle.

I settled Jack down in front of me. Jon asked, "We going to look for Barney or what?"

"Why don't you injun up on those twelve fellows tonight? Keep your eyes peeled for that Ranger; we don't want to step on his toes. He must have seen something we didn't. See if you can learn what they are up to?"

Jon nodded his assent, and we followed the railroad tracks for two hours. Suddenly, the tops of the buildings of the community seemed to jump out of the prairie. We swung wide, and worked our way back to a place where we were about a mile behind the camp Jon had seen. The only thing flat around us was the bed of the railroad track. The engineers that had built the railroad had cut right through the undulating terrain. We pulled into a gully and rested until dark.

As Jon slipped away into the darkness, I cautioned him. "Don't get lost in the dark."

Jon snorted his reply.

I had loosened the saddle on Pat and removed the packs on the two mules, which I had named "Grunt and the other Groan." He had earned the name because every time I put one pound on him more than he wanted to carry—he grunted piteously. The other mule picked up his bad habits; so he got a like name. Grunt was saddle broke, and when I rode him, he never grunted. He was just picky about what, when, and how much he carried. Actually I had named the mule for two reasons. Jon's brother Grant, who was riding with Barney, was nicknamed Grunt. Every time someone poked him in the ribs he grunted. Sometimes we called him Mule, but he became a little irritated with that name, so we lay off and settled for Grunt.

We soon had a new moon and for a woodsman like Jon it was like carrying a torch, but I worried. I knew that most likely some of those Frenchmen, like Justin Trudeau had been, were also great woodsmen.

Two hours later Jack stiffened in my arms and he made a faint whine in his throat. A rabbit whinnied right in front of me. I laughed and said, "Be careful, Jon or some Jackrabbit will hop your frame and wham—bam."

He snorted and said, "Hustle your bustle—our gang of murderers are on the move." As we saddled up Jon explained, "I was practically sitting in that fellow Brand's lap. Yep—he's a Brand. Most of the men called him Starr, but one of the Frenchmen called him Brand. They aim to bushwhack and wipe out Shannon and his clan; they don't seem to know Barney's first name. They intend to take the horses to a Cotton Brand in Denver. He appears to be the leader of this wolf pack."

"Well—aren't they a bunch of blabbermouths?"

"Yeah!" Jon replied, "The Frenchmen are all excited. The one that kills Shannon will get a five hundred dollar bonus. Starr had two men out scouting for Barney. With the scouts there are thirteen men. The scouts spotted Barney—when they came back with the report the camp went wild with excitement. Starr settled them down and laid out his plan of action. They will set up the ambush tonight and wait for Barney to walk into it tomorrow morning."

"If we get on their flanks," I said—thinking out loud. "We could give Barney a warning shot, and then with flanking fire from our Henrys, they would think they had run into an army."

Jon held up his hand and we stopped. "I had better scout a bit, or we are liable to walk into an ambush ourselves. While I am gone try this on for size. I'll go around these knuckleheads and warn Barney. I'll bring back my two brothers Chick and Jackson Lee. When you give the warning shot tomorrow Barney and Grunt will have time to drop to the ground and find cover. We will have two men on each flank slightly behind the Brands. Once Barney gets cover, they will open up from the front and we will get them from the flanks. If they try to run they will be caught in a cross fire." Jack let out a low growl and suddenly from in front of us a voice spoke up, "How about including me in that clambake?"

Our pistols swept up and the voice laughed and said, "Easy fellows it's me—Ron McMullen."

By then I had recognized his voice. I laughed and replied, "You scared the piss out of me, Ron." I was amazed that Ron had crept up so close to us, but then I realized we had both been talking when we should have been more careful, and the wind was all to his advantage.

Ron chuckled, as he got to his feet—about twenty yards ahead of us. He certainly knew how to merge in with the terrain. He said kindly, "Don't feel bad, fellows. I've crawled on my belly over half of Texas chasing Comanches and outlaws for twenty years. I reckon I got a slight edge on you younkers. Sorry to startle you, Matt, but I was just as surprised when Jon nearly ran over me. I been on Brand's trail since they left their camp tonight, but I'm not so fast trailing at night."

"What made you so suspicious on the train that you got off," I asked?

"Two gunmen walked out of the rodeo and headed for the town. I recognized one of them as being one of Brand's killers from Texas.

"That's what we thought you did, when we had time to think about it," Jon answered.

Now that you mention it, how did you fellows get off that train and get back here so fast?"

The train was no problem, we just jumped off," Jon explained with a bland face.

Ron grinned, "Are all the Cherokees brash like him?"

"His brother Chickasaw is worse than him, but some of the family did mature. As for the train, I pulled the emergency cord. You should have seen the chaos." I laughed with the memory.

Ron grinned, "That I would have liked to see. As far as the Brands are concerned, I have warrants for Brand and two of his men. I intend to get Brand alone and take him in dead or alive. I've had to do it before," he added.

"It's possible, if you don't mind taking on twelve gunnies at a time," Jon answered dryly.

"Actually it's thirteen," Ron asserted.

Jon laughed and retorted, "You do know how to get around this Cherokee."

Jon repeated his plan to intercept Barney, and Ron replied, "It's a sound plan, as long as I get Starr Brand and that gunman of his."

"Sounds good to me," I said. "Go ahead, Jon—times wasting."

Jon faded out of sight. I suddenly felt abandoned, and was glad Ron was there. I said to the Texan, "We will be able to move along pretty fast now, as long as Jack works the trail."

"You can track that fast—in the dark?"

"Well—I'm not as fast as Jon—I swear he can see in the dark—but I do pretty well especially when I have Jack to do all the hard work."

"That's quite a dog—is he as good as he sounds?"

"Ask him," I answered, "he's standing behind you."

"Oops!" Ron exclaimed. "Nice dog," he added as he skittered to one side.

"Track, Jack," I ordered and Jack pointed out the trail, and immediately took off following his nose. It's okay, Ron, we have the wind in our face now. If there is an ambush, Jack would let me know." When the outlaws stopped, we backed off and waited for Jon.

Just before dawn, an owl hooted and then hooted again. It was Jon; he had his two brothers Chickasaw and Jackson Lee with him. It was quite a reunion. The two were like brothers to me. They were both a bit awed by Ron, but he quickly set them at ease. Brand was busy setting his trap and his would be killers were making more noise then a herd of buffalos. While they were distracted, we stashed our horses well away from theirs for fear they would catch our scent and give us away. I left Jack to guard them. We had to crawl part of the way, but we were settled into position shortly after the thieves were. The outlaws had left one man to watch their horses in a small draw nearby. Chick and Jackson Lee were on the left, Ron and I were on the right and Jon had climbed to a small knoll behind us from which he could see the entire scene. Jon took careful cover from behind a fallen tree. Byron and Grunt Ridge should be coming from directly east of us driving the horses.

When our herd of beautiful horses hove into view, my first concern was that some of them might be hurt or killed during the coming shootout with Brand and his men. But then I quickly shifted my concern to Barney and Grunt. Jon had the best view, and when Barney and Grunt drove the herd within two hundred yards of the ambushed men—Jon took careful aim and placed a shot right beside the head of Starr Brand. He jerked with reaction and rolled to his left. Barney and Grunt leapt off their horses and scrambled for cover.

Ron yelled, "Starr Brand—this is Texas Ranger Ron McMullen You are surrounded. Surrender now and no one needs to be hurt. I'll give you to the count of five—then we start shooting."

Brand shouted, "Go to hell, Ranger, this ain't Texas," and he gave his reply in a volley of lead. But Brand didn't have us spotted; and their shots spattering harmlessly in the foliage all around the area. Defensively, Brand couldn't have picked a worse spot to fight from. The only thing he had taken into consideration was his cover from directly in front of his position. He was in a shallow trough formed by an ancient dry riverbed.

We each had selected one of the ambushers and aimed for their rifle shoulder. Brand's men planned to kill us all, but we had no such murderous intent. When the Texas Ranger opened fire, we all fired. Two of the men hit—screamed, and as agreed, we shot another volley at different targets. I don't think any of us felt right about shooting them from ambush, but self-preservation is the mother and father of conscience—we weren't about to let them shoot our people. Barney and Grunt had found cover behind a small knoll—like Jon, they had clear shots. Cries of distress came from the outlaw positions.

Suddenly, a horseman from the draw where Brand's horses were hidden broke into the open in a desperate effort to escape. A short pause—Ron got the range—a shot rang out; and the man toppled from his saddle. The horse ran for a short distance, then gradually stopped and fell to cropping grass.

"That was Brand's gunman. One down—one to go," Ron remarked with a grim smile.

The outlaws had no idea where we were. All our shots had come from their rear. A short pause and suddenly five shots rang out. Brand had located the flankers and the four of us ate dirt. Again the thieves had forgotten about front and rear and suddenly three shots sounded from Jon's position, and again came cries of pain. We flankers rose to the occasion and each gave Jon support fire, and ours was the most effective. The outlaws had scrambled for better cover, but their terrain was all exposed to our rifle fire. There was no escape. Then Jon opened up and emptied his rifle raking each position with a hot searching fire. Two rifles suddenly were raised in the air from the outlaw's position with handkerchiefs tied on them. A cry of rage sounded—a shot rang out—a man screamed with anguish, both rifles dropped from sight, and then dead silence.

The sharp bark of a rifle sounded; a man raised his rifle and called out, "Brand is dead—we give up."

Ron yelled, "Drop your rifles, get on your feet, and keep your hands up."

The men stood up, few hands were in the air, because their good hands were clutching their shoulders. Nine men stood, but only three were holding two hands in the air. Ron wasn't in a trusting mood. You men with two hands held up—pick up the other three men. I want to see every man."

The ambushers were beaten, and none were about to argue. A large man bent over and picked up Brand and slung him over his shoulder. When I saw all twelve men, we rose up and moved in on the group. Brand had been shot in the forehead, there wasn't much left of the back of his head. As I walked up to the men I said to the big man holding Brand, "You can put him down. What happened?"

The big fellow had been shot twice, but he acted like he had been zapped by a couple of mosquitoes. He dropped Brand and replied, "It made no sense to fight when you fellows could have killed us any time you wanted. My brother and I held up our rifles to give up. Brand roared with rage, and he killed my brother Joey. He had no call to do that. I shot Brand right in the middle of that damned star he was so arrogant about."

I liked the man. I asked him, "What do they call you?"

"I'm Jimbo Mason."

"How come you got mixed up with this bunch?"

"My family got in a feud over near El Paso, Texas. Joey and I were the only ones left; it was run, or get killed, so we ran. We ran across Brand in Kansas City. He told us you Shannons stole his horses, and killed all his men. That's why we set out to stop you. He was going to pay us fifty bucks each if we got the horses back."

We disarmed the men, sat them down, and dressed their wounds. Three men were dead. The wounded men left were in no condition to bury anyone. Jon and I dug a grave for Joey. We dumped Brand and the man Ron had shot off the horse into a crevice in the rocks and filled it with rocks. Ron checked the bodies first. He located Brand's and the gunman's identification to satisfy his warrants. Brand was wearing a fat money belt. Ron tossed it to me and said, "Maybe this will reimburse you for some of your losses?"

Barney and Grunt moved the horses to good grass—the herd was content to stop and graze. Jon and Chick brought in our mounts. Barney whistled for Jack and after their reunion, he left Jack to guard the horses.

Barney accompanied by Chickasaw, Jackson Lee and Grunt came up to us and Barney jumped down and grabbed me in a bear hug, and said, "Man, you sure know how to worry a fellow."

"I grunted and gasped, "If you don't turn me loose, you big ape you'll never have to worry again." Chick, Jackson, get me out of the clutches of this madman."

Jon looked on laughing and said gutturally, "We smart Cherokee. No fight white man's battles."

Ron McMullen grinned and said, "Are all you boys really brothers?"

'Heck no! "Grunt said, "Can't you tell the difference? I'm their handsome cousin from the intellectual side of the family.

Chick laughed, "Don't you believe him, Ron. He's actually a rodeo clown from Prescott.

"Yeah! I can see the resemblance." Ron replied with a grin. "You fellows have done a great job. It's been a real pleasure to work with you. But I'll be darned, I been fighting Comanches all my life, and they don't leave nothing to your imagination. They's savages—plain and simple. None of them have managed to make the transition and none I know speak good English like you fellers do. I've seen

119

Cherokee in the Oklahoma Reservation, and you men look a lot like some of them. But most of the Indians there still choose the Indian ways. If you fellows ever get down Texas way, you be sure and look me up. Ya hear?"

Jon couldn't resist. He looked at Ron and said, "Cherokee good friend. Yu'all come back, ya hear?"

Everybody laughed and the Texan's face flushed. After a moment, he joined in the laughter and said, "Everything in Texas is big, and nothing is bigger in Texas than a Texas Jackass."

The Ridge boys laughed so hard, I was afraid that McMullen would get offended, but he was a good sport and knew he had made a gaffe and joined in the fun at his own expense.

In the meantime Barney was still holding me in a bear hug, and he held me back and looked me up and down, "Yeah, I can see how delicate you are." With a laugh of pure joy, he slapped me affectionately on the shoulder. It was like getting cuffed by a friendly Grizzly bear.

My heart swelled, but we had business to attend to. I asked him, "What do you and Jon think we should do with these fellows and Brand's money?"

"Closest law is Denver," Barney said. They are likely to get hung there."

Jon was an excellent judge of men and he pointed out, "None of these men have any money. Two of them are gun slicks, the rest are cowpokes or miners down on their luck. What do you think, Ron?

"I agree—they'd get hung in Denver sure. In Texas—we take a man at his word. You could turn them loose on their word to go back to Kansas and get a job. I really don't know about these two gunnies. There were three of them—and we buried the one wanted in Texas. I reckon I'll be happy with whatever you fellows decide. After all, it was your horses they set out to steal."

Chick and Jackson Lee and Jon huddled for a moment and Chick said, "Grunt went to help Jack with the horses, but I know we can speak for him. "These men tried to do a bad thing, but they've all been punished pretty hard. We don't want their deaths hanging over our heads." He turned to the two gunmen and asked, "There's a question about your word—what do you have to say?"

Both men were wounded. The one most able was a tall, lanky Texan. He stood up and said, "My name is Jason Aubrey Colson. Henry Lee and me aer brothers. We grew up feuding in Texas and fought for the South—only to cum home to more feuding. We cum up north to get away from all the killen; we sure didn't better ourselves by hiring out to Brand, but," he said with a defiant air, "we're from Texas and our word's good as any man's."

Off to one side I said to the Ranger, "What do you think of our giving fifty dollars to each of these men and send them on their way. The rest of the money I intend to keep for our costs."

"I have no authority here, Matt, but I think it's a lot more than they deserve, but it's a grand thing to do. As far as yu'all keeping the balance of the money, no one's got a better right.

I told Brand's men what I was going to do. There was a look of amazement on their faces—some hung their heads. When I passed out the money, I gave big Jimbo Mason an extra fifty for his dead brother and said, "I think you're a good man, Jimbo. We're going to start up a ranch in New Mexico near the Arizona Territory border. If you ever get down that way and want a job raising horses look us up."

"You and your friends are good people, Matt O'Shannon. Reckon you know how to humble a man some. But hasn't anyone told you that's Pache country down yonder where you're agoing?"

"I hear there's some Mimbreno Apaches among a half dozen other tribes. You know—ever since I crossed the Mississippi, everyplace I go seems to be overrun with Indians—good and bad." I philosophized with a grin.

Jimbo stuck out his big hand and said, "Don't be surprised if I show up on your stoop someday. That is—if you still have one," he added with a grin?" Mason mounted his horse and rode off—he didn't look back.

Brand's men had their own rations and I read them some gospel. "You men have had your wounds tended to, and you've got some money now. Divide up the food. You've got your own horses, and weapons. I want you out of here in an hour by ones or twos. Go by separate trails, but if I catch any of you in Denver, you'll be hung or shot.

The first thing I did was stop, count the money I had left from Brand's money belt, and divided it up equally with Barney, Jon and his brothers. Then we made camp and had breakfast and caught up on our gossip.

We now had four temperamental stallions to contend with. I rode Pat, and while he could be a handful if any of the mares came in heat, I had always been able to control him, as long as I was able to separate the mares in estrus far enough away to curb his instincts. The other two stallions were young and used to traveling with the herd. With a little luck, we could control them, and if not we would cross that bridge when we came to it. Our new stallion Whip Shy was a different story. Jon solved that problem by turning his beloved Pocahontas in with the herd and he rode Whip Shy. For now the problem was solved—hopefully? I was used to sleeping on the trail with Pat hobbled close by, and Jon would do the same.

Toward evening, we began looking for a campsite, and for the first time I had a moment to dwell on all that had transpired. Jimbo had said those words again, "You're a good man, Matt O'Shannon. God, how I wanted to believe that, but all I seemed able to do was to kill or shoot more men. Not that some of them didn't deserve killing, but who was I to judge anyone?

I spotted a small run of water and rode on ahead to check it out. The run led me right to a sweet water spring sheltered in a small copse of deciduous trees. A ring of rocks laid by a former camper had been there for years furnishing a fireplace for untold numbers of campers. The terrain formed a natural bowl and with very little effort we were able to make a workable corral out of fallen tree limbs. The horses were allowed to stop and graze for well over an hour, and then we hazed them into the corral for the night. The runoff from the spring ran along one edge of the corral and the main herd was able to quench their thirst as they willed. We posted guards and made our camp away from the spring so as not to interfere with the wildlife.

Ever since Custer had been wiped out, small bands of Indians were prowling around looking for more scalps. Sitting Bull and his Sioux warriors had escaped up North into Canada. And while

Army patrols were more vigilant it paid to be careful. Indians loved good horses, and we had the cream of the crop. In addition, we had turned a gang of armed outlaws loose. True they were wounded, but we certainly didn't want to take them with us—nor could we in good conscience turn them loose in Indian country without their weapons for protection. The gang had also seen our horses and we had no way of knowing if they would try to bushwhack us again

We had set a stiff pace that day to put a lot of distance between us. Jon settled down with Whip Shy hobbled on one side of the camp and I had to take Pat to the opposite side. Over coffee that night, after Chick and Jackson Lee took first watch, I borrowed a cigarillo from Barney and after lighting it up; I began de-ticking Jack. Ticks didn't like the cigar hot foot I was giving them, but Jack kept sniffing the ticks and licking my hands in appreciation.

Barney said to me, "You sure keep a fellow guessing."

"Yeah, I like your little cigars after all. You got any more?"

"He laughed, "That's not what I meant and you know it."

"Well—when I saw how pudgy you were getting, Barney, I figured I had to keep you on your toes. Which reminds me—just because I got you into a feud with the McCoys—you didn't have to get Jon and me into a feud with the Brands?"

Barney got all red in the face. "Dad blast it, Matthew—I know I should have—"

Grunt and I started laughing and he snorted and said, "You guys never quit."

Jon came over and said, "This poor Cherokee just want to know—who going to shoot him next."

"I told you fellows that I thought it was the Brands that stole your horses—didn't I?"

"White man speak with forked tongue. He no tell why?" Jon insisted wiggling his forked fingers.

Barney was sitting on a log sipping his last cup of coffee. His face still red—he said, "I guess I do owe you fellows an explanation. After I left home, I trailed around in Colorado for two years. I became a partner with Vance Brand in a gold mine near Denver. He happened to have a lovely daughter by the name of Trinity. I was courting her when I ran afoul of her uncle. I never saw him, but everyone told me that Uncle Cotton Brand was just the opposite of his brother Vance. They all said that he caused a lot of trouble in Texas by starting one feud after another by his nasty disposition and his thieving ways. Starr Brand was Cotton's nephew, and he was as bad as his Uncle. Every time someone tried to court Trinity—Starr picked a fight with the man and ran him off or killed him. He had been lusting after Trinity for years, but of course she wouldn't have anything to do with him. She was afraid to tell her father for fear he would accost Starr and be killed. When Starr wasn't around to make her life miserable, his brother Chauncey took up where Starr left off. She was terrified of them both.

When I came on the scene and began calling on Trinity—Starr, accompanied by Chauncey, waylaid me on the street. Starr took a poke at me; when I decked him, both of them jumped me. It was a great fight, and I left them both lying in the gutter. Trinity told me later that Starr was telling everyone that he would kill me on sight. Trinity begged me not to fight him. I finally solved the problem, by telling her I had to go home to see my parents. I just delayed the inevitable, but at least with Starr's death. I now only have Chauncey with whom to contend."

I said, "There's no reason for him to take up Starr's fight, unless of course, he wants to start a feud."

"It sounds to me," Jon pointed out, "that Uncle Cotton will likely take up the fight even if Chauncey doesn't.

"It's possible, they both will," Barney admitted with a sigh. "Vance say that Uncle Chance lost three sons by his first wife in the first feuds they started in Texas, but that didn't stop the killing. The feud went on for nearly twenty years. Chance now has three young sons, Prince, Lucas and Tyrel by his second wife Mercedes. Chance vowed he would not lose another son, even if he had to chain them up in his barn, but they are just as bad as the first lot and history may repeat itself."

"No matter what, I am through handling any of them with kid gloves. If Trinity will have me, I intend to marry her come hell or high water."

"Maybe Cotton will simmer down a bit when he realizes he has lost more nephews." I suggested. "Aren't there any womenfolk in that family that can exert influence on them? Seems to me that a good woman could stop all this nonsense?"

"Cotton had two wives," Barney said. "Both died in childbirth. Vance is married to Audrey Mae. She is one-hundred-percent behind his peaceful nature and very protective of Trinity. Chance's first wife died. Mercedes, his second wife, is the mother of Prince, Lucas and Tyrel. No one can even talk to Mercedes about feuds. When a man threatened to kill Lucas, Mercedes took a shotgun and chased him out of town. Why," Barney added with a grin, "Mercedes is so dead set against violence that she would kill anyone that threatens her family."

Jon said solemnly, "She must be part Cherokee."

As usual Jack was lying between Jon and me. We had a half moon; Jack's ears jerked erect and he rumbled deep in his chest. He had scented trouble. I said casually, "I think we have visitors, fellows." One by one we broke up our circle. I dumped my coffee and pushed my cup partially under the log on which I was sitting and took up a firing position that I had picked when I first sat down.

Chick hooted once and came on in and slid down beside me. "We got trouble. I think they are Cheyenne; there's only a small band."

"I thought Indians didn't attack at night, Chickasaw?"

"Most don't, "and he added with a grin, "but some of them are changeable as the wind blows. I've been told a lot of tribes are really riled up since Custer was wiped out, and General Crook didn't fare so well at the Battle of the Rosebud. He is still exchanging barbs with the hostile Sioux in the West, while President Hayes is entertaining the Sioux moderates in Washington, D.C. Now the Nez Perce are fighting General Howard, and Geronimo, who assumed leadership of the militant Chiricahua Apaches after the death of Cochise in 1874—is making it hot for the Army down in the Dragoon Mountains in the New Mexico and Arizona Territories, which, I might add, is where we are headed. I reckon a lot depends on how successful the Army is in getting the Indians settled down on the Reservations. Some of the tribes are running scared, others are sitting back watching. The Apaches and a few of the Cheyenne, Sioux, and Arapahoe in small bands are lashing out at anyone in reach. It's a real messed up time, Matt."

"Yeah, lucky us. I guess it's wait and see what this particular band of hostiles intend. That okay with the rest of you?"

Barney replied dryly, "Do we have any other option?"

"Well—cheer up," Jon said blithely, "I have a bit of good news. While we were in Kansas City, I read that Geronimo was captured by Indian Agent Clum last winter and put on the San Carlos reservation. He broke out and fled to Mexico, so—for now—he is out of our hair."

"Uhhuh," Barney added caustically, "When Geronimo is in Arizona he attacks the Mexicans and when he's in Mexico—he attacks Arizonians. But it isn't all bad news, The Navajos went into a Reservation last year, and so far they are staying put and raising sheep."

"Well—goody goody two shoes," I added sarcastically, "all we need now is for a good wind to come up and blow these Cheyenne away." Everyone chuckled, but we were all alert as we sweated out the dawn.

Dawn came slowly but surely. The horizon was heavy with red tinged black clouds. It looked like we were going to get wet. We took turns during the night and slept. The Indians were Cheyenne. Two hundred yards across from us a few Cheyenne warriors had taken up positions at the edge of a small stand of willow trees at the edge of a small stream. More surprisingly a minor chief of the Cheyenne was sitting on his horse about thirty feet to our front. His face was not painted, and on the end of his war lance was a white clothe. I marveled at his courage and was impressed by his regal bearing. I said to the group, I'll go talk to him." He was armed, so I didn't take off my gun belt. As I arose—I gave him the sign of peace and stepping over the log I went out to meet him.

The war chief broke his lance in half as I approached—he slid off his Appaloosa mare and walked to the head of his horse and waited. My voices were talking to me and I said to him, "You speak English—don't you?"

His eyes smiled and he replied, "You are Medicine Man?"

"I am O'Shannon—blood brother to Cherokee Chief, Jon Ridge. I know some medicine. You are Cheyenne Dog Soldier. You have fought and killed Yellow Hair at Little Big Horn."

"I am Chief Lone Wolf. We have battled and killed Long Hair's soldiers. A Sioux, and great warrior, White Bull, with same blood as Medicine Man Sitting Bull, killed Yellow Hair."

"What can O'Shannon do for his Cheyenne brother?"

"We have met before, O'Shannon."

I nodded and answered. "Yes! I met the Great Chief and his Dog Soldiers less than a moon ago."

"You and your Cherokee brother honored our dead. You—good man."

"You and your Dog Soldiers are brave warriors."

"We fight no more. We go back to Reservation."

"From what I hear, it is a bad thing, but it can be better if their Chief is present to lead them."

"You speak wisely for one so young. For honoring our dead, I have come to warn you."

My ear perked up and I asked, "I thank you, Chief, but of what do I have to be afraid?"

"Twenty men lay in ambush where road forks—very near. They White Eyes like you. They plan to kill you—after we fight. No one else here," and he made a circle with his finger around his head.

I was really impressed with the Chief. I thanked him. I had noted that he looked rather peaked and slack around the mouth. I said to him, "We shot a buck yesterday. Would you and your Dog Soldiers eat with us?"

The Chief rubbed his stomach and said, "It is good."

I turned and called out. "They are friends. Make all the coffee and biscuits you can, and start roasting that hindquarter." I turned back to the Chief and was startled. Coming across the field were only eight men. Two of them were wounded. I yelled, "Barney, change that request to nine bloody rare steaks. That's the way they like them."

Before the Chief left, we gave him the rest of the buck and what few supplies we could spare. In turn he gave me his tomahawk. It was a generous gift, because it obviously had been passed down from countless generations when their tribal lands had rested far to the East. After they left, I went to my saddlebags and stashed the tomahawk, and took out two pairs of Moccasins. Tossing a pair to Jon, I asked, "How about we take a look-see and find out what kind of a reception we have waiting for us?"

Barney started to object and I assured him, "Don't worry big, brother, Jon and I can out Injun most Injuns. Be a good idea if you saddle up and move the horses out to graze. We took our rifles and were gone before he could protest. The Chief had given us good directions as to where the men were holed up. Jon found a deer path and set a good pace. Deer paths are good paths for deer, but we had to double over and sometimes crawl to get under low lying branches so as to not to make a sound as we moved swiftly through the trees growing alongside the small stream . . . In the open, we crawled, and found gullies and other cover until we were lying on a hillside just behind our quarry. They were camped in a small grove of trees beside the same stream on which the Cheyenne had camped.

I slowly swiveled my head checking all around in a last minute check. From my peripheral vision, I spotted Jack. My fault—I hadn't told him to stay when I left camp. I gave him the sign to stay. He dropped his head on his paws—watching me intently. The pristine forest had made it easy to creep up on the men. There were actually twenty-four men. Two men were obviously in charge. Two of the men were Brands—identified by men coming up to them with various problems. Chauncey and Kyle Brand; Chauncey was a big boned towhead; evidently he favored his Uncle Cotton Brand. Kyle didn't look like any of the Brands I had seen. He was slim, medium boned, and wiry built with a shock of black hair and slim facial features that most girls would call handsome. Chauncey seemed to run things, but he heeded Kyle when he did venture to speak. The sky had been black and red and threatening when we awoke. It hadn't rained since we arrived in Kansas. I didn't know it, but our train ride had carried us into Colorado Territory. At any rate, we were long overdue; as though to confirm my thoughts, lightning flashed nearby. The crash of thunder rent the air. A big thunderhead filled the sky in roiling splendor.

We could hear most of the Brand's conversation, and Chauncey growled, "They should have been here by now."

"Maybe they got lost?" Kyle ventured.

"Naw!" Chauncey snapped, "Even if they took the fork, it peters out at that old burned out cabin. They'd be here by now. Where's that damned Francois?"

Hearing his name a man jumped up and said, "Ici! Here I am, Bosse."

"I thought you said those men would be here by now?"

"Francois shrugged his shoulders and replied, "I see beaucoup Indian sign, maybeso they see—maybeso they hole up."

"Get a horse and go look. Don't let them spot you."

"Oui, Bosse. I go."

Kyle got up, lightning flashed repeatedly, and thunder boomed loudly, Kyle looked up at the sky and said, "Maybe they're sitting out the storm?"

"Damn them, and damn this lousy storm all to hell," exclaimed Chauncey.

I nudged Jon to follow the Frenchman. He was gone like a ghost. I knew Barney would move the horses out of the trees for safety and find a low spot to ride out the storm. I watched a restless Chauncey for another fifteen minutes, when I heard a branch snap behind me. I started to whirl; I saw a figure behind me and a swinging rifle butt. Suddenly my head exploded and my senses told me, I was falling—falling—falling.

I awoke when a bucket of water was thrown in my face. When I breathed in—my nose was full of water, I inhaled water, choked and gagged. My eyes flew open; all I could see was legs and more legs. I craned my neck and looked up. I was naked as a new-born-baby.

My feet had been lassoed and I was strung up like a side of beef. I looked down—what was worse I was strung up over a fire. It was very hot, but my hands were untied.

"Well, Shannon, you don't look so tough now," a taunting voice said.

Even upside down, I could tell it was Chauncey. "From where I am, you don't look so hot either," I replied. "No pun intended."

He kicked me in the head and snarled, "Pain, that's all you're going to know, smart mouth."

My head exploded with the kick. The old familiar pains that I remembered from being mugged in Leavenworth, Kansas filled my head with nauseating agony. Near Chauncey, I could see Kyle. Even upside down I could tell he wasn't too happy. They were going to kill me, but revenge came first; my sixth sense told me that this was not Kyle's way. A thought struck me—there weren't twenty-four men after all. There were twenty-five—maybe more. Chauncey had posted a guard up the small knoll behind him.

Lightning flashed, and with a crash and flash of fire; electricity struck and split a tree from top to bottom only thirty feet away knocking the men to the ground. The thunderous explosion deafened me. The storm was going to be a real tear-ass; the forest was a death trap. Men scattered in every direction, and Kyle grabbed Chauncey and shouted, "Get out of the woods."

The heavens opened up in a raging cloudburst. The fire disappeared like magic. I couldn't see a thing—blinded by blowing sheets of water. Escape was within my grasp, but I couldn't see a thing except water. I knew the tree was beside me; I began swinging myself back and forth until finally I was able to grasp the trunk of the tree. A savage gust of wind tore me loose, and I completely lost my bearings. I kept swinging—swinging—swinging. The wind was fierce and it suddenly slammed me into the tree. Stunned—my hands instinctively grabbed the tree trunk and I hung on desperately. Getting my senses back—I began climbing the tree with my hands. My feet had not been tied, but lassoed, and now free of most of my weight I found I could spread my feet—I struggled and struggled, and finally the noose opened, and I slipped my feet out. My weight tore my hands loose and I was dumped to the ground in a sodden heap.

The drop knocked all the air out of me. I had no idea where my clothes or weapons were; but I wasn't going to lose my chance to escape by looking for them. I could see the trees now, and I took off running. I ran out of the trees and onto the plain—stumbling, falling, bouncing up again and running, falling, running. The water on the ground was already an inch deep. The ground was sodden, and rain was saturating the leaves and grass—in spite of this—the pain to my bare feet was excruciating. My body was lacerated with rain and hail, thorns tore my skin and pierced my feet, but fear overcame my pain. I slowed to a mile eating pace. The cloudburst had let up; the rain still came down in torrents, but I was running easy now. I had run for an hour when I came in sight of some trees. I stopped and looked back. I was shocked to see a man on horseback riding like the maniac that he was—it was Chauncey Brand.

Just behind Chauncey, I saw Jack jumping over rushing gullies in full pursuit. I signed for Jack to run and hide. He stopped abruptly. I turned and gave it all I had running down a grade trying to reach the trees on the other side of the mountain meadow. Suddenly I was shocked—I was running toward a cliff, the rain had slackened even more, and as far as I could see in both directions—there was nothing but cliff. I could see only the tops of some cottonwoods protruding above the rim of the cliff. I made an instant decision—better to risk riding the trees down than face certain death from Brand. I increased my pace—when I got to the edge of the cliff I launched myself out into space. It seemed like I flew for at least twenty or thirty feet before I grabbed the top of a huge cottonwood. When I hit it—the top snapped off—a huge startled crow flew out cawing its outrage; I fell headfirst down through the cottonwood riding the broken off piece of limb like I was riding a wild stallion. I plunged down through the rough branches ripping and scraping the flesh from my body; my head exploding each time I hit a branch. Finally I came to rest hanging upside down, but of this—I knew nothing.

*B*IRTH OF SHAWN NACK

CHAPTER FIVE

"Hey, Cap, looks like we have visitors."

"How's that, Tally?"

"All you have to do, Cap is look."

It was Sunday and the three miners day of rest. Cap Mason put down his Ship in a Bottle project and his pair of tweezers, and looked. He jumped up, and stepped out of the tent just in time to meet Four Hands, and his brother Buffalo Who Kills Many White Men. They were two independent half-breed Kickapoo Indians. Kickapoo Indians when they wished to go on the reservation and visit and eat of the white man's meager handout, and white men when they freely roamed in Kansas, and the Territories of Oklahoma, New Mexico and Colorado. Friendly Injuns if they liked you and unfriendly white men if they didn't. Cap met them with a big smile and said, "Greetings to my Kickapoo brothers. Come to my campfire and we will smoke a pipe. He shook hands with them, and when he got his hand back, he sat them down and brought out a ceremonial pipe and filled it with crushed tobacco leaf.

His mining partners Ryan Ballard and Talley Short joined them. Company was always welcome; they seldom saw an Indian, let alone a white man in this wilderness. The two Kickapoos dressed and looked like the half-breeds they were, and they were usually welcome wherever they went. Both were shrewd, and knew the value of white man's money. They always had gold and greenbacks, but never on their person. They knew better than to flash money in the presence of a white man; no dirty Indian should have money when a white man had little or none. They both steered clear of white man's whisky. Twice they had grubstaked Cap Mason and his partners, and they had a small interest in their current strike. Some men who grubstaked miners expected a fifty percent return if the miner ever got lucky. Few ever were that lucky. Buffalo and Four Hands often helped their friends, but they were never greedy. To them, the three men were like family, and when they made a good strike, they refused to take more than five percent.

Buffalo Who Kills Many White Men could hardly contain himself. He was the more orthodox and superstitious of the two Indians. Four Hands, however, said he was worse than a squaw when it came to gossiping, but what did he know. However, like any good storyteller, he knew how to bide his time. As they sat drinking coffee after supper, he could no longer hold back the news.

He drew himself up and stated empirically, "Today I have seen the most wondrous sight. My Spirit Guides had been warning me all morning that I must be most careful midday. It had been a good morning for our mother earth. The heavens had opened up and poured buckets of water on the parched land. When the rain grows little, me and Four Hands ride to visit our brother Captain Mason. We ride below the great stone cliffs, a most dismal place full of ghosts and the gargoyles that white men speak of. Suddenly, a naked white demon flew out from the top of the cliff. He flew out over the trees and lit in the top of one of them. The tree exploded and the white demon turned into a crow and flew off cawing. He tried to put a spell on me, but I held up my White Man's Cross and we escaped his evil spell." Four Hands was nodding his head sagely as though to add his testimony to the story.

Cap Mason was captivated by the story. Indians loved to exaggerate the positive and he suspected that somewhere in Buffalo's story there was some fact. After questioning Buffalo he said to Talley, "I would like to see this marvelous sight." He winked at Talley, "Maybe you would ride with me to ward off the evil spirits."

It would not be polite to leave their guests alone, so Ryan said, "I'll just sit by the fire and drink coffee with our friends, while you two intrepid warriors save the world."

As the two rode off, Talley asked Cap, "Do you really think there's something to Buffalo's story?"

"Maybe not," Cap replied, "but it sure has me curious. Besides, it's Sunday and it's our day of rest. I can't think of a better reason to take a ride and get away from that excuse of a mine for awhile."

Cap had no trouble following the instructions that Four Hands had given him. Both men had been roaming the mountains for years looking for their elusive bonanza that most men were fated never to find. They were trail wise and experienced miners, they knew what they were looking for, which was more than most would-be-miners could claim. They both knew where the cliff fault lay; they had followed its course for thirty miles when they had first prospected this piece of Colorado over a year ago.

An hour later Cap exclaimed, "Look, Talley, is that a dog, or is it a wolf?" The animal had scrambled down a barely discernable deer path along the face of the cliff and jumped the last ten feet. The steepness of the path threw him, and he tumbled down nearly in front of them. The dog yelped, got up groggily; and shook himself vigorously freeing his coat of the forest debris.

Talley replied, "If it's a wolf, it's the first one I ever saw with a collar."

Cap had a way with animals. He liked them and they liked him. During supper the wood creatures, raccoons, skunks, and deer had edged fearfully into their camp, their hunger overcoming their instincts. The three men tossed them small handouts, but Cap never touched the wood creatures, and Talley and Ryan followed his lead. When the men hunted for fresh meat, they did it well away from their campsite.

Cap looked at the stray dog and asked, "Why in God's good name is a dog running around loose in this wilderness? Hey, dog, you look like you've had a rough time of it." He reached into his saddlebag and found a piece of elk jerky and tossed it to the animal. He smelled it and looked up at Cap inquiringly. He shook himself again and started off ahead of the miners.

Talley looked at Cap and exclaimed, "Well I'll be doggoned—if that don't beat all?"

"That dog knows what it's all about; looks like he's going our way, Talley. Do you reckon that dog is looking for the same thing we are?" And Cap left the question hanging. He dismounted and picked up the jerky and said, "Waste not—want not," wiped it off and stuck it back in his saddlebags.

They had another hour of rough going. Trees in this part of Colorado usually followed the streams; but sometimes they hugged the bottom of cliffs, which belied the water theory, but then who was to say there wasn't water under the bottom of the cliff? The only trees visible ahead were a few that seemed to snuggle up against the cliff, as though they sought its shelter.

"Look, Cap." Talley pointed and exclaimed, "The top of that big cottonwood is broke off."

The dog ran directly to the tree and began to run back and forth erratically, whining and barking, but the brush and undergrowth had created a formidable wall. The dog tried to get through the brush, but it was just too thick. Cap said, "Talley, I do think we have come to the end of our trail."

He slid down from the saddle and took a small hand ax from his saddlebags and said to the dog, "Move over, fellow, I think you need a little help."

"Look out for rattlers in there, Cap," Talley called out.

Cap snorted. "No self respecting snake would be caught dead in here."

He went to work clearing out the underbrush as he went. He worked his way close to the tree trunk, and cut off the lower branches. Talley obligingly pulled them out of the way. The dog barked and ran in deep growls of excitement rumbling from his chest. He got in Cap's way, and Cap grabbed the dog by the collar, pulled him up and saw the name Jack on his collar.

He looked him in the eyes and said sharply, "Jack, I'm trying to help him. Sit down."

Jack relaxed and barked once, as though saying, I understand. Cap called out, "Buffalo's naked demon is in here, Talley; I'll have to cut him out. I can't tell if he is alive or dead?"

It took both men an hour to cut the naked giant out of the tree. They constructed an Indian travois by cutting down two saplings, trimmed them and folded a saddle blanket to make a cot-like contraption. They ran the poles through the stirrups and lashed them tight.

.Jack ran up and licked the man's face, and lay down with his head on his master's bare chest.

Talley looked at him sympathetically and commented, "There's no doubt whose dog that is, eh, Cap?"

The two men loaded the naked giant onto the travois. Talley, panting for breath, stopped and complained. "Good Lord, he must weigh a ton."

"He's barely alive," Cap grunted, as he bent over and checked for signs of life. "He's lost a hell of a lot of blood upside down like that."

"What's him hanging upside down got to do with bleeding," Talley challenged?

Cap replied, "Nuthen! But I have to agree that's the biggest man I ever did see,"

Talley said, awe in his voice, "He's got muscles that I never knew existed. Do you think he has a chance?"

He'll live, Cap prophesied, "Any man that would jump off that cliff is too tough to die."

When they pulled back into their camp, Cap yelled, "Buffalo, come see your white demon. He's still alive. Do you think your medicine can save his life?"

Buffalo Who Kills Many White Men always bragged that if a man's body was still warm, he could bring him back to life. Buffalo came over and looked at the naked man hesitantly and then said incredulously, "He no demon; he very big white man." As though bolstered by his own words; he stuck out his chest and claimed. "I fix—he no die."

The smell of Buffalo Stew tickled my nostrils. Saliva flowed copiously in my mouth and my eyes flew wide open. Where in the hell was I? What kind of contraption was I on anyhow? I was lying on a blanket that was supported by two poles with both ends suspended on blocks of wood. A blanket covered my body and my white feet stuck out in all their glory. Looking around I realized I was in a tent. The flaps pushed apart as a man backed through the opening. When he turned he had a big bowl of steaming hot soup in his hands. He saw my open eyes and quipped with a big smile, "My stew has been known to wake even a dead man."

I felt my arm. "I sure don't feel dead," I replied with a grimace. "Where in Kansas am I?"

"You happen to be at a mine site in Colorado Territory. My name is Cap Mason. My two partners and I own the mine. It's called the 'The Mint.' At least we hope so," he added laughing. "What's your handle, partner."

"Handle?" I asked plaintively.

He laughed again and explained, "Your name. What's your name?"

The grimace slowly froze on my face. My head was throbbing. I stammered, "I—I don't know." I tried to think, but my mind was as blank as the canvas I could see above my head.

Cap Mason looked at me with empathy and in a soothing voice told me. "You've had a bad accident, sonny, and injured your head. Just relax and let's get some soup in you, so you can get your strength back."

"What happened to the big Indian, or did I dream that?"

Cap laughed and answered, "That was Buffalo Who Kills Many White Men. His care and medicine most likely saved your life. Buffalo and Four Hands, his brother, took care of you for two days and nights. They'll be back. Just eat your soup now."

I ate the soup and immediately fell asleep. When I awoke Cap was seated at a small home made table. He was pushing something into the bottle. Once secured inside he pulled on a string and sails were pulled upright and I could see it was a miniature ship. I waited until he was finished. Then I tried to sit up. Every muscle in my body screamed in protest, and I fell back with a cry of pain.

Cap jumped up and came running to my aid. "Easy does it, mate."

I grunted and replied, "I learned that the hard way, Cap. I'm starved. Can I have another bowl of that soup?' I lifted the blanket, I was stark naked and my entire body was a series of nasty multi-colored bruises from top to bottom.

He laughed. "That soup was gone yesterday. You've been sleeping for three days. I have some venison stew cooking. In the meantime, there are some cold biscuits and a comb of honey you can have for now."

The biscuits were great and the wild honey had a distinctive flavor all its own, which I knew was typical of honey gathered in different areas. At dusk, when they came in from working their mine, I met Cap's partners, Ryan Ballard and Talley Short. After the introductions, Talley asked, "Do you remember your name yet?"

"Maybe it's, "headache, I sure got one when Cap asked me that question before. My mind is a complete blank."

"Don't push it, son." Ryan advised. "You were delirious and you kept saying the word Shan or Shawn Nack You were muttering so bad it was hard to understand what you were saying. One night we had to tie you down to that travois that you're a lying on."

"Well, youngster," Talley commented, "reckon we have to call you something until you remember your name. How about we call you Shawn Nack?"

Confused, I just shook my head in assent.

Cap laughed and stated, "It's settled then. We temporarily baptize you Shawn Nack, born in a treetop and announced to the world by a black crow. Maybe we ought to call you Black Crow, or perhaps Raven would be better?"

I laughed and said, "Only under protest, Mr. Mason."

He turned and looked all around and asked, "Who you talking to? Ain't no Mister on this mining ground. Just call me Cap," he suggested with a grin.

Then he told me all that they knew about my flying adventure over the cottonwood. Miraculously I had no broken bones, but every bone in my body would argue that point. The back of my head was the worst wound I had received, but skin had been scraped and gouged off my body from head to toe. According to Cap it looked like someone had recently sewed up a laceration on the back of my head, but it had been badly battered since then. Cap had sewed up the lacerations. Talley said Cap had spent half the night sewing me back together. They quit counting after the first hundred stitches. When the finished, they washed me down with two bottles of gin.

It took a month for me to heal to where I could get up and stay on my feet. Within two weeks, I was puttering around wearing a beautifully made pair of skintight buckskin britches fringed with buckskin thongs and a matched fringed buckskin shirt, plus I had two pairs of moccasins. I was grateful for the soft buckskin. I had tried to put on one of Talley's shirts, but the harsh cloth was most uncomfortable to my healing flesh. The buckskins were gifts from Buffalo and his brother Four Hands. They had paid two horses to two Indian women to make them for me. I was overwhelmed with their gift, but I had nothing to give them in return.

Strangely enough, even though I couldn't remember my name, things I had no reason to know about, I knew the answer to. Usually, I just did a chore automatically without thinking about it. For example, I knew I should give a gift in return for the gift given me by the two Indians, for that was the Indian way. How did I know that if I couldn't even remember my name?

The Indians did not make pockets in their clothes, so I made myself a belt and a pouch to carry items in. At the moment, I had to admit, I had absolutely nothing to put into the pouch, but this was soon remedied when Cap mentioned they needed some fresh meat. I volunteered and quickly found a use for my pouch; extra ammunition. Soon I had added a piece of flint and steel so I could start a fire if needed. It is amazing how many useful items we carry in our pockets, especially when we don't have one. With the ammunition, Cap gave me a knife and sheath. "Keep it," he said, "If you are going to hunt for us, you will need a knife to gut and butcher the game"

A month later, I still could not remember anything about my past. Jack, my dog, was my only link to my past. Thank God his name was on the collar. It is man that usually trains the animal, but it was Jack that taught me all the things I had taught him in my other life. But like I said before, most things I just did by instinct. To pay my way, I began chopping wood. It would take at least nine or ten cords of firewood to last a winter. It was while I was chopping wood that I got the idea of making a log cabin for my new friends; the only family I could claim, which included two very friendly, knowledgeable Kickapoo Indians.

I broached the subject at supper that night. I could see the pleasure register on their faces. Cap spoke up and said, "We had planned to go to Denver for the winter, but that's mighty expensive. There are trading posts near where we can get supplies. He stopped a minute and said. "Shawn, I don't want to hurt your feelings, but what makes you think you can build a log cabin?"

The thought hadn't occurred to me. I stopped for a moment and replied, "I didn't know I could use an axe or a rifle, but when I picked them up, the use of them came to me as natural as breathing. How about I get started—if I flounder you can still winter in town?"

Cap looked to his partners for confirmation and seeing assent in their faces he agreed, "Sounds good to us. We have nothing to lose. Just remember—we are miners and can't afford to take time to help you. We do have tools, axes, a crosscut and bucksaw, and a couple of adz. We have some nails, but not enough to finish off a cabin"

I was young and confident and I quipped, "Never fear—Shawn is here." I already had a plan as to where I was going to get my help. I began at once. I borrowed Cap's horse and took along his Henry rifle in case I ran into any game, and walked a circle about the cabin marking the pines and fir trees I wanted and leaving enough trees so as to not strip the forest near the cabin.

It was a pristine forest, Many boles of the trees were six feet thick, but the ones I marked had boles about 20" thick, or a little better. Jack stayed right at my heels, his name was on his collar and it was my only link to my identity. He never let me out of his sight. I marked a huge, white oak to be used for the window frames, shutters, doors and furniture, I intended to make. I stopped short. What made me think I could manufacture furniture? Too much thinking made my head hurt. I shook my head free of pain and extended my circle and repeated my tree selection process.

The mining claim ran straight into a three-hundred-foot high ridge, the ore vein the miners were following had taken a dip and they were already a hundred feet underground. There was a pass through the ridge, so I walked through to the other side and ran into a surprise. A small run of water ran parallel to the ridge and disappeared right before my eyes. Nothing unusual, but what was lying on the edge of the crevice the water ran into was. I said to Jack, "I'm not a miner, Jack, but that sure looks like a gold nugget to me." He licked my face, when I dismounted and bent to pick up four of the larger pieces. The pieces of gold ore were rough, the edges sharp and they were laced with heavy stringers of what looked like gold. I stuck them in my pouch.

Curious, I followed the small run of water; it appeared to be more like an irrigation ditch than a small mountain stream. I followed it around the contour of the hill for nearly a-mile; I stopped in surprise. The creek was coming out of what appeared to be a miniature mine. I had seen pictures of the same configuration. The pictures had depicted the mines of the early Spanish Missionaries, which had a slightly slanted timbered front. I slipped out of the saddle; ground hitched the reins, slipped my rifle out of its boot, and stooped down and waddled into the mouth of the mine. The skull of a skeleton looked up at me as though surprised with my appearance. Lying beside the partial skeleton was what seemed to be a huge sparkling piece of white ore. I picked it up. It weighed at least thirty pounds. I balanced it on my left hip and backed out of the mine, only to be alerted by Jack's low growl deep in his throat. The rifle was in my right hand and I instinctively thumbed back the hammer.

I turned and was greeted by two mounted men. They were dressed different, more like lumberjacks than cowboys or miners. French! They were of French extraction. One of them exclaimed and gasped, "Mon Dieu, Shannon." He went for his pistol and holding the rifle like a pistol, I shot him out of his saddle. With my hand gripping the lever, I spun the Henry in a circle, which ejected the spent cartridge and levered a fresh cartridge into the chamber. At the sharp crack of the rifle, Jack immediately charged the second man and leapt on the horse's hindquarters and attacked the man from the rear. The horse reared interfering with the man's drawing of his weapon. With a curse, the Frenchman jabbed his elbow into Jack. With a yelp of pain he went flying off the horse.

The man's weapon came up and my shot caught him in the mouth knocking him sideways out of the saddle. I levered another round into the chamber and cautiously approached the downed men. Jack was there ahead of me. I knew if they weren't dead the dog would be at their throat waiting for my signal. Both horses had bolted, but now, attracted by the belly deep grass, had stopped, looked back and seeing that all was peaceful, began to tranquilly graze.

I tossed the huge nugget to one side and checked the men. They were dead. I called Jack over and checked him. He rewarded me by licking my face. Who were these men? Why had they tried to kill me? What did the man mean when he yelled "Shannon?" Was that my name, or a place? I stood there looking down at the two dead men. I had simply reacted to their attempt to kill me. I was surprised with the speed and efficiency with which I had dispatched two men. I hadn't known I could shoot like that. Was I then some sort of gunman, or killer that people were hunting me down to kill me? I knew it was wrong to kill, but I also knew that a person had the right to defend himself. I didn't feel any guilt, but at the same time, I didn't feel any satisfaction. Deeply troubled I searched the men to see if I could learn anything that would help me. When it came to my past—in some ways, I was like a blind man. He could not see the present—and I could not see the past.

Each man had ten double eagle gold coins on them, but there were no papers with which to identify them. I was a practical man, and I placed the gold in my pouch. One man was wearing a good gun belt. I adjusted the size and put it on. I picked up his pistol that had fallen near him. It was a brand new model 1873 Peacemaker Colt revolver. Unlike my Russian .44 cal. pistol, which a man had to thumb back the hammer to fire the weapon, this weapon, with its new double action capability, could fire by just squeezing the trigger again and again until the gun was empty.

Suddenly it struck me like a bombshell. My subconscious had kicked in and I just remembered that I had owned a Russian .44 cal. pistol. Was that the way my memory was going to come back—one little piece at a time like Doctor Elbee had told me. It could come back all at once, or come back in little pieces, or never come back at all. There—something else had come back, but who on earth was Dr. Elbee?" My head was swimming as I bent down to do my odious chore.

The one man was close to my size. I stripped him down to his underwear including his boots, which looked to be brand new. I didn't cotton to wearing a dead man's clothes, but beggars can't be choosers. When finished, I slung and tied them both over their saddles. I went back to the mine—took off my moccasins and tried on the largest man's boots. They were a mite tight, so I filled them with water and left them on. I led my horse and said to Jack, "Track." Jack picked up their trail at once and as we went I checked out the valley. It was unique. The only entrance I could make out was the one by which I had entered near the Mint Mine. I walked until the boots quit squishing and the softened leather adapted to the shape of my feet. Then I mounted to ease my aching feet, and Jack led us just beneath the rim rock following the men's trail.

On this side, the valley appeared to be edged by rim rock as far as I could see. The dead men had evidently stumbled on a narrow winding trail cut through the rock by winter ice and a niggardly stream only a few inches deep, which over the eons had formed a treacherous deep but narrow passage through the rocks. We came out of the passage, and the trail led us for another five miles past the entrance. To leave no back trail, I had led the horses on rocky terrain. I stopped and slapped the horse's butts with one of their lassoes and with a snort of outrage and fear, the horses took off running hard—the flopping up and down of their dead master's urged them on. I was sure they would keep going till they got back to where they came from. I retraced my tracks and covered the trail in the few spots scuffed by the horse's hooves. Once back through the narrow passageway, I dismounted and walked back on the rocks until I found the perfect spot. I pushed a huge rock over the hill and it thundered down the mountain smashing and tearing up an avalanche of stones that filled and blocked the passage.

I shook my head in satisfaction and said to Jack, "They seem to be looking for me, Jack. No sense in making it easy for them. Those dead men should serve as a warning to whoever wants my hide." When we got back, I rode a circle around part of the valley. I was pleased by its size and its nature bound borders. I could find no other entrance to the valley than the one I had entered by.

I returned to the old mine; picked up the nugget and rode for the place I now called home. I unsaddled the horse, placed the nugget on Cap's little table; placed an article of clothing over it and laid down on my travois, on which I still slept. I didn't realize how tired I was until I laid down. Just as I drifted off to sleep a thought popped into my head, "Love one another."

I awoke with a start when Tally yelled. "Come and get it."

The trio had erected a rain and sun shelter and under it had made a table and benches to eat from. After supper I said to them, "How long have you fellows been working this mine?"

Talley answered, "We located and filed on it last fall. We came back this spring and have been working at it ever since."

"Is it worth the effort," I asked. "I'm not nosy, but I've heard you all gripe at one time or another."

Cap laughed, "Miners are like soldiers, Shawn. We're only happy when we have something to bitch about. Actually it looks like we've hit a dry hole again. Oh, there is a little gold there, but the vein we found hasn't developed like we hoped. The ore is so poor that we haven't even bothered to haul any of it too the mill.

"I'm no miner, fellows, but could you tell me if these are any good?" I took the nuggets out of my pouch and laid them in the middle of the table.

They all picked one up, taking one look, Tally said, "Are you pulling our legs, Shawn."

"You men saved my life, nursed me, fed me and clothed me, and you ask am I pulling your leg? Wait just one minute and I'll answer that question." I left the table and went into the tent and picked up the covered thirty-pound nugget. I carried it out to the table and set it in the middle of the table. I flipped off the cover and asked, "Doe's that look like I'm pulling your legs?"

Ryan Ballard jumped up and yelled, "My God, Shawn, you've hit the mother lode."

When they quieted down I told them the entire story including my having to kill the two men. I took them to the mine and they were astounded. I said to them, "I reckon if you fellows are willing, we are partners in this if it is any good. However, you had better go into this partnership with your eyes wide open. There is someone out there that wants me dead. If you side in with me, you just may find yourselves looking up at the inside of a pine box."

Ryan usually didn't say much, but he stood up and said, "We've discussed your situation from time to time, Shawn. We three partnered up together, because we all consider ourselves pretty good judges of character, we've been together four years and proved ourselves right. We know character when we see it. Trouble follows some men like stink on a skunk, but every skunk I've ever seen carries his head high and waves his tail in the air like a flag. I ain't never seen a skunk that's ashamed of his self. You are a man with whom we could partner without any reservations whatsoever, and he help out his hand."

We all shook on it, and I was some flattered. They didn't know me from Adam and for that matter I didn't know them either. So I said, "Thank you men for your confidence. I haven't got a clue as to who I am, or who I may be. It's troublesome, but I have to live with it come hell or high water. Here's what I suggest. You fellows file on the mine and include my name as Shawn Nack. No one knows me by that name. One of those Frenchmen that threw down on me called me Shannon. It's hard to say who I am or what I am. For a while, I'll just drift. You fellows take care of my share and if I don't show up again—it's all yours. Before I go, I want to do one thing for you; build that log cabin. If I build it right over there," and I pointed: "it will cover the only entrance to the mine and the valley. I sealed off the only other entrance I could find. One last thing; how about we name the mine, "The Shamrock?""

Cap was the natural leader of the three men. He was thoughtful, and considerate, and he didn't run off at the mouth or make bad decisions. He looked at his partners and he got their nod. He said. "Shamrock it is, Shawn.

Ryan Ballard yelled, "Three cheers for Shawn Nack, Hip, hip, hooray; Hip, hip, hooray; Hip, hip, hooray."

"One more last thing," I added with a smile, "I don't know if you fellows have given it any thought, but there are thousands of acres in our valley. It has water and grass and great soil and you can see it's protected from the worst of the elements. Have you ever thought of homesteading the entire valley? Think about it. Once it is surveyed, you could all file in there and claim most of the valley."

Cap looked mighty thoughtful and replied, "That's one to sleep on, Shawn. It certainly is. In the meantime, I don't have to tell you fellows that one loose word about our bonanza and we will have claim jumpers standing in line at our doorstoop. Shawn, with your memory gone, we have to warn you that Denver is loaded with a pack of claim jumpers. They have killed a lot of innocent men and jumped a lot of good claims. The worst of the bunch is a big family that moved up here from Texas. Their leader is Cotton Brand. They have a large gang of men that does their dirty work for them."

The name meant nothing to me, but for some reason it had a deadly ring to it that I didn't like. An idea was born with Cap's warning and I said, "What do you fellows think of this idea. If anyone comes out here looking for the Shamrock, they aren't going to know exactly where the mine is. They will most likely be looking for someone operating a mine in this general area. Take turns working the Shamrock and leave one man at home to make a pretense of working the Mint, which we will change the name of with a big sign to say—The Shamrock"—.If someone jumps our claim—they will never get rich on your dry hole, and in the meantime we can take our time about running the scoundrels off.

Talley jumped up and exclaimed, "By the Lord Harry, that's a splendid idea." Talley's parents had been English and every once in a while he came up with a phrase sounding more English than American.

Ryan Ballard was laughing and he kept repeating, "By the Lord Harry, that's a splendid idea."

The next day, I rode off alone with Jack joyfully running beside the horse. I wanted to check out my new Peacemaker Colt and I

146

also wanted to be alone and try to figure out who I was and just plain meditate. I also wanted to check out the entire valley, before I started on the cabin. I learned Jack was a great hunting dog and the first time he pointed and I flushed a covey of quail, my hand instinctively flashed and my new Peacemaker colt roared three times. When Jack brought me the headless quail I wasn't surprised. I hadn't known it was going to happen, nor had I expected it to happen. At the same time my instincts told me it would happen.

By the time the miners came from work to eat, I had plenty of quail cooked and ready for a hungry man to eat. My partners never saw the headless birds. Buffalo saw them, however, and his eyes lit up, but true to his nature he never said a word. Later, he always referred to me as the Great Builder of Log Cabins, or a Ghost Hunter of Birds. His favorite for me was the Man Who Flies Like a Bird. The two Kickapoo enjoyed telling a good story and they embellished their themes with elaborate and descriptive names, and like some of the Irish story tellers I had heard, they loved to exaggerate the positive and stretch the truth far beyond its limits of reality.

Two days later Cap and Ryan left for Denver to file our claim. The three miners had checked out the old mine; they swore it was the El Dorado, or the Mother Lode itself. They had gathered up the loose gold in the old mine, which gave them more than enough to fill my needs and buy our summer's supplies. I gave them a list of the things I would need to build the cabin, which included pulleys, rope, more axes, two work horses harness, two one-man crosscut saws, several smaller items, and if possible, I hoped they could find a small foot operated wood lathe to make my pegs. Talley was the best miner of the three and he started by working from see to no see reopening the old mine. The first thing Talley found was a Spanish soldier's rusty iron breastplate hanging on a peg.

Cap and Ryan came back thirteen days later loaded with supplies, the recording of the new mine, and my wood lathe. When they left, Talley's first job had been to find the source of the water problem. He reframed the entrance and by-passed the source of the water. He moved a lot of dirt, but when he was done the spring was twenty feet to one side of the mine. Then he reworked the entrance with six-foot headers and added lagging on the sides that needed support. The original mine was only forty feet deep, and had been worked by a man on his knees. The rotten ore Talley was taking out was extremely rich and every foot he drove, the gold seam grew wider. He set aside many pieces of high-grade-jewelry-gold that would bring fancy prices in Denver and back East in Chicago and New York. Talley told me that the jewelry gold would have to be merchandised later. If the gold were shown now, it would be like sending an invitation to every claim jumper in Colorado Territory. Talley took time to do one important job. He made a big sign—The Shamrock—burned the Mint sign and hung the Shamrock sign in its place for all the world to see.

As fate would have it Buffalo and Four Hands showed up looking for his three friends. I told them "Your friend Talley will be back late tonight; the others have gone to Denver for supplies." I then engaged them in a conversation about constructing log cabins. They were a lovable pair of rogues and I had already formed an excellent relationship with them. Cap had told me that I owed my life to Buffalo's expertise in the treatment of wounds and knowledge and use of herbs.

I told Buffalo, "I have promised my friends that I would build them a beautiful log cabin. But my memory is gone and I may not be able to remember how I did it before."

Four Hands spoke up and said, "You have no problem. Buffalo has built many log cabins. He can tell you how."

"I don't know," I complained. "I think I am going to need someone to show me how, and also to work with me. My friends need a place to live. They cannot leave the mine or it will be stolen from them. With my two new Indian friend's help, I would like to make a nice home for them. If you will help me, I will pay you in gold. I will also make a place for you to live with them. Then you will always have a place to live even in your old age."

Buffalo said with great dignity. "Do not insult us with your offer of gold. If my friends and "Man Who Flies like a Bird" need our help, we are here."

"You are good friends," and I shook hands with them, and with a grin I added, "Let's go to work."

"Four Hands stopped and asked, "If you need more help, we have four friends nearby. They are thinking of going back to the Reservation, they good men, half bloods like us. We half bloods not treated well by Indians, and most white men look down on us. We work hard—no steal—good friends.

I was touched by his sincerity. I said to them, and subconsciously I began using the Indian Sign Language to embellish my words, "Buffalo and Four Hands good friends, good workers and no speak with forked tongue. We build big big cabin. Your friends—my friends. I hire all four, how long before your friends get here?"

Four Hands raised his arm and made a circle and pointed to the ground. Four men stepped out of the forest and came toward us at a trot.

Four Hands, laughter in his eyes, said, "Is here now."

After a little talk, I hired the four men. When Cap and Ryan returned, they talked it over with Talley and insisted that we all pay for the four men.

Two weeks later, the miners were amazed with the progress that Four Hands and Buffalo and I and our four new hands had accomplished on the cabin. Buffalo did indeed know how to build a cabin, but when I showed him the way I built a cabin, he showed himself to be an eager student. I seemed to learn as I worked, but this, I reasoned, had to be knowledge that I had stored from whoever I had been before I became Shawn Nack, Four Hands lived up to his name. He did the work of two men, and the four men he had recommended were eager to please and worked hard to prove themselves. The cabin progressed rapidly.

The miners were not in any rush to work the mine and get out. They had the mine of which they had always dreamed. None of them had a family, or a life to which they wished to return. They had their family with them. They decided they would work eight to ten hours a day and store the majority of the gold they mined. To announce to the world that they had a bonanza would be inviting grief. They had a place to work for as long as they wished, or until the vein ran out. I knew the house I built was going to be their retirement home, the center of their comfort and existence, and I put my heart and soul into my work.

We were all talking after supper one night. Talley started complaining. "I tell you, fellows, we have to get a ball mill or we are going to accumulate so much ore from the Shamrock that we will never be able to safely hide it."

"What's a ball mill," I asked.

"It's a contraption that miners use to separate gold from the ore. It's an iron table with a raised edge and baseball size balls that are rotated to crush the ore. It makes a heck of a lot of noise and we would have to buy a steam engine to run it. It was a problem, but I knew them well enough to know that they would keep hacking away at it until they came to a decision. Then my fertile imagination came to my aid. How old had I been when I read about the Spanish Jesuit Priests that had helped settle the New World. They had built Missions from San Diego in Old California to Sonoma in the North missing their own possible gold rush by only ninety miles away in Coloma. I remembered the small mines and the timbered fronts shown in the history books that the Conquistadores had established in old Mexico and its Arrastre that had a heavy round stone rotated on the ore by mules or even worse by Indian slave labor. The question in my mind was—where was the Arrastre for this mine?

I saddled up and with Jack leading the way I rode up to the mine. When I saw the amount of work that Talley had accomplished, I was really impressed. I knew the Arrastre would be badly grown over in the gamma and buffalo grass, but I was sure there had to be some sign of the big round stone—if the Spanish miners had taken time to build one. Jack was helping me. He didn't know what I was looking for, but he knew it was important. He barked and I jumped down and there barely discernable was a piece of bone shining through the grass. I stepped forward and went up to my knees in the thick grass. I dug around with my knife and there looking at me was the skull of a small animal. I walked over to the mine and called out. Hey Cap, I think I have found something you can use."

Cap and Talley came out carrying their shovels, and I showed them the skull.

"So?" Cap asked. "What is it?"

"I think it's the skull of a poor old burro that was killed along with his master many years ago. Come over here." And I showed them the traces of the old mill. "Have you fellows heard of an Arrastre? The Spaniards used them to break up their ore."

"I have. I've used them." Talley replied eagerly, and he began probing with his shovel. Jack barked and he was pawing at a large round mound from which he was scratching the weeds.

"Better check that out, Talley; I think Jack has just found the crushing ball." I grabbed a shovel and all three of us uncovered the old Arrastre.

Cap looked at me and panting he said, "You and Jack. You sure beat all."

I stooped down, once we had uncovered the trough, and exclaimed. "This is proof that you fellows have been blessed." The Arrastre had been full of ore when the miner and his mule were killed. I picked up a handful of ore and held it up—along with the crushed rock, I had in my hand a hundred-dollars worth of gold."

I grinned and said, "Seems all you fellows need is a new frame and a live jackass. But I'm not volunteering for the job." I stepped in the stirrups laughing, and said, "Come on, Jack, or they're liable to put you to work crushing ore."

*   *   *

Two weeks sped by and the work on the mine and the house was really paying off. Everything was going smoothly when Jack came trotting up to me from the direction of the trail to Denver. When he saw me, he turned and pointed. We had company coming. Buffalo and Four Hands understood at once, and I sent Jack to get Cap and Talley. Four Hands went over to the Mint mine and called Ryan up from the shaft.

Minutes later, Cap, rode up and stopped in a thunder of hooves, and on his heels was Talley. Jack jumped down from Cap's arms, and ran to me and sat down. He looked up at me hopefully, for a word of praise.

"Good boy, Jack," I said, and he promptly lay down at my feet.

There were ten of us now and we all got busy behind the four-foot wall already built, and pretended to be working on the wall from which point we had good cover and our rifles were at hand. I now wore my belly gun every where I went. I added a second six-gun sticking it under my belt close to hand. Cap walked over and stood by my side, his rifle leaning against his leg and the new wall of his future new home.

"Who do you reckon is coming, Cap," I asked as we waited.

"My first guess is they're claim jumpers. No one ever comes out here. It is out of the way and off the trails. I could be wrong," he said, "but I doubt it. Unfortunately, I am seldom wrong."

I laughed, "I wish I could say that."

"Not at a time like this, you wouldn't."

My mind was racing—and my head was beginning to throb again. This situation reminded me of the fact that I didn't even know who I was. Perhaps I was a killer with a reputation that would match the rep of the killers that Cap figured had been sent to try to steal their mine. Only a desperate man would jump off a cliff like they said I had done. Perhaps it had been the act of a desperate bad man? I had recently killed two men—complete strangers to me—yet they seemed to know me, and they certainly wanted me dead. Even that fact made it hard for me to justify my killing them. I couldn't think of a way to avoid our killing of these men if they started a war with us, but that did not make it any easier to accept. Every time I encountered a stressful situation, my head literally exploded, and now was no exception. My head pounded and nothing came to mind—what was a man to do?

A quarter-mile from us, four men came riding up out of a gully, I could see they were well mounted. Two pack donkeys were strung out behind the three leaders, and a fourth man brought up the rear. The donkeys were tethered to him by a long rope tied to his saddle horn. As they came closer, I could see that the fourth man was Chinese.

I thought to myself. If this man is a cook, these men were really traveling in style? It didn't take a detective to figure out that the leading men were gunslingers. The three of them had what appeared to be three model 1873 Winchesters rifles sticking out of their rifle boots. A tall man in the front wore a badge that said Marshal. On his head, he wore a black derby hat, and he wore a semi-long, black-tailed coat. He wore a pair of Russian .44 cal. Smith and Wesson revolvers in his tied-down, twin-holsters. His companions flanked him on each side, and both wore the new Peacemaker Colt .45 cal. revolvers in their tied down holsters. They both wore flat-crowned white Stetsons and I noted they also wore the extra-large-fancy Mexican spurs, often worn by Texas cowhands. The ribs on one of the horses showed his owner liked to use his rowels.

The Marshal rode right up before Cap and me, and without a greeting, or waiting for an invitation, all three men dismounted and squared off in front of us. The Marshall wasn't here to waste his time, and he stated his purpose immediately. His deputy pulled out a paper and the Marshall stated categorically, "I'm Marshall James Lee Coulter, and I'm here to take possession of the Shamrock Mine immediately. This Court Order states that the legal owner is Mr. Cotton Brand. You are to surrender possession at once."

Cap Mason said as sarcastically as he could, "Marshall James Lee Coulter—you know damned good and well that you have absolutely no authority out here. You have ridden a long way for nothing. Put that piece of toilet paper back in your pocket and go tell Brand he's wasting my time and yours."

Coulter crouched slightly and said, "Mr. Mason, are you refusing to obey a legal document to vacant this property?"

The man was not a lawman. He was a paid killer. To break the tension I said, "Marshall, the law states that only a United States Marshall has any authority outside the city limits of Denver, unless—of course—you are a deputy sheriff? What county are we in now, Bennett, or is it Denver County?"

The Marshal laughed, it was like an insane giggle and he went for both his guns. My Peacemaker Colt swept up into my hand and barked twice. Then I was standing there, the pistol back in its holster. The Marshall screamed, hysterically, "My thumbs—you crazy bastard—you shot off my thumbs." The Marshal's deputies froze—their hands on their colts—colts that were still in their holsters.

I grinned and said to them. "Go ahead, boys—you can make it." The two men's hands jerked well away from their weapons. They looked at one another for support, and then they both turned and ran.

Talley began laughing and he yelled after them. "Wait a minute, fellows—don't you want your horses?"

The Marshal just stood there—dazedly looking first at one hand—and then at the other. No matter how many times he looked—it still came out the same way—he had no thumbs. Cap turned and looked at me, as though he were seeing me for the first time.

I said, "You know, Cap, that poor Chinaman sitting on that horse out yonder is scared to death, and he don't know which way is up. Why don't you go and offer him a job, and I'll go see if I can help the Marshall."

I called to Buffalo and asked him, "Can you get me some pine resin and willow bark so I can treat the Marshal's wounds?"

"I go." Buffalo agreed, but commented dryly, "But—better you treat Marshal with lead pill."

The Marshal was docile as a baby. His bluster was all gone. He managed a whimper from time to time. I cut off two strands of buckskin from my shirt and tied knots in the middle of each one, and tied them tightly around the Marshall's wrists. The knot's pressure on the wrist slowed down the blood flow. With Cap's help I cleaned the wounds and dipped them in a Dry Gin bath, and sprinkled willow bark on the wounds. Then I sealed his thumbs with pine resin to stop the bleeding. Buffalo made a tea out of the rest of the willow bark and gave it to the Marshal to help reduce his pain.

I told the Marshal. "You obviously have killed many innocent miners and ruined many lives. For now, you will be nearly helpless. Your enemies with gather like a pack of wolves to take you down. If you are smart you'll get on a train and go east as far as your money will take you. You can find work there, and the chances of any of your enemies finding you are limited."

Coulter's malevolent eyes never left my face. His eyes reminded me of the hurt, baleful eyes of a wounded rattlesnake. I said to him. "You know, Marshall, you aren't going to be able to fire those Russian Revolvers anymore without your thumbs. Now—I'll tell you what I'll do. I have two brand new Colt Peacemakers that I will trade you straight across for those two useless Russian pistols you have. With a lot of practice you may be able to use the colts since all you have to do is squeeze the trigged gentle as squeezing the teats on a milk cow."

I put my unloaded Colts in his holsters, took his Russian 44s, relieved him of his Winchester, and put him on his horse, and pointed him north. I slapped the horse on the butt and Marshal James Lee Coulter had nary a word to say. I thought, as he rode away, was he one of the so called quiet ones, I should be wary of? For now—he was harmless, we had pulled his fangs, but the man was still full of poison and would most likely be a danger to society until someone put him out of his misery.

Cap quizzed the Chinese man to find out who he was. He indeed was petrified with fear, and thought the white devils were going to devour him. When the Marshal's name was mentioned, the little man nearly shook himself to death. His name was Chi Lin. He, and his two brothers, had worked on the Transcontinental Railroad until it was finished. His brothers were transferred with their railroad crews to work on another new railroad, but Chi Lin could never find out where they had gone.

Chi Lin spoke choppy English and claimed, "Me best dam cook in Denver." Chi proved it that night. From the two packs he had, he put together the best meal any of us had eaten in months. Talley said to him after supper. "Chi, you good cook. You want job here?"

Chi Lin drew himself up and said defensively, "No! Chi Lin already got job. Chi Lin work for Mr. Cap." Everyone laughed, but although he didn't understand, Chi Lin joined in and was very happy that every one else was very happy.

Later I said to the group. "You fellows are going to have a nice home soon. Now would be a good time to arrange to get a good cooking range for your new cook, and buy some basic living room and bedroom furniture. They have outfits in Denver that brag in their advertising that they will deliver anything right to your front door. That is—if you have one."

Ryan looked at me, and commented, "I've never seen a man so thoughtful and so handy in so many different ways, Shawn."

I figured he was talking about the shooting and I replied, "When a man has all the problems I have, Ryan. I guess it pays to have an unseen ace or two. My mind always reminds me, after such unfortunate situations as we just ran into, what our Lord said, "Love one another, as I have loved you." I just wish I could live up to what my mind tells me I should do." I stood there looking bewildered—where had that tidbit of scripture come from? Was I some sort of preacher?

Ryan laid his hand on my shoulder and said, "You're a lot better man than you think you are, Shawn. Don't be so hard on yourself. You know, as well as we do, that Marshall Coulter was sent here to kill the four of us. I, for one, thank you for my life." Cap and Talley echoed his sentiments, but it didn't help the ache I felt in my heart. Who was I? And what kind of a man was I really?

After breakfast the next morning, I said to Chi Lin, "Chi, you own two donkeys. Would you sell me one?"

Chi thought for a moment and then asked, "Why you want donkey?" His shrewd mind quickly accepted the fact that we acknowledged his ownership of the mules. If he knew the reason—then he could more readily assess the cost to the use.

Ryan Ballard took him on and said. "We have to figure a way to pay you every month. If we have the donkey, he can work for the mine, and then we can pay you for the amount of work he does."

Chi said. "Oh, I see. You get work from two and no pay for one."

"No, Chi Lin; we want to buy the donkey from you. How much money do you want?"

"No sell donkey. I rent him to you. How much you pay?"

Cap laughed and said, "I think it would be simpler, fellows, if we just purchased a donkey someplace else."

Chi, sensing he had pushed the matter too far said, "Hokay, I give you one."

We got the donkey. Over time, Chi was amply paid for his donkey. The donkey soon learned to go around and around in circles like the rest of us. In time, Chi suggested that we alternate the donkeys, and we adopted his thoughtful suggestion. Luckily, we named the stud donkey Dizzy and the dam Lizzy. We were lucky, because the donkeys bred, and nature took care of the rest. Chi Lin and the miners would soon have a welcome addition to their little family.

The two Kickapoos and I had developed a rhythm to our work. In addition, as mentioned before, I had hired four men to cut and trim trees and do all the basic work, so that my helpers and I could devote all our time to the finish work.

With our adz, my helpers and I could flatten out one side of a log in an hour. We hewed both sides flat to a reasonable sixteen inches thick, and then used ropes and pulleys to set them in place. When finished a person could not see through, nor could air squeeze its way between the two logs. We used flattened six-inch logs to finish each of the gables. The support beams were a perfect sixteen-inches-square and the flooring for the ceiling was made of flat boards two inches thick by sixteen inches wide. We used squared eight-inch logs for the rafters and roofed with one inch by sixteen inch wide boards. Cap knew where we could find a tar pit and we hauled pitch and placed a thick layer on top of the boards a little at a time and used it to bed down a slate roof. The windows we finished off with white oak frames and made two-inch thick oak shutters that, when shut, fit like a glove. The entire building was held together by white oak-pegs. Not a single nail desecrated the virgin wood from which we built the miner's fortress like home. The outside dimensions were eighty feet by sixty feet and we had built the structure on a foundation of stone. It took the three of us, with the added help of our four woodsmen, three months to build the frame and frame the partitions inside the house.

Upstairs, we made two bedrooms, one on each side of the wide staircase that was situated in front of a doublewide front door. At a touch, a six-inch wide square beam pivoted and sealed the front door shut for the night. The doors were made of three-inch by sixteen-inch wide white oak planks set into a door frame made of square ten-inch thick white oak. The doors swung on brass hinges made by a blacksmith in Denver, so finely balanced, they swung open at a touch. The two bedrooms were partitioned into simple, but very large open rooms. They comfortably held double beds, a dresser, an armoire and a mirror. The back wall opened and could be used for storage or hanging up of clothes. I made two nooks on each side of each large upstairs room. We structured two bathrooms back to back and ran the pipes down the back wall of the rooms. There was room to expand upstairs, but for now it would more than take care of the two Kickapoos and me. In the one room I built a row of two tiered bung beds so that we had plenty of sleeping space for guests.

Downstairs, we framed a huge kitchen with space for a large kitchen stove and two large ovens for the baking in one corner. I also framed an outside heavy door to a large walk-in-pantry and storage room. Under the double wide stairs, we built a comfortable room for Chi Lin. We added a set of stairs in the pantry that led to a space under the house set aside for a stone root cellar that could be built later to house beer, and wine, and sacks of flour, potatoes, apples, and other food items. I intended to build a large table that could seat at least twenty persons, and outfit the table with captain's chairs for comfort. I built two fireplaces back to back in the center of the building that provided heat for the upstairs. I furnished the room with a large round poker table and several smaller tables for chess and checkers, and purchased a pool table that someone else had to deliver. It cost a few extra bucks, but we had the cash. I told the bug-eyed miners that it would be up to them to furnish the room with some comfortable chairs and couches.

The far end of the house was to be used for entertainment. I left that up to Cap and his buddies to take care of, if, and when, the time came. At the back of the room, I built three bedrooms for the three partners. Each had a huge window looking out over the vast acreage and the mountains behind the house.

Upstairs, we had installed a row of windows the width of the rooms. The same had been done downstairs around the entire house. I installed the window bottoms five feet from the floor. Glass could be installed later. The shutters, for now, would take care of security, light and air circulation. We needed air and plenty of light to dispel the gloom of dark interiors until the glaziers delivered and installed the windows.

Before we laid the foundation, I had talked the partners into hiring a Drilling Company to come in from Denver and drill a well behind the kitchen and equip it with a windmill and a huge water storage tank. The drillers hit the sweetest water this side of Heaven at three hundred feet with a flow of a hundred gallons a minute. I scheduled plumbers to plumb bathrooms for each bedroom, plus an extra bathroom for each floor of the house. The leach fields were equipped with hotel size septic tanks, which I had installed a hundred yards down hill from the house.

I told my partners, "If Denver can have toilets and running water, there is no reason you very rich gentlemen should not enjoy your old age in solid comfort."

We had a party when we finished, and had a house warming and put out the word that all our friends were welcome. Buffalo and Four Hands did a great job and we even had a few of their Indian friends present. We were surprised when we had a houseful of young and old from as far away as fifty to seventy-five miles. I had never seen most of them before, nor had Cap, Ryan or Talley. We had asked for friends and we suddenly had more than we ever imagined.

Chi Lin did us proud and had Buffalo and Four Hands busy for two weeks before the party. I was lucky two days before the party was scheduled and I shot a young bison, which gave me food for thought. Buffalo had always been plentiful according to everyone I talked to. Now they complained that they seldom saw one. Some of Buffalo's white friends came and built a huge outdoor spit for us. Buffalo and Four Hands helped me skin and gut the buffalo. Before we were done, I was glad they did. Skinning a Buffalo was a lot harder than skinning a cow. They spitted the beast, and in the wee hours of the morning before the party, the smell of Buffalo meat could be smelled for miles. One of the last jobs my helpers and I, and our hired hands, had completed was closing off the valley beyond the house by erecting a ten-foot high timbered wall on both sides of the house. It included an extra wide gate. The wall sealed the valley from sight and denied access to that which we did not desire public access to, namely our old Spanish Mine.

We built racks in our front yard, and our guests politely left their weapons outside. Buffalo was a gem, and he tactfully sent two men packing, whom he said were not friends. I never questioned his judgment. Many of the westerners were amazed when they saw the indoor plumbing and quite a few of them relieved themselves well away from the house in an outside privy that we had previously built for our own use. The modern conveniences embarrassed them.

When we finished the cabin, the hired hands were put to work building a hip-roof barn well back from the house. We made it big with a huge haymow. We needed stables for our horses and donkeys before winter set in. We agreed that we would maintain a permanent crew of the four half-breeds, to do any farming and haying that was necessary, and maintain and guard the premises. The four men were Buffalo and Four Hand's friends, and they were intelligent, hard workers. The men started building a bunkhouse with indoor plumbing. I had to lay out all the work, especially the plumbing, which I had learned when the plumbers had installed the bathrooms in the log cabin. The men thought the bathrooms were funny and they made many indelicate jokes about the plumbing.

The ancient mine was nearly a mile from the log cabin, and so far we hadn't had any problems. Just to be sure, we built a board fence with a locked gate to insure the mine's security. We had several miles of grassland from which to gather hay. Later, I wanted to divert the flow of water from the mine to allow it to run down hill and create a small lake. We intended to fence off part of it, and supply it with ducks and geese. However, when we did create the lake, the wild ducks and geese took care of that problem and the bigger the lake grew, the more fowl showed up. Near the barn we put up a large hen house complete with fencing that we dug three-feet into the ground Next spring, we would have our own garden. I had certainly been able to satisfy my creative urge and I was tired.

Not tired so much from the work, which I seemed to gravitate toward, but from my concern about my status quo. Who was I? More importantly, what was I? So far I seemed to have been drawn to kill people and seriously maim them, which were in complete contrast to my creative talent, and who I really wanted to be. Now another name was creating more questions and confusion for me. Who was Jon? The name was beginning to haunt me. That night I had a most disturbing dream. Usually I just seemed to have one nightmare after another. This dream was different. It was about my past and answered some of the blank spaces that plagued me so badly.

In the dream I seemed to be dreaming about my past life. In it, I remember thinking: I'm a Pure D country boy and it seemed as though I had been training myself all my life to prepare myself for the future that lie ahead of me. My Cherokee Indian blood brother Jon Ridge and I had itchy feet, and whenever we had the chance we were like Ma's Wandering Jew plant that seemed to have tentacles that were peeking and prying into every nook and cranny. Yet, I knew that Jon and I had never been farther from home than Pikeville Kentucky and although we had roamed a bit in our home state of West Virginia, we were naïve to most of the outside world. Not only was I a farmer, but I was a natural born carpenter, and I had been weaned on breeding horses by my Grandpa Dillon. Except for the Civil War our family had led a rather idyllic life; at least that is until the McCoy clan moved onto Buffalo Creek. However, even before then, our idyllic pattern of life had begun to fall apart during the winter of 1876. I remember standing in the snow in my stocking feet watching our beautiful Victorian clap board farmhouse burn to the ground.

Our nearest neighbor was Oral Ferguson. He boarded Pa and me, and I remembered cutting down trees from the ridge above our house and hauling them down the steep hill and shaping and sizing them for the cabin we were building. Ma stayed with her father, Grandpa Dillon, who lived six miles away. For us to commute during the short winter days was just not practical. Pa, the Ridge boys and I, aided by the Harmon and Adkins menfolk, cut down trees, barked, trimmed, squared, sized them, and quickly put up a sizable but sturdy six-room log cabin.

I awoke with a start to the sound of Talley's booming voice yelling up the stairs, "Come and get it you sleepy head."

My head was splitting and after our breakfast, I said to my partners, "I had a dream last night. It seems, if the dream is correct that I have a Cherokee blood brother by the name of Jon Ridge and a Grandpa by the name of Dillon. Our Victorian house in West Virginia burned down and my Pa and I, and our friends rebuilt it with a log cabin in the middle of the winter. The name Jon popped into my head yesterday giving me another of my headaches, and I reckon that must have triggered my dream."

Talley shook his head in agreement and suggested. "It's possible that your building the cabin may also have jogged your memory some, or don't you think so, Shawn?

"It's so much all at once, Talley. Lots of names and lots of history. It's just too much for this young Cherokee," and I laughed.

Ryan laughed and commented, "At least you can laugh about it, Shawn. Don't forget, it's a piece of the puzzle you didn't have before."

"Yeah, Ryan, that and two cents will get me a cup of coffee in Denver. How about we show Chi Lin his surprise now?

When we showed Chi Lin his new room, he was really astounded, and rendered nearly speechless. He pointed to himself and said incredulously, "For me!" Then he brightened up and said, "I no spittee in your food—ever—."

I don' think he meant it as seriously as it sounded. But it had been said and the miners, his employers had heard him.

Talley looked shocked and said firmly, "See here, young man that is quite shocking. The very thought sickens me. I really expected much more from you."

Ryan was shaking his head and said forcefully, "I say, Chi Lin, we can have none of that. My parents taught me when I was very young to not even spit on the boardwalk. It was held to be that disgusting. To even think of spitting on someone's food is repulsive and disgusting, and to do it in anger is reprehensible. That won't do—that won't do at all."

Cap Mason took all this in and looked Chi Lin up and down as though he were sizing up an insect. "Chi Lin, you are an excellent cook. You are a hard worker and none of us have ever found reason to find fault with you. Do you understand me?" Poor Chi Lin would have crawled into a hole if he could have found one. Cap pointed his finger at the Chinaman and stated, "You understand this. If you ever say that word again, let alone do it, I will cut off your Queue and kick your butt every step of the way from here to Denver. Then I will kick your butt on a train and kick your butt all the way to San Francisco, where I will kick your butt onto a Chinese Clipper and send you back to where they spit in food in China. Do you understand me," he thundered. Poor Chi could only shake his head. No one was ever known to have heard him use that dreadful word again.

The house was finished, and while we had all been, so to speak, camping out and sleeping in the up stairs, we now moved in lock, stock and barrel, as the old saying goes. We had a most successful house warming. That first evening, all alone as a family, I thought everything was running perfect. Suddenly, Jack came up to me and pointed. My heart sank—was it never going to stop? I alerted the men, but I wasn't really worried. This time we were well prepared and snug as a coon in a hollow tree.

I had purchased a dozen brand new fifteen shot Winchester, Henry 44-40 rifles. The Henry was the one I was partial too. The Henry rifle had an outstanding brass frame and a 24" octagonal barrel. I had even included four Henry carbines with the twenty-inch barrels. I had also purchased two cases of metallic-casing, rim fire ammunition. These are the rifles that the Rebs used to say toward the end of the Civil War that the Northern Soldiers loaded on Sunday and fired all week. We placed them in gun cases at strategic points inside the cabin to facilitate accessibility. Now alerted, we closed the shutters, and inside our fort, we were nearly invulnerable, unless someone had a cannon.

This time, our enemies came in strength and they had changed their tactics. They had filtered in through the trees at dusk, and slipped into the mine plainly marked The Shamrock. I guess they were some proud of themselves. We could see men trying to climb up the face of the steep cliffs on either side of the Mine, but after three of the men took bad falls they gave up. They weren't rock climbers, nor were they even miners, at least good ones. They were low class thieves.

Cap Mason opened a rifle port and called out. "You men are trespassing. That mine belongs to me, Cap Mason, and my three partners. We are filed legally in Denver and your acts make you claim jumpers. Cease and desist immediately, or we will fire on you."

One man laughed contemptuously and fired his rifle at the rifle port. We immediately fired a broadside from every rifle port on that side of the house. Our four hired men had taken positions on the wall and opened fire when we did. An intruder cursed with alarm and another one yipped with pain. We had just fired in their general direction in an attempt to scare them off. They retreated inside the mine and we could hear them begin blasting and working the mine. Unless we wanted to make an assault on the mine, for all intents and purposes the mine was theirs; something to do with the old axiom, possession is nine tenths of the law. At least it is when there is no law within a hundred or so miles, and when we had no intentions of risking our lives for a worthless mine. It would be a lot different if the men learned of the old Spanish Mine, to which we had made our legal claim. For now, we sat back right comfortable and allowed them to beat their brains out.

We kept an eye on their activities, but they were smart enough not to try to storm the house. I was interested in one man who appeared to be in charge. If I did not miss my guess, he was a Brand. He was tall and slim, but well built with broad shoulders and slim tapering hips. I noted with interest; he wore his two pistols somewhat like I did.

I saw him eyeing the house thoughtfully, but he was careful to keep his distance and tried not to bring attention to himself; especially when he was checking out the house. As the days passed, I guess he begun to figure out that since they could find no gold that there was a reason for the fortress like house and the solidly built high fence.

I told the partners my thoughts, and Cap, thoughtful as always said, "We knew when they came that we couldn't fool them for very long. What do you boys think," he asked turning to his friends and partners.

"Nothing we can do, but fight for what's ours." Ryan stated positively.

Talley asked me, "What do you think they will do, Shawn?"

"If the beast runs true to form, Talley, greed will overcome any shreds of decency or fear that they may have. From what I have observed of the man I presume to be in charge, the man whom I believe to be Chauncey Brand, I think he has concluded that since they have found no gold in the mine that there has to be a reason why we have the house and fence blocking off everything else. He will most likely try to breach our fence."

"By George, I think you're right, Shawn." Ryan stated somberly. We have the wall well defended from the house and from the back of the fence. We can stop any attempt to burn the place, but there is one thing we have all overlooked; dynamite and kegs of black powder."

Cap looked disgusted, "For mining men—we should hang our heads in shame. The powder house is on the other side of the mine. They have access to it, but we don't. But one thing is in our favor. In the past three days, we haven't shot at them and they are getting careless. They are walking around out there like they own the place.

"But, we did think of the dynamite," Talley assured Cap. "The thing is—how can we defend the house and fence from being blown up? However, their carelessness can be the end of them, if we go about it right. What's your opinion, Shawn?"

"I think we should try to take them from outside the house." I suggested, with a touch of regret in my voice. I didn't know how I knew, but I knew I could eliminate every man out there operating from the cloak of darkness and using the stealth I knew I could utilize. I asked the two Indians, "Buffalo Who Kills Many White Men—and Four Hands—will you fight with me tonight?"

"Yes—Man Who Flies Like a Bird—I will fight the demons and the white eye thieves with my white brother," replied Buffalo.

Four Hands grunted his emphatic, "Yes—we go—and our friends you hire, they go too."

At dusk I took the six men aside, and explained my plan. "There is no moon tonight. Brand's men have been careless. They don't post guards, and they wonder around half the night drinking, playing cards, arguing and fighting. I don't want them dead. I want to set an example for those hard cases in Denver. If at all possible, we will take them on one person at a time. We will take a supply of rope with us, knock them on the head, carry them off, and tie and gag them. Two men will guard them. When we capture all twelve of them, we will dump them in the Mint Mine for safekeeping. Then, if Buffalo and Four Hands will carry a message to all the miners in the area, we will try these claim jumpers in a Miner's Court. Their punishment will be decided by the Court."

"Is good!" Four Hands grunted.

When darkness fell, the seven of us, and Jack, slipped out of the simple exit I had provided for and faded into the black shade of the forest; a forest with which all of us were familiar. It was chilly and would soon be bitter cold. Indian summer was nearly over and we could expect our first snow anytime. First snow sometimes came in September, and other times in October. I was a warm-weather-man myself, I could wait.

The claim jumpers hadn't brought any lanterns with them. They depended on the ones they could confiscate; consequently, they only had three lanterns, which they had found in the mine and tent. One, they used to light a makeshift bar and another, to light their seemingly never-ending poker game and the third, Brand kept in the tent that Cap and his buddies had lived in for months while trying to develop the Mint Mine. Chauncey Brand was a loner. There were cots and the simple comforts of three hard-working men inside, but Brand did not share. For three days the men had worked the mine and came up short. It was when Brand gave up on mining that I realized our time was short. Brand could not afford to idly stand by. When he decided to act; he would come—decisively—and some of our people were sure to be hurt or killed.

Four Hands and I worked together with the four new hires. After we sized up the area, we decided to use the mine as our staging area. Buffalo would stay in the mine and Four Hands and I would bring him the unconscious men. I didn't want to ruin my pistol, so from the mine we found two picks and removed the handles. I stumbled over a sleeping man; he cursed me and I put him back to sleep. Buffalo chuckled and whispered, "Me fix him!" Three men were sleeping their drunk off, and Four Hands kindly put them into a deep sleep and tied and gagged them securely. Most of them were sound asleep and we made quick work of them.

Only the last four men posed any sort of a problem. They were playing poker. Four card sharks had cleaned out the rest of their buddies and they were now in a dog eat dog poker game to see who got all the money. The fourth man left to relieve himself, when he did Four Hands rapped him on the head and gave him a soft rock to lay his head on. After he was tied and gagged, three of us came up behind each of the remaining men simultaneously and put them to sleep. Once we had the eleven men tied up in the mine—that only left Brand.

I boldly walked into the tent. Brand was reading by the light of the lamp, and ignored me until I picked up the lamp with my left hand and said pleasantly, "Brand." When I took the lamp, he jumped back knocking over the bench he was sitting on, and stood poised—ready to draw.

"I told him, "You have a choice, Brand. You can lift your hands and turn your back to me—or you can draw that gun your fingers are itching to draw. Just one bit of advice. I'm the one that shot off both of James Lee Coulter's thumbs." I gave him a moment to think it over. Then, I said factually "If you think I was just lucky, you can try your hand."

I really did not wish to kill Brand. But something made me give him a choice. Did I want to test myself against him?" No—I knew positively that I could outdraw Brand. If I had it figured right—Brand was going to get his just punishment without any help from me. Brand glared at me, but when he saw Buffalo standing behind me, his common sense told him he had better comply with my choice. He slowly turned glowering every inch of the way. He never knew when Four Hands stepped in and put him to sleep.

I left Buffalo and Four Hands in command of their four friends to guard the prisoners and returned to the cabin. Talley was worried and complained. "It's been so quiet. Is everything alright?"

"More than alright, Talley; the three men gathered around me, and I filled them in. They approved my plan, and I wrote two letters, one in English and one in Spanish. As owners, we signed them. Cap and I returned to the mine. When we got all the men squared away, I told Buffalo and Four Hands. "You better get started. You have a lot of territory to cover. I gave them the notices written in both English and Spanish to present to the miners.

SEPTEMBER, 13, 1877
TO ALL COLORADO TERRITORY MINERS
A MINER'S COURT WILL BE HELD TWO DAYS HENCE
ON SEPTEMBER 15, 1877 AT 9 A.M. AT THE
SHAMROCK MINE.
ELEVEN MEN AND THEIR LEADER,
CHAUNCEY BRAND, WILL BE
TRIED FOR CLAIM JUMPING.
THIS CHARGE IS MADE BY:

OWNERS OF THE SHAMROCK MINE
AND THE MINT MINE

SIGNED:
CAP MASON—TALLEY SHORT—RYAN BALLARD—SHAWN NACK

I told Chi Lin of our plans and that he would have as many as two hundred men to feed, and that he would have to start now to prepare to feed so many hungry men.

Chi Lin looked at me intently and then said, "You no tease Chi Lin?"

I held up my right hand and said, "No tease. Get to work."

Forewarned of the extra mouths to feed, Chi Lin picked two of the work hands and said to Cap, "I use—hokay."

Cap replied. "Okay," and asked him. "Do you need cow now?"

Chi smiled happily and said, "You bet, boss." He added, "Winter here now, we need go Denver hop, hop. Need stock up."

"Okay, Chi."

Cap asked me, "Shawn—would you like to go to Denver with us? We need to buy a wagonload of food. I swear it's like we're feeding an Army."

I hesitated. Was I ready for that? No telling whom I might run into? Friends would be welcome. Enemies, I could be dead, and never know why. I laughed and quipped, "I'm game, Cap—if you promise to take care of me."

Cap grinned, and retorted. "That's a joke. I'm going to take Chi Lin along to take care of both of us. I promised him he could look for his brothers. We'll give him a day to visit China Town. Maybe we can hire another cook to help him out."

"Good idea, Cap. I have already started expanding the bunkhouse. What do you think about building a small house for Chi Lin later on?"

"Yeah, that's something to think about," agreed Cap.

I smiled; Cap always wanted time to think about things, before he made a decision.

Miners came trickling in early on the fifteenth. By nine A.M. we had a hundred and twenty-nine miners in front of the cabin eagerly anticipating the trial. Talley set up the porch with benches and chairs to serve as a Miner's Court Room. The Miner's Committee would serve as the jury. Their top foreman acted as the judge, and he appointed a miner to serve as a defense attorney and another to serve as a prosecutor. The miners were called by their first names only. Their last names would remain anonymous. The appointed defense and prosecution men were given an hour apiece to prepare their offense and defense.

The prisoners had hobbles on their feet and their hands were tied about a foot apart. Brand refused to talk to anyone. He never said a word before or after I had captured him. I went over and told him, "Brand, your silence is utter nonsense. These men have established a Miner's Court; think, man, think. Your Texas pride will only get you hung. Cotton Brand isn't going to show up at the last minute to save your rotten hide. It's your last chance to speak up and save your butt." As I walked away, I looked back at him, and I knew I had wasted my time. His jaw was set like granite and not even the grave was going to make him budge.

There were eleven victims and twelve thieves. Brand refused to say one word and was dressed like many of the ranch owners I had seen, which was a shade better than the men that worked for them on their ranches. We were dressed like the mining men we were, and to us; the thieves looked like hard-case, low-life bums. Some dressed casual like the cowboy with a neckerchief knotted around their throat, a denim shirt, faded denim trousers, and cowboy boots. A few were miners and looked much the same as the men that were trying them. Three of them wore city clothes and derby hats worn cockily to one side of their heads.

I was the prosecution's first witness. I told them. "This is not the first time the Brand family has tried to steal our claim. The first time they sent four men led by a gunman by the name of James Lee Coulter. He had a phony piece of paper trying to claim our mine. When Cap Mason refused to comply with the phony order, Coulter drew both his guns to kill him. Only thing was, I was faster and shot off both his thumbs."

The miners all broke out laughing and the Judge rapped on the table with his Peacemaker and yelled. "Order in the Court." The acting judge was a hard rock miner. He was burley and rough on the edges, but I could tell the miners had chosen well. He said to me. "That's right good shooting, sonny. Go ahead with your testimony."

"The second time we had trouble was a week ago. Chauncey Brand was in charge. He had eleven men with him and they sneaked onto our mine when it was dusk and took over the property clearly marked as the Shamrock Mine. We had just finished supper when we heard them working the mine. Cap Mason yelled and told them to vacate the property. They laughed and fired at us. We shot back and nicked a couple of them. They ducked inside the mine, took it over, and kept on working it. They didn't find any gold after three days. By their actions, we thought they were planning on attacking us, so I took some men with me that night, and we captured and tied them all up and sent out letters for a Miner's Court. That's about it your, Honor."

Cap Mason and his two partners, the four work hands, and the two Kickapoo Indians all testified to the same story in their own words. Chi Lin spoke up and said, "The bad men steal boss mine. They shoot—we shoot back. I see—my own eyes." And he pointed to his eyes. The miner's laughed, and I could tell the miners were even taking the Chinaman's testimony seriously.

One after another, a dozen different miners took the stand and swore that Chauncey Brand and his three gunmen had run them off their mines at gunpoint. Three other men testified they had been shot, and four others claimed their partners had been shot and killed. I know the committee was impressed, but they were even more convinced by our four ranch hands, who told it like it was. The story told gutturually but graphically by Buffalo and Four Hands made points, for I saw some of the miners nodding their head in agreement with the testimony.

Many Western white men held most Indians, especially half-breeds, and Chinese people in very low esteem. They were considered heathen, pure and simple, and neither race was considered citizens of the United States. Their testimony would not have been acceptable in a regular court of law. However, their testimony was just as damning as far as the miners were concerned, because they had had enough of the Brands and their murderous ways. They would have believed anyone, because of the circumstances, and their own prejudice regarding the Brands and their cronies. They were getting a fair trail, but definitely, with prejudice.

Brand, and three of his men, had an extremely ugly reputation among the miners. Two dozen men got up and each testified that Brand and his three men had beaten them and stolen their life's saving, or that they had been victimized by them in one way or another. Each was a hanging offense as far as the miners were concerned. The sentence was fast and harsh. Brand and his three men would be hung. The other eight would be shot. The Committee named off two execution squads of a dozen men each. The squads put the men on their horses and rode them deep into the dense forest. We never heard any rifle fire. Brand and his henchmen were found a week later hanging from trees on a trail that led into Denver. We heard from a miner that the other men were made to dig their own graves. The eight men were made to stand in front of their graves they had just dug. Eight men of the execution squad drew short straws. On command they each shot one of the men so that their bodies fell into the grave they had dug for themselves. The miners shoveled in the dirt and no one ever found their graves, and no one ever looked that we heard about.

Miner's justice was harsh, swift and sure.

I wasn't looking forward to our trip to Denver. I was dissolute over the loss of my memory. The name Jon had haunted me. Then I had had the dream, and I now knew, thought I knew that Jon Ridge was my Cherokee blood brother. I now had reason to believe that my grandfather's name was Dillon, a good Irish name, and that I was evidently born in West Virginia, yet, dreaming of all these things did not help me one whit. I still did not know who I was, or whether I was a killer, or a saint, a good man, or a bad man. Nothing seemed to help me with my dilemma. I had made some wonderful friends, made a lot of money, and at least proved that I was not a coward, and that is where I had to leave it hanging, for better, or for worse.

It proved to be a long, hard, six day trip. I knew it would be even more difficult driving a wagon coming home. Coloradoans drove their wagons everywhere. Yet, there would be no real roads for years. In the meantime the natives just made do. I didn't want to go, because of the unknown. I didn't know who I was, and at times I was rather afraid of what I might find out.

*   *   *

Chi Lin was like a little kid when he saw—his city—once again. We took him to China Town and I told him I would pick him up the next day to help him check on his brothers. The first thing Cap and I did was stop at a store that sold Western haberdashery. We each purchased ourselves new, flat-crowned, black Stetson hats. When I put mine on—it felt like it had grown there. Fall was upon us, and Cap and I each purchased heavy outfits and changed into one of them at the store. It was already getting cold at night and Cap purchased winter clothes for his partners, which included long johns and warm sheepskin winter coats for the entire crew. Talley had made me a new holster for my Russian .44, and as I tucked it away under my vest—it felt comfortable; Cap did the same with his pistol. Our other holsters, and weapons, we stashed in our soogans during our stay in Denver. Once we got into town, Cap told me that no one wore holsters on their hip and most men wore what we back home had called, store broughten clothes and derby hats. The thought hurt, where exactly—was back home? Was it West Virginia as I had dreamed?

The boardwalks and the streets were heavy with the flow of horses and people. As Cap and I made our way through the pedestrian traffic looking for a place to eat, a big man with a handlebar mustache and a Lone Star badge on his chest was loping along at a cantor when he saw me. He looked surprised, and called out, "Matt" It can't be? Matt! Is that you?" He twisted around in his saddle and craned his neck back to see. He was surrounded by horsemen and couldn't ride free.

Surprised, I looked around—had that man been talking to me? I asked, "Cap! Did you hear that? Was that fellow talking to me?"

"What man, Shawn? Cap asked as he looked all around.

"Nothing important, I reckon, Cap," I said with a sigh, as he herded me into a famous restaurant named Charpiot's just in time to miss seeing the rider come back. He was frantically looking up and down the sidewalk

An attractive young couple was led past us by the headwaiter. The man caught my eye. He nudged his lady friend and whispered in her ear. She stopped abruptly, turned and looked right at me. She gasped, stepped back and said, "Pardon me, sir, but I have a friend who has a picture of his brother that is an exact image of you?

174

Cap and I both rose to our feet and I asked the gentleman, "Won't you join us, we just came in.?

He looked uncomfortable, but she gave him a slight nod and he answered, "Yes, but of course. The perfect solution, I would venture." He seated her and remaining standing.

I introduced us. This gentleman is m partner Cap Mason and everyone calls me Shawn Nack.

The man replied, "The lady I am escorting is my daughter, Miss Trinity Brand. I am her father, Vance Brand."

My face reflected my feelings when he mentioned the name Brand. Vance Brand saw my reaction and said with great reserve, as we seated ourselves, "I hope the name Brand did not offend you, sir?

"On the contrary, Mr. Brand, "We could never be offended by a lady as lovely as Miss Brand, or by the father that brought her to us."

Trinity flushed beautifully and replied. "You Irish do have a way with words."

Cap added, "We live in the wilderness about six days ride from here, we have heard of the good name of Vance Brand; and everyone speaks with admiration of your lovely daughter."

Brand laughed with pleasure and replied. "With all the flattery we are receiving, Trinity, I believe this lunch will be one that we will long remember."

I turned my head to Trinity and said, "In reply to your question, Miss Brand,"

Suddenly a man lunged up to the table and ground out in a harsh voice, "I'd like to hear the answer to that question myself, you Papist pig."

Trinity recognized who it was, she kept her poise, but I could tell she was angry. Her eyes snapped with irritation and her voice would have frozen the blood of a thousand better men than he, "Kyle Brand—how dare you."

Vance Brand rose to his feet, his face, dead white with rage. He ordered, "Kyle Brand, you know that your cousin and I are Catholic. You will leave this room at once, or you will answer to me personally."

Trinity Brand's face drained of all color. She gasped, "No, Father, no!"

I could tell she feared for her father's life.

A man dressed in cook's clothes; wearing a large white cook's cap stepped in between Kyle Brand and me waving a big butcher knife and said to me, "You will leave my restaurant at once. Then he turned to Kyle and said, "I should have known you would be the middle of this trouble. Get out! Get out! And don't come back."

Kyle stuck his nose up to the Frenchmen's face and snarled. "I'll go and I'll have this stinking place closed down. Who wants to eat your lousy prison grub anyhow?" He stalked out, his face convulsed with anger.

With a bow to Trinity, I followed him outside. He was so angry that he walked a block before he turned and saw me. I hadn't wanted any scene near Trinity Brand that would reflect on her reputation. He stopped abruptly—stepped out into the street and said, "Now you Papist hog, I'm going to fix you so you won't make any more Irish baby filth. People scattered.

"Just one thing you should know before you pull that gun, Brand. Your brother tried to steal our mine and a Miner's Court found him guilty and strung him up. He is dead—dead—dead—"

Kyle's face flooded red with rage and he drew. He wasn't any better than the other Brands. There was one shot—he just stood there staring at where his thumb used to be. Then he screamed, "My hand—you Papist son of a bitch—I'll kill you." But the pain doubled him over in agony."

I heard a man say, "How did it happen—that tall fellow never even moved. Look! He's just standing there."

I stopped a man that appeared to be a good citizen and asked, "Would you please take this man to a doctor?" I turned and pushed my way through the crowd that had gathered, and headed for the area people referred to as China Town. I didn't feel bad about shooting Kyle, and for the first time, I didn't feel guilty, but I was hungry. Was I becoming acclimated to the taking of the blood of my fellow man? I shook off the thought. I hadn't looked for the fight, but I sure wasn't going to run away from one.

I had had my first lessens with bigotry in—where had it been? There went my memory again, but for some reason I knew that many people hated Catholics. Why, I didn't remember, but I had learned much about Denver since I had ended up in the Colorado Territory. Ryan had warned me before I came to Denver that there was a group of Papist haters in Denver that brought discredit to the entire Territory. Then the thought occurred to me. Why had he warned me about Catholic haters? I wasn't Catholic. Hell, I wasn't any denomination that I knew of. Ryan said there was even one newspaper that dedicated itself to propagating hate mongering in edition after edition. I couldn't even remember its name, but who cared. I didn't hate Catholics or any religion. I didn't even know what affiliation I had been, or for that matter whether or not I had ever had one. I knew I believed in God. I could recite the Pater Noster, the Hail Mary and the Glory Be, but that pretty well summed up my knowledge of religion. It really didn't matter—for now; I had to find Chi Lin in China Town.

I located Chi Lin and he was his usual sanguine self. His cheerful demeanor helped snap me out of my doldrums, I asked him. "Something has puzzled me, Chi Lin, why did you bring up that word? That word," and I laughed, "that you can't say."

Chi Lin looked at me skeptically. When he was sure I wasn't angry, he answered, "Me no mad, Mr. Shawn; white man always make joke about Chinaman doing that. I say as white man joke."

"That's what I thought, Chi Lin. I'll set it right with the others. Do you like living in America, Chi Lin."

"Oh yes, Mr. Shawn, velly velly much."

"What do you think you need to make it perfect, Chi Lin?"

"My brothers gone; I no can find. No family here—no family in China—all dead." He looked at me hopefully, "You my family now?"

"I have no family, Chi Lin. No remember anything. We family—yes," and I gave him my hand. He broke out crying. To cheer him up again, I told him, "You need wife—make many little Chi Lins."

He giggled, "It cost much money, I save."

"You have a girl, Chi Lin? Where?"

"She here, must give papa five hundred Melican dolla. Don't know Melican name."

"It's called a dowry, Chi Lin. You're my family. I'll pay your dowry.

Cap found us in China town and he said to me, "Ryan warned you about the bigotry here, Shawn. I guess he knew what he was talking about.

I nodded and said, "I got thinking about that Cap, and what I don't understand is why he singled me out to tell me about Catholics?

Cap smiled and replied, "Ryan really likes you. He told me that when I first brought you back to camp, and you were delirious for two days, you were raving out of your head. You said many things that are associated with Catholics. He noticed that when we say grace at meals that you usually cross yourself, which only Catholics do that we know about. It's little things, but when you are cooped up with a small group of people, you begin to notice their mannerisms much more so than when you are among a crowd of people. He thinks you were at some time in your life a Roman Catholic. He thought we should warn you of the bigotry that is sometimes prevalent here, so you didn't get yourself in over your head by the first incident that you might run into.

I smiled grimly and said, "He must be clairvoyant." And I told him about the shooting incident."

"Dad blast it," Cap exclaimed. "I had a feeling that I should go with you, when you charged out of the restaurant. But I stayed to try to set things straight with the owner. He said to tell you that you are welcome to come back anytime.

"That's not likely, Cap." And I brought him up to date on Chi Lin.

I had talked to Chi Lin about how much groceries we would need. I had thought that Cap and Chi Lin were a bit off on their calculations. I convinced Cap that one wagon was not going to be enough, especially with the harsh terrain that we had to navigate and with the extra mouths we had to feed. I reminded him we would need good hardy wagons to haul the ore from the mint and the ore that they had taken from the Shamrock by use of the arrastre. Ryan had explained that the Arrastre would get most of the gold, but not all by any means. That which was left, we began piling separately to be hauled to an Orr Mill later on.

Cap and I negotiated for two Conestoga wagons and eight draught horses, and then we attended the wedding—Chinese Style—firecrackers, dragons, Chinese wine, mass excitement and celebrations. Afterwards, we filled our two wagons with enough supplies to more than last the winter.

We checked out of the City Hotel and set out for home. We barely had enough gold to pay for everything. Vance Brand had taken care of Sheriff David Cook's inquiries, so I knew the law didn't want me. Sheriff Cook told Cap that Kyle's losing his thumb might take some of the meanness out of him. Unfortunately, in all the hustle and bustle, we forgot all about the Vance Brand family regarding our conversation about the picture. I didn't think of it until we were nearly home. My memory was still a nebulous thing at best.

On the way home, I told Cap about his misunderstanding with Chi Lin. Cap was a great man. When we got home, he announced that I could start building a cabin for Chi Lin and his bride as a wedding present. She was very shy, but Cap gave a reception for the newly weds, and we sent out word to all the known residents in a fifty mile radius. Quite a few people did come for various reasons, but not nearly the turnout that we had hoped for.

Cap reminded me that many people did not like the Chinese and considered them heathens. But at least, it made Soo Lin feel more at home. Chi Lin ran the kitchen and Soo Lin ran Chi Lin; I was her big brother, but with reservations. She made it quite plain; we four bosses were Number One.

I loved horses and every horse I had—I spoiled. I had purchased a case of sugar cubes and two potato sacks of apples just for them. The draught horses had grown their full winter coats and one mare had beautiful long white hair flowing from around her head, mane, and tail. She had a super personality. It snowed before we got back. We had to stop, and I attached skids to the wheels. In some ways the skids helped, but in others they were a pain in the butt and hindered our progress.

When I finished putting on the snow runners—and the skids, the lead horse actually stopped and turned her head and whinnied, as though she were saying thanks. I named her Grace. She was the leader and she set a steady pace that the other horses immediately fell into. She nipped them to let them know she was the boss—they all gave in gracefully—and she became the acknowledged leader. Once she knew what I wanted her to do, she picked her own trail. She saved her team again and again by her judicious judgment and saved us hours on the trail. There was no road, but she knew where one should have been, and as the snow grew deeper, it became obvious why they called those magnificent beasts, draught horses.

When we got home, we were happy to see our huge larder and pantry filled nearly to the capacity. Cap came for me the next day. He had just learned that a rancher was coming up the Cheyenne Trail with fifteen hundred head of Texas Cattle heading for Montana. He had lost time and had been caught in the snowstorm. He stood to lose every head he had. He had sent some men out trying to find a buyer at two-bucks a head, the going price for hides. Did I want them? I went out and threw a saddle on Grace. I needed big horses to buck the drifts and I took her seven companions with me. At first I tied them together. But I quickly found out—where she went—they went, which was fine with me.

Two days later I found the owner. The steers were spread over a four-mile area trying to find food. They were tough Texas range cattle and knew how to dig down with their hooves to find grass. They would survive. I roped a dozen of them from throughout the herd and checked them close for Hoof and Mouth disease. They seemed to be okay. I agreed to pay Dobby Keyes the two dollars a head he had asked for, delivered to our valley. He agreed and with the six cowboys he had left we set out. Six days later I helped drive them through the gates and into the big valley. It took another two days to get them spread out sufficiently to find grass for them all. I invited Keyes and his men to be our guests for a few days to rest up. He gratefully took me up on the offer. He was amazed with our cabin and our indoor plumbing.

While we were in Denver, Cap and I had learned that cows were going for twenty dollars a head. I talked to Cap and his partners and we agreed to pay Keyes $10.00 a head. Dobby got choked up trying to thank us.

After a couple of days I was really impressed with Dobby's six cowboys. I had seen them work with the cows and it had been tough work to get them here and even tougher to get them spread out over our valley. I talked it over with Cap and our partners all agreed they were men of character. I offered them fifty bucks a month and found, and after they talked it over, they agreed to work for at least a year. Suddenly, we were ranchers with fifteen hundred head of cows and a crew of six to manage them. We also had four half-breed Kickapoo Indians as ranch hands.

That night after supper, Talley said "I have a surprise for you, Cap. You remember those mining experts that came out here to jump our claim?"

Everyone shook their head yes, and with a grin he took up a bag he had hidden and dumped it on the table. It looked like rocks to me and being impetuous, I said so.

Talley laughed and said, "Thank you, Shawn, that's just what those claim jumpers thought. They knew very little about mining. They were blasting holes all over the place. This happens to be the prime gold ore we were looking for, and those idiots found it for us. What you didn't know, and what they didn't know, is that in most gold ore the gold is not visible like it is in white quartz ore. It's often hidden in diorite, limestone, and even slate. As the old saying goes—Gold is where you find it, but you better be a miner, or you won't know it when you see it."

He started laughing so hard I thought he would bust a gut. "Gentlemen," he said with a flourish, "We now have a Bonanza and a Mint choked plumb full of gold ore and fifteen hundred cattle out there in our new cattle ranch; and all this is just for us poor old prospectors. Fellows—we sure have a lot for which to be grateful.

We all said with enthusiasm,

"Amen!"

7HE LONER

CHAPTER SIX

The next morning I got up earlier than early and told the cow hands that they would be taking their chuck in the cabin with the rest of us—when possible. "First," I suggested, "let's get acquainted. My name is Shawn Nack. I'm one of four partners that run this show. I'm in charge, but the other three partners are also your bosses. They are not likely to bother you, but if they do, and you don't agree with what they say—you bring it to me. We have four ranch hands—one of their jobs will be to take care of the haying and the farm's work next season. They are good men, they do their work and the first time I hear of them, or any of you calling each other names, the man that causes the trouble gets his walking papers. I can whip any man here and I can outshoot any one of you. If you don't believe me and want a demonstration—just sing out. I paused and looked around—I wasn't kidding—they got the message.

We have a Chinese cook and his wife, who live in the big house. They are good cooks, they are nice people, treat them with respect. If you can't treat them with respect—keep your mouth shut or draw your time. We have two Kickapoo Indians, who live here off and on. They are part owners. They are our friends. We are one big happy family here. Your pay will be fifty dollars a month. We have two mines here. They are none of your business. If I catch any of you in or near the mines, you'll get your walking papers. If you want to play poker, the game is limited to matches or beans, or penny anti poker, if the foreman agrees. There will be no guns carried on your person inside the bunkhouse. I hired each one of you men, because you looked to me like you know your business. I don't like to be wrong, so show me what you can do. Are there any questions?

"Yes sir." A tall drink of water stepped forward and pointed out. "So far all we've ridden is the horses we rode in with. We'll need a change of hosses from time to time."

"Thank you, Slim. May I ask what happened to your horse ramuda?

"Kiowa got them just before you showed up. We were too short handed to chase them. If we had—we could have lost the herd as well.

"It sounds as though old man Keyes, if he ever had any luck—it was all plumb bad. I'll take care of the horse situation just as soon as possible. Anything else? If not—let's eat."

Chi Lin was waiting for my signal, and he immediately struck the iron triangle with his iron bar.

Hungry men don't talk much, and believe me those men were always hungry. Chi served pancakes and the men tore into those stacks like ravenous wolves—soaking them with gobs of butter and hot syrup and washing them down with cup after cup of scalding hot coffee.

When they were finished, except for the belching, I divided them into two groups and I told them, "I want you fellows to separate those cows into two herds. Put all those old mossy horns and young steers in one herd, and put all the good breeding stock into another. We are going to herd the better stock closer to the cabin. Once you have the cows separated, they will hunt for grass that isn't buried and look for shelter from the wind. Be on the lookout for some young bulls and don't castrate them all". Even an old one might still turn a cow's heart.

Slim, if you want the job you're Ramrod of the crew. Judd, you act as foreman of your bunch, and you'll get thirty dollars a month more. Slim you get fifty dollars a month more, but you'll earn it. I may not be around much. If that happens; you'll report to Cap Mason. Once we get the fences built. We'll build a couple of line shacks, and horse sheds and then begins the real work, I want you cowboys to breed us bigger, and better stock that has more meat on them than horns, and I grinned. Those cowboys went to work like a bunch of kids going on a holiday.

Slim and Judd came to me after supper and Slim said, "Could we have a minute, Shawn."

I took them into the recreation room and asked, "What's on your mind, fellows?"

"We are going to have to spread these cows out right quick, or they're going to get mighty hungry. There's not enough grass for so many cattle. We want to spread the cattle out for about five miles, while they are still strong enough to travel. We saw a tent out front. If we could take that we could set up a camp two or three miles up the valley and operate from there. One of your ranch hands used to be a cook. If we could take him as a cook, and a load of grub, we could make out for the winter. Next year we can cut enough hay to supplement the herd. I reckon you plan on selling the steers and if you do we can easily make out. The only problem I can see right now is a lack of bulls to take care of all of those ladies, and we need those horses yesterday."

"That's an awful lot for one minute," I commented with a grin. "We just picked up twelve horses; just don't take any of them into Denver." And I told them briefly about the claim jumpers, and added, "Some of them might be cutting horses if you're lucky. "I also picked up eight draught horses in Denver, none of which are cutting horses. Leave the pretty one named Grace here for me. They've been broke to saddle and they can handle the snow and drifts better than your cow ponies. We have our own horses, which you can use for now, but alternate and stable a couple of them here. This will give you a total of twenty-or more horses to work with. I will start the ball rolling to get you some more cutting horses with some beef on them. Your smaller cow ponies are going to take a beating in all this snow.

Cap had come in and was listening and said. "The tent is yours, fellow, and anything else you need. I think you boys said you need a bull. Come here"—he said, and he led them to the door. Standing in the front yard was the biggest bull I had ever seen. A huge brindle bull at least 17 hands high, with a pair of horns that spread more than nine feet wide. When he saw us he lowered his head, pawed the snow and let out a bellow that shook the house.

"Where the hay—did he come from, "I asked?

Slim looked and laughed. "That old reprobate must have followed us all the way from Texas. I've seen him on the range a thousand times. He must have looked around and found himself all alone and decided to follow all those pretty cows. Those old bulls can track better than any Indian. Old man Dobbie Keyes is going to have a stroke when he finds out his best bull is gone."

We were all laughing, and I asked Slim. "How much do you think he weighs."

"Most folks say, he must go at least 1800 lbs. A grizzly jumped him one time and he gored and stomped him to little pieces."

I said, "You fellows get your horses and we will haze that amorous bull through the gate and up to his lovely ladies and just let nature take its course. If Mr. Keyes shows up, we will take care of that situation when he gets here. If we don't hear from him, I'll try to get a message to him and make him an offer. That is—once I have talked to you boys on how much he's worth."

"I went out and saddled Grace and helped Slim and Judd round up the horses and readied one of Conestoga wagon as a Chuck-wagon. I heard a ruckus and saw that Slim and Judd were having trouble getting that big bull through the gate. I yelled to Slim. "Go get a few of those cows and bring them down here. We will use them to lure him through the gate. A half hour later Slim hazed the cows near the gate, and I rode up behind the bull and whacked him on the rump with my lariat. The bull spun and swung his horns catching me on the back of the head. I went out of the saddle like I'd been shot and landed on my face.

When I was able to get back in the saddle Slim and Judd had the bull with the rest of the cows. Slim told me later. "Grace is a good horse, but getting dumped like that would never have happened to you with a good cow pony." I believed him, but that didn't help me with my thumping head. One of these days someone was going to hit me on the back of my head once too often. I was still dizzy and off and on, I was seeing red and white lightning flashes.

I found Chi Lin supervising the loading of the food on the Conestoga. I talked to Goober Thorp about subbing as a cook and offered him another thirty dollars a month to help him make up his mind. It took us a week to get the animals separated. Goober knew what was needed and he soon located a gushing spring that had found its own natural drain. Goober set up his tent a quarter mile away and bragged,

"You give me a little help and I'll have water at camp site and a good sized pond down yonder to water the cows and the horses." I sent him two of the half breeds to assist him, and he went right to work.

Slim and I spread the cows out from that point on for another three miles. Judd took his batch of cows straight ahead for three miles and then began spreading them out until he rand out of cows. In the meantime Goober set up his tent and cooking fire, and moved the Chuck wagon. The cowboys had all tossed their soogans in the back of the Chuck-wagon. The first time I stuck my head in the back of the wagon the tangy smell of sourdough tickled my nostrils. I knew we would be eating biscuits in the morning. Goober cut enough saplings to make a reflector and rigged up a spit and began cutting firewood. He even dragged in logs for the cowboys to sit on, which made me happy that I had paid him an extra thirty dollars. By supper time he had steaks and potatoes and a big coffee pot filled with hot—hot coffee. The smell of hot, fry-pan cornbread set my mouth to salivating. Goober was off to a great start, but the boys knew they wouldn't get steak every night. Cowboys lived on beans and anything the cook could add to that is what made him a cook.

It took us two weeks to get the cows spread out and teach them to find the holes that we had chopped open with axes so they could drink. The men were good at their jobs, and when I left Slim and joined Judd, he had done equally well and I noted from time to time that the big Brindle bull was doing his share with the greatest of enthusiasm. After supper the boys all jumped in and made a stone boat for the cook so he could bring in wood as needed. It was a good natured crew; they worked and joshed each other with idle banter. I had been lucky to get so many good men with so little effort on my part. At least I was lucky on some things. My head was still flashing lightning from my run in with the bull, and I was having irritating flashes of memory again that did nothing but depress me.

The next morning, I said, "Take over, Slim." I rode back to the house and was pleased to find Buffalo and Four Hands just finishing their breakfast. I could tell that they were not their usual good-natured selves. Four Hands said. "We hear you have many wa-haws."

"Sure do, Four Hands. The boys and I brought 1500 head. That whole valley over yonder is full of beef.

Our people starve. White agent says no wa-haw come. He lie. He sell wa-haws. We see him.

"Do you know where the white men and the wa-haws are now?" I asked.

"Buffalo exclaimed, "I know. I follow."

"Are the men and Wa-haws off the reservation yet?"

"Buffalo thought for a moment and replied." They go Denver, high up, snow heavy. They go slow. When close—they kill Wa-haw, cut up and take meat to Denver in wagon. They no on reservation now."

"How many men, Buffalo?"

"Four."

"You have plan, Buffalo?"

"Learn white man plan. Wahaw stop soon. Small valley—have water and hay. Four men come from Denver with God Damns. They kill Wahaws little bit. Put meat on God Damns and sell in Denver."

"Just what is a God-Damn, Buffalo, I asked with a frown.

"Big freight wagons, Shawn." Four Hands explained. Men drive wagons, crack big whips, and yell God-Damn all the time. Indians think big wagons called, God-Damns."

"I understand, Four Hands. Only careless white men use God's name as a cuss word. We will call the freight wagons by their right name. We don't wish to offend the Great Spirit of all men when we are about to ask for his help on this journey that we take—okay?"

"Buffalo smiled and said, "Okay! We go now, okay?"

"Okay", I said laughing, and we started packing our things.

Ryan joined right in, saying, "It looks to me like you're short one man." We selected the biggest horses we had, and Chi Lin helped pack our two donkeys with food and our bedrolls we tied on the back of our horses, which the cowboys called soogans. Within half an hour we were on our way. Buffalo said, "We go little valley and wait. We fight who come first."

"What happens," I asked him, "if they all come at once?"

"We have one damn good fight," Buffalo answered with a huge smile.

I stepped into the saddle and my senses spun. That damned head again. If it wasn't some berserk Brand smacking me on the head, it was a cantankerous bull.

Two nights later, hidden in the trees, we lay on our soogans waiting for the herd to arrive that we could now hear coming from just over the hill. Jack lay snuggled up to me; the warmth of his body was most welcome. The weather was warm comparatively speaking—about 40 degrees I would estimate, and the humidity was heavy. I wouldn't be surprised if it rained tomorrow, but most likely it would get colder and we would have more snow. The thieves had evidently used the valley before. They had picked well, the snow was not deep, and this end of the valley was thick with trees. It would give the thieves good cover, and the cows would have shelter, grass, and water. There were signs among the trees that showed that animals had been butchered here before.

With a bellow from the driven cows, the herd flowed up and over the hill and poured down into the valley. They began milling, as if they knew they were at the end of their journey. One man stayed with the cows and the others rode to the creek and dismounted, unsheathed three axes, and they began cutting holes in the ice. The mounted man kept the herd back until they were mounted and then they all headed for their old campsite, which we knew was located at the edge of the stand of trees. They quickly started a fire, and the first thing they did was to put on a pot of coffee to brew. We had scouted the area, and we swung in behind the trees and walked right up on the men still numb from the cold and tired from the trail.

Their guns were all inside their coats and their rifles were still on their ponies, and when I yelled, "Move and you are dead." They froze into position, except one man, who started running for his horse. "Jack," I called and like a flash Jack darted across the fire and leaped on the man's back. He fell flat on his face and I called out, "Don't move or the dog will kill you."

One at a time, we called the men to one side and made them shed their coats. Then we carefully disarmed them. The man on his stomach was last and when he came up to the fire—it was Kyle Brand. I shook my head and said, "Now why am I not surprised to find you here. I see you are now using a Colt Peacemaker, instead of the Russian .44. Well it is a bit difficult to thumb a Russian Colt if you haven't got a thumb. I just bet you this colt has a hair trigger. Then you don't have to squeeze too hard to get off an accurate shot. I dumped the cartridges out and tried the action. The action was so fluid I commented. "Man, you will have to be careful with this pistol, or you will shoot off your big toe. Then you would be as toeless as you are thumbless." I deliberately had no mercy on him. If hate could kill—I would have dropped dead—his face was a mixed fury of passions.

We gagged and tied each man to a tree back in the woods apiece. One man we tied and gagged sitting down facing the fire with his back to the expected entryway of the wagons. We moved our soogans up closer to the fire, which we had built up so that the clearing was clear as a twilight evening. We wanted to see well enough so we didn't kill a friend; but not too much light, as to give ourselves away to the expected thieves.

I was restless—and I paced up and down. I was always on edge when I was faced with the thought of having to hurt someone, but tonight my head was throbbing with that old familiar throb. That blessed bull. I still hadn't made up my mind what to do with the captured thieves. In situations like this my mind buzzed like a beehive. The name of Barney kept plaguing me. Then it was Jon and Dr. Elbee and Marshall Clemens. Tonight a new one had burned into my thoughts, The Reverend Denver McCoy and there seemed to be McCoys of every name and description. What was the name of my mother and my father? And who in God's Good Name was Juliette? Suddenly Jack growled and I sensed a difference in his growl. He was pointed behind me. My .44 Russian flowed into my hand and when I turned I was holding it dead center on Jon Ridge.

Jon grinned and said, "You going to shoot me, Matthew?"

Jack ran and jumped into his arms, and was whining and kissing his face. Jon dropped him and he said cheerfully. "Well, Jack knows me even if you don't."

My head was smashing, my friends gathered around me and suddenly I was being sucked down into a vortex—around and around and around and I had never hit bottom when I collapsed and fell. I wasn't unconscious, but at best I was an invalid; at that very second a voice called out, "Hello the camp. We're coming in."

Jon had watched the previous action and knew these men were facing more trouble. He quickly explained, "I am this man's friend. The dog knows me. You have trouble coming. Let's take care of that first."

Ryan nodded and acted decisively. He called out. "It's clear, Come on in."

Led by Ryan, they all filtered back through the trees and flopped down on their soogans—their weapons at the ready. Ryan stood to one side making sure the trees gave him some cover. Jon crouched watching Ryan for his orders. Two huge freight wagons each pulled by four beautiful draft horses came slipping and sliding down the slope, held back by the handling of an excellent pair of teamsters. When they pulled up the two teamsters got down, and stepped over to one side out of harms way—but no one else dismounted. Ryan yelled, "Where the hell are the rest of the men you were to bring. We ain't going to cut up all these beeves by ourselves."

"We're just the teamsters." The man answered. "There are six men on those wagons with their rifles pointed at you. It seems you didn't give the right password."

"What the damned hell are you talking about? Ryan snarled. "When Kyle Brand hired us three men for this job, he didn't say anything about a damned password. He and his bunch were so shot up, they were lucky to tell us anything. We been promised a hundred bucks apiece to wrangle these mangy critters up from the reservation. Who's going to pay us?" He demanded wrathfully.

When Ryan said three men, Jon tapped Buffalo on the shoulder, and they all slipped off into the woods and took up firing positions behind and to one side of the wagons taking cover behind the trees, waiting for the showdown.

It was obvious that the men in the wagon were confused. They were a leaderless batch of scoundrels who didn't know what to do next. Prudently Ryan stepped behind a tree and called out. "You boys in the wagon listen to me. The men that drove the herd here are all prisoners. No one is going to get paid. My men have you in their sights. You are sitting ducks in those wagons. Take your coats off. Take your weapons off and one by one get down off those wagons and walk over to the fire and squat with your hands clasped behind your heads. I'll count to ten, and then we begin shooting. He didn't have to count to three before the first man jumped out, ran over to the fire, squatted and clasped his hands behind his head. Five men came out. The sixth man tried to sneak out the back of the wagon, but Jon shot his finger as he grasped the edge of the wagon. He screamed and a few seconds later he jumped out the front and ran to the fire and squatted—blood dripping down the back of his vest.

Ryan called out to the teamsters. "You teamsters told me six men. If you lied to me and one of my men gets hurt—I will hang you both."

The one teamster was a cool one; he answered calmly, "I told you six. Six came out. If there's more in there, I don't know about it and you can go to hell with your threats."

"No threats, sonny. That's a promise." Ryan checked inside both wagons. He found them empty except for the men's clothes, weapons and butcher's ware.

He called out, "Okay, men—all clear. Take the men one at a time and tie them tight. Get the gags off those other men and you teamsters are going to work whether you like it or not. Jon, go take care of Shawn."

"Shawn," he responded. Is that what you call him? His name is Matthew Michael O'Shannon and I am Jon J. Ridge his blood brother."

Buffalo looked surprised, he asked, "You Indian?"

Jon said, as he hurried away to find Matt, "I'm Cherokee."

Buffalo caught up with him and said, "Me Kickapoo. Me help you with Man Who Fly Like a Bird, he big friend of Kickopoo."

They found me holding my head and rocking back and forth in pain. Jon ran to me, and Jack whined his welcome, but he wouldn't leave my side. I looked at Jon and complained, "You make my head hurt." I cried out, "Go away—you're a figment of my imagination."

Buffalo told Jon, "He hurt his head when he fly off cliff. He no can tell who he is. We name him Shawn Nack."

"We better get him to a Doctor in Denver," Jon said. You stay with him. Hold him down if you have to. I'll get a wagon."

My head was pounding, and I tried to ignore them. Just the sound of their voices made me clutch my ears with both hands. A few minutes after Jon left, a big voice boomed out, "What the hell's going on down there?" Then there came a crescendo of shots, men shouting and a sudden scream. The firing tapered off and the booming voice demanded, "Kyle, why are you tied up like a hog being taken to market?"

Buffalo said, "We lose war—I get horses." Seconds later, he rode back and helped me into the saddle. The irritating voice boomed again and yelled. "There's more of them—kill them all," a wild rash of firing sent bullets crashing all about us. There was a sodden blow and Buffalo grunted. He grabbed my reins and galloped with me in tow. I hung on grimly. Something bad had happened, and I was too incapacitated to help. When I woke up, I was in my own bed and I could hear rain drumming on the roof. I looked all around and there was not one leak. I reared up in bed. Where was Buffalo? Then I saw him. He was sitting up in the bed across from me. We were home. Jon—I had seen Jon—or had I? I must have been dreaming.

Buffalo said. "Man Who Flies Like a Bird, lives. That is good."

I got up. I was a little dizzy, but otherwise I felt good. I could hear someone on the stairs. I asked, "What the devil happened, Buffalo?"

Cap Mason came in and said shortly, "You got Ryan Ballard killed—that's what happened." His face was torn with emotion and he turned and stomped back down the stairs.

I stood there frozen. My penchant for violence had finally caught up with me. Someone else I loved had paid for my lust for blood. I walked over to Buffalo, and asked, "You okay?"

"Just little bullet. No hurt," the Kickapoo claimed.

"Is Four Hands okay," I asked?

"He too wise to die." Buffalo said proudly. "He take care of you and me."

I clapped him on the shoulder, "You are both great Warriors, Thank you. By the way—what happened to Jon? I did see him didn't I?"

Buffalo replied, "Jon good friend. He go Denver—get Doctor for you."

"Give him my regards, Buffalo. He's a full-blooded Cherokee. He's my blood brother. Where did they put Ryan, Buffalo?"

"Him downstairs, Big room."

I put on my long underwear, dressed in my buckskins, put on my heavy woolen socks and boots, strapped on my two Russian .44s—my belt knife, and gave Buffalo the Indian sign for goodbye. Cap had given me a stash of gold and cash, and I bundled it in with an extra outfit, then walked downstairs and asked Chi Lin to prepare a two-week pack of food for me, and then reluctantly walked into the reception room.

There laid out in a pine coffin was my friend and benefactor—Ryan Ballard. My eyes brimmed with tears. I knelt and prayed a rosary for my dead friend. When I was finished, I rose—kissed him on the forehead and said. "I'm sure sorry, Ryan." Sorrow could not begin to define my feelings. I was completely and totally devastated."

I went to the barn and saddled Grace, I would need a horse that could handle the heavy snow. I packed my saddlebags with 500 rounds of .44-40 ammunition, cinched down the packsaddle on another one of the draught horses, slipped my Henry Rifle into its boot, and rode out to see Slim. I nodded at his salutation and said, "Talk to Cap, but I am sure he will agree. Round up a hundred and fifty head of those steers and have Four Hands guide you to the reservation. Wait at the Reservation line and he will get Indians to take them off your hands. Those Indians will starve if we don't help them."

"Sure, boss," he said, "that's a nice thing to do. Glad to help."

I started to ride off—stopped—and turned and said, "One more thing, Slim, my name is Matthew Michael O'Shannon, just call me Matt." And I turned and rode off. Slim caught on quick.

Slim called after me, "You're a good man, Matt. It has been a pleasure working with you."

I finished packing and left the house I had helped to build, and had learned to call home. I called Jack and he jumped up to me, I caught him and put him across the saddle in front of me. Then I rode out—enough good men had died because of me. If anymore died, it would be, because I didn't have any choice, and they wouldn't be my close friends or family. There had to be a curse on me. I didn't look back. I couldn't.

To the North, Pike's Peak dominated the horizon. I angled southeast and headed for the Cheyenne Trail. I had started this journey with the intent of settling in the Southwestern New Mexico Territory. I might as well go and see what it looked like. The rain had pretty well washed away the snow. The thought made me smile. The cattle would be able to get to the grass now. If they were lucky and the rain let up, the cowboys just might be able to cut some grass, but the odds weren't good. The streams were running over their banks and I had to adjust my route many times to meet the terms of the terrain. The main thing was—I was moving—and I was alone, which was just the way I wanted it. No people—no trouble—no responsibilities for someone else's life. When I started out, I had put on my raincoat, but I left the middle button open so I could reach inside to get to my belly pistol if needed. It might slow me down a mite, but I had practiced for this very contingency.

Fog set in and dusk came on with a rush, but I was ready. I had picked out a dry spot under an overhanging rock that wasn't going anywhere. I cut a small windbreak with my hatchet—built a small fire and put on my coffee. I settled for a few pieces of jerky for my supper, as did Jack. I had no appetite, but at last I had my memory back. With the new tragedy added to all the old ones, I didn't know if it was a curse or a blessing. I didn't like to run out on Jon, but the way the deck was stacked, I was sure he would be safer without me. I seemed to attract death for my friends like a lightning rod attracts lightning. Why the hell had I been in such an all fired hurry to go after the Indian Reservation beef herd? Why hadn't I just sent the Indians steers from our herd like I had just done before I left? If I had Ryan would still be alive and Buffalo would not be lying in bed with a bullet wound.

My memory was back, but with it came the memories of my life's work—my horses. I was homesick for my horses, especially Pat. I wondered if I was right in going alone on the trail? I really missed Jon. Jon had wanted to settle in New Mexico. Had he arrived there, settled in, and then came back for me? I had just been getting to know Barney after he returned from Denver, and here we were separated again. Tiffany was certainly a beautiful girl; I couldn't help but wonder if they had set the date yet. Then I remembered that deep commanding voice from the other night. Had that been Cotton Brand? Whoever he was, he had certainly turned the tables on our plans. From under the overhang were some small dry dead branches. About thirty feet out from my camp, I scattered a path of the dry twigs in a semicircle about my camp. The fire died out, I rolled out my soogans, took off my boots and my hat, spread my raincoat on top of my soogans, and lay back with my pistol near at hand and was gratified to see a few stars. Jack snuggled up to my side, and I drifted off to sleep.

I awoke to the sound of a crackling fire and the smell of cooking bacon. I eased up my hat with my pistol in my hand and was greeted with the welcome sight of Four Hand's smiling face. He held up a twig and said with a mischievous look. "Thanks for leaving dry twigs so handy for fire."

I jumped up with a laugh and exclaimed. "Four Hands!" Jack was sitting by the Indian, and I swear he had that same mischievous look on his face. "What brings you to my camp so early," I asked. The sky was just breaking light.

"Cap Mason send me. He sorry for big mouth. Want me tell you—come home. He speak from hurt in mind—not from heart."

I was really touched. Four hands had said Cap's words of apology far better than he could have done in person. "Thank you, Four Hands. You tell Cap no apology is necessary unless it is one from me. No man has ever had better friends than those I made in the Valley of Green Grass and Spanish Gold." I entitled the valley the way I would always see and remember it and the endearing friendships I had made there in such a short time were firmly etched in my heart for eternity. Jack gave a low growl, and from the corner of my eye, I saw a flash of movement and the ominous click of a pistol hammer thumbed back. I dived at Four Hands and rolled us both into a small gulch made by a small stream. I came up with my pistol flaming and the ambusher's shot and mine blended into one roll of thunder. I felt a whiff of air as the assassin's bullet fanned my ear. I heard the sodden sound of my bullet hitting solid flesh and a cry of fear and surprise.

Jack was crouched by me, and I said, Jack, scout." Jack disappeared without a sound and two minutes later, he came back and lay down and looked up at me. It was his way of saying, "It's over."

Four Hands reached out for Jack and he went to him, and lay down next to him. The Indian said, "Good dog." And Jack reached up and licked his face.

I said, "Jack, track", and in a half crouch he crept away and I followed him. He led me from in behind the ambusher, Jack knew he was dead, and had scouted out the position. The man lay flat on his back, a round bullet hole right in the center of his jacket, the look of surprise on Jerry's face did soften it somewhat, but even in death Jerry still had a hard look to his features. I checked his pockets, which revealed he only had the usual trivia. He had a nice jack-knife, he was wearing, a used but nicely made gun belt and clutched in his hand was a new looking Colt Peacemaker pistol. I unbelted the holster and finally got some answers when I found he was wearing a money belt containing two-hundred dollars in twenty-dollar gold eagles. It seemed to be the price of the proverbial, Thirty Pieces of Silver. I was not surprised to find he had three throwing knives in a neck sheath, and sleeve sheaths, and a nicely sheathed hunting knife in his belt. What was revealing was a reward notice put up by Cotton Brand offering five-hundred in gold coin for Byron or Matthew O'Shannon Dead or Alive for horse stealing.

From what I knew of the Brands I wasn't surprised, but I was surprised he was so brazen. I knew it wasn't legal, but if Byron or I protested to the law, Brand would swear he hadn't had them printed. In the meantime—we O'Shannons had a price on our heads that would tempt a lot of low lifes to shoot us on sight. I'm sure Brand had the word out on the street that if we were found dead he would make good on the offer. So far, no one knew I was an O'Shannon. I had earned a new name of which I was not ashamed—Shawn Nack. Until the Brand threat could be met head on, I would use my new name. But, the question was—how had Jerry found me?

Jack found Jerry's horse. I was shocked when I saw her. It was Lucy, one of Jon's Arabian breeding horses. When she got my scent—she nickered and readily accepted my hand and a lump of sugar. How did he come by one of our horses? The Ridges and O'Shannon's needed a reward notice for Jerry instead of the one Brand issued for us. I guess the old saying was correct. It pays to advertise. Four Hands came over and shook his head in sorrow. To set him straight, I said, "He was a bad man; Four Hands. He got what he had been asking for all his sorrowful life."

"No! Four Hands not sorry he die. I sorry I led him to you. He come house pretend he friend of man named Matt O'Shannon. Your friend Jon saw him and challenged him. But man say all mistake and he leave in hurry. He follow me, too much mud to cover trail, me sorry."

"Jerry is no one's fault, but his own, Four Hands. Tell me, how bad was Buffalo's wound?"

"Doctor say, Buffalo's wound serious, but he live." I gave Four Hands Jerry's jack-knife, and his Peacemaker colt and belt, and the four knives. I showed Four Hands the Arabian mare and told him, "Jerry stole this horse from my blood brother Jon Ridge. It is a very valuable breeding mare. Will you return this horse to Jon when he returns? Also please tell my friend Slim Albright, to keep it confidential about my real name. Tell him about the reward notice—he will understand."

"Cap Mason send you package." Said, "Please forgive, you friend, please come back."

I took the package and stowed it away in the bottom of my saddlebags. I would check it later. "Tell him, I have many problems to sort out. Tell him I definitely will come back."

I had not been surprised to learn that my would-be assassin was our old troublemaker Jerry. I was actually surprised that he had lasted this long. I found a crevice in the rocks and wrapped Jerry in his blanket and buried him under a mound of rocks. I didn't know his last name. I did say a prayer over him. It was a sad commentary to note that there was not much chance that anyone that he ever knew—would ever know, or even care that he was dead. After that thought, I said a rosary for him. Four Hands rode north and Jack and I rode south.

As is often the case in Colorado the sun came out and dried the terrain. The small streams became fordable and the next evening, I cut due west and the nest day I crossed the Central Pacific's railroad tracks and the next evening I rode into the small town of Pueblo, Colo. I hadn't seen a single person since Four Hands and I had parted. For one thing when I saw a cabin or any sign of people, I swung wide and went around them. I wasn't anti-social, but I had a lot on my mind to sort out. It seems that when I did socialize. I always seemed to end up in some sort of trouble. I seldom if ever went into a bar. I did occasionally drink a beer, but what attracted me, as I rode into Pueblo, was a simple sign on the window of a bar that read—Coffee and Donuts—and I did have a sweet tooth for donuts. I hadn't met a single cowboy that didn't love "Bear Claw" the cowboy's name for doughnuts.

I left Jack lying across the saddle on top of my sheepskin coat; I ruffled his head and said—"Guard." The bar was clean. I found the usual room-length bar facing me on the right side of the room and took a seat closest the lone bartender. I noted four men playing poker and the barkeep was with two customers down the bar. He walked up and said, "What's yours, friend?"

"Your sign—Coffee and Donuts—caught my eye. Coffee black and two donuts please."

"Sure thing, buddy," and he filled a big cup and speared two donuts onto a plate—set them before me and smiled and said, "I swear—I think I'm in the donut business. Every since my wife talked me into putting up that sign, I sell more donuts than I do booze," he complained. She makes the donuts fresh every day. No complaints so far," and he laughed.

He looked like a big Swede, his shirtsleeves were rolled up and his arms were all muscle. It was good to hear a pleasant voice and I grinned and dug into the donuts. They were better than good. "These donuts are great," I told him, "my compliments to your wife, sir."

The front door slammed open and three men burst into the room. They either had been drinking or were being intentionally rude. One man slapped his hand on the bar and said, "Three black coffees and six of those bear claws, Swede."

"Sure, Buck, that will be Six Dollars please."

"What do you mean, Six Dollars? Have you jacked up yer prices?" Buck snarled.

"Sure haven't," Swede answered pleasantly." It's still a buck for a coffee and two donuts. You forgot to pay me the last time you gentlemen were in."

"Okay! Buck agreed, "We'll pay you when we leave."

Swede grinned pleasantly and said, "Sorry, fellows. It's pay in advance or no donuts."

I sensed there was more behind their actions than just donuts.

While talking Swede kept busy wiping and fussing behind the bar. He saw me tense up, and he gave me a slight negative shake of the head.

Suddenly, the three men fanned out in front of Swede. Buck put his hand on his pistol and said with a snarl, "I've killed men for saying less than that."

Swedes big hands moved with blurring speed and he swung up a double-barreled shot gun aimed right at Buck's middle button on his shirt, cocking it as he swung it up—he said casually, "You were saying something about killing someone. Would you like to complete that thought?"

Buck's companion Dink Wagner managed a squeaking sound and he ducked out the front door. Skip Roper just as casually dropped his hand from his gun and looked at Buck doubtfully.

Buck replied, "You heard me." And he started to leave.

Swede said. "There you go again, Buck, with that bad memory of yours. You owe me three bucks."

Buck tried to stare him down, then reached into his pocket and threw down three silver dollars. He said as he stepped away from the counter. "You haven't heard the end of this."

Swede said pleasantly, "Give Joe Binder my best regards, Buck."

"I will, Buck replied, "and he has a long memory."

"Yeah, I know," Swede said, "but it's not nearly as long as his greed."

I didn't question Swede. I had involuntarily nearly gone to his aid. He nod staying my hand, or I might have found my nose in someone else's problems. I had to learn to control myself, or I would find myself the Sir Galahad of every person in trouble in the west. I finished my donuts and drank down the last drop of coffee and spun a silver dollar across the counter to Swede. "Again, my best regards to your wife, Swede. Listen to her, and you'll be a rich man." I advised with a friendly smile.

As I approached my horse a man followed me out of the bar and remarked. "You a friend of Swede's?" Then I noted the Marshall's badge on his coat.

"Those donuts and coffee were my first introduction to him, Marshall. He seems a likable sort."

"I'm Pat Desmond, Marshall around here. For a moment I thought you were going to take a hand in that squabble."

"I've a soft spot for any man caught in a sucker play like that, Marshall. I didn't see you inside."

"Neither did Buck Dixon or his cronies. My back was to the door, but that mirror in front of me told me a lot," and he laughed. Buck came close that time, but he will make a fatal error one of these days and I will rid the town of his cheap theatrics. That your dog? Keep an eye on him. There's some mean folk around and lately a couple of them have been poisoning dogs."

"Jack catches rabbits. He won't take food from anyone but me. Thanks for your concern. Can you steer me to a Hotel and a restaurant. A nice rooming house would be better."

I could tell that Pat liked me and the feeling was mutual. He asked me point blank, "How good are you with those canons you carry?"

I felt comfortable with Pat and I grinned and replied, "A man never knows that unless it's after he's the last man standing. I reckon I'm better than most, but there is always someone out there that's better. If I were back east I would take them off and never put them on again. Out here, I would feel undressed without them."

Pat nodded thoughtfully and said, "I feel much the same way. There's plenty of work around here, for a man that can handle himself. Miners and mine owners are always looking for guards, but they are careful whom they hire. If you're interested, I'd vouch for you."

"I'm right flattered, Pat. Thank you! I'll keep that in mind. Right now I'm cold, I'm tired, and I just want to take it easy for a while."

"Best you try Mrs. Gibbons then. She only rents six rooms. She just lost one roomer. He grubstaked a fellow, and he hit it big. He left to help him out."

"Mrs. Gibbons hesitated when I said I had a dog, but that he was house broken. I thought I understood and suggested, "My dog can stay in your stable, Ma'am.

"No! No!" She exclaimed. "We love dogs. Someone recently poisoned our dog, Maximus. We were broken hearted."

"Ma'am, if your former roomer comes back, I will move on."

"No, that's not it either," she replied with a little laugh. "It's my older daughter. I keep hoping she will come home. She's living with her father for now."

Somehow her last statement did not ring true. Honest people have trouble telling lies. I spoke up, "Same promise, Ma'am."

"Good," she said. "Simple rules, Mr. Nack. No drinking in the house, no overnight friends. I feed two full meals a day, and a midday snack. I don't wait meals, and I can't tolerate bad language, or chewing tobacco. Smoking is alright as long as you are neat about it. The charge is five dollars gold coin a week in advance, plus a dollar a week for the dog, and a dollar apiece for the horses. No refunds for missed meals. Coffee is always on the stove. I change the sheets once a week. Do you want to see the room, Mr. Nack?

I shook my head, I felt like I was at home. Mrs. Gibbons had two children, a boy Charles, 13, and a daughter Marie Elena, 16. Both were out, I would meet them at supper. I paid Mrs. Gibbons for two weeks and by the time Mrs. Gibbons rang her small dinner bell. I had all my gear squared away, had fed the horses some hay, and curried them both down. Grace loved the attention; both horses nudged my hands for a piece of cubed sugar.

Mrs. Gibbons had built in her back porch. It was a handy place to wash up for supper. Eight wash bowls with roller style pitchers of warm water were attached to the wall, with towels hanging conveniently from a rack with a mirror over each towel holder. I washed up and upon my entrance every one rose and Mrs. Gibbons said, "Our new resident is Shawn Nack. Shawn please meet Gabe McCoy and Tuck Doyle. This is Marie Elena, my daughter and this is Michael my son, and she reeled off all the names. Then she led a prayer.

"God is gracious, God is good. God we thank you for this food. Amen"

My hair was longer, I was dressed in buckskins, and I had matured considerable. Gabe looked a bit more mature, but if he recognized me, he didn't let on with as much as the blink of an eye. We had only met once or twice, and any other time I had seen him had been at a distance. As far as I was concerned, the war between our families was a nightmare from my past that I never wished to relive. Marie Elena was a flirt, but not for me. She had eyes only for Tuck Doyle. He was about twenty. He had a shy way about him that I knew she must find attractive. He was clean cut with a strong jaw, a friendly grin and a nice head of hair. Gabe was slimmer, not nearly as dapper looking, as he had been, when I first met him. His eyes were guarded and pain filled.

People in the west seldom asked a man where he was from. They would ask what you did for a living, so I was not surprised when Michael asked me. "Are you a scout for the Army, Mr. Nack?"

"No, Michael," I smiled and answered, "but I have some very good friends in the Kickapoo Indian Tribe. They made this outfit for me."

"Gee! That sure is a swell outfit, Mr. Nack."

Mrs. Gibbons gave Michael a slight shake of the head for his use of 'swell' and then said. "It's a beautifully made garment, Mr. Nack. It must have taken days to cure and fit."

"It cost my Indian friends two horses, Mrs. Gibbons."

"That's a lot more than we pay for a suit here," Tuck Doyle exclaimed incredulously.

"I hate to think how much it will cost to clean," I admitted with a smile.

"The Indians in West Virginia used to wear them and let the rain clean them," Gabe McCoy offered.

I never let on, but why would he so obviously call attention to West Virginia if he were trying to travel incognito? In stead of reacting, I decided to just go along. Maybe—just maybe—he hadn't recognized me? It certainly wouldn't hurt to just play along, so I said, "It's too cold to do that now, Mr. McCoy. I hate to think how bad I will smell if I have to wait till spring." I added grinning. "Does there happen to be a good Chinese laundry in town?"

"Yes," Gabe replied, "I'll be glad to show you where it is."

"Thank you," I said and Mrs. Gibbons led the conversation far a field. It was obvious there was not to be any direct confrontation. Not yet anyhow.

I wasn't afraid to go with Gabe, but the thought of the two of us going somewhere together was a novelty that I had never contemplated as possible. Was he as naïve about my identity, as I had dared to allow myself to believe? Only time would tell. One thing of which I was reasonably sure, Gabriel McCoy might be a lot of things, but he was too proud of his own ability to ever shoot me in the back. At least—that's what I kept telling myself? Gabe, by virtue of the gossip mill, had a reputation in Pikeville, Ky. as a ladies man. If he was, I had never seen or heard of it in Buffalo Creek. But we had never really learned anything about his true nature since he had arrived in Buffalo Creek. He had kept a very low profile. All we knew was that under the despotic leadership of his minister father the Reverend J.D. McCoy that he had exploded like a vial of nitroglycerin dropped in the middle of the Battle of Gettysburg when his father started killing O'Shannons.

We saddled up the next morning and Jack assumed his usual seat lying in front of me. I had taken a pan bath the night before and changed my clothes. I stuffed my laundry in my saddlebags, and Gabe led me right to the laundry. I didn't know if they knew how to clean buckskin suit, but the Chinese man assured me that he could. His name was Chang lei do, and I asked him if he knew Chi Lin, and I told him about Chi Lin's problem. He promised me that he would be on the lookout for his brothers. As I left, he said, "You wait—you see. buckskin soft—like baby's bottom."

When I came out, I said, "Thanks, Gabe, I think Chang will do a good job."

He was standing relaxed by his horse and said, "Glad I could help you, Matthew. Did you come here to finish the job, or is our meeting just an accident?"

I looked him in the eye and said, "I left all that hate and killing back on Buffalo Creek, Gabe. I had hoped that you hadn't recognized me."

"You are a man that stands out, Matt. No chance that I could pass you by. As far as my family and I are concerned, Matt, what's done is done, and better forgotten."

I gave him my hand and said "Gabe I have never heard more pleasant words. Are you speaking for the rest of your family?"

"I am for those with me, but we are out of communication with the family back on Buffalo Creek. We've heard by the grapevine that the rest of the family moved back to Kentucky, but not near Pikeville. My biggest problem is trying to get enough work for the boys with me. I'll take you over and introduce you to my ex sister in law. There's three ladies altogether. They run their own still and use the moonshine to supplement their own beer bar. I'll let them speak for themselves. They tell me they are peaceful. Four of the boys are still in school. They are growing like weeds; you will see that I have too many responsibilities to be concerned about anything else. It took fifteen minutes for us to get to the bar located just outside the city limits. The more I saw and learned about Gabe the more impressed I became. Gabe led us up to a roughly thrown together log cabin. Smoke poured from the chimney above us.

"Here we are," he said as he slid out of the saddle. He threw open the door of the cabin. Inside was a bar made of boards laid on top of empty beer kegs. The floor was dirt with saw dust strewn to sop up the mud and spilled booze, a crude bar at best. It was heated by a big cast iron stove standing in the center of the room, and vented through the ceiling. The bar was empty of patrons. "Girls," Gabe said, "meet Shawn Nack alias Matthew O'Shannon."

Sandra looked me over casually and said, "I know all the whys and wherefores of why your family took a beating before you boys decided to fight back. I only wondered why it took you so long to retaliate?"

Kate declared heatedly, "Daniel was a good husband. If you hadn't killed that old buzzard of a father of his, I would have." She looked at Gabe and said, "Sorry, Gabe."

Patricia just looked me up and down and added, "They said you were a big one with horns and deadly eyes. You don't look like you have horns. You look more like the Teddy Bear type to me."

I replied, "I'm more like a pussy cat, Patricia, I have had all the Teddy Bear stuffing knocked out of me. I see you girls are following the customs of the Old Sod Widows in Ireland who had to support themselves by opening a Sheebeen usually in an old barn. Their fathers taught them the trade. Let me have a taste of that mountain dew that you ladies call moonshine."

Patricia poured me a generous portion and said, "That will be two-bits, Shawn." I grinned and tossed her two-bits and took a sip and said, "Ladies that is the best Tennessee Sipping Whiskey I've ever tasted. I sipped on my drink until it was all gone—even though every drop burned like fire. But it was first class moonshine and few bars in the west could say as much. I commented,

"Did you girls know that the early bartenders out here took a bucket of alcohol or prune juice, or whatever came along and laced it with a cut up pound of chewing tobacco, the head of a rattlesnake, and a couple pounds of red peppers. They boiled the tobacco and red peppers to get the strength out, added a bottle of Jamaica ginger, two bars of soap, and two gallons of molasses. Then they dumped in thirty gallons of branch water and let it ferment overnight. Some Mexican bartenders stirred in tarantulas and centipedes to give them flavor."

Patricia laughed, and said, "That tops all the stories the miners and cowboys tell. You'll do, Shawn."

I asked Patricia, "Did your Dad teach you the trade?"

"We first lived in Harlan County, Ky. And we grew up helping Daddy make his Shine." Mom got tired of his being chased by the Sheriff and made him move us back to Ashland, Ky. We lived with our Uncle Carl Giesling; we were also related to the Mays on Buffalo Creek."

I grinned at her, "Now isn't this cozy. We were also related to the Mays a couple of times removed."

Pat beamed, "I guess that makes us kissing cousins," and she blushed.

The girls deserved better than fate had dealt them. Yet, they weren't asking for handouts and were struggling to bludgeon their way into what was strictly a man's world. As I mentioned before, I am a bit impetuous. So I suggested, "Would you girls be interested in a business proposition? I understand Gabe has some boys that need work, and I happen to know that the McCoy boys are top-notch workers. What do you say if Gabe and I team up and build you a bar of which you girls could be proud? If you don't like what we build, you don't have to take it. If you like it, we will abide by your girl's decision as to what is a fair deal?"

Sandra looked at me speculatively and said, "Your feet sure don't grow no moss, Shawn Nack. We'll talk it over tonight."

The next morning, Gabe and I rode back to the bar. Sandra confirmed that they were more than willing to accept my offer. I said to Gabe, You've had the night to think it over, Gave. "What do you think of my plan? Ideas just suddenly bombard me like this. I have the money. You have the work force. I have the knowledge how to build the bar" I held out my hand and offered, "Partners?"

He looked at me completely dumfounded, a gamut of emotions flooded his face. Neither of us really knew anything about the other, but for the first time since the McCoys had descended on Buffalo Creek; I had met my nemesis and found that I actually liked and trusted the man. I guess my impulsiveness must have caught him entirely off guard. The women were looking at the two of us rather incredulously and seemed to be holding their breaths. All at once the entire scene struck me as rather ludicrous, and I started grinning and repeated, "Partners! Yes or No?"

He laughed, "You're a real man, Shawn Nack. I can't think of a better way to end a feud that neither of us wanted. Partners—yes." and he gave me his hand. It was just as firm as I remembered from our first encounter. The girls broke out laughing and voicing their support.

Suddenly, he was all business. "We are going to need a lot of trees, and I know where we can get them." he said. "There are two prime pieces of property that I know of that are loaded with Douglas Fir. There is good water and if we cut careful we can save the forest and save the land. All we have to do is for each one of us to Homestead the property."

"Why don't we form a company," I suggested? I have enough cash to build a sawmill; then we could do some real building. Each one of your brothers, Gabe, and you, but not me, I'm just a child," I added with a grin, "and any of the girls that are twenty-one can file a homestead. We will build a small house on each homestead plus the necessary outbuildings. If we form a company we can protect everyone's rights and still come out smelling like one of those Wall Street Magnets. Later, we can go right into opening a furniture manufacturing company, and the boys that like farm life can raise horses, grow hay and corn, or whatever they would rather do." I didn't have to push Gabe, he was grinning from ear to ear.

At first the girls balked. None of them wished to live alone that far from town. But my mind raced faster than my mouth. So I suggested, "Look, Gabe has four young teen-agers going to school, all with the name of McCoy. Gabe has proven that he is a good father, but the boys could certainly benefit from a women's touch."

Patricia began laughing, "Whoever told you that the boys are Gabe's teenagers. They happen to be our sons." And she nodded towards Kate.

They read the confusion on my face, and they all began laughing.

"That's a good one on me.," I gasped laughing. "Tell me what else I don't know before I make a complete rear end out of myself."

Patricia came to my aid, "The twins are mine. I'm a bit older than you boys," but she added with a coy smile, "I know I look a lot younger. I married into a different family of McCoys that also lived on Buffalo Creek. Strangely enough my husband's father was also named Denver McCoy. After all the trouble on Buffalo Creek, people began connecting my family with Gabe's family, and my two boys were being picked on in school because of their last name. Gabe and Sandra had dated a few times and when he decided to pull out of Buffalo Creek with part of his family, he invited us to go along. I was sick of the killing, my husband had died of Typhoid Fever, so I sold out for the little I could get, and Sandra and I, and my two boys joined the McCoy exodus. The other two boys are Kate's sons.

I chuckled and said, "Is my face red? If not—it should be. I admit I am a bit impetuous, but I don't usually blunder as badly as I did this time. The question remains, Patricia, are you and Kate willing to homestead two parcels of land? The Company we form will pay the gong price for timber, and the money will be reinvested in the Company less our immediate expenses. Gabe will select the trees we need for future growth. Once we have cleared off the land, we would have a home and great place to raise horses, farm, raise hay and grain, or whatever." I was talked out. "So sleep on it, I suggested, and give us the verdict tomorrow."

I arranged to meet with the four McCoy brothers. I wanted to make sure that they would join our group, and more importantly that the feud was over. I didn't have a death wish, and I sure didn't relish getting shot in the back. I did not intend to start a business with men that viewed me as an enemy. I was pleasantly surprised. The men were the same ones that had ridden with Gabe when they tried to raid the Wayne County Jail. I learned that Gabe had picked his brothers that were single for that raid. They were Samuel, Shadrach, Micah and Isaiah. They were older than Gabe, who was barely twenty-one, but the acknowledged leader of the group. They were all in their late twenties. They were McCoys, and as such were loyal to the family, but they hated their father. They would not desert the family, and the only way they could fight back was to refuse to get married and have children that J. D. McCoy could dominate and ruin for life. The religious training that J.D. taught actually saved his life. His sons could not and would not kill their own father, nor could they desert the rest of the family. One by one they shook my hand and thanked me for freeing them from their father's tyranny.

We contacted Pat Desmond the next morning, and when he knew what we needed, he gave us the name of a young, honest, upstanding attorney. Within two days we had the basic contract written up. The attorney guided us on how to properly apply for homestead property. The only stumbling block proved to be me. I was the only one that wasn't twenty-one. But, the attorney got around that stumbling block by signing on the homestead with me with his written promise to deed it over to me once it was proved upon. Our block of eight homesteads took in a good chunk of land. Gabe knew good land and good timber. The only problem was that the property was nearly twenty miles from Pueblo. Gabe had picked out the best for us. The Homestead Act of 1862 allowed a family 160 acres of land. The family had to live on the property and develop it, before they could get full rights to the property.

The next day the girls agreed to our plan. I put up nine-thousand-dollars, and everyone signed the papers. It took a lot of planning and time to get organized and in operation. Gabe and Sandra proved to be the best in detailing the needs for the Company, so we voted them our confidence and I set about finding a good mill man. As far as I was concerned, everyone came out a winner.

We had twelve-hundred and eighty acres of prime timberland located about twenty miles from Pueblo. There were decent trails to the area. A sawmill was delivered to us in one week by the railroad. A month later we had the homesteads settled. We began erection of the Sawmill in the middle of the property, and we finished the work the day before Christmas. We celebrated Christmas together as a business-family-group. We named the Company, The West Virginia Sawyers.

I hired an experienced mill man and it promptly paid off. He saved us his annual salary the first month by his expertise. He lived alone and we later built him a small house by the mill. We built simple four room cabins and the necessary outbuildings on each homestead. Once we decided where the hay and grain was going to be grown, we could decide where to build the barns. I wanted to build the bar with dried logs. Our mill man took us out on our property and he found enough sound felled trees that we were able to build the bar with dried logs. In one pond the mill man found many trees that Beavers had felled years before. The pond was fed by frigid cold mountain water and the logs had been preserved by the cold. When cut, I knew I was going to be able to build the prettiest bar in Colorado. The wood finish would be fantastic. That is if I had analyzed the wood correctly.

We not only needed wood to build, but it seemed everybody in the Territory needed our uncured finished lumber. We soon had a dozen men working including Gabe's four brothers and the mill was a little gold mine in itself. In three months we had built nine houses and outbuildings, and I had put the finishing touches on the bar itself. Gabe's twelve man crew and I finished the bar in record time. Sandra, Patricia, and Gabe and I were elected to run the enterprise and one of our first decisions was to promote Isaac Solomon. We put him in charge of designing and setting up the lumber yard and to determine the size cuts we would need based on the orders we were receiving. Later, he and Gabe would work together to develop forestland to be cut and logged. We also decided to build an office building at the mill and run the business from there.

The three girls named their bar "Kentucky Moonglow," and it was an immediate success. Patricia and Kate would run the bar, since Sandra was tied up with the mill supervision. With the Railroad so handy, they stocked the bar with a wide range of bourbon, Vodka, Gin, a nice selection of wines, Champagne, and of course cold—cold—beer.

Their most popular beverage was their Kentucky Moonshine labeled "Moonglow." The girls sold it for ten cents a shot, and the Federal Revenue agents were quick to show up and slap a tax on the distillery. The girls had to raise the price to fifteen cents a shot.

We installed a brass foot rail and shiny brass spittoons were placed at appropriate places. We installed full length mirrors behind the bar and they really lit up the room. Patricia hired a huge loveable, but tough, Norseman, as their head bartender. His name was Skippe Skerry. Barefooted, he stood six-foot—six. He weighed two-hundred-and-seventy-five-lbs, and he didn't have one ounce of fat. Kate blushed every time he spoke to her. We had built three rooms in the rear. In the far corner of the bar, we had installed a heavy door and loading platform. The platform had a dumbwaiter that let down into a deep storage beer, and wine cellar. On the far side of the bar, we had created three rooms; a large meeting room, and an office. As an after thought, we added large rooms with a corridor that led to large modern toilet facilities for ladies. Completely separate, a door opened into a room with plumbed toilet facilities for the men. The leach field and septic tank were installed a hundred feet from the building.

Gabe and I stopped by after the grand opening and with a wink at Gabe—I said to Patricia and Kate, "How would you girls like to take a first class trip on the Central Pacific and with connections ride on into Ashland, Ky. You could make a quick visit to see your mother. From there, I bet you girls could get yourselves invited to several Breweries and Whiskey Distillation Plants. Then when you get back, you could start building your own distillery."

Patricia caught on real quick and punched me on the arm. "Oh you fellows have to have your little fun."

Kate was looking real thoughtful and said, "You know, Pat, I bet we could do just that." She pulled Pat over to one side and they began talking about the mountain water. Gabe nodded to me and as we left the bar he said, "You know I think those girls took you serious." We looked back and as we went out the door both girls pointed at us and laughed.

We walked away laughing and Gabe commented. "You know, Matt, I bet you a hundred bucks those girls could build a distillery."

Gabe's brothers were working in the mill and hauling lumber to our new customers in Pueblo and the surrounding area. They were also working their homesteads on their off days. The girls, after the first month, began taking turns with Gabe to run the bar, and we had our own Buggy Service to run us back and forth to our homesteads. Two months later we built a school house and an attached home and we, and our new neighbors, contributed enough funds to hire a school teacher, Patricia and Kate had their sons transferred to the new school.

We no sooner left the bar than Joe Binder walked into the bar with his three hirelings tagging along. He said in a silky voice, "Good day, Ladies. I'm Joe Binder. You certainly have a nice bar here."

Kate stepped up to the bar and replied in her rich Kentucky accent, "Well thank yo, Mr. Binder. What kin I do fer yo boys today?"

"I really like yer bar—how much aer yo asking fer it?"

"You are wasting your time, Mr. Binder. The bar is not—and has never been for sale. Is there anything else I can do for yo boys?"

Dink Wagner leered at her and said, "Now thet yo dun sed it, honey—thar's several things I can do fer yo—thet cum ta ma mind."

Kate replied, "I doubt that. It takes a man to do most things."

Buck Dixon and Skip Roper laughed at Dink, but Binder's face flushed and he snapped at Wagner, "You apologize to the lady at once," and his hand was near his gun. Dink didn't budge.

Skippe had edged his two hundred and seventy-five pounds up behind the girls, and he said, "Did I hear someone speak cross to you, Miss Kate?"

Kate flashed a smile of gratitude to Skippe and said, "Nothing, I can't handle, Skippe."

Red faced, Dink said surlily, "Sorry, Miss—nuthen meant."

"That's all right, Mr., Wagner. You are all new customers. The first one is on the house. Now what will it be?"

Joe Binder said unctuously, "That's very nice of yo, Ma'am. We heard of yer Moonglow. Let us have a shot of that."

Kate set up four shot glasses and deftly filled them to the brim." Kate walked over and was talking to Skippe when a tremendous explosion rocked the town. Kate looked to Skippe and said expressively, "What on earth was that?"

Skip Roper put his hand over his mouth and giggled.

Binder glared at him. Defensively Skip downed his drink with a gulp—then he exploded, "What ta hell is thet," he demanded, gasping for air?

Kate couldn't resist, "Like I told Mr. Wagner, it takes a man to do most things."

Binder looked apprehensively at Skippe—grabbed Skip Doyle's arm and hustled him out the door.

Outside, Doyle shook off Binder's hand and yelled, "Fer two cents, I'd go back in thar and larn that bitch a lesson."

Binder snapped, "Shet yer stupid face, Skip. We dun exactly what we cum for."

"Whut's thet?" Dink asked.

"An alibi, yo stupid ass," Binder retorted, and stomped off down the street.

Buck Dixon punched Dink hard on the arm and snapped, "Yo aer a stupid ass. Did yo see the size of thet big gorilla working behind thet bar?" Neither of them noticed that Kate, from the door, had witnessed and heard the entire conversation.

Gabe and I, galvanized by the explosion, spun our horses around. Wood and debris was still flying through the air from a building far down the street. We raced down the street. It was Swede's place. We hit the door running. We pushed through the wreckage. Gabe yelled. "Anybody need help?"

We heard groans and movement from several spots. I pushed on through the maze of broken lumber and heard a moan. Inside a small office and beside a big safe, I found Swede trying to get up. I gave him a hand and he gasped, "The safe must have protected me from the blast. There were four other fellows in here; they just came in for donuts and coffee.

Gabe hoisted a man in his arms carrying him out the door. Swede and I found an inert body. Swede groaned in sympathy, as he checked the man for injuries. I slung him over my shoulder and waded my way out of the splintered building, as I exited the ruins I saw Gabe rushing back inside. I no sooner had laid the man down, than a man ran up with two buckets of water, and wordlessly handed me one. We both headed for the hot spots. The building wasn't ablaze yet, but there were a dozen places beginning to flame up. We doused what we could and headed outside for more water. We met others on the way in with full buckets. It looked like the entire population had assembled to help, and they quickly formed a bucket brigade passing the full water buckets into the building. I went back outside to check on the people we had carried out. One man was dead. Another was sitting up dazedly and two others were talking to Swede.

I joined them and asked Swede. "What happened?"

"Someone must have opened the back door. I always keep it locked. A man tossed in what looked to me like a bundle of three or four sticks of dynamite; the fuse was sputtering. I jumped to the side of the safe and then all hell broke loose. That's all I remember until you pulled me to my feet.

Pat Desmond had come up in time to catch Swede's story. He asked Swede, "Do you know why anyone would want to do this?"

Swede swore and said, "Damn it, Pat, you know who did it, as well as I do."

Pat said patiently, "Did you see who threw the dynamite in the door, Swede?"

"I can't swear to it, Pat, but it looked like that fellow Dink Wagner."

"Why do you think Dink Wagner is involved, Swede," I asked?

"You saw him in here with Buck Dixon and Skip Roper causing a row a few months back. They work for Joe Binder. He has been trying to buy my bar, but that is just a cover. I'm a partner in a hard-rock mine and he has been trying to force me to sell my shares to him. If he gets his foot in the door, he will get rid of the rest of the owners. He has done it three or four times, and the other partners all disappeared. Unluckily for him—the mines all failed, and he didn't get a plugged nickel. Pat knows all about him.

"I sure do. He never leaves any witnesses or evidence that I can use to arrest him."

"Pat," Gabe said, "Shawn and I have a little time on our hands. Why don't you deputize us and we will begin an investigation on Joe Binder and his men. As we told you the other day, Binder tried to buy our Saw Mill. Isaac Solomon shot at a man that dropped a can of Kerosene that same night after we turned down Binder's offer. Pueblo has too much to lose to disregard the threat that this man poses."

"I don't think the town council will want to pay you. They expect me to get the job done."

"We don't need money, Pat. Just swear us in and we will report directly to you."

We began by questioning every person that had gathered to help put out the fire. No one had seen anything, but finally we got lucky. John Scarbury admitted, "Yeah, I did see something rather strange. I saw that bunch that hangs around Joe Binder. Dink Wagner is a filthy bugger. He wears the same stinking clothes every day of his life. He wears a beat up derby hat with a broken brim, and a filthy sheepskin coat that has the right sleeve tore off at the elbow and it's woven together with a buckskin thong. He claims to be a miner and wears miner boots that look like he picked them up out of a trash can. His blue jean overalls are ragged and have every stain on them known to man; they stink like urine. There are several drunks in town, and I could swear I saw Bull Whacker Davis wearing Dinks clothes staggering down the street behind Swede's place.

I looked at Gabe and exclaimed. "If we can catch Davis with those clothes still on—we might wrap this case up real quick." I turned to Scarbury and asked, "John, could you show us where we might find Davis?"

"I would do anything to help Swede. Let's go."

We found Bull Whacker passed out in a stable behind a row of bars. He still had the overalls on. The rest of Dink's clothes were scattered about the stable, where the drunken man had evidently tried to shed them. We dumped Davis into a wheelbarrow and carted him to jail. Pat jumped up and exclaimed, "I don't want that stinking drunk in here."

Then he saw the clothes and when we explained, he began laughing and said, "Let's take him out the back door. There's a stable there, and I'll chain him to a log and cover him up with horse blankets until he sobers up."

Gabe snorted. "The longer we wait, the more time it gives our suspects a chance to run, or figure out a way to beat the charges. Shawn and I will sober him up. Could you have a gallon of black coffee sent over and we will go to work."

We got the coffee and cups. Jack went to sleep in a corner of the stable. We stripped the drunk down to his underwear, looped a lariat around his chest, and threw it across a rafter. We suspended him standing up. It took about ten buckets of ice-cold water before he snapped out of his drunken stupor. We cut him loose, and let him dry himself with horse blankets. We began pouring hot coffee down him as fast as he could swallow it. After he heaved the third time, his eyes began to focus and he began to fight. Pat came in just then, and he punched Davis in the stomach. He doubled over retching, and heaved again.

Pat just shook his head and said, "I'll be back. You boys have a real chore on your hands." He was right, and more than once we rued our volunteering to get Bull Whacker sober. It was a nasty, heartless, stinking business.

Three hours later Davis was relatively sober. We got Desmond and he started grilling him. Pat never let him know a man was dead by his hand. He began begging for a drink, and he finally cracked up completely sobbing and begging for just a wee nip.

I felt sorry for him. He had been badly used by Joe Binder. Davis would pay a terrible price for the cheap case of whiskey that Binder paid him to throw the dynamite. Marshall Pat put it all down on paper, and Bull Whacker signed it.

Scarbury had stuck it out with us and the three of us witnessed the document. Pat went to the judge to get a warrant, and while he was gone, we took Bull Whacker to a bathhouse, and paid for a hot bath for him. Then we had him shaved and given a haircut, and he put on some clothes Scarbury had rounded up. Bull Whacker Davis looked like an entirely different person, although a bit green about the gills.

I said to Gabe, "I don't think we did him any favor by cleaning him up. He would have received more sympathy from a jury in his former condition."

Gabe nodded his head sympathetically but said, "You're right, but nothing will save Davis now. Just one question? How are we going to apologize to those horses for using their blankets to dry him off?"

When Pat came back with the warrant, and as he set out to serve the papers—Gabe and I sided him. The first thing we learned was that Pinder and his gang had been in The Kentucky Moonglow having a drink with his men when the sound of the explosion had ripped through the quiet of the morning. We went there first—hoping for a lead.

Kate laughed when Pat asked her if Binder and his men had been in. She told us, "They were here alright. That idiot Skip Roper actually giggled when the explosion went off. Binder was his usual oily self. He wanted to buy the Bar. There were five of them. It was the first time I ever saw Dink Wagner wearing something besides those rags he usually wears. He smelled some better," I might add. Something besides Dink didn't smell right, so when they left, I followed them to the door, and she repeated the conversation she had overheard.

Pat said, "You're sure Binder said, "We got exactly what we came for." And then said, "An alibi, you stupid ass."

"I'll write it down right now, so I don't forget it. I would swear to that on a stack of Bibles," Kate affirmed resolutely.

Pat looked grim when we came out of the Judge's office. He now had a warrant for each of the five men for murder. He commented, "I have a bad feeling. Those boys aren't going to give up without a fight."

"That's alright," Gabe replied glibly, "there are only five of them and there are three of us."

Pat stopped and dismounted. He took his gun belt off and extended the size. Then he put it back on over his coat. Gabe and I took off our heavy coats. I had Jack get down and I tied the coat to the back of my saddle. Gabe did the same. "Track" I said to Jack and pointed, and he fell in along behind us.

Gabe gave me a cocky grin, as we fell in behind Pat, but I noticed that his eyes were deadly serious. Pinder had homesteaded a place well east of the railroad tracks, and Pat set off at a canter, which pace quickly ate up the distance. We had just crossed the tracks when we turned into a draw and there they were all bunched up waiting for us. Binder said something—and his men spread out in a row and waited. It reminded me of my meeting with the McCoys at the Little Sandy River.

I said to Pat, "If they make a fight of it, I'll take the two on the right, Gabe you take the two on the left, and Pat you take Binder in the middle. Binder is the only gunman in the bunch.

Pat grunted his assent—he stopped us about forty feet from the group and said casually, "Howdy, Binder. We were hoping to run into you. We want you boys to come into town with us. We have some questions to ask you about that explosion this morning."

Binder had a contemptuous leer on his face and he replied in his usual self assured manner, "I don't know why you would do that, Pat. I'm sure you know by now that we were in the Kentucky Moonglow when the explosion went off."

Desmond was in a no nonsense mood. He snapped, "Binder, we know all about Bull Whacker Davis. I have his confession, and I have a warrant for your arrest, and the men with you. Unbuckle your gun belts, and let them drop or you will be shot."

Binder went for his gun, he evidently thought he was a gunman, but he wasn't even close. Pat took his time and Binder's first bullet struck the ground in front of his own horse, then Pat fired and shot Binder right through the heart. Binder slid out of his saddle—dead—long before he hit the ground.

I was faced with Tuck Doyle and Buck Dixon. They were so slow that I had to shoot the pistols out of their hands. Then, when they each tried to draw a hide out gun, I shot them both in their elbows. Tuck sat transfixed, and began screaming with pain. Buck flipped backwards off his horse and began running and I shot him in his right heel. He went tumbling over and over and then lay flat on his back mouthing every cuss word he had ever learned. I was amazed at his repertoire.

Gabe was faced with Skip Roper and Dink Wagner. Skip got his hand on his peacemaker before he made his peace with his Maker.

Dink threw himself from the saddle and took up a fetal position on the ground and began crying out, "Don't shoot. Don't kill me."

Pat got down and put irons on Tuck, Dink and Buck, and dragged Buck back to the horses. I glanced at Gabe and he was eyeing me curiously. Up until that moment, I don't think he had any idea how well I could shoot, or how well I would hold up in a confrontation. As far as that went, the same could be said about me in regards to his ability, but I had always figured that Gabe was a hand with a pistol and I hadn't been wrong. He was good—very good.

Pat looked up sourly at Gabe and me and growled, "Look at all the work you fellows done caused me. I don't know whether to thank you or shoot you."

Pat was close-mouthed, and he never told anyone who did what, for which I was most grateful, as was Gabe. The town people were amazed at how quickly the mystery of the bombing of Swede's place had been solved. As far as the town was concerned, Patrick Desmond was the town hero. That didn't help the victim, but the town was generous and took up a sizable collection for the man's widow and two children. The Doctor didn't broadcast the details of the men's injuries, and the three men were tried and quickly condemned to die on the gallows. A week later the grisly deed was done, and the townspeople would talk about it for years, but the men themselves were quickly forgotten. Buck Dixon remained cussed to the bitter end. His last words were a torrent of abusive profanity.

Bull Whacker Davis had no idea what he was doing when he threw the dynamite that destroyed the donut bar and killed an innocent man. The dead man left a wife with two children to support. There was no conceivable way for her to get a job to support herself or her children. We all knew that. The fact that he was drunk out of his mind does not make it right, nor does it excuse the dastardly deed. But, Pat Desmond was not just a lawman; he was a lawman with a heart, and a lawman with an excellent sense of justice. Patrick charged Davis with being drunk and disorderly and after talking to the judge, Davis was put in the County Jail for six months. The judge also placed him on probation for life; never to drink again, to obtain gainful employment, and to support his victim's wife and two children until they were eighteen years of age, and then to continue to support the wife until she died, or until she remarried. If he broke his parole, he would be charged with murder. Bull Whacker was not a stupid man, nor a bad man. He sobered up and never took another drink as long as he lived. He drove a logging wagon for forty years for the West Virginia Sawyer Company.

Even with the solace of Gabe McCoy's forgiveness and the forgiveness of the rest of his family that were present in Pueblo, I still couldn't make myself enter a Catholic Church. At least I had solved one problem. I wasn't killing people when I didn't have to. Maybe someday my soft heart would get me killed. If it did—I sure as hell wouldn't know about it in this world, and whatever was waiting for me in the next would just have to run its course, which in my opinion is true about everyone. At least Mom and Dad and Grandpa would know that I had tried, as would the good Lord. After my head wound healed and I remembered who I was, I did keep my promise to Father Tom. I said my Rosary every day.

The next week, I rode out to my homestead. I had wasted away half of the day, when I decided to check out my 160 acres. I took a canteen and a pack with some food and some walnuts, and tossed in a prospector's hammer. Then I said, "Come on, Jack, let's take a walk and see what we have." I started walking through the trees. The forest was pristine. In places there were briars and underbrush, and in others it looked as though someone had cleared out all the underbrush and carried it away. It reminded me of a big park. However, the scene I liked best was the when I found myself in a stand of huge pristine trees. Trees that had suffered the ravages of nature were lying all around in impossible looking positions, some leaning up against and supported by neighboring trees, others had fallen and some were rotted and covered by nature's blanket of small fungus, moss and undergrowth, and others were just beginning their journey to replenish the rich Coloradan soil. I determined that this pristine section of my land would never be touched by the hand of man, and as long as I lived it never was. All too soon I found myself climbing an incline and then I was walking among big boulders and quartz strata that quickened my interest. I came into a beautiful glade. A square shaped boulder sat in the middle just as though it were saying, come on over and rest awhile. I tossed my pack on the rock and got out a sandwich and shared it with Jack. Then I took out a handful of nuts and began cracking them on the rock with my hammer.

The rock was soft and crumbled under the soft pounding. I ate the nutmeats and picked up the hammer. My hand froze. I had seen gold before, and while I certainly was not a miner, I knew I was sitting on a chunk of gold ore that appeared to be fairly rich. I sat there thinking of the fickle finger of fate. Some people spent their entire lives looking for gold, and never found it. Now, twice in my short life, I just walked up on it and there it was for the taking. I had never wanted to be rich. I just wanted to raise horses and earn a good living doing what I loved to do best. I didn't even have to file a claim. The gold was on my own property. I walked around for another hour or so and toward evening I returned to my cabin. I opened the door and as I stepped inside my foot caught the doorsill and I fell to my hands and knees. The crack of a rifle was synonymous with my fall and a bullet shattered the doorframe. I crawled into the room and turned and slammed the door shut with my foot. Jack was growling deep in his throat. It grew dark and I opened the door a bit, and said to the dog, "Jack, scout." He crawled out on his belly and disappeared into the inky blackness. When he came back, he didn't point, so I knew the person was gone. I closed the shutters, lit a lamp, kindled a fire, cooked my supper, ate and shared it with Jack, smoked a Mexican Cigarillo, rolled up in my bedroll and went to sleep. My last thought was—it certainly had been an interesting day.

The next morning I asked Gabe to call for a meeting of the West Virginia Sawyer Company Board of Directors. We held the conference in the meeting room in the rear of the Kentucky Moonshine Bar; The three girls were already there. Shaddock, then Samuel, Micah and finally Gabe showed up with Isaiah. The fact remained—the principals were the Board of Directors.

"Well, as the old story goes," I said as I opened the meeting, "I have good news—and I have bad news—which one do you wish to hear first?"

Patricia laughed and said, "We hear bad news all the time, especially in a bar, I, for one, would like to hear the good news. Her charm was contagious. Everyone chuckled and in chorus they began saying—"The good news—the good news—let's hear the good news."

"The good news," I said, "is—we may all become very rich—" and I dumped a large bagful of the gold ore on the table.'

The girls all gasped and Patricia picked up a piece and exclaimed. "It's beautiful."

Everyone then thronged about the table and picked up pieces of ore marveling about how pretty it was. There is something about white quartz gold ore that enhances a person's eye for beauty. Some person's greed is accelerated to such a fever pitch by gold that they lose complete control of their sanity. I was lucky; I had never had that misfortune. Kate asked the right question, "Shawn, you said we could all be rich. What does that mean?"

"It means that I found it on my leasehold, which means we all share and share alike."

"But, Shawn," Sandra asked, "if you found the gold on your property how does that effect us?"

Gabe answered for me. "Sandra, when we formed the Company, we all agreed that any yields from our individual leaseholds would be common property. This is an unexpected yield, but it does fall under the provisions of the contract we all signed."

I laughed and said, "How much money can one person spend? We are already getting wealthy from the profits of our Saw Mill, and the girls Bar."

"I don't know how much money one person can spend," Micah said, "but it will be fun to find out."

Everyone was laughing and chuckling and admiring the ore, when Gabe spoke up. I knew Gabe well enough to know he was a real skeptic at heart, and he said, "Now let the other shoe fall, Shawn. What's the bad news?"

All eyes were on me and I said simply, "Someone tried to kill me last night."

Patricia gasped, and I thought for a second that she might faint. But she was made of sterner stuff, and she demanded angrily, "How could you give us all this good news when all the time your life might be in danger?" Patricia glared at me with eyes filled with concern.

I had a deep feeling for Patricia, but had never been willing to express it, because I carried such a heavy load of guilt. I still was not ready to reveal my true feelings to anyone, so I replied, "I apologize to all of you. I just thought the good news would help dispel the bad. Besides he was a lousy shot," and I exaggerated and spread my hands wide and added with a grin, "he missed me that much."

"Oh you men!" Patricia exclaimed with a little laugh to cover up her true feelings. "But the fact remains. If someone tried to kill you—who do you think it was?"

"For heaven's sake?" Kate breathed with deep concern. "You don't think it's one of us—do you?"

I explained in all sincerity, "The thought had occurred to me, but that is all it was—an unbidden thought. I honestly think of all of you as family. The truth is—my brother has had trouble with a family in Denver by the name of Brand." I gave them a brief explanation of the trouble Byron had in Denver, and how it had affected Jon Ridge and me, and then continued my explanation,

"I believe some feuds often get started rather innocently, others because there were evil people involved. But even for an innocent feud to continue there has to be proud, evil men, who put honor, pride and decency before love and concern for their fellow man. This does not mean that evil should not be challenged or fought, but it is very easy to mistake revenge for justice. Before Almighty God, I still cannot separate the legality of my actions against J. D. McCoy, as to whether it was revenge or justice. It's like a black cloud that hangs over my head. I carry it with me to this very day. I still don't know."

There was a stark silence when I finished. Then Gabe stood up and said, "I can only speak for myself, Shawn. When I left West Virginia, I left as a wanted man. I am still wanted, but I have heard that the Governor may step in and declare amnesty for all concerned parties. I have had plenty of time to think for myself. The Parson was wrong. He led us down the path of perdition all in the name of religion—his religion. Thank God I never rode with him when he killed your grandfather and your parents. I don't know what it was, but something held me back. He did talk me into going with him when he attacked your home. I can only apologize. My family paid the price. At first I wanted revenge and I rode roughshod over the law in Wayne County. I was dead wrong. Like you—all I can do is repent and try to figure out what to do now. I started by bringing as many of my family as would come with me to a new land to get a fresh start for us all. I don't allow any hate or bigotry to be expressed in out group. I have tried to teach those who followed me that we must first start out with loving one another and allowing it to grow into the community in which we have chosen to live. We have made many friends here. The best friend I have ever had is the man I tried to kill. You forgave me, Shawn and I have forgiven you. That is all that I think God expects of us as long as we continue to love our neighbors as we love ourselves. What do you think, Shawn that we can do to help you with your present problem. How can we stop this killer?"

Emotion had welled up—I cleared my throat and replied, "My dog Jack is my best defense. He has smelled the scent of the person that tried to kill me. Early this morning Jack led me to the place where the would-be-killer laid last night. If one of you were the person that shot at me—Jack would have led me to you this morning. All I can ask is that we all be alert to those persons about us, and advise me if anyone acts strangely. In the meantime, I will contact our Attorney and see if I can find us a good and honest mining man to develop our claim. I love you. God Bless you all."

A few minutes later I closed the meeting. I had a good idea who was after me, but I certainly did not intend to allow anyone in my new group of friends to become involved in another feud. They had moved here to find love and friendship, and from what I had seen, they were doing a fine job of doing just that. But I had a lot to learn about people and friends. Before I was much older I would need every friend I had.

7HE HUNTED

CHAPTER SEVEN

The next day I contacted Maximillian W. Van Fossen, our attorney, and told him of our need. We needed a knowledgeable mining man to develop our new bonanza. Maximillian replied, "You are in luck. The son of a good friend of mine just showed up on my doorstep. He just graduated Cum Laude from the Colorado School of Mines and is looking for employment. His name is Sylvester Vandegard Spencer. Would you be interested?"

"If he's a friend of yours, I couldn't have a better recommendation. What do you say, Gabe?"

"Trot him out," replied Gabe with a grin, "and let him impress us."

Van, as he liked to be called was impressive. He stood five-ten and weighed two hundred pounds of solid bone and muscle. We had lunch with him and his handshake was like iron. George told us, Van had been a Boxing and Wrestling Champion at college. He gave us his credentials, and ended his summation of his credits with, "I transferred to the Colorado School of Mines the last two years and graduated Cum Laude. What do you, gentlemen have in mind?"

I laid a piece of quartz on the table and said, "That's a brand new find for us and you are a brand new Mining Engineer. Would you like to look over our prospects and tell us what you think? We will pay you $200.00 a day for your time."

"You've come to the right man. There is nothing I would rather do than get in on the ground floor. When do we leave?"

"Right now, I said, "Just as soon as I finish this cup of coffee."

When we stepped out of the restaurant, the distant crack of a rifle sounded just after the bullet popped over my head and shattered the window of the restaurant. Jack jumped off the saddle and ran to me protectively. We all had ducked instinctively. I turned to Gabe and exclaimed, "See—I told you they didn't try to hit me the last time. That bullet hit too high. Excuse me a minute, Van, while I take care of the window." I went back inside and tried to smooth things over and told the owner to send the bill for repairs to me at the Kentucky Moonglow.

Van was remarkably composed for an Easterner. He asked Gabe. "Is he always this calm when someone tries to kill him?"

Gabe chuckled and answered, "No sense getting all upset. That restaurant owner was angry enough for all of us."

The first thing I did was to report to Marshal Patrick Desmond about the harassing fire I had been receiving. As I walked out of his office a bullet hit the doorjamb and showered me with splinters. As I brushed the debris from my clothes, Pat shucked his pistol and pulled me back inside.

I grinned and said, "I guess that removes any doubts you might have about it being an accident. The first attempt was made on my homestead twenty—miles from here. Then it followed me here. I went back home and have just returned, and as you can see, the shooter has located me once again."

Pat and I lined up the trajectory of the bullet and came to the conclusion that it had to have been shot from at least six or seven-hundred-yards away. We dug the bullet out from the back wall and discovered it was another slug from a sharps rifle.

"They are obviously using sniper's sights," Pat had growled as he dug out the bullet. "There are plenty of Buffalo hunters that can shoot that well," he added, I could see that he was uncomfortable with the thought.

*   *   *

That afternoon Van and Gabe and I, stood looking at the block of quartz. Van took his rock hammer and dug around the bottom of the huge rock. "Something is not right, yet there is lots of loose quartz around the bottom," he murmured, "Mother Nature dumped this stone here, and time has reshaped the rotten quartz from a huge round boulder obviously from a mother lode ten-thousand years ago to its present nearly squared shape. I will have to dig more under the stone to be sure, and I will need a sieve to salvage the rotten quartz. I am reasonably sure there is not a vein under this slab of quartz."

He walked along the ridge I had noticed before and dug and scuffed the top layer away as he went. There were many round stones, clay, sand and gravel. "This long mound is a terminal moraine," he explained, "carried here by a glacier the last ice age from that direction," and he pointed north. That quartz could have been carried for hundreds of miles, or for a short distance. If you wish, I can check it out for a day or two, but it doesn't look like you have struck it rich. As of now, I would declare it a freak of nature. It's your call, but it will cost you two hundred a day to find out," he added with a grin. "I estimate your piece of ore is worth about eight or nine hundred-dollars, more or less."

I looked at Gabe and said with a grin, "Easy come—easy go. If it is okay with you, I will cover the expense from my share of the profits. I don't hanker to get rich anyhow."

Gabe shrugged, "I'll go with you, Van for a couple of days. I don't think a tenderfoot should be working alone out here when there may be a killer running amuck"

"Company is always welcome, and I can teach you all about geology to keep us occupied," Van said with a note of relief. I had invited Van and Gabe to stay at my cabin for the night. It beat making a cold camp, and it gave me company. I asked Van, "If we get snow, is that going to cripple your efforts to run down the gold source?"

"It won't help," Van explained, "but for what I am looking for it may not make a difference. Let's hope it doesn't snow. "There are certain geological signs I can look for, but from what I have already seen, I will call a halt tomorrow night unless I get lucky, so don't count on anything."

"I won't. You fellows be mighty careful out there. If these people are who I think they are—and you make a strike—they would kill you in a heartbeat and try to jump the claim."

They were inquisitive when I took out a couple of white bed sheets and started cutting them up. I told them, "Jack and I are getting tired of being shot at. Sooner or later, whoever is out there will end it with a kill shot. I happen to be a pretty good woodsman, and with Jack's help, I am going to try and put an end to this nonsense. If it snows, a pair of white pants and shirt will blend me in with the snow. They have to leave a trail, I have a good pair of snowshoes, and if Jack gets tired I can carry him on my pack."

Gabe said, "Why don't you wait and I will go with you. I do pretty well in the woods."

"Thanks, Gabe. But those boys you're caring for need a father image. You and Van be cautious, these guys may not care who they shoot at." He started to argue and I said, "You know as well as I that this is a personal fight. I have an idea who it might be, and I will be better off out there by myself. Thanks for offering, but I don't want you involved in another feud. Not now—not ever."

We talked while I made a simple white covering for Jack. I packed food for four days, and stowed extra clothes and the camouflage suits into my pack. When the fire had died down, I slipped out a back window, saddled Grace and headed off into the wind. I figured there were three or four of them. The shots had been coming too fast today for one man to move around so quickly. Yesterday, we had received a light snowfall. By noon it was gone. They had to be riding horses. I hoped for at least a few inches of snow, then, they would leave a clear trail. Horses would have to find grass to eat if it snowed heavily. The bushwhackers would have to chop holes in the ice for them, if it remained below freezing. Within a few days, I figured they would ride into Pueblo to find a warm place to sleep and a good place to eat. Pat Desmond had every restaurant and every hotel in town alerted to notify him of any new tenants or new diners.

We didn't get the snow cover, so well before dawn, Jack and I rode back to Pueblo and moved cautiously to about 1500 yards across from the town. There I found a high point from which I would be sheltered from all points and before dawn I was bedded down.

I had my field glasses, and canvassed the area around me carefully. My caution paid off. A quarter of a mile behind us, I saw a man riding cautiously toward Pueblo. He rode nearly another half a mile past us and then began looking for a good vantage point from which to shoot. He hobbled his horse in a thicket and with a canteen and a canvas drop cloth dangling from his left hand—his sharps rifle in his right hand—he crept forward and crawled underneath the low hanging branch of a blue spruce—he spread out his canvas, crawled on it, and began sighting in his rifle.

An hour later, I was standing fifteen feet from his left rear, and I had positioned myself so that anyone covering the man could not see me. Jack was sitting by my side, when I said to the man, "I have my rifle pointed at the seventh vertebrae right between the middle of your shoulder blades."

The man stiffened with shock. "Which one of the Brands are you?"

The man didn't answer. I told him, "That Brand pride has got one of you hung, another one shot by his own men, and the third one I shot his thumb off. All I have to do is squeeze the trigger, and you'll be dead. I'll dump your saddle in a defile and turn your horse loose. It's not likely that anyone will ever find your body. I'll give you one more chance. "Which Brand are you?"

A muffled voice replied, "I'm Tyrel—Chance's Son."

"Does he know you're here?"

"No!"

I took an educated guess and said, "So Kyle talked you and your two brothers into stalking and making my life a living hell. When was I going to be executed?"

"The end of this week on Saturday night."

"By whom?"

"Kyle!"

"Are you willing to tell Marshall Desmond that?"

There was long pause before he answered, "Yes!"

"Just one last piece of advice, Tyrel, if you refuse to tell the Marshall the truth, I will follow you and shoot both of your thumbs off, and then blow both of your kneecaps off. I'm through playing games. I'm declaring an open season on all Brands, except, of course, Vance Brand and his family. Now just relax. We won't pull out of here until after dark. In the meantime, you can tell me where your brothers and Uncle are, so I don't have to kill anyone."

I turned Tyrel over to the Marshall just after dark. He complained good naturedly saying, "Why can't you bring your business during Banker's Hours like any civilized person."

"Why, Pat, the mayor himself told me you sat around on your duff most of the time with nothing to do." I'm just trying to keep you from getting bored."

Pat grunted, "Life was quite pleasant until you showed up. Trouble follows you like odor does a skunk. Gabe came in and interrupted our enlightened conversation, soon followed by the Mining Engineer.

"I hoped I might find you here," Gabe said.

"All the bad guys hang out here," I acknowledged. I shook hands with Vandegard and asked, "Well, Van, did we strike it rich, or are we back to being hard working peons again?"

He laughed and said, "Your gold nugget is just that—a gold nugget. The biggest darned nugget I'm likely to ever see. Unfortunately there is nothing under it but dirt. Gabe and I looked hard for the source, but all we came up with was an out cropping of coal."

"Coal!"—I laughed—I thought all the coal was back in West Virginia and Kentucky?"

"Oh," he replied easily. We have a bit of coal here and there in Colorado. Did you hear that Andrew Carnegie, the multi-millionaire, who had invented the Pullman Railroad Car, was going to build a steel mill in South Pueblo? Carnegie uses the new Bessemer Steel making process, and is building plants all over the country. It might interest you to know that once Carnegie builds his mill coal will be in great demand for his new factory. In the meantime, with the railroad at your doorstep—coal can be shipped anywhere, but it costs like hell. I'm afraid that if this vein of coal is as good as it looks you are going to have to get used to being filthy rich. Just don't plan on selling it to the railroad?"

I grinned at him. "Well I guess that includes you. You've just become the manager of a rich coal mine if you want the job. And just why can't we sell our coal to the railroad? I though they were already burning coal?"

He laughed, "It's the wrong kind, but never fear, it will have a good market with residential users. And yes, I will be delighted to develop your Coal Empire."

On the way to the Marshal's office, the night before, Tyrel and I had passed St. Ignatius Parish Church at Thirteenth and West Streets. I closed my eyes until we had ridden by. Each time I passed the Catholic Church, I was reminded of what I had lost, and couldn't seem to find again. Was I going to be forced to kill again, or was it my time to turn up my toes? I shook my head. Jack sensing my concern reached up and nuzzled my hand. I forced myself to clear my mind. Only the Good Lord knew what was ahead for me, and he and I weren't on speaking terms.

The next morning before dawn, I checked in with Pat Desmond. Tyrel wasn't the hard case his cousin Kyle was, and he had kept his word. He said to me, "You could have killed me out there and nobody would have blamed you. My mom told me Kyle was no good, but I had to learn for myself. We were all supposed to meet tonight at the Kentucky Moonglow. If you came in—Kyle was set to kill you."

Pat commented, "Confession is good for the soul, Tyrel. You done the right thing," and he patted him on the shoulder.

Shawn, why don't you stay inside here today out of sight, I'll send out for food. Then, about dusk, we'll take a ride together over to the Moonglow," he asked—and assumed—as he tossed me a marshal's badge.

"Got one of those for me, asked a familiar voice from the doorway?" Jon Ridge was standing in the doorway with Jack in his arms. Jack was licking his face.

We met in the middle of the room and I clasped him to me with one arm and shook his hand with the other . . . I said, "Pat, meet my best friend and partner Jon Ridge. Where in thunder did you come from, Jon?"

"I've been looking for you, Matthew. You're always in trouble, so I came to the Marshal's office figuring he could save me a lot of time. As usual, I was right," he smirked with a satisfied smile.

After darkness set in, the three of us rode up and fastened our reins to the hitching rail in front of the Kentucky Moonglow. I gave Pat the key to the back door; after a couple of minutes; Jon and I nonchalantly entered the bar. The bar was a thumping and a jumping, from the music being played by the musicians that Sandra had hired.

As we bellied up to the bar, Patricia saw me and gave me a big smile and said, "Don't just stand there, get in here and give me a hand."

She poured our drinks and I leaned forward and said to her, "Trouble—get ready to duck,"—and I gave her my most engaging smile. Pat was smart. She hustled off to take care of a customer—keeping one eye of concern on me.

We had added tables and captain chairs for our customers, and Sandra had hired a fiddle man, a piano player, and three waiters for the weekend evening trade. In addition, we had hired a man that could sing ballads better than most.

Jon nudged me and murmured, "In the middle of the room, Matthew."

I searched the room using the room length mirror. I had just located Kyle, when suddenly he and his two cousins rose from their chairs and Kyle shouted, "You maimed me Matthew Shannon. Now it's your turn. Turn around and . . . "

I tossed down my drink—Kyle was still yelling—I saw the Marshal about half way down the bar—and I murmured to Jon, "Just like old times," we both turned, and we both had six-guns in our hands—it's lucky we did. We were facing three shotguns—Kyle was still shooting off his mouth instead of his gun. Three Brands died with a surprised look on their faces, as they were each knocked down from the force of two, 44 cal. slugs in their chests. I half turned—only to see Patricia standing with her hand raised to her horror stricken face.

Marshal Desmond called out in a loud voice, "These are the men that have been stalking Shawn Nack and firing shots at him all over town. Shawn Nack and Jon Ridge have been deputized. This has been a legal shooting." The men responded by cheering and yelling.

Patricia called out loudly, "Drinks are on the house. Let's hear some music out there." Then she came over and took my hand and said, "You okay?

"Sometimes, Patricia, I wonder if this killing is ever going to stop? I had no quarrel with those men. I had never even met the two men with Kyle Brand."

She patted my hand, "I think that some men are just born evil, or mean, or whatever." Don't let it get you down. There isn't a blessed thing any of us can do about men like that. Gotta go," and she left to meet the demands of her customers.

Pat Desmond was still giving orders, "You men there—take hold of those bodies and get them outside. Jimmy, go get your wagon and take these men to the mortuary."

Skippe Skerry hauled out a small barrel of sawdust and scattered it on the huge pools of blood. In ten minutes the mess was cleaned up. The three of us rounded up Brand's horses and stabled them near the jail. I had been doing a lot of thinking about young Tyrel Brand, the sole surviving member of Chance Brand's second family. I talked to Marshal Desmond and told him about the Brand family. I also told him about Tyrel's mother Mercedes. "Tyrel is her youngest son. He is only seventeen years old. If you agree, I will withdraw my charges and put young Tyrel on the Denver and Rio Grande tomorrow morning and ship him home to his mother."

Pat looked at me with a rather skeptical look on his face and said, "Anything you say, Shawn. I hope you don't die regretting it. Keep in mind one thing, old buddy—nice guys like you die out here a lot faster than us hard cases."

The next day I told Tyrel, "Prince, Lucas and Kyle came at us last night armed with shotguns. I killed Kyle. I hate to tell you, but Lucas and Prince were also killed."

Tyrel took it hard that his brothers were dead, but expressed no sorrow over Kyle. He looked at me, his eyes brimming with tears, "I reckon we all asked for it. What happens to me now—a rope—or jail?"

"I've heard your mother Mercedes is a good woman, Tyrel. For her sake, I'm withdrawing my charges against you. In an hour you can escort your dead kin on the train back to Denver. I suspect your mother will beat you half to death, but other than that, I reckon you will live to see your grandchildren grow up. Tell your mother I'm truly sorry about your brothers, but they gave us no choice. One more thing—tell her it's not over until Cotton Brand's in jail, or hanging at the end of a rope." Tyrel looked at me puzzled. "What's Cotton done? I haven't even seen him since we moved to Denver from Texas"

From what I've been told, Tyler, he's supposed to be a holy terror and behind all this trouble."

"If he is"—Tyrel said, "it's news to me.

I put Tyrel on the train to escort his dead kin back to Denver. I joined Jon for breakfast and I asked him, "I'm dying to know where our horses are. Tell me what's happened to them?"

Jon grinned, "Well after you took up flying, we looked all over for you. We never dreamed that you dove off that cliff. None of knew you could fly, so we never looked past the cliff. My brothers thought you were dead, but Barney and I kept telling them that you would show up sooner or later. Barney is now engaged to Tiffany Brand. According to the authorities, Cotton Brand is still the miserable low life that he has always been. The Sheriff and all the police in Denver claims that he runs all the graft and vice in Denver."

I grabbed Jon's arm grinning, and said. "You Indians love to drag out a good story. Damn it—Jon—where, for the love of Pete, did you take our horses?"

Jon laughed outright his eyes crinkling with humor. "Quit worrying. Our horses are in a gorgeous canyon in New Mexico Territory. They are as safe as the Apaches allow us to think they are safe. Geronimo is in Mexico, but that doesn't mean he can't raid back across the border. I have Pat stabled near here and if you promise to be good, I will take you to see him."

"What?" I shouted and jumped up. Everyone looked at us in astonishment. I turned red and exclaimed with an embarrassed laugh, "Please excuse me, I have just received good news."

An elderly lady smiled and stated firmly, "You go ahead and yell. We rejoice with your good news. By the way—is the good news a lady?

I began laughing and said, "I'm afraid not. It's good news about my thoroughbred Palomino Stud.

Everyone began laughing and clapping. Still red of face, I made a little bow and said, "Thank you one and all."

When I entered the stable, Pat saw me and began whinnying and tried to crawl over the door of his stall. I opened the door and threw my arms around his neck. The stableman came up—scratching his head—he complained, "I figured nobody could ride that horse—let alone hug him. Reckon I've seen everything now."

I stayed for an hour with Pat and made over him, curried him, and fed him a lump of sugar every once in a while. While I was working with Pat, Jon brought me up to date. I asked him, "How is Barney's romance coming along. Have they set a date?"

"Nope!" Every time they set a date, Cotton comes up with more of his shenanigans. He trades with the Indians—sells them rotgut whiskey and rifles—and keeps them riled up most of the time. He has the Arapahoe, Cheyenne and Utes in his pocket. Gossip says that the only person able to keep Cotton from taking over the town is David Cook. David was appointed a Major General of the Colorado Calvary, and he was elected Sheriff of Arapahoe County. He also owns the Rocky Mountain Detective Agency. Gossip says that Cook is trying to get appointed as a U. S. Marshall. Brand has a loose knit band of cutthroats to do his dirty work He owns several bars, cathouses, and he owns several legitimate businesses, yet he has managed to keep a very low profile, and no one is sure of what he does own. Most people regard him as one of their most prominent citizens. Yet I have never seen him, nor has anyone seen him that I have talked to."

"I have had enough of Cotton Brand, Jon. As long as he lives, he is going to make the O'Shannon's as miserable as he can. I'm going to Denver and contact Sheriff Cook. With his help, I'll see if I can get myself appointed as a deputy. Then I'll rid Denver of the thorn in its side. You want to go along for the ride, partner?"

"Jon snorted, "You don't need a partner—you need a nurse-maid. You don't get out of my sight. Every time you do—you get into trouble."

I laughed, "That's what I need alright—a Cherokee nursemaid."

Two men had entered the stable and were listening to our chatter.

They stepped forward, and Buffalo Who Kills Many White Men, accompanied by Four Hands, said, "You both need Kickapoo nursemaid. We go too."

Four Hands asked, "Where we go?"

Jon and I answered in unison—Denver

Later, as the four of us rode to the train station, I had time to think. Just who was this mysterious Cotton Brand? Everyone seemed to know, or at least to believe that Cotton Brand was the king pin behind all that was evil in Denver. Yet when I tried to pin them down—not one person had ever seen the man, or knew anyone that had, or even knew how to get in touch with him. Were these stories just more gossip like it had been with Gabe McCoy? Was the man really as evil as everyone said? For that matter, did the man even exist? Little did I know that I was soon to learn the answer to my every question—much to my dismay.

*D*ENVER QUEEN CITY OF THE PLAINS

CHAPTER EIGHT

It was after 10 PM when I heard the key rattle in the lock, and the door swung open. I waited till it was closed and then I whispered, "Barney—it's me—Matt. Turn the lights on—then close the window blinds. As usual your place is being watched."

Barney snorted, and mumbled, "Tell me something I don't already know." He turned one light on low; pulled the shades, and I stepped out of the closet with a big grin. He grabbed me and gave me such a hug I thought my ribs would crack. Thanks for the letter. I acted on it immediately." he said in my ear, "it has been six months where the heck have you been."

"I won't be here for long—if you don't turn me loose," I managed to gasp. "I hope you don't hug Trinity that hard."

He chuckled. "Always the comedian," and he murmured to himself, "don't ever change," and he grinned all over himself."

"My Kickapoo friends and Jon are camped outside of town waiting for me."

"Kickapoo, what kind of Injun is that?"

I laughed, "You asked that the last time I was here. Your education is dreadfully lacking,"

"How do you keep getting into my room," he asked curiously, "I have both keys to my lock."

I waggled a skeleton key before his eyes, "The same way I did when I saw you the last time. There's a lot you don't remember about your wayward brother. No mere lock can keep out "Man Who Flies Like a Bird." Seriously, besides wanting to see you, I'm here to report to Sheriff Cook.

He took me by the arms, and we squatted facing one another. "There is a lot of catching up—then we will talk about Sheriff Cook."

I told him what had happened to me since I saw him last. "I didn't tell you in my letter, but Kyle Brand recruited three of his nephews and tried to harass and then kill me while I was in Pueblo. To make a long story short, you can scratch three more Brands." I tried to move on, but he insisted I tell all that had happened.

When I finished, he exclaimed, "That sure beats all. I've been here nearly four years, and I've done better than most. You've been here less than one year and you've made two fortunes, and along the way killed some of the worst skunks in western history. Now you come breezing in here with your tail on fire, and want to take on the most dangerous outlaw in the west. Yeah, 'Man Who Flies Like a Bird,' you keep on with this undercover work and you are going to get yourself killed," he groused, as he pulled me to my feet. He hissed in my ear, "And God help Cotton Brand whoever he is?"

I sat in the hotel's straight back chair, after Barney left to get Sheriff Cook. The longer I sat—the harder the rungs became. I couldn't walk about the room, when no one was supposed to be there. My brother was being watched much more closely than I had heard. It had been hard for me to part with my new friends in Pueblo. Every time I made friends, it seemed for one reason or another that I had to move on. I guess it's a good way to make a lot of friends, but hard to establish any lasting relationships. Gabe had insisted that he come with me to cover my back. But Gabe's entire family rotated around him. He was the hub in the wheel. Like it or not, he was the father and big brother image for all his brothers and cousins. I knew if Sandra had her way, he would soon be a husband. The company we had formed needed strong leadership; Sandra and Gabe were those leaders.

My parting with Patricia had been rather awkward. I certainly wasn't worldly-wise about women, but I wasn't so naïve that I didn't recognize a woman's interest in me. I had been more than just interested in Pat. She was everything a man could desire in a woman. Pat was an outstanding beautiful woman, slimmer than most young women of our era. She had slim features and a glorious, head of jet black hair. She had a special quality that reminded me of someone or something, and for the life of me, I could not put my finger on it. When I couldn't figure something out, it was usually so close that I couldn't see the forest for the trees. I could not allow myself to become interested in anyone, because I had more dirty linen hanging over my head than a Chinese laundry washed in a month. Furthermore, I couldn't shake my gloom and doom demons long enough to give my heart to anyone. Then again—maybe she just wasn't the right woman for me. As mixed up as my thinking was—there wasn't any way I was going to get involved with Patricia and mess up her life with my baggage. Was it just the situations that I could not control; or was it my black-Irish instinct to fight anyone that threatened me or mine, or, for that matter; anyone that needed my help? My thoughts came to a screeching halt. Someone was trying to open the door, and they weren't doing a very good job of it. I ducked into the closet and held the door open a crack to see.

It was a pretty girl. As the light caught her face I could see the heavy make up. She looked to be a dance hall girl. She walked over to the bed and sat down. A moment later I heard the sound of tearing cloth. And then we waited.

Fifteen minutes later the sound of heavy footsteps—the noise of the key in the lock, and then the door swung open. The girl jumped up, and let out a scream chocked off by my hand clamped over her mouth. I said to the startled pair, "Sheriff Cook, I think I have a customer for your jail." The girl quit fighting me when she heard me say Sheriff Cook.

I removed my hand, and the harlot sobbed, "Thank God, Sheriff you got here in time to save me from this maniac."

Barney had been busy and the light flared up as he put the chimney back on the lit lamp. "Sheriff, I said grinning, "That's the first time I ever saw a sobbing, molested woman without a tear in her eye," and I took my thumb and made a swipe under her dry eye.

Sheriff Cook snapped, "That's enough of that garbage, Madge—we saw what happened. It's fortunate that Mr. O'Shannon has a bodyguard. Now get out, and report to me at the jail tomorrow morning." As she started past him, he stopped her and said, "You must be dimwitted to take a job like this, Madge. Nobody in this town is going to believe that a man like O'Shannon would try to molest a dance hall girl, now get." And he gave her a slight push down the hall.

As soon as she left, Cook suggested. "I just saw the cook leave as we came in. Let's go downstairs and help ourselves to some coffee. We can talk in private down there."

Cook was a good listener. I told him, "As I told you before, the Brands started a feud with my brother over a personal matter. The Brands carried the fight to me and my friends while I was still enroute to Denver. We had no idea that Barney was involved in a full blown feud with the Brands. The Brands attack us no matter where we are, or what we are doing. I'm sorry to say, there are a lot less Brands today. However, everything that my men and I could find out about this gang is that the Brands are the rooks and bishops in a much bigger game. The top gun appears to be a man reputed to be Cotton Brand, and his organized band of troublemakers. Everything we have found out since I saw you last is that Cotton Brand is just a name to throw off suspicion of the person that is really in charge of this operation. As you told me in the beginning, the gang is real enough, and they are always bragging that the man in charge is Cotton Brand. Yet he is nowhere to be found. He owns a nice home, but no one is ever seen coming or going from his house. With your help, we were able to get some personal banking information on him, but while there are substantial deposits made from time to time to his account there have never been any withdrawals, nor has anyone at the bank ever seen the elusive Cotton Brand. Someone else opened Cotton's account, and is making the deposits. No one remembers who opened the account. As far as Cotton Brand is concerned, he is like the little man that never was.

This gang has been riling up the Indian tribes so they can profit through the sale of rot-gut whiskey and weapons. We have learned that the Indians are being led by renegade white men and half-breeds to attack specific incoming and outgoing Denver freight wagons. The renegades are said to give the Indians cheap gaudy stuff and the main cargos are taken into Denver and sold through legitimate businesses. We know who they are because we planted good merchandise in freight wagons that was stolen, and it turned up and was sold in competitor's stores. It has taken us several months to build this case. We have invoices and witnesses to the sales of these items.

Your own organization has reports of several miners in outlying areas that have been reported killed and their gold stolen. We have learned the number of miners reported killed is just the tip of the iceberg. News from the mining areas trickles slowly into Denver, and unless you are there, going from mining camp to mining camp, it is hard to get the complete picture." I took a map of the known area and showed them our findings. There were dots all over the map. I told them, "Each dot represents a miner killed and his gold stolen. The gang members try to cover up the scene of the murder and try to erase all evidence of a mine ever being there. From what we can ascertain through my Kickapoo Indian friends, it seems that the Brand Gang has enlisted a splinter group of Arapahos led by an Indian that calls himself Chief Black Cloud. We think he is an educated half breed that is using renegade white men and half breeds to recruit young hot blooded Indians to kill miners to get their gold so they can buy rifles and whiskey. The renegades spy on the miners from a distance with binoculars. When they figure out where the miners are hiding their gold, the renegades then guide the Indians to that camp, kill the white men, plunder the camp, and cover up all signs of a claim The Chief uses the gold periodically to buy whiskey, rifles and ammunition from the gang. We think the Chief and his half breeds are only using part of the gold for rifles and whiskey. We can't prove it, and it only makes sense when you start adding up all the claims these Indians have robbed.

We are familiar with the area now, and with your guidance, we can lay an ambush for this group and put them out of business. I have two Kickapoo and one Cherokee, and I have grown up in a Cherokee environment. We make a good team. You deputize us and we will bring you evidence to not only stop the Indians, but also put a crimp in the Brand Gangs activities. Jon Ridge and I know Blackstone's Law Book inside out. We know the Rules of Evidence, so you can rest easy about our not arresting the wrong people. We only need to catch one or two of these groups in the act and with the evidence we already have, and the evidence you have, we can put these people away for good. So what do you think," I asked and sat back to give him a chance to reply?"

David Cook turned to Barney and asked, "Does your brother carry on this way all the time?"

Barney replied rather primly, "He does talk a lot—now that you mention it."

"Matt," Cook said grinning, "Technically, you and your men have been sworn in since your letter to me through your brother arrived six months ago. You have been deputies without pay. But, I hired you as detectives working for my Detective Agency. You all have six months salary due you—plus you are all eligible for any rewards that are outstanding. Keep these badges hidden until you need them," and he handed me four badges. "I have a man whom I will introduce you to; he will act as your liaison man. His name is Dennis Hobbit. He handles horses for those a step or so outside the law, but only because I set him up in business to help me run down wanted men. Go to his place any time after dark, and you can pick up horses or supplies. Ignore any others that might happen to be there. Don't talk to him unless you are positively sure you are alone. All I need now is for you to catch the renegades in the act of selling the rifles and whiskey to the Indians.

"You fellows have done an excellent job. It ties in with all that I know. I have an area where I believe the Brand Gang and the Indians meet to conduct their business. It is a large area, but with your special skills, you should be able to pin down their meeting place. Take a month's supplies and check this area carefully," and he drew a large circle on the map. If I don't hear from you in a month meet me back at Hobbit's place.

I reported back to the others. "We're in business, and have been for six months," I said laughing, and I handed out the badges. I explained Cook's instructions and said, "There's a trail north of here that Cook wants us to keep an eye on. Anything that comes up, we are on our own, as to how we handle it."

Dennis Hobbit equipped us with three pack mules, and a month's food supplies. We rode until late afternoon the next day before we began looking for a good spot from which we could observe any freight wagons, or mule trains that might look suspicious. We scouted the trail, and set up a listening post on a bluff that overlooked a busy intersection. At night, we split up in pairs, so that we could follow anyone that went in either direction on either trail. Jack loved our game, and was a real asset. With him on the move scouting around—no one was going to slip up on us. A few cowboys coming and going kept us alert and on our toes. A couple of ranch wagons loaded to the top of their three-foot-high gated sides passed by loaded with months of grub for their ranch, they were always guarded by several cowhands. Four small, well-guarded herds of steers passed us going into market. Denver was a big city, and the sale of beef kept many a rancher in business.

Before dawn broke, we took to the brush and kept to patches of forest when possible. Each hill we crested, we stopped, and Jon and I checked the terrain carefully with our field glasses before we crossed over. An hour later, I sent Buffalo on ahead to scout for us. He was a master of any terrain, and when alone, he blended in with the flora as naturally, as though he were one with the fauna of the locale. An hour later, as we paused before cresting a hill, my glasses picked up Buffalo. He circled his hand above his head and then pointed to his feet. Buffalo wanted us to join him.

When we rode up, he said, "Brush is all trampled down. Wagon tracks go east off trail into trees."

Take a look, Jon. You know what we need."

Jon took Jack with him; we didn't see him until he appeared in some open beaten-down underbrush, and they began looking for tracks. Then he turned east—he and jack jogged out of sight following the wagon tracks. When he rejoined us, he reported,

"Good eye, Buffalo. I followed the tracks for half an hour. The trees are sparse, because the land is so rocky, and the trees mostly grow along the streams and rivers. The tracks go over a small rocky ridge, and after five minutes, they stop at the edge of a small stream. The stream follows the contours of a cliff for several miles. There is a small grove of trees, and a mountain meadow at the campsite. That's where they have been meeting. There are Indian pony tracks all over the place, and there are deep tracks from heavy freight wagons. They have camped there several times, and I found the remains of many fires. I picked up this piece of a broken arrow, and this medicine bag. The Indians have been posting warriors on the rocky ridge, as a rear guard."

Four Hands took the items and said. "The arrow is Arapaho, and the medicine bag is Sioux."

"The first thing I think we should do is circle this area and check it thoroughly so we know every bit of the area in case we need to get out fast. Once we are satisfied, we will do the same with the campsite. Then we must check the other side of the creek that cliff across the creek offers us some good possibilities to eves drop, attack, or defend ourselves. How recent are those tracks, Jon?"

"None recent. My best guess is at least a month—maybe more?"

Once we checked the top of the cliff, I was satisfied. There was no sign of any Indians having been on top of the cliff. We had to ride three miles to find a way to the top. I took out our map and pinpointed our present location. We were close to the middle of the circle that Sheriff Cook had drawn. Jon laughed and said, "That's one Sheriff I'm glad is on my side."

Buffalo took one look and commented. "General know what he do. Is good."

I nodded and said, "Here's what I think we should do. If anyone disagrees speak up. We have access to water. We will camp well back of the cliff, and take turns standing guard near the cliff edge. If the renegades show up, we will have to decide then, as to how we will handle the situation. We have enough food for two more weeks. Let's get comfortable."

Trees edged the meadow on the creek side with mostly willows and some cottonwoods hugging the banks of the stream. Behind our cliff position, the land sloped away a quarter of a mile to a huge mountain meadow. We all found protected firing positions along the cliff edge. Then we sat and waited—hoping for something to happen to break the monotony. Ten days later, late afternoon, Buffalo, who was on guard came back and said, "They come!"

Two heavily loaded freight wagons lumbered up to the side of the stream; the drivers yelled, "Whoa!" The wagons answered the description given us by David Cook. Each wagon carried two men armed with rifles and belted pistols. There had not been the usual joviality or chatter on these wagons. They were all business and exceptionally alert as they stepped down stomping their feet awake. One man walked out to the middle of the field and picked up a twenty foot pole. He tied a white cloth to the top, and inserted the bottom into a hole prepared for it. The white flag fluttered in the breeze, an open invitation to someone. The men unhitched the horses, left the harnesses on them, and staked them out where they could graze.

We crawled with Buffalo to our selected firing points. The freight wagons had pulled right up to the bank of the creek where the willows had been tramped down from previous visits. An hour later, we picked up a long line of Indians riding down a switchback trail on a hill about a half-mile northwest of us. A few minutes later about fifty Arapaho Warriors rode up whooping and hollering and crowded around the two freight wagons. An Indian chief wearing a distinctive war bonnet jumped down facing the man from the lead wagon. One man began talking to the chief with a great many gestures and use of his hands.

Four Hands told us, "Their Chief is Black Cloud. We know him—he half breed like us. He warrior like Geronimo, no real chief. He full of hate. He talk young hot-blooded warriors to follow him. He no welcome with Arapaho Tribe. He raised in Baptist Missionary School. He speak good English, but pretend he dumb Indian when talk to white man. The white man is using sign language; he speaks some Arapaho. He say, Chief Black Cloud is a great leader. Armed with white man's weapons, he can stop the white man from stripping the earth of its yellow metal, fouling the streams and killing the buffalo."

Four Hands exclaimed, "Man trade Indians Henry rifles. We call Henry rifle 'Yellow Boy,' because receiver brass. Indians get Yellow Boy, they better armed than soldiers."

Jon muttered, "Brand must be out of his mind. That's the rifle, near the end of the Civil War that the Confederates claimed the Union Soldiers loaded on Sunday and fired all week."

"If you really want to get angry, Jon, get angry with the Military. They still arm the soldiers with single shot, breech loading trapdoor; Springfield rifles that use .45-70 cartridges The Indians will have fifteen shot lever action rifles that use the same ammunition as the Russian .44-40 pistol.

Four Hands shushed them and continued, "White man tell Arapaho, kill miners and take gold. Arapaho pay Brand's men with gold. One of the white men set up a table and was quickly weighing out the gold on a small set of scales.

Through my binoculars I could see the Arapahos were paying four ounces of gold for one rifle, and one-hundred-bullets.

"Look—see there," exclaimed Four Hands, "four half-breeds. They spy on miners from the hills with spy-glass. They see where miners hide gold—they lead Arapaho to kill white men and steal gold." An hour later Four Hands grunted again "Now look see—men sell whiskey jug for one ounce of gold."

Buffalo asked me, "What you do? We no fight so many."

"You forget, Buffalo, that we've picked the field of battle. We are on a thirty-foot cliff, and the closest trail up here is three miles away. We will fight dirty—just like they do. We'll wait until they get drunk. Then we shoot—then we run like hell."

Buffalo grinned and asked, "Who we shoot?"

"We shoot the horse handlers first and stampede the horses. Then we shoot the leaders. We will try to kill the four half-breeds, the four white renegades and Chief Black Cloud. The rest we will only wound in the legs. We don't want to massacre the entire bunch. If we have to, we will kill their horses out from under them. We will empty our rifles—reload and maim as many Indians as we can—then we head for Denver. Jon will register at the American House Hotel at the corner of 16th and Blake. Buffalo, Four Hands, and I will meet our contact Dennis Hobbit, and tell him what we have accomplished. He will find a place for Buffalo and Four Hands to hole up. I will then register at the same hotel Jon does. Hobbit will tell Sheriff Cook what's going on. The miners have to be warned. I imagine the Sheriff will have some more work for us to do. We keep a low profile until the Brands are in jail or dead."

Half the Indians were already drunk. As soon as they got a bottle, two Indians paired off, and they began taking turns at the bottle. However, Chief Black Cloud was no fool. He and twenty of the Indians were not drinking. They spread out and casually formed a defensive perimeter. I tapped Jon on the arm and said, "Look at that, Jon. That Black Cloud is a fox."

Four Hands said, "I no understand. Indian no discipline. They want whiskey. They take whiskey."

"Black Cloud has a remarkable control of his warriors. It goes against everything I have learned about Indian behavior." I observed thoughtfully.

Jon chuckled and commented, "That Chief speaks better English than we do, Matt. I just wonder when he graduated from West Point?"

"He most likely went to the same school as Chief Joseph of the Nez Perce. I just read that Colonel Gibbons has chased him all the way across the country from their Reservation in Washington State, when the Chief decided to take his people home. He is badly outnumbered, but the Chief has whopped them every time the Army attacks him."

The four white renegades were not drinking. Cotton Brand had them well disciplined. Within an hour thirty Indians were staggering drunk or passed out on the ground. They were whooping and hollering and having a hell of a good time. It seemed a shame to ruin all their fun. I called out to the others, "These men are worse than killers. We don't dare allow them to walk out of here able to sell guns to Indians, who would in turn kill innocent men, women and children. I want all the leaders with holes in them. It's your decision—fire when ready. We were less than a hundred yards from the main body of men. I steadied a bead on the Chief legs, and then shifted my aim and shot him between his eyes. I could not risk allowing him to live. He had too much control of his men for me to risk his living to give them orders.

Jon and the two Kickapoos had stampeded the horses. The four half-breeds fell dead of lead poisoning and within thirty seconds three of the renegades were dead and the fourth wounded. The twenty sober Indians disappeared at the first shot, and were already returning our fire. We were looking down on them and it was hard for them to find cover. We shot at thighs, ankles, and shoulders—the damage was devastating. They had only clumps of grama and Buffalo grass and scrub brush to find shelter behind, and most of that was trampled down from previous visits. We were all crack shots and the Indians never had a chance. Several drunken Indians snapped out of their stupor and began firing at us, but we stopped them cold by shooting them in the legs and shoulders. The Indians that remained in one piece were going to have a hard time taking care of that many wounded men."

Cease fire," I called out softly. "Anybody hurt?" I asked.

Buffalo said, "Chief bad Indian. He half breed like us. He bad Injun, now he good Injun."

Jon grunted, "I got creased a couple of times. That one Indian down there had me zeroed in, and I had to take him out."

I noted the regret in his voice, and I said, "Get the horses together, will you Jon? I'll be down in a few minutes." I waited; it was suddenly going from dusk to dark. Across the creek, I could hear them cautiously moving about. Then what I hoped for happened. The one renegade had to have a light. He lit one lantern, and checked his companions; they were obviously dead. He sat the lantern on the wagon seat, and went back and lit the second lantern on the other wagon. I steadied my rifle on the side of the tree I stood behind. Angled down, the bullet sliced through the lantern and the seat, and the wagon was quickly engulfed in flame.

Suddenly a shot sounded from behind me, and the second lantern exploded into a ball of flame. Jon chuckled and said. "I figured that was what you were up to. You always want to hog all the fun."

We could see figures scurrying about, and then someone jumped into the wagon to save the whiskey and rifles left in the wagon. We both fired and heard a cry of anguish. We peppered the entire area emptying our rifles, and then took off running down the hill. The fire lit up the sky outlining the trees from across the creek into stately monuments. The sound of the ammunition exploding was like a tornado shattering a town into a thousand bits and pieces. We leapt on the backs of our horses and thundered off with Buffalo Who Kills Many White Men chanting a Kickapoo war song as he led us back to Denver.

The next morning, after my usual shave, I went downstairs for breakfast. Jon was already seated and reading a newspaper. I walked over and said, "Jon, what a pleasant surprise. I never expected to run into you." Jon had registered as John Rogers and I had registered as Shawn Nack.

Jon looked up in surprise; jumped up and exclaimed. "By golly—if it isn't Shawn Nack. Last I heard you were getting rich down in Pueblo." He asked, "Won't you join me?" We shook hands and sat down as a waitress came bustling over to take our order. She was all eyes and smiles for Jon. We settled for steaks, eggs and country fried potatoes, and I told her to bring us a big pot of red hot coffee.

We were eating a piece of blueberry pie when I said, "We have to go back, Jon.

"You reckon there will be much left?

"We have to have evidence for the Sheriff. If word of this action leaks out and he is connected with it, he must have proof of his righteousness, or he might find himself in an embarrassing situation."

"When do we leave?"

"Now's as good a time as any," I said stuffing the last chunk of blueberry pie into my mouth, while pushing back my chair, we saddled up and headed for Dennis's place. We took a wagon, and Buffalo insisted on driving, his horse tied to the back of the wagon.

Jack, and I, and Four Hands scouted the route carefully. We cut across country so that we came upon the Indian's camp from the north. I stopped every few minutes, and checked the terrain carefully. Buffalo and Four Hands stood guard a good two-hundred yards away, one north, and one south. I sent Jack slinking through the woods looking for signs of the enemy. Then we closed in on the scene of the action.

The ashes of the wagons gave up lots of evidence. We found the ruined frames and barrels of forty rifles, and I even found an intact box of .44 cal. ammo that had been blown out of the wagon when the lantern exploded. The Indians had not buried the three white men, but they had taken their dead and wounded with them. We wrapped each of the dead men in a blanket and laid them in the wagon. The Arapaho had also taken the four half-breeds with them. We checked the area where the drunken Indians had been and found several artifacts to take with us as proof. Broken crocks lay everywhere; and we found one jug still full. There were the double tracks of a dozen travois leaving the area, mute evidence of the carnage we had created.

We were getting ready to leave when Jack came up to me, then turned and pointed. We all took cover. Jack had started off and finding himself alone, he turned and looked back. Ron grinned at me, and we realized the dog wanted us to follow him. Ron and I trailed Jack cautiously, and he led us to an unconscious white man. It was the head teamster. He was still alive. Sheriff David Cook was going to be one happy lawman. Buffalo dressed his wounds and I blindfolded him and tied him securely. I sent Four Hands on ahead to tell Dennis to find and send Sheriff Cook to meet us on the trail into Denver.

We took our time and a few miles out of town, the Sheriff stepped our from behind some boulders and said, "Pull in here, boys, while we have a powwow."

He took a careful look at the renegades and said. "I know them all. They each have a price on their heads" You boys get out of sight, and he pointed to the wounded man. The less he knows the better. He dragged the leader out of the wagon, dumped him on the ground, and removed his blindfold. He took a canteen of water and poured it into the man's face. "Quit playing possum, Blackjack. It ain't gonna to do you any good."

"Who the hell is playing possum, Sheriff," he sputtered with a whine. "I been shot three times, and my merchandise and goods been stolen or burned. I got a bill of sale for all my stuff. I was taking my goods to Leadville to sell to those miners up yonder. Are those men I heard the yeggs that set upon an innocent merchant and nearly killed me?"

"Aren't you leaving out the parts about the Arapaho, the half breeds, the gold, the rotgut whiskey, and the rifles, Blackjack," the Sheriff asked? He questioned the man for five minutes and didn't even learn his real name. The Sheriff came back to us and said, "I'm getting nowhere fast."

"Let us go back with you," I suggested, "only this time we will put sacks over our heads so he can't identify us to any of his gang . . ."

"What's his last name?" I asked the Sheriff.

"Blackjack is all we know him by," he replied.

Jon laughed, "He's from near Parkersburg, W.Va." We played baseball against him. His name is Jimmy Woodson. Seems some of his family settled near there. He was quite a pitcher."

We went back with the Sheriff and Jon said heartily, "Hi Jimmy how's things in old Parker's Ferry? Have you played any baseball lately?"

Blackjack gave a slight gasp and said nothing.

"Now that we know your name, Blackjack. I'm willing to bet you have a record there. You may even have a reward on your head?" Sheriff Cook suggested.

Blackjack's face turned ashen white. "You dumb snoop, you got it all wrong," He snarled.

"Reckon I'll send a wire over there, It might be worth my time," mused the Sheriff.

"I'll make you a deal, Sheriff," Blackjack said pleadingly. "I'll tell you everything you want to know, which will be enough to hang me—but only on one condition. Whatever you learn from that wireless don't go no further than you."

Cook nodded his head and said, "It's a deal—but only if you tell me the truth of what I need to know—and then only if you hang."

"The boss of our outfit is Tornado Slim. He never leaves Denver. That's all I know."

Cook laughed. "I know Slim. I know he works behind the scenes in an awful lot of shady deals, you have told me exactly nothing." Sheriff Cook sat down and wrote out a message. He handed it to me and said, "Would you have one of your men run this up to the telegraph office and wait for a reply. Have him send Doc Newsom to the jail, we will be there shortly. Tell him it's me asking."

"Now, James, suppose you tell me who you got the rifles from?"

"Slim told me to pick up two wagons and take them to just past the crossroads and turn right and go to a creek and stop. I didn't know what was on the wagons."

"You just told us that you were a merchant on the way to Leadville, and that you have bills of lading for all your merchandise. You lie so much, you should take notes to keep your stories straight. We have four witnesses that saw you take rifles and whiskey off the wagons and sell them to about fifty Arapahos for four ounces of gold for the rifles and one ounce for the whiskey."

"They lie. I never done no sech thing."

Jon exclaimed, "If he says I lie—I'll have to shoot him again." He whipped out his pistol and laid it on the nose of the renegade.

"I can't allow that while I'm here," Cook stated firmly, "I better leave and allow you boys some leeway." Sheriff Cook said, as he walked away. "I haven't got much time fellows. Do it quick."

Jon thumbed back the hammer, and when the man didn't blink he pretended to slip and discharged the weapon beside the man's head.

James Wood grabbed his ear and screamed with pain.

Sheriff Cook walked back calmly and lit up a cigarette. Five minutes later he said, "Can you hear me, Blackjack?"

Blackjack nodded sullenly, and rubbed his head.

"I want to apologize. I told them to shoot you. I didn't mean to cause you any pain." He looked at Jon and said harshly, "Do it right this time," and he started walking away.

"Don't bother, Sheriff," Woodson stated, "I'd rather be hung than go through that again."

"Tell it straight, Blackjack, or I'll just let them hang you now and get it over with."

"I do work for Slim. But I'm a cautious man. I followed him one night, and he led me right to the source. He takes his orders from Cotton Brand. We used to take orders from his kids, but that Shannon guy killed them all off. Damn him all ta hell, we had a good thing going until he came along. I've been selling rifles and whiskey to the Indians since that new Winchester came out in "73." I ain't one damn bit sorry I done it. All I done was give the Indians a fighting chance," he claimed in false bravado.

"That don't cut it, Blackjack. There is no such person as Cotton Brand. Who did you see? I'm getting sick and tired of playing games with you, Jimmy. Give me the straight goods or I'll leave you to the tender devices of these fellows."

"I'm telling you the truth. I followed him to that big house they say belongs to Cotton Brand. I looked through the window and I saw Slim talking to a big man sitting back in the shadows. I couldn't see his face, neither could Slim. So help me God that's the Gospel truth."

I saw Jon nod his head, and from what I knew it sounded like the truth. The Sheriff shook his head and said, "I think you're telling some of the truth. Nobody in their right mind would trust a thief like you with anything important. A lot of men died out there last night, and a lot of innocent people will die from those rifles you sold to the Indians. James Woodson, alias Blackjack. I have no choice but to charge you with selling rifles and whiskey to the Indians among a dozen other charges."

The next day we received the news. The Prosecuting Attorney could not charge Cotton Brand with anything, which of course was obvious. Woods hadn't seen Brand's face. The word of a man like Blackjack against a reputable man like Cotton Brand would never hold up in court in any event.

I told Byron, "We are back to square one. But at least we have stopped this particular group in their tracks and have them up on serious charges. It's better that we keep our mouths shut in public, and keep as low a profile as possible."

Blackjack's trial was swift and sure, and the testimony we had gathered against Tornado Slim was enough to get him twenty years in prison. Our evidence against James Woodson was devastating and the newspapers had a field day. A week after he was convicted, Blackjack was hung by the neck until he was dead—dead—dead—.

Sheriff Cook left the telegram from West Virginia about James Wood laying out where I could see it. Woods was wanted for the murder of his own wife and child, but you can only hang a man once—if you do the job right—and Arapahoe County did it right.

*   *   *

Byron was in the Cattle Buying Business. He represented the interests of a small Meat Packing Business that furnished beef to several large cities including Chicago. They specialized in prime beef, and Barney had to be most selective when it came to buying high-grade beef. My brother had earned himself an excellent reputation in his chosen field, and he was well paid for his expertise. I remembered the fifteen hundred head of cattle that my partners and I had purchased. I talked to Barney about them, and when he showed an interest, I invited him, his fiancée, and her father to come along and make it a holiday-business trip.

Trinity and her father were entertaining friends who owned a ranch near Santa Fe, New Mexico Territory. I had not met them, but invited them to come along with us and make it a hunting safari. They were delighted, and our entourage included Jon and I, my two Kickapoo Indian friends accompanied by Barney, Vance, Trinity, and her four Spanish friends. Barney hired six men and two Chinese cooks to tend the four wagons loaded with tents, equipment, food, and presents for all my friends at my former home. When I learned of all the people we would have along, I asked Trinity to help me buy extra presents for everyone that was to attend. I sent a messenger with a letter to Cap and Talley to announce our coming.

The night before we were to leave, Jon and I were invited to Vance Brand's home to meet their guests. Brand had a beautiful Victorian two-story home loaded with gingerbread, as we boys used to call the fancy wooden frill that edged the outside eves etc. The house was located conveniently near Saint Patrick's Catholic Church in North Denver. Unlike most of the immigrant Irish that settled in Boston and New York, the Irish that settled down in Denver were acculturated, and except for their excessive drinking habits, I was pleased to see that the Irish were well accepted in Denver. The ladies were not yet present when Jon and I arrived. Vance introduced Jon first, "Don Patrick, meet a full blooded Cherokee Indian, Jonathon Ridge. He is a member of the family, and Mathew's partner."

Then he said to his friend, "Don Patricio Miguel Valesco, I would like to present to you Byron's brother Matthew Michael O'Shannon." Patricio wore just enough Spanish clothes to let you know that he was a little Irish, and a little Spanish. I noted that the people here didn't generally speak of the Spanish as Mexicans, unless you were in the manual labor sections of town. "My pleasure, Don Patrick," I said as I shook his hand. "I must say, you look more Irish than I do."

"I should, Mathew, my father was a "Brick House Irishman from County Clare Ireland."

"And," I added with a laugh "My Great, Great Grandfather was Lace Curtain Irish from County Cavin, Ireland."

"Don't leave me out," grinned Jon, "my Great, Great Grandfather was Chief of the Cherokee's, U.S.A."

A sweet vibrant voice broke into our conversation. "Well then, that should make us one big, happy family."

I half turned and three visions of loveliness so filled the room that I was rendered speechless. The visions swept forward, and the eldest said simply, "I'm Victoria, Patricio's sister and duenna for these two lovely young ladies. I took her hand and my eyes met and clung to Victoria's for one wonderful moment. Laughingly, slightly red of face, she disengaged my hand, and at the same time smoothly transferred my hand to her niece's hand saying, "This young lady is my niece, Teresa, and this little sweetheart is my niece, Lucy." Patrick's youngest daughter blushed and took our hands, and by this one act of gentility enslaved Jon and me forever. Teresa was eighteen, had graduated from School, and was every bit the charming young lady. She had all the earmarks of a real heartbreaker. Lucy was sweet sixteen and never been kissed, or so I assumed.

Teresa and Lucy didn't walk off, but stayed with Jon and I. Teresa said, "We are all ranch girls, and we are delighted with your invitation. We love to hunt, and we all learned to ride before we could walk."

Lucy, like her sister Teresa was straight forward, and very direct and to the point. Lucy said, "You can ignore Victoria. She runs the house, but Teresa runs the ranch." I got from Lucy that she and Teresa were both Tom Boys, and that Victoria was the accomplished Lady of the family.

Lucy was irrepressible, I asked her, "And who do you run?"

Teresa laughed, "Lucy runs us all, Matthew, or at least she thinks so."

Teresa's eyes boldly checked Jon and I, she knew how to handle herself, and she asked us. "I do hope you have some good horses for us to ride. We wear skorts, and ride astride the horse."

"Jon," I suggested, "Lucy, your thoroughbred Arabian, would be a great horse for her."

Lucy de Valesco giggled and exclaimed, "You have a horse named Lucy?"

"I did, Lucy. But, didn't I tell you, Matt. Someone stole her."

I struck my forehead with the heel of my hand. "I forgot to tell you. I got her back. Barney, didn't Four Hands bring Lucy to you?"

"He sure did, Jon, I give her back to you with the greatest reluctance—even though she eats like a horse, and I can't keep enough sugar in my pocket to keep her happy."

Jon's face lit up. "How in the world did you get Lucy back, Shawn? I spent a week looking for her, but it rained and washed out all the tracks."

"Remember Jerry? He stole her, and unfortunately for him, Jon, we crossed trails. He saw the error of his ways and gave the horse back to me, I asked Four Hands to return her to Barney."

Four Hands and Buffalo, dressed to the nines had come in and Buffalo said, "Jerry no steal again, he try bushwhack Shawn Nack, Man Who Flies Like a Bird."

I tried to catch Buffalo's eye, but like Cap, he was a storyteller, and I doubt I could have shut him up even if I choked him, Which,

I felt like doing. The ranch girls were fascinated; they asked just the right questions, and goaded Buffalo until they got the entire story of my flying naked through the trees and my fight with Jerry.

When he finished Teresa looked at me and said, "Well aren't you a caution. I never dreamed you were that Shawn, the Man Who Flies Like a Bird?"

I flushed like a school girl and growled. "I flew just like a dodo bird and lit on my head. I am now just as smart as Barney, Jon and my two Kickapoo Indian friends. Now that they have told you all my secrets, I will introduce them to you.

The story broke the ice, and we had a delightful evening. The next morning, our Safari pulled out for the plains for some great hunting. Knowing they were ranch girls, I rode my stud Pat. This can sometimes be embarrassing to those not accustomed to ranch life, but which ranch persons just ignore, and accept as a matter of course. We had a big ramuda of horses, but we had two horse-drawn Phaeton Carriages if the ladies got tired of riding. Victoria and her father, and Trinity and her father did indulge themselves.

Two Chinamen were driving these rigs, and did a good job, as well as proving to us that they were indeed great cooks . . . "Do you speak English," I asked them?

"Speak good English. Work on railroad many years. My name Kee Lin and my brother is Jo Lin."

"And your third brother is Chi Lin, and he works for me and my partners," I told them.

They exploded with excitement. I explained. "Chi Lin has looked for you boys for long time. He is married and has a baby." It took me a while to get them settled down. I turned away and nearly trampled Teresa and Lucy.

"That was nice of you," Teresa said, "the Chinese fare badly with most Americans."

I grinned self-consciously and replied. "It just comes natural for us to treat all people as equals. My Mother and Father were always helping people, and we were always taking them somewhere, or helping out someone. The Cherokee are like that, they help others all the time. They make great neighbors. My Mother must have delivered half of the Cherokee children. The night she and Dad were murdered, they were off helping a river woman deliver her baby. A gang of thugs killed them on their way home."

"Oh! I'm so sorry," Lucy exclaimed and she instinctively laid her hand on my arm. Teresa is like that," she explained." She is always dragging home both human and animal derelicts."

Two days later we got exceptionally lucky. Jack, well in front of us, pointed. When we snaked forward, I was surprised to see a small herd of about thirty Buffalo leisurely grazing in a small lush valley. How do you want to hunt them?" I asked the hunting party.

Teresa replied, "Well, I for one don't wish to shoot a sitting duck, as it were. Let's go in at a run, and get our game sporting style."

And that's what we did. We allowed the women first hunt, and the three of them charged down the slope at a dead run. Each girl picked out a young calf and rode up beside them; amid thundering hooves each got their game. These ladies were born to the land and fit in the hunt as though they were warriors of a tribe of Indians. We men thundered past the girls, and each got a bull. Our safari men came up and began skinning the buffalo and butchering the meat. Buffalo and Four Hands had contacted their friends, and they were trailing well behind our safari. After we carried off all the meat we could use, the Indians made short work of what was left.

Six days later, loaded with game, we cut back west, and Buffalo led us right to my former home. When I saw the huge lodge, my eyes brimmed with emotion, but I made sure no one saw me acting like such a baby.

We made a great entrance thundering up to the hitching rail, and jumping out of our saddles. Cal Mason grabbed me and swung me around in a circle. He whispered in my ear. "Thank God you came back. It was as though I had lost a son. I'm so sorry for my rash words."

"Thank you, Cap. You make a great father."

Talley Short gave me a big hug, and said, "Welcome home, Shawn, we missed you."

Chi Lin ran out and hugged me by grabbing one of my legs. He hadn't grown much. When he saw his brothers, I thought he would have a stroke. He would rattle on as fast as he could talk in Mandarin for a while, and then cry, then grab my leg, then hug one brother, then hug the other one. He was a basket full of Chinese happiness. The members of our Safari watched in fascination, and I saw the girls wipe away a few tears. As the madness died down, I grabbed them one at a time and managed to get everyone acquainted. Teresa seems fascinated. I explained, "Most western men do look down on the Chinese. They treat them like dogs. I wasn't raised that way. They are fine people, and, while they do work for us, they are like family."

Tally Short showed our guides where to put up the tents and insisted that the ladies take over the bedrooms downstairs and the men would all sleep upstairs. The girls were impressed with the indoor bathrooms. The smell of roasting beef permeated the air. Talley had built a huge roasting spit that could cook an entire beef. Before long we were all standing in line with our plates filling up with heaps of savory food.

The next morning, after breakfast was squared away, Cap Mason took over. He gave our guests the grand tour of the beautiful cabin that Buffalo, Four Hands and I had built. I was delighted with the glass windows that had been installed during my absence. Cap kept saying, Shawn did this and Shawn did that, every time he did I would gladly have dropped through the floor. Then he made a quick tour of our mine, The Mint. It was a repetition of Cap's saying Shawn did this, and Shawn did that. He told them about the Mint and our calling it the Shamrock in order to throw the Brand spies off. Of course, he had to tell them all about the battles we had and the consequent Miner's Court.

After breakfast, Cap led us through the back door, and we found our horses all saddled and anxious to go. Pat nickered and came to me and nuzzled my neck. I fed him a lump of sugar, and then mounted, and pulled Jack up in front of me Cap pointed out all the improvements, and we stopped and Talley told the story of the lake that was already showing the promise of being the deep lake that I had envisioned.

Cap next led us to the Shamrock Mine. He told the story of my discovering the mine, and my coming out of the mine with the nugget in my left hand, and having to kill two unknown assailants with the rifle in my right hand. He ignored my protests with a big grin, he had a good story and was a good storyteller, and he didn't hesitate to embellish the weak points. When he finished, he gave each person a beautiful piece of jewelry gold. The women were all thrilled with their gifts, and Cap got all of their attention. Barney was enjoying my discomfort just as much as Jon was. Then we rode out into the valley. I was impressed with all the improvements. Slim Albright rode up and met us with a big smile. He stuck out his hand and said, "Welcome home, boss."

"Good to be home, Slim. You must be a tough ramrod. It looks like you didn't give those poor bulls any rest at all." The bulls had been busy and there was a bonanza crop of young calves running all over the range. The cows had thrived on the buffalo and gamma grass, and were fat and sassy looking. "You and your hands have done a mighty fine job, Slim."

Barney rode up and introduced himself to Slim and said, "I knew Shawn was great at raising horses, Slim, but I never knew he could raise cows. I'm impressed, Slim. If the entire herd looks this good, "I'll be one of your best customers."

"Slim knows who raised these cows, Barney," I said," and it wasn't me. Slim and his cowhands have done a great job, and each time we make a sale, he, and his boys, will get a nice bonus." Slim grinned his pleasure.

We rode the length of the naturally shaped valley that had been formed between two steep slopes. It was close to six miles long on this side of the house, and ranged from two to three miles wide There were six springs, and the cowhands had walled each one with white quartz. They then piped it to a large metal water tank below. The spring itself was left for nature's creatures. Four additional, extremely large, hay barns had been built spaced along the valley. The ground floor had been left open so the cows could find shelter during the winter or hazed inside during severe blizzards. The southern end of the barn was left open, the northern end walled up. A couple of walls had been erected inside so the cows could always find a place out of the cold winds. I noted, Cap had invested and stored several reaping machines to cut the hay.

"Slim," I called out, "Where's that big brindle bull that knocked me silly the last time I was here?"

"He's most likely up one of those canyons guarding his cows. We had a puma sneaking around, and he got one of our calves. "Big John" has been hunting him ever since."

"One thing you might do when you get time, Cap, I suggested, is have those four hands build a small dam at the end of each one of the branches that run down off the mountain. It gives the cows more watering holes, plus it saves the water from running off down the mountain. It soaks right back into the ground in time and helps keep the springs from drying up."

The end of the valley had been fenced off. Two double-wide gates had been provided for easy access. Slim said, "I took you up on your homesteading idea, Shawn. My 160 acres begins where the valley floor opens up into a beautiful meadow. I have a small cabin just ahead. I've planted soybeans on most of the land. Cap said he would be my best customer."

Cap Mason came up and added, "Like you suggested, I homesteaded our home area in our three names, which includes the house, outbuildings, and the two mines. This valley of ours goes on past our house for three miles. I talked Judd Jenkins into homesteading at the end, and we have a fence like the one here at the beginning of his property. I'm sure you noted that the sides of the valley have been fenced off with natural barriers. The men used downed trees and heavy brush to seal off the branch runoffs or small canyons that weren't desirable. The canyons that we used are box canyons and have excellent graze. They nearly double the size of our holdings.

As you suggested we dammed up the area below the house, where it makes that dip, and directed the run off from the mine into it. It proved to be a bigger job than we figured, so we paid an engineer to dynamite a few overhangs. He put those draft horses to work to sled down some big rocks to fill in the base of the wash. We got rid of most of our slag pile from the Mint Mine by hauling it all down to the wash. We can safely back up twenty feet of water. The engineer used concrete to make spillways to carry off any excess water, so we don't overload our earthen dam. With the snow and rain and natural runoff, we already have a nice sized lake that will guard us against any bad draughts. Talley has been busy stocking it with bass and trout, so if anyone wants to drop a line while they are here—we have the fishing gear."

"We have a herd of a hundred horses running in the valley below the new lake. It took a hell of a lot of work to seal off that section. Horses aren't as docile as cows when it comes to staying home."

"What is Judd growing on his homestead?" I asked Cap.

"I asked him to grow corn, Shawn. With all these horses, we're going to need a heck of a lot of corn. The four farm hands put in a four-acre garden for our use. They added to our fruit cellar, and I purchased eight hundred quart and half-gallon mason jars. I have already hired Kee Lin and Jo Lin. They are coming back once they close out the work they were doing in Denver. They will do most of the canning."

That's okay, Cap. But I have already hired Kee Lin to be my cook in New Mexico. Jon has us a place all set up down there. Jon's brothers expect both of us down there yesterday."

Vance Brand caught us all together and suggested. "You have your land pretty well protected, but there are a lot of "Land Sharks" out there looking for places like this to come into the middle of, and file a homestead claim. Get yourselves a good Real Estate Attorney in Denver to arrange for you to buy or lease this land from the Government, and you can save yourselves a lot of grief."

"Thanks, Vance," I said, "that makes a lot of sense. Maybe you can point us in the right direction to find such an attorney?"

He grinned, "You're looking at him. That's what I do for a living. Pay me a two—hundred-dollar retainer and I'm yours."

Barney laughed, "There's nothing like keeping the money in the family."

"I'll have to give you two-hundred more, Vance. Jon and I have a place all set up down in New Mexico."

Vance Brand grinned and quipped, "Lord Byron and his brother, Man Who Flies Like a Bird, have spoken. Let it be so." Vance teased Barney from time to time calling him Lord Byron, and now he was already picking up my bird name. The title fit Barney and after awhile we were all doing it. I was already stuck with my 'bird 'name.

Jack squirmed when he heard Barney's voice, and I let him slide down. He ran to Barney, who grinned and said, "He knows his master's voice." Jack jumped up, and Barney caught him, and was rewarded with a kiss for his efforts. "Such sloppy affection," he groused.

After supper that night, Vance Brand stood and tapped the side of his glass with his spoon and said. "I have a little announcement to make. "I am happy to announce that my daughter Trinity and his Excellency Lord Byron have finally set a date for their long anticipated marriage. They wish all of you to attend their nuptials next month on Saturday the 25th, followed by a Mass to be held at 10:00A.M. at Saint Patrick's Parish in North Denver. The Reception will be held after the Mass at my home in North Denver. The happy couple will honeymoon in San Francisco for two weeks.

Everyone cheered and congratulating the happy couple. Barneys face was wreathed in smiles and Trinity's face was flushed and happy. Cap called out, "Chi Lin break out the Champagne."

Cap sidled up to me and said, "I never get a moment in which to speak with you privately. Now your brother tells me you are all leaving tomorrow morning." While he was talking he was leading me into his bedroom. I was surprised, as he closed the door; I could see that he had divided the room in half. The front section was a nicely laid out office with a beautiful Oak Roll-Top-Desk set up against the wall. We sat and a timid tap came on the door; when Cap said, "Come in."

Chi Lin came in, his face beaming. He had two champagne glasses filled to the top. He giggled and said, "No want you miss toast."

"Thank you Chi Lin. Sit the drinks on the table here."

Cap lifted his glass and said, "Here's to Byron and Trinity."

After we drank, I raised my glass and said, "To Ryan Ballard. A blessed—good man. We will always cherish his memory."

Cap said, "Amen!" We both drank with tears in our eyes.

"Ryan had no family," Cap said. "He left his assets to his three partners." Cap took a bank book from a pigeonhole and handed it to me. Several entries had been made, and the balance column read $158,125.00 dollars.

Cap was watching my reaction, and he laughed and said, "It's real. That's your Savings Account deposited with the First National Bank in Denver. From the looks of it, you will be a millionaire before long. You need to go see the bank people in person, sign some papers, and open a checking account. You might need some cash before then," and Cap handed me a stack of bills with a wrapper that said $5,000.

Cap sat back with a satisfied smile set on his face. I hear your partner Jon has already found you a site for your horse ranch. Congratulations! Don't forget—this is your home. I hope you will be spending more time with us. Is there anything you would like to have done while you are gone?"

I grinned. "Cap, you know that I always have something on my mind, how about we give Slim and Judd a hundred cows each, so we can have some struggling rancher friends down the road." I took about half of the money Cap had just given me—put it in my pocket, and gave the rest back to him. Split that between Slim and Judd. We don't want them to struggle too much."

The next morning, we ate an early breakfast; amid the tears of Chi Lin, and the smiles and heartfelt wishes of our friends, our Safari Party left for our trip back to Denver. We hadn't been gone for more than an hour. Those of us wishing to hunt were spread out in a skirmish line with Jon and I in the middle. Jack pointed and I kneed Pat up to Jack and said, "Flush them, Jack. He sprang forward and a huge covey of quail erupted at our feet. I got off four shots and Jon shot three times, and there was a scattering of shots on down the line. Jack placed four quail at Patrick's feet and three at the feet of Pocahontas, then he raced down the line placed two quail at the feet of Barney's horse Mike, one at the feet of Teresa's horse, and the final two at the feet of Don Patricio's horse.

Barney explained to Vance and Patricio what had happened, and how Jack always kept count, but said nothing else. Victoria came over to see Teresa's kill, but by this time Teresa had come along and was looking at the headless quail that Jon and I had shot.

Victoria rode up, laughed, and said, "I see you have Jack trained well. He gave you the most quail."

I smiled and replied, "Jack is one smart dog, and he knows who feeds him." I slid out of my saddle and tossed Jack one of the quail. He disappeared into the brush to have his breakfast.

Suddenly Victoria gasped, "My God—you shot their heads off. No wonder you can kill men so easily." She wheeled her horse away and galloped down the line to where she stopped, and I could see Trinity comforting her.

Teresa, with fire flashing in her eyes exclaimed, "Please excuse her, Shawn. She went to a boarding school back east, and she came back a spoiled snot. That's real shooting—you to Jon." She looked me up and down; shot an approving glance at Jon, and said, "You fellows are real cowboys," and she raced off her laughter trailing along behind her.

Jon looked after her approvingly, "Now there's a girl you could cotton to, Matt. She's all women and tough as leather."

"What about you? You gonna stay single all your life?"

"Oh—didn't you know—I've got one all picked out?"

I was surprised. Jon ran deep. He didn't tell me everything right away. He always waited until the situation was ripe. I snorted, "Who's going to look at a runt like you. Last I heard Mama Ridge couldn't even get one of your 'kissen kin' to date you."

"Patricia said to say hello the next time I saw you."

"Patricia who?" I demanded.

"Patricia McCafferty—who else? You introduced us down in Pueblo."

"Moonglow McCafferty," I shouted? "Well I'll be tee-totally damned." I laughed and slapped him on the back. "That's great—that's wonderful," I declared. "She's perfect for you. I'm glad you asked my permission. I'll give away the bride."

He snorted. "I should never have told you. I might have known that you would try to hog all the limelight."

"What do you think a "Best Man" is for?" I challenged. "Besides, she is my partner. I have to protect her best interests."

"That ends this discussion, because I," and he pointed to himself, "am her best interests."

"What do you have to say to that—Mr. Sharpshooter?" Teresa asked, as she rode up.

"Not a thing, Teresa. I never argue with a woman."

"You're smarter than I thought," Teresa murmured. She flashed me a golden smile, as she rode on. Teresa always seemed to be handy when anything came up, but she was still too shy to just come up and ride with me. Every time I tried to ride with her, it was the same thing in reverse.

"There is one thing in which your partner Patricia never confided with you, Mr. Sharpshooter," Jon said with a hint of mystery.

"Maybe so," I replied, But, as my partner, you are going to have to get used to being rich," and I tossed him the check book Cap had just given me.

Jon took one look and replied. "I have to admit that caps the Coal Mine in Pueblo, but this is one thing you can't cap. For your information Patricia McCafferty's maiden name happens to be Whitehead, She is a full blooded Cherokee, and her roots are even deeper than mine."

My mouth fell open and I doffed my hat to him and said, "It couldn't happen to a nicer Cherokee. And yes, her being Cherokee is much more important than being a partner in a rich coal mine and a partner in two gold mines. You have always been luckier than I, especially when it comes to women. I bow to my superior," and I swept my hat in a wide sweep that startled Pat and he humped and bucked a couple of times just to let me know how frisky he really was."

Teresa descended on me again and said gaily, "First it's coal mines then gold mines and then you can't even control your horse, or your women. I'm beginning to think you do need a keeper." And she rode away laughing.

We had a great time hunting the rest of the day. It was a constant stream of game all morning. As usual the later the day, the less game we saw until evening came and shadows began to fill the valleys. A herd of antelope took off running, and several hunters wasted their lead. The plateau leveled off, and the herd was running hard nearly three-hundred yards away. Jon lowered his 24 inch Henry rifle, set the sights, wet his index finger, and held it up gauging the velocity of the wind. Then, quite deliberate, he leveled his rifle aiming carefully, and then took his shot at a big running buck in the middle of one of its amazing strides. To me the buck appeared to be a moving dot on the prairie. I wasn't surprised to see it tumble over and over. I had seen Jon shoot deer at four-hundred-yards before. Everyone was amazed. They all came up to Jon and congratulated him on such a magnificent shot. We camped near the spot where the antelope and taken its final leap.

Buffalo looked the buck over and commented; "Only one who has the eyes of an eagle can put bullet in heart of that which I can barely see."

Four Hands looked at the antelope—then at Jon and said, "We have—Man Who Flies Like a Bird, and his companion—Man With Eyes of an Eagle—we are most fortunate."

Vance Brand began clapping his hands and calling out, "Bravo, Bravo." Everyone joined in, but I noticed that Tate Slocomb, the leader of our guides and porters, was standing to the rear—he was frowning—he was not clapping—he was not calling out, Bravo. My sixth sense kicked in; I instinctively knew—'Something from Denver was rotten as hell.'

I turned to Jon and said, "That's one hell of a shot, brother." As I passed him, I whispered, "Something's wrong, watch Tate."

"Thank you, brother, I will." Jon replied casually.

Jack was at my heels, and I said softly, "Jack, guard." The dog stopped and looked all around, and then looked back to me. Casually, I said, "Come on, Jack," and when he was at my heels I repeated the command, "Jack, guard." This time Jack never broke stride. He had the message. That evening I had the opportunity to warn Barney and Vance. Vance tried to stop me, but I walked on past him and muttered, "Be casual, Tate's a rat." Barney' usually relaxed posture stiffened, and I knew he was reviewing his knowledge of the men he had hired in Denver. Not for one second would he not take my warning seriously. He had lived with Ma and me for too many years and seen every one of our premonitions too well demonstrated to ever doubt us.

Was Cotton Brand up to his usual tricks, or was I letting my imagination run away with me? Mom told me to always trust my instincts. She told me that when she first started having her flashes that she had been just as troubled as I was. I had learned to do just as she said. How can one separate instinct from a premonition? I never did, and I had never had any reason to regret it. Because of my instincts, I had learned to take nothing for granted. Every night before I went to bed, if at all possible, I checked my weapons, and I often said my rosary while I was working. I often wondered if I was not being warned by my Guardian Angel instead of just having a premonition. There was really no way to tell the difference. After we began having troubles with the McCoys, I also started checking my weapons every morning when I got up. Was this the mark of a gunfighter, or was I just being prudent?

The first chance I had, I told Barney and Jon of my concern. They both knew of my gift, and had seen it in action with my mother and me over the years. We took turns checking the camp all night. When I rose in the morning, the first thing I did was put on my hat. This I had learned to do since I came west. When I awoke, I woke with my every sense alert and demanding. I checked my revolvers carefully. My Russian pistol had an eight-inch barrel and a better range than most pistols. It commonly shot a .44-40 Henry rim fire cartridge using the common black powder, metal cased shell. Smith and Wesson had made two-hundred thousand revolvers for the Russian Army. The weapon had won gold medals in every contest for accuracy at the Moscow International Exposition of 1872. I knew Jon and Barney would be just as careful as I was, but I could not be sure of the rest of our group. In addition we had four women to protect.

I talked to Buffalo and Four Hands and told them, "Take no chances. Get us back to Denver as quickly as possible. My instincts tell me we are on a war footing. Don't trust Tate, or any of his men, but protect the women and the Chinamen. Be sure to recheck your weapons, but do it under cover."

Buffalo gave a muffled Kickapoo curse and exclaimed, "My rifle is empty." It was the same with Four Hands. They quickly reloaded.

I said, "That settles it; I'm getting rid of Tate and the men with him right now. Back me up." I shucked out my rifle, and as we went toward where Tate and his men had camped, I warned Barney to get the women out of danger. Tate's camp was a sham. It looked like six men still sleeping, but when I kicked one of the figures it revealed bunches of grass made up to look like a sleeping man. In the darkness of night it might have fooled us.

I gathered all our people together and told them, "Everybody please listen. We may be in serious trouble. Tate and his men are gone. Check your rifles, they may have been unloaded. Take just what you need. Leave the tents and the wagons, we can send men back for them. Barney, would you take two men and the two cooks, and get some food together. Store the food and our soogans in just one wagon and harness to it the four draft horses. We reassemble here in ten minutes."

Patrick asked, "Matt, why did Tate leave the horses and the food?"

"Because Barney and Jon and I were up and making the rounds all night. Buffalo and Four Hands were the only ones close enough to their camp for them to take the risk to unload their rifles. I think their intention was to unload them all, but Jon and I were too close for them to take the chance. Something is going to happen, my instincts are screaming, but I don't know why. We have to be careful of an ambush. It will either be Brand's men, or the Arapahos, or both. Let's post two guards now and eat breakfast. Tie the horses securely. If we are attacked now, we have water and a good field of fire."

Don Patrick took the horses and led them to a low point in the streambed. He tied each one securely to the willow trees along the bank. When done, he came to me and said, "The ladies and I will watch the horses."

Kee Lin and Jo Lin went to work. They cooked a simple, but filling breakfast, and immediately began cleaning up the utensils. Teresa and Lucy jumped in with a will. Don Patrick's three girls all wore gun belts as naturally as the men. I saw Barney talk to Trinity. She went into her tent; she came out armed the same as the Velasco girls. With the help of the women; everything was quickly cleaned and packed in the wagons. I knew Don Patrick had extra rifles and I asked him, "Don Patrick, if you would be so good as to outfit the two cooks with weapons. Make sure they know how to use them."

The Don laughed and said, "I gave them weapons and lessons the first day. They can take care of themselves if it comes down to that." Our mounts were saddled, the wagon loaded, and horses harnessed to the three wagons. I turned and said to the group, "Unless someone has a better idea, I have asked Buffalo and Four Hands to scout and lead the way. Jon and I will ride in front of the three wagons—then the women—then the rest of you fellows can cover the rear. If we are attacked Jon or I will call out what to do. Let's keep bunched up. We don't want to be caught spread out. Make sure you have plenty of shells in your pockets, and make sure you have your canteen on your person, and that it is full of water. Any suggestions? Any questions? Okay—let's ride."

It was noon before Buffalo spotted an Arapaho, and only another Indian could have done that. Soon another young brave appeared and he had on war paint, and immediately took a shot at Four Hands. He and Buffalo returned fire and he disappeared. Buffalo told us, "He young fool warrior. He's out ahead of his war party trying to get his first scalp. You wait—we go—look see."

Jon shook his head. "Better we stick together, Buffalo. We know they are out there, and with those shots, they know right where we are."

"Jon's right, Buffalo. Pick us out some high ground, or, better yet, someplace with water and shelter for us to hole up in." It was a hot day and I didn't want the women and horses to have to lie out in the hot sun. The Indians had lost their opportunity to jump us unprepared. That gives us a chance to pick our own battleground. Obviously, their plans had been interrupted. As we proceeded, we began to pick up the sound of regimented rifle fire. Half an hour later,

Buffalo and Four Hands came out on a small rise. They pulled back taking cover. They signaled Jon and me to come up and survey the situation. Two things were instantly obvious. Spread out in panorama was the source of the rifle fire. A squad of soldiers was ensconced on a small knoll. Five men were lying in a prone position. Kneeling behind them were five more men. Standing behind them was a grizzled Buck Sergeant n command the five men fired, and while they reloaded, the kneeling men behind them could fired on command. It was well controlled, aimed fire, and only when needed. Below the top of the knoll a soldier was holding the reins of their horses.

While the Indians wanted glory, they did not want to die getting it. The soldiers had seen them first. They had taken a defensive position, and were waiting for them. I could see six Indian bodies. I figured the Indians had been within fifty yards of the soldiers before they were fired on. The Indians were now about two-hundred and fifty yards away. Most of them had taken shelter in a small draw. When they showed themselves, the Sergeant in charge fired on them. What the Sergeant didn't know, but what we could see, was that half the Indian force was going around them hoping to take them by surprise from the rear. Unless we did something, the soldiers would be wiped out. If I did help them, I was placing our entire party at risk. There was no doubt in my mind that this batch of Indians had been looking for us when the soldiers stopped them.

"What do you think, Jon?

You always know the right thing to do, Matt. Just do it, and let the chips fall where they may."

The soldiers had single shot weapons. Their average was three shots a minute, six at the most. Their Sergeant had increased that with his tactics, but I knew the Arapaho had sixteen shot Winchesters. The soldiers wouldn't have a chance. When I first came west and learned that frontier soldiers were only armed with single shot weapons—I couldn't believe it. Trust the Army to do it the Army way, which from what I had learned, there was the right way, the wrong way, and the Army way.

Jon stayed with the two scouts. I returned to our group and led them back down the slope until we ran into the creek. We turned and followed the stream until we came to a small grove of trees, mostly willows, a few scrub-oak, and every so often a cottonwood. The position was far from perfect, but it should provide adequate cover for our needs. The stream curved, and the winter run offs had created a bank four and five feet high and across the stream was a jumbled nest of rocks. The position had good possibilities. I explained to Barney, Vance and Patricio the situation and they agreed,

"Get the soldiers down here, and we will teach those Indians how we can talk with a Winchester, "Barney said with his lop-sided grin. "I'll take care of our defenses here—get going."

I headed up the slope toward the sound of the intermit firing. Jon spotted me and I gave him the sign to assemble, and pointed to our new location. In another few minutes I was in sight of the besieged solders. I fired my pistol in the air three times; the soldiers jerked around alert to a possible new danger. I pumped my rifle over my head several times and then pointed to where I had seen the encircling Indians. I then gave him the sign to assemble with my group. In a minute the soldiers were mounted, and thundering down the slope toward me. I knew the Indians would be right on their heels.

Barney had worked fast. He had the entire Safari Group ensconced on the edge of the stream where a shelf had been created by high water. Barney had strung the wagons behind the position and ran the horses across the stream into the protection of the rocks. The stream made a right turn and piles of debris were heaped on the inside turn of the stream. Bedrock was exposed, and huge boulders dumped by the glaciers added to the debris. It was a better fighting position than I had first thought. If we were threatened with being over run, or encircled, we could regroup amidst the boulders; it was good shelter for the horses. I rode right to the corral, Barney had set up. Jack jumped down, and I said. "Stay, Jack, guard." Jack lay down on a shelf, from where he could see the horses, and any approaching danger. The Cavalry slowed, and came in wary of a trap.

"Relax, Sergeant. I called out. These ladies won't hurt you."

He looked around and saw the women, and his face picked up a bit of color. "You didn't know it," I told them, "but you saved us from the trap those Indians had set for us. You can see our defenses. If you agree with my plan place your men in the rocks to cover our horses and our backs. We all have Henry Rifles, but for your information—so do the Indians. We will give them a good reception—if you back us up."

He grinned and ordered "Dismount" put your horses in the corral, Private Barnes; you are detailed to guard the horses. Men, form up in the rocks. Be quick, the vermin are at our heels."

The Arapaho were already half way down the slope. A War Chief had stopped on a high point five-hundred-yards from whence he could direct the attack. I yelled, "Jon, see if you can take out the chief."

Jon stopped, set his sights—tested the windage—aimed and took his shot. The Chief swayed on his mount, and then toppled off his horse. The Arapaho were spread out coming straight in whooping and uttering blood curdling cries—determined to overrun us in one sweep. Well over a hundred painted Indians were coming intent only on killing and taking scalps. At one-hundred yards Barney yelled fire. Eleven Henry's belched fire, and I saw seven Indians knocked off their horses, and two others trying to stay on their ponies. Behind us the Sergeant yelled "Fire" and six saddles were emptied; one warrior sped toward us with his arm flopping. Our second volley wasn't as effective, for the Indians were taking evasive measures, but I saw saddles being emptied with our combined sustained fire. With the withering fire the Indians wheeled away into a long line and swept past us firing as they went—some with outstretched arms aiming the rifles like a pistol, others aiming from the shoulder, and a few fired at us from under their pony's neck.

We were crouched behind the bank of the stream, and screened by the low-lying brush, the Arapaho only had a small target to try to hit from the back of a running horse, but they had practiced doing just that for years. The smoke from our black powder shells further screened us, but it also cut down our visibility. The Indians thundered past us and disappeared into a draw. As the smoke cleared, I counted the bodies. Fifteen dead or wounded Indians lay in the hot sun to remind us of our own mortality.

I stood up and walked down the line of defenders. Barney had placed a man between each woman, then the two Chinese, and then me. The soldiers were behind the rocks and none had been killed. We only had one casualty; Jo Lin. Kee Lin was trying to bandage his arm when Teresa ran up with a first aid bag that we had made up back at Cap's place. She cleansed the wound with whiskey. When Jo Lin cried out—Teresa gave him such a smile that he settled right down.

Kee Lin said, "Jo Lin get excited when Indian come. He stood up and shoot—bang—bang—bang—until all bullets gone. Then he get hit."

"Good man, Jo Lin," I said grinning. "You'd make a good soldier."

"Everyone reload." I yelled. "Get a drink of water, and rest while you can. No doubt they'll be back."

The Sergeant came up shook hands and said. "Those women of yours can sure shoot. I'm Sgt. McDermott. We were sent out to look for these Arapahos. I was told there were only a few of them. When we ran into them—it was fight or die. Who made that great shot that killed War Eagle.?

"Ron Ridge! Ron, meet Sgt. McDermott. They shook hands, and I asked the Sgt. "Do you think they'll be back?"

"No telling what they'll do. Killing their Chief may make a difference."

"What do you and Buffalo think," Four Hands?

"Man With Eyes of an Eagle, kill Chief War Eagle. Indian no come back until new chief appointed to lead them. We kill many Indian—bad medicine for Arapaho—maybe no come back."

"Ron, what do you think," I asked.

"Four Hands has said it very well. We wait. If they don't come—the Kickapoo and I will scout and see if they are gone? Sgt, if I may suggest, Could you put a couple of men where they can see around that bend in the creek. Those Arapaho could creep up the bed of that creek and catch us from the rear."

"Suggestions like that, Mister, could keep a man and his hair together a lot longer." He grinned and said, "You're a lot smarter than that new bobtail Lieutenant, we just got from West Point. Thanks for the advice; I'd better get back to my men." He saluted Ron with a grin and trotted off.

"You girls okay? I asked.

Trinity smiled and said, "It's a bit livelier than Denver on a Saturday night."

Teresa with an impish grin said, "Victoria has been finding out how easy it is to take a man's life with all of her expertise. What was the count, Vicky, two or was it three?" Teresa gave me an innocent look, and slid another round into the loading tube on her Henry.

Victoria glared at her and said, "You should know, you got more than your share." She muttered, "You really can be a brat."

Lucy looked a bit pale, but she was still flippant, "All is well in the Velasco family, Shawn, as you can hear." I grinned when she called me Shawn. After all the stories, I guess they were all confused as to who I really was. Well—at least as confused as I was.

I laughed and called out, "You ladies are great. Keep your heads down." I was concerned about them all, but it was only when Teresa obviously put up a defense for me that I felt my pulse pump a little faster. She was an extraordinary girl, but then—they all were."

I said, "Barney, you'll have to be the referee for these girls."

His lop-sided grin said it all, "You seem to be the bone of contention, referee your own squabbles."

Buffalo commented dryly, "Better for Man Who Flies Like a Bird to fly while he can."

Don Patrick looked at me quizzically and muttered, "I figured when it happened it would be another Irishman."

"You okay, Don Patrick? That one looks like it had your name on it." A 44-40 had left a long groove down the right side of his head. It was oozing blood."

"I'm okay. It didn't have my name on it." His girls all clustered around him, but it was Teresa that grabbed the first aid bag and the next thing I heard was, "Damn it, Teresa that hurts."

"Oh don't be such a baby, Daddy." I heard another curse, as I went over to see how the soldiers were doing. One man had been hit high on the shoulder, but it wasn't serious. When I left Teresa was dressing his wound.

Three hours later they came again. They had picked a new chief. Jon nailed him through the chest at three-hundred yards.

The Indians stopped, and milled about. They picked up their latest Chief; laid him across his horse, turned and slowly rode away.

Buffalo looked and exclaimed succinctly, "They go." That said it all—the fight was over. The Indian's medicine was not good. It was not a good day to die. The following evening we rode into Denver with all of our tents, gear and wagons. I was a person not subject to bouts of depression, but as we rode through the city to Barney's and Vance Brand's residences, a pall of gloom overwhelmed me. Was Cotton Brand up to some new deviltry, or was I beginning to let the man get to me? I shook the thought off, what would be—would be—. I knew I had to be as alert as possible. Jack as though sensing my milieu raised his head and licked my face. Jon was riding beside me, and I turned to him impulsively and said, "Jon—something is very wrong—knowing you are my friend and partner is a great comfort to me, and I know your strength will help see me through whatever I am sensing."

Jon reached over and put his hand on my shoulder and said, "Matt, those senses of yours have saved our hind ends more than once. We both will have to be alert."

Teresa was riding on my left, and had overheard us. She reached out and put her hand on my hand holding the reins and said, "You can count on me, Shawn. I, too, feel a sense of foreboding—something dreadful—I think."

*   *   *

Barney drove me to the City Hotel in his surrey. I was renting my room by the month. Barney had the room to put me up, but I was used to my privacy, and he was always entertaining someone. City Gaslights lit up the area, and my head was nodding from a full two weeks of exertion. I had stabled Pat when we rode into town, and Jack was staying with Byron. "I think I'll sleep for a week," I growled as I slipped out of the carriage. "Thanks for the ride, Barney. Careful does it," I admonished.

He laughed, "Who are you kidding, you'll be up with the chickens, and I'm always careful," he responded.

He clucked to his horse and drove off. The clerk was evidently sleeping. I walked on past the desk. I wearily walked up the steps to my room on the second floor. The hallway gaslight was turned down so low I could barely see to get my key into the lock. I was tired, and my senses were not helping me. I stepped into the room; someone grabbed me, and a fist grazed my jaw. I saw a big head and planted my fist right in the middle of it, and had the satisfaction of feeling the nose squish flat. A second head filled my sights and I hit him with my left and I saw a blur from my right eye; for a split second I recognized the on coming sap. My head exploded, and the dim light flashed out.

*   *   *

I awoke with a jerk. My head snapped forward; my neck caught the full impact wrenching a groan from my pursed lips. I tried to open my eyes, but something was wrong. My left eye was covered. Across from me I could see vertical bars. I turned my neck; I was looking at more bars, and the back of a hairy neck. It was the back of a man driving a wagon. Two draft horses were sliding, slipping and falling, but, in spite of any obstacle, they made steady progress up an impossible trail. My hands and feet were manacled with chains that rattled with every move of the wagon—then the facts hit me like a clap of thunder. I was in a wagon used to haul prisoners. I was the only passenger. I was manacled hand and foot, but I had a limited use of my hands and feet. I felt my head. I had a huge bandage that covered most of my head. It crossed over and covered my left eye and part of my mouth.

The driver heard my groan. He swiveled his head and saw that I was awake. He stopped the wagon and got down. Once he did, I could see that the wagon was following a path barely more definable than a deer path. The driver opened the door at the back of the wagon; got in and sat down facing me. "Awake huh? Dingus must have really conked you a good one." He took a knife and cut a rope that was tied around my chest and one that was tied around my waist. He explained, "I tied those there to keep you from flopping

277

all over the wagon. The boss said to treat you right. See that tank above your head? That's water. That tube there is how you drink. It had a simple snap on it to shut the water off. You screw up, and you ain't got no water."

It reminded me of a snap on an enema tube. I tried it—my throat was on fire. The tube fit the small opening at the corner of my mouth. The water was hotter than the seven hinges of hell, but it was wet. It was a big tank, so I sprayed a little water on the tank, and it condensed so fast that I realized my supply of water was too limited to use mother-nature to cool off the water.

He grinned—a cheerless look—and said. "You got the hang of it. Don't give me no trouble, and I will let you out at night, so you can sleep on the ground. I'll feed you in the morning and again at night. You gotta take a crap—or take a piss—let me know. Don't stink up my wagon, or I'll beat you like an egg-sucking-dog. My name is Goober. Your name is Mudd. It is the only name you will be called. Answer to it, or you will be beat. Do as you're told and you will be treated right. You will work like a dog sixteen hours every day—seven days a week—you will be fed decent food unless you act up—act up and you go hungry for a week.

"What work? I managed to mumble through the bandage.

He grinned, a mirthless grin at best and replied. "You'll find out soon enough."

"Why the;" and I pointed at my bandages.

His eyes got ugly, "Don't screw with that bandage. If you do—a doctor will have to put them back on to save your miserable life," and he laughed.

He was so matter of fact about my expected treatment that I had no doubt that his word was like a contract. He locked the door—got back into the drivers seat; with a jounce and a jerk, we were on our way again. I sized up the inside of the wagon carefully. Everything was in place and working perfectly. I studied my chains inch by inch. They were brand new—made of the best steel, and made by the best manufacturers. Careful not to make any noise—I put the maximum pressure I could exert on each chain—there was no give—no possible way I could free myself unless I had outside help. I soon found out how Goober got his name. He loved peanuts. He had a hundred pound potato sack full of peanuts, and he was addicted to eating them. He left a trail of hulls all the way from Denver to our final destination. My heart jumped. He was leaving a trail even a child could follow. That is—if anyone was looking?

Just last night—at least I think it was last night—I had sensed something was going to happen. I had asked Jon for support for what—I knew not. I had been careless last night thinking I was going to the safety of my room. With Brand there had been no safety for any of my family, or friends since I had first heard the name from Barney. Was he safe—or was he in a jail wagon like me being transported to some unknown place of confinement? I was thrown forward—when I reached the end of the short length of my chains, I was jerked short. I gasped with pain. Pain was my only comfort as the journey went on all day in the hot sun with no respite from the heat or solace for my fears.

The next day was worse, as Goober wended his way up a pass. Huge boulders were everywhere. The pass had to have been formed by roaring cascades of water rushing off the mountain every spring. A mountain stream roared down the far side of the pass, and Goober had to make impossible detours to avoid the stream. Twice we had to cross the roaring cataract. Each time riders appeared to help the driver make the crossing. They were equipped with block and tackle, and during the trip I counted six different men. Whoever was ramroding this outfit was not sparing any expense to have me transported incognito to my destination. The men were not traveling with us, nor were they within my sight during the day. They were tough looking able men, who disappeared as soon as the need for them was gone. I watched the terrain carefully—coming and going. A good man in the wilderness always noted the terrain where he went and where he had been, so that he could traverse the route in case he had to return. Utah juniper, pinon pine, and willow abounded along the stream including the occasional cottonwood.

Goober knew where he was going. When he had to ford a stream, or a river, his route took him to a ford that was passable. We only saw one man, other than the men that were at Goober's beck and call. The one pilgrim we saw was a prospector who wanted to be left alone. He respected the rights of other man to that same privilege—he passed us without so much as even a 'grunt.' By this time I had figured out why my face was bandaged so heavily. If any one saw us—all they could say was they seen an injured man being hauled off to the hoosegow. I could only wonder where on earth a calaboose could be in this wilderness?

As we drove higher I noted big sage, ponderosa pine, mountain juniper, and alder, which grew at about six-thousand feet. I knew I was near seven-thousand feet when I saw spruce and aspen trees. As we worked our way higher, we passed through gambel oak and white pine mixed with ponderosa and douglas fir, which, I knew if we rode much higher would give way to the ubiquitous spruce and woody shrubs. The air grew thinner and the horses labored at their daily task for another two weeks.

When we did stop, we were still in pine trees; I figured we were no higher than ten-thousand feet. I was bruised and sore; hurting in every muscle and bone of my body. We were deep in the mountains of Colorado. Goober had driven southwest; the best I could figure. From Denver, we had been going up—up—up—. It was cold at night, so I figured we had to be at an elevation of nine or ten-thousand feet. A thumping noise became more evident all that day. When we slept that night, I could feel the thump-thump-thump of a stamp mill reverberating like the beating of a heart. Late the next day, the source of the noise was obvious. A large eight stamp mill hove into view, the noise was thunderous. Goober drove right on past, and he stopped at the entrance to a mine.

"What mine is this, Goober," I asked.

"It ain't got no name," he snapped. Then he laughed, "Just call it, 'The No Name Mine.'

THE MYSTERY OF THE NO NAME MINE

CHAPTER NINE

The huge head-frame had no name to enlighten him as to where he was. The slag piles told me the mine was several years old. It was a chore to walk, my legs crippled by the ride, but Goober had no patience. He yanked me out of the wagon, and pushed me toward a steam-driven elevator. My eyes raced around the terrain. There was a huge bunkhouse, and an equally large mess hall. The mine had an eight stamp mill operation. They could handle sixteen tons or more of ore a day. All around the area I could see beautiful seams of white quartz. It had to be a gold mine. On an opposite hill, I could see a small log bunker built into the hill. It was padlocked; a red flag flew above it. It had the appearance of being a powder bunker. There were other buildings, all part of the mine complex, except for one that had to be a large stable. Open doors on the hayloft disclosed stacks of bailed hay, so they must have a lot of horses, yet there were not many in evidence. There were not many men in sight, but there were three guards in a bunker located off to one side. The cook house was active from which good smells emanated—wafted to us by a kindly breeze.

Goober steered me around the elevator and walked me straight back. In the shadows I could see what I figured to be the original strike tunnel. From what I could see it went straight back into the hill. At the entrance, I stepped aside as a man pushing an ore cart exited the mine. I shot a quick look at the ore. It was gold bearing ore, and it didn't look that great. A hulk of a man met us at the tunnel entrance. He was five and half feet tall and his shoulders were three feet wide and he went straight down and it was all muscle. He looked me up and down and said, "Men call me 'Brute Smith'. Your name is Mudd. Your prison number is #10. Your fellow inmates are prisoners found guilty of murder—same as you are. Your job is inside this mine sixteen hours a day. At the end of your shift, you will be locked up in a cell inside the tunnel. If you get sick a Doctor will come and attend to you. The food is plain but good. Cause trouble and you will be beat. You get clean clothes and a shower once a week. There are inside privies. On Sundays you get an hour to pray. There is a Bible and candles by each cot for you to sleep on. There won't be much time for anything else. Your sentence is hard labor the rest of your life. If you don't work you don't eat. If you refuse orders, you don't eat. If that don't teach you—you will be beat every day until you decide to follow the rules. This ain't no health resort. Work hours are 6 AM till 10 PM.

He turned and said, "You there, Amos, here's the keys and chain. Chain him with the new prisoner Mulligan and put him to work—his vacation is over. His name is Mudd, and he is #10. Amos equipped us with miner's hats and attached lights, which threw a cone of light in front of wherever our head was pointed. I was only familiar with two sizes of Carbide lamps with which we were furnished, one had a small reflector, and one had a large reflector. We got the large reflector, which threw a lot more light. The light container held a supply of carbide and water. The simple controls determined the amount of water allowed to mix with the carbide, which made a gas that was inflammable, a flint lighter was attached to the reflector that allowed the gas to be ignited. The flame was reflected and threw a good light in front of the miner permitting him to see well enough to do his work.

Amos said, "Light your carbide light and walk straight down the tunnel, Mudd." A hundred feet later the passage was blocked by bars. This place was beginning to look more like a prison each step we took. Heavy one-inch thick iron bars sealed off the tunnel. Amos opened a door that had an efficient lock that looked impregnable. We went through and soon came to a cross tunnel that was equipped with a set of mine car rails. The round shaped eight foot tunnels were cut through hard rock through which no shoring was needed . . . It was impressive. A hundred feet into the tunnel it emptied into a hundred-foot wide chamber that I learned later had been what miner's call a glory or bonanza hole. The miner's had taken a million dollars out of this one hole. It was about thirty-feet high, the room was lit by lamps set into the rock walls of the room. Bars separated the room into a barracks on one side, and a mess hall on the other. Twenty cots were laid out in the barracks in military style. I noted nine cots were made up, the rest were empty. The far side of the chamber was made into a dining room equipped with tables with benches on each side.

Amos said, "This room will be your cell at night. You get fed at 6 A.M. and 6 P.M . . . The grub is good. We eat here too. You get an hour each meal to wash up, eat and go to the bathroom. Get regular or crap your pants. No breaks when you are working, except to take a piss. The foreman designates where the piss-buckets are kept. Alright, let's go." As we left I noted in the middle of the ceiling was a ventilator shaft about three feet in diameter that had been barred on this end.

I kept my mouth shut. I figured anything I had to know, I would be ordered to do, or I would learn from the other prisoners. I wasn't going to make my life here any worse that it already was. Everything I saw, I checked carefully to see if I could detect any flaws that might help me get out of this place. Amos took us back to the cross tunnel. We turned, walked another hundred feet, and came to another cross tunnel. A pair of tracks led the way. He gave us a hand lantern to carry, which helped a great deal. We passed two men pushing a loaded mine car, so I figured we were getting close.

This mine had been here awhile, for this much tunnel to have been dug. There must be another slag pile someplace. We came to another cross tunnel, turned left, and suddenly we were at the tunnel face. Men were working. Two men were hand-drilling steel into the face of the mine. Two men were filling an ore car, and four men were working as a team erecting headers and footers, and putting in lagging where needed. This part of the tunnel was going to need a lot of shoring. They were building six foot sets, which meant I would be bent over much of the time, what with my 6 foot 4 inch frame. It was not the first time I had reason to regret my height.

The first thing I heard—then saw—was a small bird cage. In it were two canaries. They were hopping around and singing happily. I knew if the canaries dropped dead, it meant gas was in the tunnel. If we were lucky, we would have time to run like hell. If we had the time or sense, we would turn off our lamps, so as not to ignite the deadly, explosive methane gas.

As we approached, a guard stepped out of the shadows, his lamp shining in my face, and said, "What ya got fer us, Amos?"

"Another killer, Jingo. Name's Mudd # 10."

Amos explained, "Dutch is in charge. He is a miner; he is not a jailor, or a guard. Do whatever he tells you, and, as a miner, you just might stay alive."

Amos called out, "Mule, get over here."

A big burley, heavily muscled man walked over and snarled, "What now?"

Amos hit him in the mouth with his rifle butt. He looked down at the brute of a man, and said mildly, "How many times do I have to tell you # 9—a bad attitude is not good for your health. Your name is Mule # 9 . . . Now get up—and shut up."

Amos called out, "Shaw # 2, bring that chain over here."

Amos took the six foot chain and clamped and locked it on # 9's left leg, then clamped and locked the other end to my right leg. Whomever I had been captured by—was certainly not taking any chances of my getting away. However, desperate men will always find a way to thwart their captors. I was not going to be stupid like # 9, and get my brains knocked out, but from the moment I awoke on the trail—my one thought was, and had been—escape—. I knew very little about Colorado. I did know that the town of Leadville was said to be at the ten-thousand foot level, and located southwest from Denver. Goober had traveled generally southwest from the time of my capture, up—ever upward from Denver. I had to be within one or two days of a mine or a small community. It might take time—but I would find out. It might take time—but I would escape.

In addition, I had friends on the outside—friends that could track a rattlesnake across a bare rock. My heart swelled with affection when I thought of Barney, Jon, Buffalo and Four Hands—and of course the best tracker of all—Jack—. I knew none of them would rest until I was located and freed, but in the meantime—my every waking moment would be devoted to freeing myself, and the men with me. I believed I knew who was behind the plot to incarcerate me. It had to be 'Cotton Brand.' I had never met, nor even seen the man. Yet his tentacles of evil seemed to extend behind every rock and into every canyon of Colorado.

A man, with an air of authority, joined us while the chaining took place. Amos said, "We got you a pair of mules this time, Dutch."

Dutch asked, "Why the chains, Amos? You know I don't allow chains in here."

Amos put his hands on his hips and tried to stare Dutch down. "Damn it, Dutch, look at the size of these bozos. We need these chains."

Dutch ignored Amos and said, "They come off tonight. Mudd you and Mule start at the bottom of the learning ladder. Your first job is 'Mucking'. We keep a plate of quarter-inch steel lying in front of the face of the mine. After the ore is blasted, it will fall on and cover the plate. It's your job to get down on your knees and shovel the ore into the ore cart—one man on each side of the cart. Today you'll have to coordinate your work, because of the chains. One of your jobs will be to help move the iron plate to the face of the mine before the powder man sets off his charges. It's a four man job."

Mule glowered, but did as he was told, but as we neared the face of the mine he moved and took up the left side to the rear of the cart. Dutch told him, "That won't work, Mule. Get on the other side of the car. As he crossed over he jerked my leg painfully, and I nearly fell. I dropped to my knees. In spite of Mule's bullheadedness—I tried to fall into a rhythm of work. Every time I did, Mule would do something different. It slowed the work and made it extremely painful for me. I knew it must be hurting the mule-headed man as much as it did me, but he was determined to cause trouble. He was full of anger and despair; he was ready to lash out at anyone or anything to vent his rage. Dutch had to attend to the steel-driving men, and as he walked off, he said, "You men have to learn to work as a team. Amos keep an eye on them, I have to go help the drill men to pull steel."

As soon as Dutch moved out of hearing, Amos started for Mule ready to slam him with the butt of his rifle, but I said, "Amos, is it all right if I settle this in my own way?"

Amos stopped in mid-stride, and looked me over carefully. Seeing that I was playing by his rules he smirked and replied, "Why yes, Mudd, you can. Let's see what you can do?"

I said, "Mule, you can act like a jackass and cause us both a lot of pain, or we can work together, and make it easy for one another. What do you say," and I held out my right hand. He did just what I expected him to do. He threw a right hand straight for my head. I caught his right with my left—grabbed him by the throat, and lifted him off the ground. I slammed him hard against the wall of the mine, and held him there. His face soon began to turn purple and I relaxed my grip, and asked. "What's it going to be, Mule—war or peace?"

Mule gasped, "Peace!" I dropped Mule and turned back to my work position.

I glanced at Amos; I detected a gleam of malice in his eye, and he started for me with his rifle poised for a shot at my chin. I said casually, "You know, Amos, if I get hit for breaking a rule, I will accept it as part of the game you're playing, However, if someone were to hit me for no reason, sooner or later I will be able to get my hand on his throat. I can crush a man's throat in less than a second. It wouldn't make any difference to the dead man if I were killed a minute later by one of his friends—he would still be dead."

Amos stopped abruptly. He looked at me keenly, and I saw the malice fade into a calculating gleam in his eyes, and he chuckled; "Now I know why Brand had you kidnapped and went to all that trouble to get you here unseen. You must have been a real pain in his ass." He turned to the miners and snapped, "Shows over, get back to work."

Tom # 1 drifted over, and with a friendly smile said, "Be careful, Mudd, don't bump the sides of the tunnel. You might cause a cave in."

Once Mule got over his churlishness, we made a good team and churned out the work as Amos said, "Like a team of Missouri Jackasses." I still don't know if we were being insulted or praised. It really didn't make any difference. Even as slave labor, I would rather work than be idle. Even if I had to work with no compensation, I liked to work, and so did Mule. We became good friends and even better friends when I started talking to him about how we were going to escape. The first night I was surprised after our second shift was finished. Amos came into the barracks and took off our chains. So Dutch was the boss.

Amos said, "You boys behave yourselves and the chains stay off."

I replied, "Well now, Amos, that's mighty white of you. Thank you." It never hurt to be polite, and I had been taught to never look a gift horse in the mouth. Mule mumbled something derogatory, but Amos let it pass.

Mulligan told me he had worked for Cotton Brand, but as a cowman, not as a thief. As foreman of one of Brand's ranches, he learned too much for Brand to trust him. Mulligan, the day before I arrived, was suddenly imprisoned, and forced to work as a slave—a real shock; from ramrod to mucker without any warning.

"Just what did this mysterious Cotton Brand look like?" I asked Mule. My curiosity knew no bounds. His name was well known in Denver, yet no one I had talked to had ever seen him.

"Hell, I don't know" Mule answered. "I said I worked for him, but I never saw him. His brother Chance handled all his business. Chance wasn't too hard to work for, but his wife was a holy terror.

"So you're that Shannon feller the Brands hate so bad." Mule marveled. "You should have heard the things Cotton's men used to say about you. 'They said you were a wizard with a gun and a devil in a fight.' 'Did you really shoot Kyle Brand's thumb off?'"

"I had no choice. It was kill him, or wound him. I chose the latter, for all the good it did me. I had to kill him a few months later when he tried to kill me with a shotgun."

287

"No wonder the Brands want you dead, I guess this mine is the worst thing they could think of to satisfy their hate for you."

"It's a mistake, they will live to regret, Mulligan. My friends and family will never quit looking for me, and I will escape.

"That's for sure," growled Mule, "that's for damned sure."

The other prisoners were a wealth of information, especially for a person that had been deliberately left in the dark about every thing. Every prisoner, I learned day by day, had run afoul of Cotton Brand. Most of them were prominent men that had been competitors, or in business with Brand. The mine we were working, according to miner's gossip, had never been filed on. However, it was said that Brand had one of his trusted men homestead the property, and that he would sign it over to Cotton when the Homestead was proved up. Somehow that didn't make sense to me. Cotton obviously wasn't a trusting man. Brand, the miners said, had owned at least a dozen good mines, mines that he had stolen from their owners, and then resold at a handsome profit. If true, why had he kept this mine—why? It sounded like just so much more gossip to me. Nothing added up.

One of the prisoners was named Crenshaw. He had been a bookkeeper. He had learned too much about Cotton's crooked interests. Before he could turn him in, he found himself working as a miner in Brand's hidden mine. He was now Shaw # Two. The rumors ran rampant. Some of them were true. At least the ten men being held here were most likely telling it like it was. But, as I quickly learned, a lot of what was said was just plain gossip, hot poop—right from the number one hole. Gossip—not hope—springs eternal, at least so it seemed inside the mine.

Actually the ten of us became the closest of friends. We worked, ate, and slept together. For a short time each night, we talked, and formed a trust and protectiveness for one another. Then we began swapping ideas of how we could escape. The big surprise was Tom # 1. He had been the first person kidnapped in 1872. His name was Sebastian Tomas Velasco whose brother was Don Patricio Miguel Velasco. I was really surprised; he was Teresa's uncle. He was full of questions about his family, and I told him how smitten I had been with

his niece Teresa. I related to him the details of our trip; the battle with
the Indians, and he pumped me for every little detail. Information for
him about his family, was like water for a man crazed with thirst in the
middle of the Mohave Desert. I learned he and Patricio had another
brother by the name of Joaquim. Sebastian and Joaquim had attended
the University together and had both graduated as geologists. In the
spring of 1871, Joaquim had been hired to check a gold prospect
by Stefan Baca, a friend of the family. The client was supposed to
have a map to an excellent mining prospect. The Colorado Territory,
since gold was discovered in 1858, was full of hustlers and miners
selling phony maps and claims to the gullible public. It was debatable
how good the map was, but Baca had excellent specimens taken from
the proposed location. Joaquim and Stefan left together with several
mules loaded with equipment to make the survey. Stefan fell seriously
ill with malaria. Urged on by Stefan, Joaquim hired a miner, and
proceeded to look for the mine. They were never heard of again. The
following year, Sebastian Tomas Velasco rode the stage from Santa Fe
to Denver to initiate a search for him.

   Denver was the last place that Joaquim had been heard from.
Sebastian Tomas Velasco hired David Cook's Detective Agency to find
his brother. David Cook had given the assignment to John Divers,
David Cook's most experienced detective. Divers learned that Stefan
Baca had died from malaria, and the trail had died with him. Sebastian
and Divers from Denver in the spring of 1872 to find the lost brother,
and they in turn had simply vanished. Cook's best detectives had been
unable to develop a lead. According to Sebastian, before Joaquim left
Santa Fe, he had shown his brother a map of where he was going. It
was not an exact location, but it was good enough that Divers thought
they could locate the mine. They did! When Divers confronted the
men working the mine, they had shot and killed him, and Sebastian
was imprisoned. After a few months incarceration in a tool room, he
had been put to work in the mine. Gradually the mine had taken on
the appearance of the prison that it was today; instead of one prisoner,
there were now ten prisoners.

   Before long, I had learned that Crenshaw had worked for the
Brands in Texas, as well as in Denver. He had been like one of the

family and had worked for Chance Brand for years. Shaw knew me as Shawn Nack. He didn't know that that I was Matthew O'Shannon. From my habit of self preservation, I had only told Mulligan my real name. From what Shaw told us, I had the impression that Shaw, in spite of his imprisonment, was still convinced that Cotton Brand was at heart—a good man. Shaw told us,

"It was that ridge-runner Shannon family from West Virginia that caused all the trouble. The Shannons claimed that Cotton started a feud with a Byron Shannon over his wooing the hand of Cotton's niece Trinity Brand. But Brand learned that Shannon was a scoundrel and after her father's money. Cotton and his brothers Starr and Chauncey stood up for their niece, and ran Shannon out of town. When Byron Shannon returned, he brought his brother Matthew with him. It turned out that they were both fast gun hands. That is why the Brands started hunting Byron's brother Matthew Shannon. From what I heard they ran into a wildcat. He killed Able Brand, shot Kyle Brand's thumb off, and then maneuvered a Miner's Court into hanging Chauncey Brand. It's said that Starr Brand was killed by Texas gunmen in a bushwhack led by the Shannons. Then Kyle Brand, Chance's brother, talked Chance's three sons, by his second wife, to back up his play to kill Shannon. The only one that survived out of the second branch of the family was Tyrel."

Mule looked at me and I just shrugged my shoulders. There was plenty of time to set Shaw straight as to the facts as I knew them.

"What happened to the first branch of Chance's family," Mule asked.

"They were all killed in a feud down in Texas," Shaw explained.

I asked Shaw, "What did Chance do when his sons were killed?"

"He was hit plumb hard, Shawn. Reckon he went a little crazy. He took a shotgun and killed the gunman and his entire family in the middle of the night. He blew the father all to hell and then shot the man's, two teen age boys, and he even killed the man's wife. Then the entire family of Brands packed up and lit out for Denver. I was the family bookkeeper and I was just bundled up like part of the furniture and taken along. The neighbors had enough of the feuding and were just behind them with a lynch rope when they all cleared out one jump ahead of them. Cotton Brand had moved to Denver months before. I don't think he ever found out about Chance killing that woman. Cotton kept to himself and had little to do with his family. That was until—

"What the hells all that noise in there," Amos yelled as he held up a lantern peering through the bars? Lights out means—shut up and go to sleep.

It wasn't until two weeks later that Amos disappeared long enough for us to continue the conversation. Mule was determined to find out all the facts and only Shaw could tell us if we kept him on our side. It was not time to start an argument about the feud between the Brands and the Shannons when Shaw was still half way convinced the Brands were telling the truth.

One night Mule asked Shaw, "If you're such buddies with the Brands, why did Chance Brand have you put in here with all of us killers?

"I asked Chance why, and like always he said it was Cotton's decision. I had only seen Cotton Brand a few times and I never had an opportunity to talk to him. After Chance's family was nearly wiped out, Chance said that Cotton decided that his enemies, instead of being killed, would be kidnapped and incarcerated in his mine. Chance told me that Cotton Brand said; why not kill two birds with one stone. It was hard to get miners to come to his unknown mine. Cotton Brand, from all I heard, is a good man. It's said he trades whiskey and guns with the Indians, but I think that is just more Shannon talk. I would never judge Cotton Brand as being a killer. In Texas it was his brothers and nephews that did the feuding. Cotton Brand has never been a bloodthirsty person. Chance says that all Cotton ever wanted was to punish those people that cheated him out of his just due, but he doesn't want anybody starved or brutalized. When he set this place up, he insisted that no one be killed or tortured, he just wants his prisoners to pay their debt for killing his family and foiling his plans. He doesn't think like we do. I believe he is a little mad." After he said that he added, "Maybe he is a killer, but he sure don't act like it."

Mulligan looked at Shaw intently, and told him, "You are either stupid, or rather naïve, Shaw. Do you know who Mudd #

10 really is?" Mule had asked me if he could divulge my real name. When a man is forty-feet down a thirty-foot well it really makes little difference who knows his real name. Whoever had put me here—sure as hell knew who I was.

"No, I never heard of Mr. Mudd until he came here."

"Mr. Mudd, for your information, Mr. Shaw, is that mad killer Matthew Shannon."

Shaw's face drained white, and he turned to me and stuttered, "I I'm sorry, Mr. Shannon, I was just repeating the stuff I've seen and heard in Texas and Denver."

Who told you all that information about the Shannons, Shaw," I asked.

"Why I guess most of the information came from Chance and his wife Mercedes.

I smiled, "It serves to prove one thing, Shaw, Don't believe anything you hear and only half of what you see. As for the person operating as Cotton Brand, the actions attributed to him are not good—they are evil. He has the blood on his soul of every man killed since he began his struggle for power. Napoleon Bonaparte never personally killed anyone that the history books that I've read talks about, but he is responsible for the blood of thousands of men all because of his lust for power. In my opinion, he and men like Brand, are the personifications of evil. Yet, don't forget one thing. Not one of us prisoners has ever seen Cotton Brand. Not one of us could tie him to a single crime. He is like the little man that was never there. He appears to be as blameless, as this mine is nameless.

I never corrected them on the error they made regarding my last name. The least anyone knew the better. Shaw's story did bother me. There were people that regarded me as a killer. That did not rest well with me. The facts were simple, if you carried a gun—someone could easily be killed. If you killed someone in self-defense—you would be labeled with the stigma of a killer by some—others might understand that you had no choice—but you would still carry the "Mark of Cain" to your grave. What most people don't know is the astounding number of persons killed with the knife—not the gun? It's the killing that earns a person the "Mark of Cain"—not the gun—nor the knife. Cain had only his bare hands. Thank God our soldiers and law enforcement officers are not tarnished with the label of being killers. One thing did bother me. Everyone said Cotton Brand was responsible for all their problems. Yet, not one person could tell me that they had done business with him on a person to person basis. I know I never had. Cotton Brand was like a ghost. Perhaps that was the way he wanted it? Perhaps?

The ventilator shaft intrigued me. It was barred on this end, but I was sure I could tear it out of the ceiling, if I could just figure how to get up there. We were about two hundred feet beneath the surface. By looking up the shaft, it looked like it had a wire screen over the opening—that should present no problem. It looked to me like I was about thirty feet from the route to freedom.

Two weeks later, Dutch put Mule and I to work on the ore cart and two weeks later he changed our work schedule. Dutch was an easy man to work for. He had a lot of patience and was a careful man. I never met any careless men in charge in a mine. He told us, "I want you two to work on the timbering. The work is done on the theory of a square, like a bee's honeycomb, which gives the most resistance to the pressure from all sides of the ground. The other men of our crew are small in stature and the caps and posts take a lot of strength to handle. They weigh about a hundred and twenty-five pounds to one-hundred and fifty pounds each. We are in a bad section now that is going to need consecutive sets and lots of lagging. You have to learn when to put lagging on the cap, and when to put it on the walls to keep the rock from slabbing off., and mud and loose rock from pouring in. We do the driving of lagging or spiling with 2"x 9" boards. You have to drive wedges behind the lagging to keep it tight against the sets. In the loose stuff we are working in, we will use a square set. Two posts, a cap and a sill. This ground swells a bit and you will have to learn when to leave spaces between the cap lagging and the sill lagging. Don't worry, I will work right with you at first, and if you are not sure about anything, be sure to ask. I think you fellows will do a great job."

"We'll do our best, Dutch." I told him, "You show us what to do and we will take it from there." Dutch was a good boss, and Mule and

I worked hard for him. I figured we might as well learn something, since we had to be here anyhow. Besides, I felt we owed Dutch. True, he was a member of Brand's team of cutthroats, but he saved us from the brutality of the sadistic guards time and again—especially from Amos. I promised myself that I would someday repay him for his kindness to the prisoners.

Mulligan and I worked well with one another. In no time we were slapping up sets and spiling lagging, as fast as they were needed. Dutch soon had us doing all the jobs except handling the dynamite. Brand was afraid that if any of his enemies handled the powder man's job that he could use it to assist him in an escape. Of course, he was absolutely right. It developed that our ten men became so adept that we were standing around part of the time with nothing to do. The ore, at best, was not better than a half an ounce per ton. Then the ore became so bad that it wasn't worth the money to process it. We drove the tunnel for a quarter of a mile before we ran into some decent ore again. The vein was still there, but at times it became pure white quartz with no sign of that gold that can be so elusive to man's efforts to get rich. I wondered how the Superintendent of the mine, with his professional crew of miners was performing? They would be following the primary vein that would yield the most profit.

Dutch told us, "The vagaries of a vein are nothing for you to be concerned about. You will find that this vein is going to tease us to distraction. Just when we are ready to throw up our hands in frustration, we will hit a hot pocket. The last pocket we hit was a half-million-dollar bonanza."

We learned a lot. Sometimes we hit hot veins that splintered off; some went up and to the right or left, and some went down. We had to follow these stopes, and if they went up, we used ladders to follow the vein. Stopes would usually go up for fifty or a hundred feet and then usually petered out. We had to build a wooden stull to catch the ore as it was blasted from above. A stull had to be built about every thirty feet and lagging put on it. To build a stull we had to cut a hitch in the wall and slip in a timber and wedge it from the top end against the far wall. Then we made a chute with a shutoff to funnel the ore down into an ore cart. The further we went into a stope the more stulls and chutes had to be built to catch and hold it firm until the next load of ore was ready. Ladders were often necessary. These stopes were usually rich with ore, or they were not worked. They were always marked and might be worked at a later time. It was a pleasure to work them. Mule and I would have a good laugh later that night when we were going to bed about our excitement for gold that we would never benefit from. It was ironic, except for the fact that each day Mule and I came closer to our goal of escaping. Two months later, we looked at one another and knew we were ready. All we needed was the appropriate night to stage our escape. The pre made ladders for the stopes were ready made for our escape.

The next morning, Mule and I had just cleaned up the ore from the blasting from the night before. I was digging a drain alongside the wall to carry off any seepage. In this section of the mine we were only building square sets where we thought they were needed.

Suddenly my hand froze. Under my hand was a wall of near pure gold. I looked around, Dutch was gabbing with Amos and another guard. "Mule," I hissed. He looked up; I whispered, "Help me lag this mud run."

I grabbed a canvas bucket; scooped up a bucket full of mud and sloshed it on the vein of gold. It took three buckets to cover the vein. With a big grin Mule shouldered a cap and held it while I set the sill and then placed a post under each end of the cap and shimmed them tight. Then we grabbed lagging and covered up the wall—wedging the lagging to keep it up tight against the posts. Curious, I took my miner's hammer and tapped the wall of the tunnel that we had done the day before. I looked at the chip; the underside was ribbed with gold. A crack suddenly broke and ran at an angle across the tunnel wall threatening to slab off. Mule sloshed mud on it, and we quickly put in a cap and a sill and lagged another six feet of wall shut. If we could help it—we wasn't going to make Brand a rich man.

I kept an eye on Dutch and once he turned to come over when Amos called out, "Mr. Brand, one more thing." I stared when Dutch turned and went back.

When Dutch did return, he commented, "You guys been busy while I was gone. He checked the lagging and said, "Good job, those damned mud runs can kill a man."

That night, I thought Mule would bust a gut laughing. I had to shush him for fear the guards would come to check on us. I didn't tell Mule, but if my theory was right, we had just covered up the new route the vein had taken. If it was as good, as I thought it was, it was the proverbial Mother Lode. Nor did I tell what I had heard Amos call Dutch. I couldn't afford to allow Mule to blow his top and ruin my plans. But it did give me a lot to think about.

The next day we heard Amos and his back up guards talking. Amos said to the guards. "Tomorrow is August 1st, the second anniversary of the Statehood of Colorado. Cotton said he was arranging to send out some girls for us men, and that we could have a real bash." I looked at Mule and winked. We would be in the escape business at ten o'clock tomorrow evening.

By midnight, August 1st, not a guard could be seen. The sound of their revelry resounded up and down the tunnels like the eerie wails of banshees. We alerted all the men. Mule and I took hold of the gate barring our quarters and lifted. The gate lifted right out of its brackets and we eased it to the floor. Our captors had made their first mistake in building our cage. In minutes we had three ladders and nailed them together with lagging on their sides to make us a thirty-six foot ladder. We knocked out two rungs and the ten of us raised the ladder and inserted the open end into the metal grill that covered the air vent. Mule held the ladder and I scrambled up the rungs to the barred vent. I yanked on it, but nothing happened. Mule climbed up and handed me a six foot long—two inch thick pry bar. In another minute I had the grill hanging on one edge of the ladder. I crawled up the shaft with my feet on one wall and my back on the other. With my height it was mighty close quarters. In minutes I was twenty feet up the hole. I called down softly and said, "Come on up, Mule, the air is wonderful.

In five minutes there were six of us in the air vent. Several men were bitching because dirt was falling on them from the effort of those above them. I stopped and said, "Keep quiet! We've been dirty before." I ascended another ten feet; the top was not more than twenty feet above my head. I could taste the free air. I pushed hard with my legs; and tried to inch my way up. I felt something give. I tried again and without warning I fell through the wall of the shaft and landed in mud and water. Fetid air swooshed out the hole and gained freedom up the air shaft.

From below I could hear shots and Amos bellowed. "You men come on down or I start shooting." He laughed, "It will be like shooting ducks in a shooting gallery."

I called out softly. "Mule—you and one other man come on up. I think I'm in an old mine." So much dirt was raining down the shaft that I knew no one could look up and see what was going on. Mule clawed his way into the tunnel and crawling right behind him was Rat # 6. His name was Joseph Ratkowski; he was Polish from the Old Country. I found a muck-stick; a shovel with the handle cut halfway off. Muckers used it to shovel muck working from a kneeling position. I had learned its use by hard work. It was the first mining tool I had mastered, as a mucker. The word mucker means a low person, and mucking was considered the lowest job in a mine.

I dug a trench to the wall of the shaft to drain the tunnel. A couple of men were still in the shaft; their cries of indignation resounded up the shaft, as the cold water and mud cascaded down upon them. I said softly, "Sorry guys, maybe it will distract Amos and his men."

Mule and Joe were looking all around; their lights picked out the decomposed bodies of two men. One man lay up against a post and I checked his pockets. I found some papers and put them in my pocket; but I hesitated about turning him over. Suddenly I got an irresistible urge to do just that. My sixth sense was telling me, *Do it—turn him over.* Then I noticed that the body was lying in a peculiar position. The man had died with his hand pressed up against his neck. I took the shovel and turned the body over. Something was protruding from his mummified neck. I pulled it out. It looked like a long pin; I stuck it in my miner's hat.

The only thing noticeable about the corpse was that he had red hair. I put the thought out of my mind. Every time I turned around, I was relating whatever happened to my past. What was it that Luke wrote in the Bible that Jesus said, "Let the dead bury their dead." I would have to remember that. The other man was lying face down with a miner's pick protruding from the middle of his back. I found his wallet without any trouble. I removed the pick; took the mud-stick and used it to roll the body over. The odor was nauseas. I gagged, and quickly checked the cadaver's pockets. There was nothing of importance. I threw some dirt on the bodies, and the cloying smell of death was partially blotted out. The bodies would have to be retrieved later. We walked to the right—on down the tunnel, which appeared to lead to the entrance. We labored through the muck for a hundred feet until we ran into a wall of rock and pieces of timbering. The entrance had the appearance of having been blown shut. We turned and retraced our steps to the shaft; it had grown ominously silent from below. Suddenly Amos bellowed up the shaft. "You three come on down, and it will go a lot easier for you." Dead silence.

I could faintly hear Shaw's shrill voice exclaiming, "I told you, Amos, three men got out. I was a good way below them, but when I looked up, all I could see was a man's legs disappearing out the top." I heard the sound of a fist hitting flesh, and Amos' angry voice screamed. "They may have got out, but you're going to wish to hell they hadn't."

Then, again, we heard the sound of flesh hitting flesh. Fred # 3 spoke up whining, "I thought you said Mr. Brand didn't want anyone hurt?" There was a dead silence, and then the sound of a shot. Then all we could hear was the fading away of voices.

"Damn! I exclaimed. "I never thought of one of the fellows getting shot."

"It could have been us," muttered Mule. "How're we gonna get outta here?"

"Let's see what's down this way?" I headed down the tunnel; I stopped and exclaimed, "Wow! Look at this." There was the face of the mine, but the vein, the men had been following, had suddenly turned straight down; the vein was rich beyond belief.

Mule whistled, and Joe said, 'We haven't seen anything that nice."

"That's why that poor fellow back there got a pick in his back." I said. "Look—on this side of the face—I can see daylight ahead."

Mule muttered, "That bum murdered his partners, and dug his way out."

"And that, fellows, is why Brand never filed on this mine," I declared succinctly

"That bastard murdered his own partners," muttered Mule. "Shaw was wrong about Brand. He is capable of murder."

"This murder fills in the blank portion of Sebastian's story," I commented. "One of those dead men has to be Joaquim."

Mule replied, "Enough talk let's see if we can get out of here before daylight, or it means another night with these stinking bodies. God have mercy on their souls."

Taking the muck-stick Mule began digging and enlarging the old escape tunnel that Brand had evidently dug to make his escape. He pushed the dirt back behind him; Joe and I kept pushing it behind us as we dug our way to freedom. Brand, when he had hit air, realized he had come out on a steep slope. He had backed up a few feel and dug straight up. In a minute, Mule stuck his head out and looked around cautiously. He exclaimed and said, "What the hell?" Then he crawled out.

I was right on his heels. As my head cleared the hole, I felt a familiar tongue licking my face, and I said, "What kept you so long, Jon?"

Jon whispered, "Not so loud, Partner. There's bad company all around."

I grabbed Jack and hugged him. He was so ecstatic that finally I had to order him, "Guard, Jack. He immediately settled down, and began nosing around doing his job. I pulled Joe out of the hole, and told him, "My friend is here—keep quiet." I whispered to Jon, "Anyone with you?"

Jon chuckled and whispered, "About half of Denver, and the rest of Colorado. Let's get out of here. Jack, camp." And Jack traversed the hill for ten minutes; then cut straight down the hill. Later we came to a small canyon down which a small stream of water tumbled, jumping and bubbling over the stones from where it plunged down a natural chute thirty feet long, where it poured into a deep pool. As Jack turned into the canyon Jon reassured us. "Don't worry it has a back door."

From the shadows a familiar voice spoke, "Aha! Man with Eyes of an Eagle has found Man who Flies Like a Bird."

"Buffalo!" I exclaimed, "Who Kills Many White Men, it's good to hear your voice and I grabbed him and gave him a big hug.

"Ugh! He exclaimed. You strong before—now you Man With Arms of Steel. I stay here—go—your friends wait for you." It was a deep canyon. We finally made a turn and there tucked away under a big overhang were clustered my friends, and some men I did not know. With a scream of joy, Teresa jumped up and ran and threw herself into my arms.

"I knew Jon and Jack would find you," and she kissed me on the mouth. Not a kiss of passion, or one of friendship, but one of possession. I didn't mind one bit—she felt like she had always been a part of my arms.

Jon laughed, "He didn't need saving, Teresa. He was crawling out of a hole when Jack found him."

She laughed, "Looking at the size of him, I don't think it was a rabbit hole."

Then I was surrounded by friends. Four Hands was there. He was even smiling, as he jumped down from his perch on the wall and shook my hand vigorously.

Barney grabbed me and gave me one of his exuberant hugs. He didn't mangle me like before. Holding me by my shoulders he stepped back and said, "Now you are the one crushing bones. Let me look at you—you've put on twenty-pounds of solid muscle and I would swear you've grown an inch." He turned to Teresa and said, "You will have to get him a new wardrobe—he is nearly indecent."

Then I was mobbed by my friends. Cap Mason and Talley Short, Chi Min and his brothers—Jo and Kee Min. I was surprised to see Slim Albright and Judd Jenkins, Pat Desmond, Gabe McCoy and two of his brothers, Samuel and Micah, Vance Brand, and Don Patricio. All were armed to the teeth. Then I saw Patrick in the rope corral. He had smelled me, and heard my voice; he was acting out his joy. I went to him and he took my miners hat in his teeth and tossed it away. Barney slipped me a piece of sugar. When I gave it to him—Pat shook himself all over, and ran excitedly around the corral scattering the other horses and mules.

David Cook came up and said, "It looks like you have solved the case of the kidnapped people," and he introduced me to the four agents he had with him.

"It's better than that, David. Don Patricio, I have good news for you and Teresa, Your brother Sebastian Tomas is alive and well. There were ten prisoners. Sebastian was Tom # 1, and I was Mudd # 10. Sebastian was captured at the mine trying to find his brother. The guards killed Divers. Sebastian was locked up for months in a tool room until his captors could contact Brand, and find out what to do. Brand couldn't turn him loose. Sebastian knew the truth about the mine. That's when Brand came up with the idea of imprisoning men that got in his way. You won't believe it when you see the inside of the mine. One section of it has been turned into a prison."

"Let me introduce you to my friend, a fellow prisoner Mule # 9. His name is Haley G. Mulligan. He was the ramrod for one of Brand's ranches. He found out too much, and he was imprisoned the day before I arrived in a prison wagon—bars and all."

"This man is Joseph Ratkowski, as known as Rat # 6. He was older than the rest of us. His family emigrated here from Poland. His father and mother homesteaded near Denver, and proceeded to develop an exceedingly productive Produce Farm, which found a ready market in Denver. When his father died, Joe inherited the farm, and six younger brothers and sisters to raise. He refused to sell to Brand, and Brand had him kidnapped. Brand now owns the farm, and Joe doesn't know where his family is?"

"I do," David Cook interrupted, "His older brother John works for me as a detective, and he takes care of the family."

"Thank God," Joe exclaimed, and added, "thank you, Mr. Cook."

I circulated around thanking all my friends for coming to my aid. Then I went back to see Cook. It was full daylight now. I took the papers out of my pocket that I had found in the mine, and gave them to Cook. "I think you, and I, and Don Patricio's family should take a few moments and check these papers," and I explained how I had found them.

Don Patricio became agitated when he saw the papers. His eyes filled with tears as he verified that these were the papers that Joaquim had taken with him to Denver.

I said to Cook. "What do we do now? I'll be damned if I'll leave those men imprisoned, while we go back to get a warrant."

David Cook grinned and said, "Cool off, Matt. We have proof that men are being held prisoner here. We also have proof of murder. I also took the precaution of getting a Federal Search Warrant based on Don Patricio's complaint to me as Sheriff of Denver County."

I'm not angry, Sheriff, just determined." I asked him, "How many of Brand's men have you spotted outside the mine?"

"We have seen more than a dozen men, Matt. I was surprised to see so many men conducting a search in such a remote area. In addition there are ten men or more posted as guards on the outside of the mine. The bunk house and mess hall will bunk and feed close to a hundred men. Of course, twenty or thirty of them may be miners. There is no doubt in my mind that the men out searching were looking for you three men?"

"So what are your plans, Sheriff Cook," I asked.

"We don't have much choice, Matt. I'll take my four men and proceed to the mine and force entry if necessary and free your friends."

"If you do Sheriff, you will be shot to pieces. These men are outlaws. They have been here a long time and have had a lot of time to figure out their defenses. I think you will find that at least half of those men will be staked out in strategic points, and you will be under constant sniper fire. When I arrived, I saw bunkers with guards in them that looked mighty efficient. You should see the inside. This mine and its defenses have been well planned. Your idea would most likely work under ordinary circumstances. No doubt you have used it before, but I ask you—how many of Brand's men have you arrested in Denver?

"What does that have to do with anything," Cook asked—a bit on the defensive.

"You didn't answer my question. How many?"

"None! Cotton Brand doesn't run the usual band of outlaws inside town. He's too smart for that."

"Exactly! You know, for a man that had created so much havoc in the City of Denver, I'll bet that you have no idea of what he even looks like?"

Vance Brand was standing near, and he answered, "My brother Cotton is very ordinary looking. He purchased a house in North Denver, but he is never home. I have only seen him once since he moved here from Texas. He never married, and has always been a very peaceful person. Have you ever seen him, Sheriff?"

"No, I never have. The descriptions I get are all the same. He is a quite ordinary looking man that could pass us on the street, and even if we knew him, we could pass him by. He has brown hair."

"That rang a bell," I declared, jumping to my feet. "All this time I thought he was named Cotton because he was white haired," I turned to Vance Brand and asked, "Where did he get the name of Cotton, Vance?"

"It's a nick name he was saddled with over in Texas, Matthew. He was the Cotton King in the Southern Plains where we lived. Robert Nathanial Brand is his real name. He was a kind, hard working farmer. His brothers and nephews kept involving him in feuds with other families. His brother Chance saw that he couldn't stop the feuds, so he decided to profit from them. Any killing done was thought up and carried out by Chance, or his sons, or by my brothers. For some reason Cotton always got the blame. Our brother Chance ran a gang of killers. I guarantee you, if there was any killing done—it was done by Chance. He is the second oldest brother, but he has always been the dominant one in the family."

"Where does Chance live, Vance," Cook asked? "I've heard of him, but nothing derogatory."

"He owns a cattle ranch east of Denver. He and his wife Mercedes run it. She is quite a rider and cattlewoman. She is a worse tomboy than Teresa and Lucy—if you can believe that? They have just one living son, Tyrel." He laughed and added, "Mercedes is quite eccentric. When she wears her skorts, she still insists on wearing her lady's hat."

"Okay! Enough on the Brands for now," Sheriff Cook exclaimed. "what were you saying, Matt?"

"May I suggest that you first allow my two Kickapoo Indian friends to scout for you? They will take Jack with them. When they come back they will tell you where, and how many outlaws you have to contend with. Jon can hit a running Antelope at four-hundred yards. A lot of us are crack shots. We can incapacitate most of them before we get close enough for them to shoot at us. What do you think?"

"I should have had you with me when I first took over the Colorado Cavalry. It's a good plan, Matt; will you ask your friends to assist us?"

Buffalo and Four Hands nodded all through Cook's request. When he finished they simply said, "We go!"

I said to Jack, as Buffalo and Four Hands rode off—"Jack, scout."

Jack cocked an eye at me and Buffalo called, "Jack". He took off running and Buffalo patted his saddle. Jack jumped up, and Buffalo settled him down in front of him, and they rode off.

David Cook watched, and as they rode off—he scratched his head and said with a laugh, "Maybe I should have hired that dog instead of you and Jon?"

Jon murmured to me, "Maybe you and I should have done that scouting?"

I shook my head, "I don't think so. We're good, but they are better. I should have checked to see if they had a pair of binoculars."

"Don't worry. I gave them both a pair before we started looking for you."

"How soon were you on my trail?"

"We checked all the obvious things in Denver. David Cook was a real help. He sent all of his unassigned agents into Denver checking every dive and every possible suspect. Two weeks later, when we determined that you weren't in Denver, Jon took Jack and began to circling the town. From the beginning, I never believed that whoever kidnapped you would keep you in town, but we had to exhaust that possibility. Too many things could go wrong. Jack picked up your scent a few days later. We were lucky it hadn't rained. I went back and told Barney to get your friends together, and I would leave a trail for them to follow. Within three days they were all assembled, and with Don Patricio's help, they acquired a buckboard, and a string of horses and Mules all loaded with supplies. Then they strung out following my trail. From the start we began seeing peanut shells. After awhile they were the only trail we could pick up. That's mighty rough country out there. Don Patricio tried to keep Teresa at home, but she said something to him, and he never said another word. By the way, Barney thought you might need these, and he handed me a duplicate set of my Russian revolvers and holsters. I strapped them on and checked the pistols. To me they were a thing of beauty.

I said, "Thanks, David, if I had a hat now, My cup would runneth over."

Teresa came walking up just as I spoke. She whipped a black, flat-crowned Stetson from behind her and said, "Your every wish is my command. I love your hat pin," she declared with an impish grin, and with a tinkling laugh she slipped away. I started to put the hat on and something gleamed. Stuck through the front of the hat crosswise was a sparkling hat pin. The decorative piece was a beautifully wrought, deep-red, chunk of garnet. Was this one of hers? Then it hit me. Teresa had picked up my miner's hat and found the pin from the mine. Bless her, she had cleaned and polished it. I left it in the hat—it was safe for now.

Later that evening, our Kickapoo friends returned. They had crawled the last half mile to get close enough to the mine to detect its defenses. There was a trickle of blood running down Four Hands ear. Their clothes depicted the rough passage they had taken. Jack's tongue lolled from the corner of his mouth. When we gathered to hear the scout's report, he dropped gratefully at my feet and went to sleep.

When we were all assembled Four Hands spoke, "Sheriff, wise man. He listen. Man Who Flies Like a Bird spoke wisely." The Indian took a leafy branch, and scoured a clean space on the sandy terrain. "Here mine," and as he spoke he drew a picture in the sand of that which he spoke. "Above mine is two men with Gun that spits fire, Gun guarded by man on each side, and he marked the positions. Two men guard back of mine. Three men guard path to mine on each side—here and here. All men in little houses dug into ground made of logs. Top covered with grass—hard to see. Little houses open all around—so can see," and he made a circle with his finger above his head. Big sign at both ends of path. Signs say, Go Away or We Shoot. I got too close, and man shoot," and he pointed to a bloody crease on his scalp.

"That's one hell of a good job," Cook said in all sincerity, "our thanks to Buffalo and Four Hands." Marshall Desmond and Barney O'Shannon both have a bout of fever, and I suggested they guard the camp, but they are both here and ready for duty. Cook stepped behind the sand map and asked, "Matt, would you and Jon and Gabe step over here with me, and I would like my detectives to move over here where we can all see. You three men and my four men are all crack shots. Unless someone has a better plan, I think we should start off with what Matt suggested. We need to take out these twelve men with long range rifle fire before we make our final assault. Matt, would you, Jon, and Gabe take out the Gatling Gun? We can't take any chances of just wounding those two men. If they get that gun into operation, they could chew us up. To be safe, the gun itself must remain dysfunctional, once the men are taken out. The rest of the men have to be put out of action, and killed only if necessary. The men in our group will have to block anyone from coming out of this end of the bunkhouse. With all these guards, there have to be more men to relieve them. There may be twenty or thirty men or more in there. We could have our hands full. Once all the outlaws are apprehended, or killed, we will assemble on both sides of the mine entrance and decide our nest step. Remember this—other than my instructions regarding the Gatling Gun—we are the law. We are here to arrest these men if possible—at the same time, I am not asking any man to risk his life. Once I have ordered these men to put down their weapons—your lives come first—their's last. Are there any questions? Are there any suggestions?"

"Sheriff Cook, do you think the rest of us came here as decorations," Teresa asked. "We insist on being included in your plans." There was a loud chorus of approval.

Cook laughed, "Oh, believe me. I have duties for all of you. As for you, Miss Teresa, you are designated Doctor and Nurse for anyone that gets hurt, and I hope the three Chinese gentlemen will join you as litter bearers and assistants. Don't forget the outlaws may need medical attention, and we certainly can't neglect that unpleasant duty. Remember, treat them as prisoners, and don't take any chances. If they are conscious, have one of your men hold a weapon on the prisoner until you can put the proper restraints on them. Once treated, place them under guard. I'll give you some handcuffs to put in your wagon. You can start, Teresa, by treating Four Hand's head."

"Marshal Desmond, will you take the rest of the men and leave now. We will start out in half an hour. Your primary job is to circle around the mine out of their sight, and post at least four crack shots behind the bunkhouse. If any one tries to get out, they must be stopped. There are twelve guards outside and eight men inside the mine that we know of. That means there may be another twenty men in that bunkhouse that are the relief for those twenty men. We have to be careful. There is a complete shift of miners that work the other side of the mine, and from all I've learned so far, they appear to be honest, hard working men that have no idea of what is going on.

Our success depends on our keeping the men in the bunkhouse pinned down. Marshall, you are our cavalry; any action you take will be done as a matter of expediency. Something always goes wrong in the best of well laid plans. If any of the men get out of the bunkhouse, you are to take them out or capture them. Just don't get in the line of fire of our men. You know where they will be. Is that agreeable with you?"

"You are the General—General Cook." Desmond replied with a grin.

Marshall Desmond gathered all of his men around him and using the diagram that Four Hands had drawn in the dirt, he went over his plans with his group of men. He had a good group of men. Barney said to him, "I thought you had a fever?

Desmond grinned and replied, "I see you also have had a miracles cure." In spite of the bravado of the two men, I could tell the fever had taken, and was taking its toll. Their faces were pale, and I saw Desmond's hand shake. I was proud to be one with such men—especially my brother. Ten minutes later the Marshall swore his men in as deputies and pulled out.

Teresa had immediately organized the Chinamen and prepared the buckboard to be used as an ambulance. Chi Lin began barking orders to his brothers in Mandarin. They soon had the medical supplies at hand, and were busy tearing up a white sheet that Teresa had in her sleeping bag. We automatically separated into groups, and Teresa collared Four Hands and fixed his ear in spite of his verbal protests.

When she was finished, Four Hands looked at me and said slyly, "This woman make good wife for Man Who Flies Like a Bird."

I laughed! Teresa flushed—slapped his arm and said, "Shush, or I will bandage your mouth shut, you are supposed to be wounded."

We saddled our horses, and Jon tossed me a Henry carbine and asked, "Do you remember how to load that, or do you want me to show you how?"

I laughed and replied, "You only say that because you know Indian children are never spanked."

Gabe joined us and held up a Sharps .50-130 rifle. That Gatling Gun is my meat. This baby will tear it to pieces."

"Welcome, Gabe. Glad you thought of it," Jon said.

General Cook called out, "Does everyone have extra boxes of rifle and pistol shells?" Does everyone have a full canteen of water—on your person? Four Hands will guide us to where we leave the horses. The Kickapoos will lead each person to their shooting position. When finished, they will report back to Matt and Jon. When you hear three shots the party begins. Any questions? If not—one last thing. All you civilians raise your right hand. We did, and the Sheriff swore us in as deputies. He raised his hand over us and said, "May Almighty God protect us in what we are about to do." We all said "Amen>" A half-hour after Marshall Desmond left, General Cook looked all around and said, "All right men—let's kick some ass."

*   *   *

Teresa flinched when the sound of three well spaced shots sounded the beginning of the battle for the No Name Mine. Amid the sound of the beginning battle, she said to Chi Lin. "Okay, fellows—let's go and get our feet wet."

Jon had a Henry 24" rifle. His three-hundred yard shot took the Gatling Gun ex-Army Sgt. James J. McGuffy right through the bridge of his nose. He was dead before his knees buckled; he fell straight backward. As Jon shot, he breathed a prayer, "God forgive me!"

At our first shot, Buffalo and Four Hands began crawling to their assignment.

The startled face of the Gatling Gun's Sergeant's assistant, Dippy Cartier registered surprise, but the .44 slug from Matt's Henry rifle never allowed his mind to complete the thought that made his head turn. "Matt muttered, "Poor bastard." The bullet severed Dippy Sloan's spine—he never felt a thing—never had a chance to make his peace with his Maker.

Gabe's first shot knocked the Gatling Gun off its stand, his rapid fire, second, third, and fourth shots kicked the weapon all over the gun emplacement.

I said to Jon, "I think you have competition."

Jon said humbly, "Believe me—I'm impressed."

At the rear, left flank emplacement, John Pee Pee McMahon was lucky. Just as Cook's marksman fired, Pee Pee bent to pick up his canteen; a slug from a Winchester 73 rifle caught him in the left shoulder and drove his rotor cup through his shoulder. Brag Tyson, his companion, was more mercifully dealt with. A Winchester 73 .44 cal. rifle lead bullet hit him on the left side of his head, and blew out what few brains he had left.

At the same time Sheriff Cook had crawled down and taken cover in a small rivulet to the side of the three men who were in their shelter defending the left flank of the mine. Cook stuck his head up and yelled. "This is Sheriff Cook. Come out with your hands up, or you will be shot."

Ex British Left'tenent Bradford Sibley McQueen, cashiered for Immoral Conduct Unbecoming an Officer of Her Majesty's Royal

Army yelled, "Go bugger yerself, Sheriff dear," and he and his two men fired a volley at where the Sheriff's head had been.

As if on command, Cook's two detectives popped up from the front, catching the outlaws facing the wrong direction. With two shots they killed ex-Left'tenent McQueen and Killer Jonas McCafferty. Peter Ryan, a seventeen year old, would be bad man, screamed, pissed his pants, threw up his hands and blubbered, "I quit—I quit."

On the right flank the three guards in their shelter swiveled their heads as one to cover the action to their left. That's when Buffalo and Four Hands slithered through the open shelter and dispatched two men with as many knife thrusts. Charlie Josephen and Nate Baker died with hardly a whimper. Goldie Koenig, a sadistic women beater, had a brief second's warning. He whipped around only to meet Buffalo's knife as it plunged into his solar plexus. Buffalo brought the blade up high—felt the heart—then twisted the knife. Koenig knew he was dying in the second it took him to fall free of the knife. His life flashed before his eyes, his heart emptied itself before he hit the floor. In the fleeting mini-second before he died—like many doomed man facing eternity—he screamed.

Wiping his knife on Koenig's shirt, Buffalo asked Four Hands. "Why Sheriff yell before he shoot?"

Four Hands replied, "Sporting White Man think he must first give bad man chance to kill him."

As Four Hands was speaking, Jon's rifle cracked and Sgt McGuffey's rear guard on the right flank—Jimmy Trueblood—gasped as he was knocked on his back. A clean shot through his right shoulder put him out of action. He lay moaning clutching his mangled shoulder.

I shot a second later and Robert Smyth, the Sgt.'s companion, and the last rear guard, jumped up and screamed holding his shoulder. "Jon," I complained, "I never was as good of shot as you, but maybe that fellow will live long enough now to make new friends in prison?"

"My guy isn't dead," Jon protested. I shot him in the shoulder. He went down because I meant it—not like that half-hearted shot you made."

Gabe swung his Sharps .45 to cover the bunkhouse just in time to catch the first outlaw bursting through the door with a rifle in his hand. The Sharps bullet picked the man up and threw him back to where his dead body blocked the door. Gabe shot again through the open door, and a man screamed. A rifle barrel appeared and shoved the dead man out of the door. Gabe shot through the wall where the man should be; he was rewarded with another yell of pain. The door slammed shut, and Gabe's fourth shot drilled right through the center of the door. The door remained closed.

Jon and I joined in by placing shots just inside of each side wall. The shots went through the board walls, and kept any brave men from trying to get out of the windows. We heard several shots from the rear of the bunk-house, and knew that Desmond's men were doing their share. A white flag was stuck out the front door, and Sheriff Cook yelled. "Take off your gun belts—throw down your rifles. Come out the front door one at a time—slowly now." The outlaws came out slowly. Most of them were wearing just their pants, some had boots on, but it looked like the war on the outside was won. Desmond's men came in from the right rear and took the men into custody.

We cautiously assembled on both sides of the entrance to the mine. The men inside could see us from within the mine better than we could see them, so we kept to each side of the entrance. So far, we had not seen any activity from the entrance, nor did anyone fire at us from inside the mine.

Cook's face was pale as he came up. He said, "I'll never get used to having to kill or be killed." He turned to one of his detectives and said, "Fred, Would you go up to our cavalry and ask Desmond to check and see if there are any of the men in their holes left alive. If so, collect them here at the entrance, put a guard on them and attend to Miss Teresa's welfare. After we go in, I will assign two of my men inside as guards."

The Sheriff's men collected around him, and Jon, Gabe, Buffalo and Four Hands were loosely assembled around me. I looked around for Don Patricio—spotted him and motioned him to join us. Before we entered the mine Sheriff Cook turned to me and asked, "What can we expect inside, Matt?"

"There are two sections," I replied. "There is a tunnel to our right and a shaft under the A-Frame to levels down below. The tunnel that goes straight ahead is the prison complex. The men, other than the prisoners, are supposed to be regular miners. They should all be in the tunnel on the right and also in the levels below. If so, they should be no trouble. Until we know for sure, I suggest we approach, or let them approach with caution."

Cook said to the guards, "If any miners come along, check them for arms. Then order them to sit down by the Tool Shack over there, and stay there until we get back. Shawn you and your men lead the way."

I laughed and said, "I will, Sheriff, right after we open the Tool Shack, and I issue you Miner's helmets equipped with carbide lamps, and I show you how to use them. Don't forget it gets mighty dark in there."

"Save yerselves the trouble," Amos called out. "We ain't gonna fight no damn army." So saying, Amos came walking out of the tunnel with his hands in the air followed by his seven men with their hands held high. Sheriff Cook and his men checked them carefully for hidden weapons and began cuffing them.

I walked up to Amos and asked, "Where's Dutch, Amos?"

"He's the foreman here. I ain't got no idea where he is"

"Where are the prisoners, Amos?"

"What prisoners are you talking about, Buster?"

I eyes him patiently and replied, "The seven men that you were guarding when I left here yesterday, Amos.

"I ain't seen you before in my life, buster. We ain't got no prisoners here—just miners.

I knew Sheriff Cook had heard every word. I had seven friends whose lives Amos did not hold as dear as I did. I called out. "Sheriff, would you please take those prisoners outside. They are beginning to stink up the place."

In response, without a word, the Sheriff and his men began herding the men toward the entrance, Amos started to fall in with them. I pulled out my Russian .44, cocked it and stuck it on the end of his nose and said, "Not you, buster." I called out and asked, "Have you got all the prisoners we captured with you, Sheriff?"

"Sure do, Matthew. Let me know if you find any more."

"Amos," I do declare, You must be getting feebleminded. First, I want to introduce you to Don Patricio. He is the older brother of Tom # 1. If all else fails, he has asked me to turn you over to him, which, I promised to do. Have you forgotten that little conversation you and I had four months ago when I first met you?" I grabbed him by the throat and raised him to his toes. "Now I'm going to relax a minute, while you cogitate and rethink your rather tenuous position. Then I am going to give you one—only one chance—to reflect on what you say. Oh—by the way—my friends here would clear the mine first, and then go outside so they could tell everyone that there were only seven—not eight outlaws that gave themselves up to the good Sheriff." I turned to my companions and asked them. "How many prisoners did you men see?"

They answered in unison—"Seven!"

"You see what I mean?" And I gave him a little shake to jog his memory. "Now I am going to set you down; I sincerely hope that what I hear you say will be, "Mr. Mudd, I made a terrible mistake. The seven prisoners are safe. I'll quit screwing around; making you angry, and tell you where they are. Do you think you can remember all that?" I gave his throat a near mortal squeeze and turned him loose.

He fell to the ground breathing hoarsely, and began blubbering, "Mr. Mudd, I made a terrible mistake. The seven prisoners are safe; I'll quit screwing around; making you angry. They're tied up in the Superintendent's office, I'll show you," he cried scrambling to his feet. I shoved him in the direction of the Super's office. I kicked the door open, and there, sure enough, were the prisoners—all tied up and gagged. Buffalo took Amos by the scruff of the neck, and held him.

"Estabian! The Don called out excitedly, and he rushed to him and cut him loose. Don Patricio clasped him to his breast; exploding in sobs and thanking God. Estabian was too overcome with emotion to speak. After we cut the rest of the men loose, they all crowded around me—hugging and trying to kiss me on the cheeks and venting their thanks.

The one man I was surprised to see all tied up was Dutch; he had been shot in the shoulder. He shook my hand, and I said, "I have a feeling—and I pointed to his shoulder, that is a result of the shot I heard when we were making our escape."

"Amos started to shoot Shaw. I grabbed the gun; it went off, but it stopped anyone else from getting killed."

"You stick with me until this is over, okay?" Dutch nodded his head in assent.

I yelled above the uproar, "How would you men like some sunshine and fresh air?"

They cheered and picked me up bodily and rushed for the entrance yelling, "Hip, Hip, Hooray, for Mudd # 10, over and over." It was a gratifying moment when we charged out of the mine into the bright sunshine and fresh air. The seven men nearly dropped me when the bright sunlight nearly blinded them, but I managed to regain my feet.

Teresa screamed with excitement when she saw her Uncle Estabian. She threw herself into his arms. He was still too filled with emotion to speak. When he finally got control of himself, he called out and said, "We all have so much for which to be grateful. In gratitude let us kneel and thank Almighty God for his Infinite Mercy." Estabian led us in saying the Our Father, the Hail Mary, and the Gloria Patria.

Afterwards, I asked Teresa to tend to Dutch' shoulder. When he was taken care of, I murmured to Jon, and he left. A minute later he returned with Vance Brand. I said, "Vance, I have someone I want you to meet," and I stepped from in front of Dutch. Vance exclaimed, "Cotton! What in the hell are you doing here?"

"Why, I live here, Vance. I have ever since I opened the mine. Actually, the man I hired as Superintendent, James Leverton, opened the mine. He had his men teach me how to mine. He and Chance nearly came to blows when he learned that Chance had contracted with the State of Colorado for prison labor. Chance had ordered the Superintendent to guard the men as prisoners and to make them work. He was ready to quit. I settled the problem by creating two operations. I took charge of the prisoners in a separate section of the mine. The men Chance hired as guards were too rough with the prisoners, so I had to take over as foreman, and I saw to it that they were treated fairly."

"Thank you for freeing me, and taking these rogue guards into custody. But now I need some answers. Why did you have to shoot the guards that were guarding the mine? Has the world gone crazy? Were the guards outside in on a plot to seize the mine? I just don't understand."

"The State of Colorado and the Federal Government has that right, Mr. Brand. I'm Sheriff Cook of Denver County. I have a Federal Warrant to search these premises for men that have been reported kidnapped and held here. Your guards resisted—we had to shoot some of them. The men held with you in that shack claim to have been kidnapped including the men you know as Mudd # 10, Mule # 9, and Rat # 6. What do you have to say to their charges?"

Dutch was completely confused, but before he could speak up again; Sheriff Cook called Estabian over and asked Dutch, "This man came up here looking for his brother with one of my detectives—John Divers. Estabian says one of your guards killed Divers, and imprisoned him on August 30, 1872."

Dutch shrugged and replied, "I agree that the first time I saw Tom #1 was about the end of August 1872. My brother Chance made all the arrangements in Denver with the authorities to transport him here. Chance told me that he had been incarcerated by a legal Court of Law. He said that our mine would be paid to house and guard prisoners. They were to work sixteen hours a day. I didn't like the idea. I had a serious argument over the issue with Chance." He turned to his brother Vance and said, "You know how bull-headed Chance can be when he has a wild-haired scheme. He and I argue about it every time he comes up here."

"All I could do, after Chance left, was to make sure that the men were not mistreated. But that damned Amos was a mean son of a bitch, and I couldn't be everywhere at once. I helped the prisoners every way I could. We all ate the same food. With time off for two meals, I gradually cut their work load down to twelve hours a day. The mine Superintendent has the legal papers on the men. That's all

I know. I can testify that all the men you mentioned were all good workers. I never heard of Divers."

Cook called each of the prisoners over to see if any of them had ever seen Dutch before they were imprisoned. None of us had even seen him before we were transported to the mine.

I said to Cook, "Why don't the four of us take Dutch into the Super's office and interview him privately. There's a lot here we don't know about."

A few minutes later, we seated ourselves, and Sheriff Cook proceeded to interrogate Dutch. Cook said, "Dutch, Please state your name and address."

Dutch replied, "I've lived here since July of 1871, that's when I opened the mine. My name is Robert Nathanial Brand. Some people call me Cotton. The miners that taught me how to mine called me Dutch. I've gone by that first name since about the time the mine opened.

Who owns this mine, Dutch?"

"My brother Chance and I are partners. I used my money to open the mine. I run the mine and Chance handles all my business arrangements. It costs a ton of money to open a mine, that's why Chance needed me. I gave Chance my Power of Attorney to act for me. Vance here knows I am not good at business stuff. I was a rancher before we all left Texas. I don't fit in well with city folk."

"How did you make your strike?"

"My what?"

"How did you locate the mine?"

"I didn't. Chance did."

"How do you and your brother split up the profits?"

"We share fifty-fifty after expenses. Every month my share is deposited to the Colorado Savings Bank. It's located at 401 Blake Street in Denver."

Cook was getting exasperated. He said peevishly, "In my opinion, for an intelligent man—you have allowed yourself to be manipulated like a two-year old child."

Cotton Brand was an extremely well controlled man. He looked Cook in the eye and retorted, "Did you know, Mr. Cook that you are an insolent Son of a Bitch? I like to think of myself, as a gentleman, perhaps not as well versed as some, but never the less—a gentleman. I have patiently answered all your questions and cooperated with you trying to clear up this abominable mess the best I could. For my thanks—you insult me—my ignorance of the situation does not make me stupid—but your arrogance causes you to act like the rear end of a south bound Jackass—in my honest opinion—Sir."

Cook looked pained. Then he said sincerely, "I deserved that, Dutch. However, the serious problem I have at hand may have made me over zealous. My most sincere apology, Sir."

"Accepted, and what may that problem be, Mr. Cook?

"Murder, Dutch! I'm afraid your mine was purchased with the blood of two innocent men." Cook turned to me and said, "Matt, will you tell this gentleman what you and Mulligan found when you escaped?"

"Glad to, David. When Mulligan and I escaped through the air vent, we fell through the wall into the caved in discovery shaft that had been initiated by Joaquim Velasco, and his friend, we don't know his name. A third person murdered the two men with a miner's pick after he had blown the entrance shut. That person then dug a thirty-foot tunnel and escaped."

Dutch exclaimed, "Oh my dear God. Those poor men—their poor families." He was bewildered and said sincerely, "Is there anything I can do? What does all this have to do with me?" The horror of the situation was beginning to sink in.

I told him, "Dutch, immediately after the murder, you and your brother hired a crew and opened the mine making a new entrance that your Superintendent recommended. A month or so later Estabian Velasco hired David Cook's Agency to help him find his brother. He and agent John Divers located this mine. While making inquiries Divers was killed by one of your guards. Estabian was locked in the Tool Shed for several months. When he was let out he was told that he had been charged with murder, and would have to work in the mine as punishment. A couple of days later,

Dutch, you were introduced to Estabian, as his civilian foreman, and Amos and other men were assigned as his guards."

Cook looked at the bewildered man and asked, "Dutch, who introduced you to the man you knew as Tom # 1, and to Amos and the other guards?"

Dutch was getting agitated and said, "Chance did, but a couple of the guards were already here. Chance hired them to guard the mine, and the gold shipments."

"That helps a great deal, but as you can see, Dutch," Cook added, "there are still a lot of unanswered questions."

"I've told you all I know. I will have to talk to Chance. Perhaps he can shed some light on the subject."

I looked at David; he threw up his hands in resignation. "Dutch," I said, "You are like an innocent lamb being led to slaughter. Your love for your brother Chance Brand is most commendable, but while you have been isolated in this desolate area we believe your brother Chance has been using your name and committing one crime after another. All ten of the prisoners had trouble with a person called Cotton Brand, and they all ended up here. David can prove some of this now, but it will take a thorough investigation to learn all the details and the extent of your brother's perfidy."

Dutch passed a shaking hand across his brow and exclaimed, "You can't be serious. I don't believe it. Why would he do murder and involve me? If he needed money, I would have given him all I had."

"Greed, Dutch. Everything we have learned points to your brother Chance, as being the main suspect in the murder of the two men that actually discovered this mine. The ten men incarcerated here were all victims of Cotton Brand. That's why I had Vance identify you. However, not one of us ten prisoners identified you as Cotton Brand. Mulligan and I became suspicious, because the guards seemed to be afraid of you. At one time or another one of them would refer to you as Mr. Brand, or would call you Cotton. Nothing added up. It wasn't until Cook and I got our heads together that we were able to partially figure out what has been going on."

Dutch groaned, "What do we do now?"

Cook said I'll leave my four men here to guard the mine and the miners. The Superintendent is a capable, honest man. He will be in charge until the Colorado Authorities can sort out who gets the mine, the money etc. I'm afraid that when we get back, the authorities will most likely freeze all your assets, except for enough money to keep the mine running, until this mess is cleared up. The Super tells me they have a weekly stage service here, so the miners could get recreation in Leadville. That is where we are all headed except for those who wish to return on their own horseflesh. Matt is paying for the transportation of his nine friends back to Denver, where they can get in touch with their own people. I'm sorry, Dutch, but I have to take you into temporary custody until the District Attorney can sort out who is guilty and who is innocent."

Before we leave, Sheriff," Jon said, "Maybe Dutch could tell us the Prison Wagon driver's full name. All we know is he ate a lot of peanuts."

Dutch smiled. His nickname is Goober. He's addicted to peanuts. His name is just as peculiar, His parents named him Happy Moon.

Jon grinned, "Goober in his many trips up the trail paved it with a generous layer of peanut shells. Each time we lost the trail, Jack picked up the Goober trail, and we have him to thank for finding Matt as fast as we did."

. As they walked out the mine entrance, Jon told me and my group of friends. "Before we left Denver three prominent men mysteriously disappeared. Their circumstances were similar to Matt's. Now we know that every time Goober came to a stream that he couldn't cross by himself—six men appeared and helped him. We all think that it is entirely possible that Goober and his six cronies are on their way up here now with those three men. We want to lay an ambush for them and arrest them if we can. Sheriff Cook has approved the idea, but he wants us to set the ambush someplace within a few miles of the mine. Buffalo and Four Hands have agreed to scout down the trail for ten miles, and set up a listening post. They will be able to give us ample warning if Chance Brand's men are spotted."

When we came out of the mine, I was surprised to see that my friends had been busy. The dead men were laid out in a row wrapped in blankets. All the weapons, ammunition, and equipment had been gathered and piled on a wagon. Mulligan, Estabian, and Ratkowski, and the other seven prisoners had gathered together.

I looked at Jon and said, "Well, Sheriff, it looks like you and Jonathon have been busy little bees. Whatever you are planning, count me in."

"We did!" Mulligan said walking up, followed by the rest of the former prisoners. "We elected Pat Desmond to lead us. Don Patricio and Vance Brand are our elder statesmen. We can't get rid of Tom Estabian; he has a score to settle. His pretty niece Teresa refuses to go home without her Daddy and Estabian and someone I'm not allowed to name. Crenshaw and Ratkowski have a real grudge against Goober and his buddies. Cap and Talley say they can't leave their partner here, because he needs a keeper. Slim Albright and Judd Jenkins tell me that cowboys are loyal to the brand, and they hurried to assure me they did not mean Cotton or Chance. Gabe, Samuel, and Micah McCoy claim they are your partners and they are here to make sure you don't break the partnership by getting yourself shot. Chi, Jo, and Kee Min told me they are family—and in China—families always stick together. Then the other prisoners—Crenshaw, Hess, Steiner, Brewer, Hoffer, and Marsh say that they want to serve up a hot-lead sandwich to Chance Brand and his men to show their appreciation for the hospitality they received at the mine. They refuse to leave until the job is done, and so do I. So altogether, we have a small army of thirty-four men that are willing, if need be, to take on the entire Colorado Territory."

"That's great." I agreed. "I suggest that any person that is short of weapons that you help yourselves from our ample stock of weapons stacked on the wagon over yonder. We will see if can round up some of the guard's horses to pass around where needed. Once we are properly equipped, then Marshall Desmond can take charge and try to organize his volunteers into a cohesive fighting force. Just make sure we have plenty of canteens. Jon says we already have pack mules loaded with supplies, so, once we know what to do, we can soon be on our way."

Jon came up to me pleased as Punch. He said, "Hey, Matt. Look at this. I picked up a Sharps .45-120 rifle with a two power sniper's scope."

The rifle was a beauty, but my mind was filled with a jumble of thoughts. Two hours later, we were mounted and ready to go. My mind was still swirling around like a whirlpool.

Jon gave me the outraged look he always gave me when he was about to work me over verbally. He knew me like a book, and was aware I needed something to bring me down to earth. He sized me up and stated empirically so all could hear,

"Matthew Michael O'Shannon, I can't trust you for a second. Here I thought I was your only partner. Now I find that as your partner, I have more partners than I can count, and my family has grown tremendously. Since all of you folks are mostly family or business partners, I now confer upon you all the honorary title as members of the Cherokee Nation."

Everyone cheered and clapped.

Barney said dryly, with his crooked grin, "You kids have had your fun, now let's get on with Posse business."

I called out, "Barney's right, but now you all know why I never let Jon out of my sight. Let's go blot some Brands."

Most everyone chuckled at our nonsense, but posse business was serious business, and we all set too with grim determination.

Buffalo and Four Hands went to Desmond, and after a brief talk, they rode up to me and said, "We go—okay?"

"Be careful, my Kickapoo brothers."

As we gathered to move out, I said to Teresa with an inviting smile "Come ride with me, my little Cherub, your father and brother have promised to ride along as chaperons." She gave me her long eyelashes and said, "I would be delighted to ride with The Man Who Flies like a Bird and Cackles like a Hen."

Desmond led us down the trail for an hour, before he found the ideal place for an ambush. He was a meticulous man about the safety of his men and horses. Just behind the ambush site, he found a gentle swell where the horses could be hobbled and staked out on a long leash so they could eat and relax. He added a rope corral and assigned Teresa with her medical group and their equipped wagon to a place behind the Posse in the shelter of the same cover as the horses. Four people to care for the wounded and—or—four rifles to protect the horses. There were still Arapahoe and Utes of the Shoshonean Tribe in the area to contend with. The Marshall was checking the position of every man when we left.

Desmond had agreed that after the Kickapoos returned that the four of us would return down the trail. When the men following the wagon passed us—we would follow them and hit them from behind when Desmond sprang his ambush. And also, if needed, we would prevent the outlaws from fleeing from the ambush.

Two hours later Buffalo and Four Hands galloped up and Four Hands told Desmond, "Wagon come—one hour—no see men following wagon."

Jon, and I and our Indian allies took our leave, and started down the trail. I asked Jon, "Desmond said there were Indian pony tracks back there—did you see them."

He laughed and replied, "I guess we all did except you. You were too busy romancing Teresa to see anything except stars. Desmond laughed when I told him about the tracks. He chided me, 'What took you so long? Gabe, and the two Kickapoos, told me about the tracks as soon as we got here.' It seems we have about twenty Kiowa on a raiding party. Desmond warned us to be careful. He says the Kiowa have the reputation of being the best light cavalry in the world. He warned all of us that the Kiowa have killed more white people than all the other Plain's Tribes put together."

I was instantly concerned about Teresa's safety. "With twenty Kiowa running loose, why the hell did Desmond leave Teresa with the horses? There is only Chi Min and his brothers to protect her."

"Easy doe's it, Matt," Jon cautioned. "Desmond put Judd Jenkins and Slim Albright in charge of our little ramuda; they been over the hill and down the trail a few times. As an extra precaution, he is positioning Barney, Micah, Samuel and Hoffer in the rocks above the ambush area. From there they can cover both the trail and the horses. That's ten rifles in the hands of people that know how to use them. Teresa can take care of herself when it comes to slinging lead. She killed at least three Arapaho in that last scrape. Have a little confidence in your own people."

I knew he was right, but I couldn't help but wonder how he would feel if Patricia McCafferty was back there. My senses were fully alert, but I was not getting any negative vibes that I would ordinarily have if any of my family was in danger; and in my mind and heart—Teresa was definitely family. I tried to put the matter out of my mind. We had enough problems on hand, as we headed for our appointment with fate and its fickle finger.

Desmond had agreed that Ron and I, and the two Kickapoos, could ride down the trail a mile or so and stake out in the trees. After the outlaws past us, we were to fall in behind them to cut them off if they turned tail and ran. I had a bad feeling. If we were right and these men were on their way, for some reason I didn't think it was going to be as cut and dried as it had been previously. My senses were literally screaming at me. I told my friends. "My senses have me on edge. Be careful—I think we may run into a hornet's nest."

Four Hands grunted and commented, "We hear Man Who Sees Tomorrow. We have big battle—that is good. No time to be careful—we make war."

I grinned at Jon, and shook my head—he just smiled. We had not gone far when Buffalo suddenly swung off the trail and said, "Here—good place to wait," and without our acknowledgment began looking for a place to hide the horses. He was right. It was perfect. No doubt he had picked the place previously. Ten minutes later we heard a man cursing his mules, and I recognized Goober's voice. We had been lucky. Ron's intuition about the three men had been right on the money. A few minutes later Goober passed us—still cursing the mules, and making good time. He hadn't changed a bit—big, tough, and mean, but I had to admit—fair. There were four prisoners—not three in the wagon—and they looked as wretched, as I had on my way to my unknown fate. But fate had been kind to me—I hoped fate would be just as kind to the four men, as I saw the wagon pass out of sight up the trail. The question was—just how far back were his helpers riding?"

Goober was evidently anxious to reach the end of the trail. He was not the only one. He had just rounded a bend when Buffalo announced, "They come!"

"Eight—There were eight men—not six. I noted their mounts were some of the best horseflesh man could buy. These were outlaw horses—horses that had bottom to carry a wanted man a long way fast. Behind them a Mexican peon led four pack horses whose packs hung slack. The men had a mean, hungry look. They were the hawks of the human race. Their eyes were wary and constantly checking the terrain about them. Once undercover, we had broken off branches and brushed away the tracks of our horses. The settling dust had done the rest. We each held our animals close—ready to pinch off their nostrils if they started to snort a greeting. When they disappeared from sight, we made ready to follow them, when Buffalo hissed—we stopped dead in our tracks, and the Kickapoo whispered, "Wait." Jon and I had heard it too—an iron horseshoe striking rock. Was it from up the trail, or were there more men coming? I pointed down trail; Jon shook his head in agreement. Minutes later we had our answer.

Four additional lean, hard-looking men rode into sight and everyone looked to me. Should we take them on, or were there more men behind them? I couldn't allow more men up the trail to support those who had already gone ahead. If we shot now—it could warn the eight men that had gone on ahead. We had to take the risk. As the men passed us, I mounted, and everyone followed suit. Just then the distant thunder of guns sounded from up the trail, and I barked, "Now—and I yelled as we thundered out behind the men, "This is the law—put up your hands."

In response to the firing—the outlaws stopped dead in their tracks. They reacted instantly to my command; as one—the men slapped leather, drawing their pistols, as they wheeled their horses about. As their weapons came up two saddles were suddenly emptied as our four pistols filled the air with hot lead. One man was knocked backward, caught his balance and got off a hasty shot before he fell. The fourth man slumped forward in his saddle, his pistol fell from his hand; he grabbed the saddle horn to stay seated. Then we were among them; Jon and I jumped down and covered the downed men. Buffalo shoved the one man from his saddle; Four Hands leaped down beside the man that had just fallen. It was over that quick. Buffalo remounted and kept checking the trail. The first two men were hard hit, but might live to hang. The third man died cursing us through his smashed teeth. The fourth man snarled, "Where the hell did yu'all come from?" The one hasty shot fired had zipped through my right ear leaving a neat hole—it was bleeding profusely. The man exclaimed heatedly, "I don't see no badges."

"Pat Desmond has the only badge we need." I snapped.

"Desmond, hell—no wonder I feel like I ran into a hornet's nest."

The sound of the firing from up the trail petered out—and it was suddenly deathly still. Buffalo grabbed the reins of my horse and led him to me. Pat was spooked by the shooting and the smell of blood. "Easy, old fellow," I said and petted him and gave him a piece of sugar. I said, "I think we better load these fellows on their horses, and check up on the rest of our folks."

Pat Desmond limped out to meet us when we rode up. "We had us quite a ruckus. There were eight of them, and they were the deadliest bunch I ever ran into."

"You're limping," I said, "you hit bad?"

"Nothing bad, that bastard Colson grazed my foot."

"What about Goober?

"He war'nt no trouble. Crenshaw ran out and caught up the mule's reins. Mulligan was on Goober before he could let go the reins. As you know Goober is a big man. Mulligan picked him up off his seat and threw him fifteen feet through the air. When he hit he was looking into the muzzle of Mule's .45 colt revolver. While Mule and Crenshaw tied and gagged Goober and hid the wagon, Ratkowski and I were smoothing out the signs of the wagon being run off the road, when Barney called down the slope, "Men coming."

We hid the brush and ducked out of sight. When I had cover, I looked and coming up the trail were eight of the toughest looking hombres I've seen in a coon's age. They were as jittery as a coyote trying to steal a cougar's kill. The lead man was Mark Colson. A cold blooded killer wanted in three States that I know of. He was a cagy one. I swear—the devil protects his own. Colson sensed the trap, his eagle eye spotted the wagon rut we didn't have time to brush out; he drew his gun, yelled "Ambush," and fired right at me. I nailed him dead center. Four of them, drew their pistols and tried to escape up the trail. Just around the curve we had hauled a dead tree onto the trail, I had two men, Gabe and Estabian posted there to prevent any men from escaping. There was a passel of shooting; later, when I could, I checked and all four were down. Two were dead and Bull Rousch and his brother Mike were seriously wounded. Gabe was hit in the left shoulder and Estabian caught one in the leg, but they had the situation well in hand. The posse opened up on the rest of the outlaws, only one man, Tod Joslyn, had the sense to throw up his hands; the rest died with their boots on."

I went to the prison wagon. The four men looked at me fearfully. I told them. "Relax, Gentleman. Marshal Desmond and Sheriff Cook are ramroding this outfit. You are free men as soon as I find that rascal Goober." I heard a muffled roar and behind a bush I found Goober tied up like a fat hog on the way to the slaughter house. When I took off his gag, Goober let out a roar of rage, I barked, "Shut your mouth, Goober."

He looked up; the shock of seeing me rendered him speechless. The key to the wagon was around his neck. I released the prisoners—picked Goober up bodily and threw him into the prison wagon and locked the door. I told Goober, "The same rules you gave me and these men apply to you, Mr. Happy Moon. Kidnapping should get you life. Let's see how 'Happy' you can be while we transport you to jail in Leadville."

Teresa had her hands full with the serious wounds of the shot up outlaws, but was valiant in her effort to aid the injured men. Chi Min proved to be as dedicated as Teresa. Between the two of them, aided by Chi Lin's brothers, they saved the lives of the badly hurt men. When she was treating her Uncle Estabian's leg he yelped with pain. Teresa teased him saying. "Oh did I hurt the little bambino, I'm so sorry."

Estabian laughed and declared, "Hurt me all you want, my beautiful niece, for today I'm a free man."

All the wounded men were housed in the bunkhouse in which the guards had been quartered. The dead outlaws were given a Christian burial. Some of the kidnapped men, sore and bruised from riding in the prison cart, preferred riding the dead men's horses to Leadville than riding the stagecoach. Sheriff Cook had finally obtained the services of a Doctor from Leadville. He mended the torn flesh of the outlaws from the gunfight at the mine. The doctor went right to work on those we carried in and commended Teresa and Chi Lin for their efforts to save the men. In spite of their work, one of the men died from loss of blood.

James Leverton, the superintendent of the mine, was not only a good man, but he was also an efficient one. He assigned eight of his miners to remove the dead bodies from the discovery mine. He went along to verify the find, and to take notes of all that he found. Gabe intended to identify the redheaded man if possible and Don Patricio and his family would remain to escort the body of Joaquim Velasco to Leadville. There the body would be prepared by a mortician in a sealed lead coffin, for shipment to Santa Fe. Once home, the family intended to bury him in the family burial plot in hallowed ground in the Catholic Cemetery. At home, he would receive a Requiem Mass for the dead.

The arrival of a stagecoach in most towns was nearly as exciting as the event of a train arriving at the depot. The arrival of a stage at a mine in the wilderness was a major event. Most of my friends, and all the miners, were eagerly awaiting the stage. Sheriff Cook and Cotton Brand were expecting to begin their trip to Denver on the return stage. Chi Lin came pushing through the crowd to tell Teresa that one of their patients had died. Tears welled in her eyes; she turned to me. I took her in my arms and comforted her. Just as she stepped back and wiped her eyes, we heard the thudding of horse's hooves, the sound of the stagecoach horn, and the shouting of the driver, as the stage came to a grinding halt twenty-feet in front of us.

The driver tied off the reins; climbed down and lowered the doorstep. He opened the coach door. A man stepped out with his head lowered, his face covered by his Stetson. He turned to assist his companion down the steps. The lady had deep auburn hair and when she looked up, I was impressed. However my impression faded, as I detected the hard look on her face, and the stern lines about her mouth and eyes. Gabe was standing beside me, and I heard him gasp as though he had been kicked in the stomach. He grasped my arm and muttered, "Watch yourself."

The man turned; I knew immediately that he was a Brand. For some reason Dutch and Vance were the exceptions. Perhaps they took after their mother's family, but all the Brands with whom I had the misfortune to meet, except Dutch and Vance had that same hawk-like, superior look of the man in front of us. Stepping down behind them was Tyler their son, and behind him were three hard-bitten men that reminded me of Mark Colson, the hard-case gun slinger that Marshall Desmond had killed.

Cook moved up beside me and said, "That's Chance Brand and his wife Mercedes. The kid is Tyler their son, and those hard cases are Chance's men, Skip Banks, Drago Sloan and Whit Ketchem.

Before I could react, Dutch stepped forward and said in his deep, rich voice, "Well, what a pleasant surprise. It's my dear brother, and his lovely wife Mercedes along with their handsome son, Tyler. And who are these gentlemen, dear brother? Don't tell me you need a body-guard?"

My closest friends, recognizing the peril I was in, began filtering slowly through the crowd to get to the front of the throng of men.

Chance stopped short and eyed his brother sharply, "You trying to be funny, Dutch."

"You know better than that, Chance. You've told me a hundred times, I have no sense of humor. I do have a question for you. How come you call me Dutch now? You used to always call me Cotton?"

I saw Chance and his wife stiffen with surprise. His bodyguard sensing trouble began to slowly spread out.

"I wasn't aware that I had, Cotton. Someone called you Dutch; somehow it fit. I've been calling you that for years.".

"Six years to be exact, every since you stumbled on this mine and cut me in for half."

"What the hell does that mean?"

"It means that someone has been using the name Cotton Brand. You sent ten men here saying they were convicts sentenced legally by a Judge in Denver. They all claim that they had trouble with a person calling himself—Cotton Brand. Afterwards, they ended up in here doing time for crimes they never committed. Sheriff Cook has checked the prison records filed here, and they are all fraudulent."

A cunning look came over Chance's face, and he said, "I don't know anything about convicts, Cotton. You're the only Cotton Brand I know of."

Dutch shook his head sorrowfully, "Now you shame both of us with your lies. There is something you don't know about me, Chance. I never signed a legal paper in my life with the name Cotton Brand. As you know, my legal name is Robert Nathanial Brand. All my legal transactions in Colorado and Texas will bear that out. Sheriff Cook has already verified that fact. The Sheriff found that it was you that filled out and filed the mine application. Your handwriting shows you filled in my name as Cotton Brand. When Matthew O'Shannon escaped, he and Mulligan and Ratkowski fell into an old mine. They found two bodies. One was Joaquim Velasco. He had papers on him identifying him, and showing the location of the mine. The other man was red headed, but his wallet did not have his name in it. It did imply that he came from W. VA. That leaves only you to answer the question. Did you murder those two men to get this mine?"

Chance's face went deadly white. There was no way out. He calmly stated, "I admit I did ya wrong, Cotton, and I am sorry as hell. But I swear to God, I never killed those men."

I could see Chance was going to pull his gun. I had seen too many men with that desperate look in their eye, I called out, "Easy doe's it, Chance, I know you didn't kill those men."

Chance's hand quivered over his weapon. I said, "If you want to commit suicide, Chance, go ahead. I looked around me. Twenty guns were pointed at the small group around Chance. If you don't want to see your wife, your son, and your body guard killed, you better let me handle this. His body slumped in resignation. His hand fell away from his weapon. I smiled and shifted my gaze to Mercedes. I commented, "That's a beautiful hat you have on, Mercedes."

She looked at me quizzically, and replied, "Well thank you. Do I know you?"

"If you don't—you should. I spared the life of your son, Tyler."

Chance's jaw set. It wasn't from shock. It was rage. He snarled to Mercedes, from the corner of his mouth, "Careful—that has to be Matt Shannon."

Mercedes' face grew taunt, "If you are that killer Matt Shannon, you killed my sons Prince and Lucas?"

Pat Desmond stepped out and said, "No, Ma'am, he did not. I'm Marshal Desmond, of Pueblo, Colorado. I killed one of your sons for trying to shoot Matt Shannon in the back with a shotgun; my Deputy Gabe McCoy shot the other one." Mercedes gasped when she heard the name Gabe McCoy. "Deputy Matt," Desmond added, "during that same incident shot Kyle Brand for the same despicable reason."

Before Mercedes could get her breath I added;" Mrs. Brand, that's a beautiful hatpin you are wearing."

Exposed, and no longer wearing the label 'lady', she snarled. "My hatpin is none of your damned business."

Ignoring her outburst, I added, "It's garnet isn't it? Like me, you must have been born in January. By the way, I have one just like it," and I pulled the pin from out of the front of my hat and held it up. "I found mine. It was stuck through the neck of your red-headed kinsman. He was lying dead next to Joaquim Velasco, who had a miner's pick stuck in his back."

She screamed, "You son of a bitch, Matthew Shannon, Daddy should of killed you too;" Mercedes arm shot straight out, and I knew I was too late. She was wearing a gambler's mechanical sleeve gun, said to be the fastest draw in the west. Gabe's gun suddenly erupted beside me, and Mercedes was slammed sideways. Her right shoulder blossomed blood. Chance tried to help her, but she knocked his arm away, and she fell on her side. Her knees gradually came up until she was lying in a fetal position. Pitiful sounds began coming from her twitching figure.

Gabe said, "Sorry, Matthew, my twin sister is an evil woman. She left home when we were still very young. She hasn't improved any with age. I have no doubt, as to whom, the red-headed man is in the mine. When the Parson saw the beautiful full head of hair that my twin sister was born with, he named her Jezebel. He said nothing good could come from a woman born with hair like that. He talked her down a lot, and she became just what he had prophesized. When she was fourteen, she ran away with her cousin Aaron—another scraggily red-headed malcontent."

Sheriff Cook, spoke to his men; they picked Mercedes up and carried her to our little makeshift hospital. They handcuffed a suddenly meek Chance, and took him into custody. As they carried Mercedes away, I saw her eyes. They were eyes born in pain, and eyes so filled with mental and physical anguish that they wrenched my heart. The anguish in her eyes reminded me of my own conflict with confession and the Catholic Church.

Mulligan was a devoted Catholic, and a man with rare catechistical skills. He and I and Estabian had become fast friends and being Catholic, we had talked many times during our dull drudgery in the mine about many things—including my conflict with my faith. It was hard to believe that I had left home only a little over a year ago. Like Barney had said—in the west it was often—kill or be killed—. The only man that I had hated and killed was Parson J. D. McCoy. That hate had faded over the past year to just a painful memory. There was no room left in my heart for hate. I had been met with so much love and goodness from so many different people over the past year that the memory of the meanness and evil that I had encountered along the way was now—just a haunting memory. The thoughts of my original quest—was I—a good man—now seemed unimportant. How many times along the route of my trek had I heard someone say to me—you're a good man? That too was not important. With the help of Mulligan, and the friends I had made along the way, I had learned one very valuable lesson. What

people thought could be, and often was important, but it was my
Maker's opinion that really mattered. I hoped someday to hear Him
say the words, "My good and devoted servant—welcome—you are
a good man."

Teresa holstered her peacemaker and said petulantly, "Hey!
Wake up—what are you dreaming up now?"

I pulled Teresa around facing me, and replied, "I do believe
that little scene we just witnessed marked the end of our immediate
troubles. Here I was—standing with you like a big clod thinking,
but not saying, the things that are really important. I have hopes
that this moment is going to be our beginning. I was thinking—if
you want me too—that I would escort you and your family to Santa
Fe. Along the way, I would sweep you off your feet, find a priest,
marry you, and allow you to break me to harness the rest of my life
along with all those beautiful horses that I have stashed in the New
Mexico Territory."

I caught her to me and added, "That is exactly what I was
daydreaming about. But I forgot to include my plans for our having
six sons and six daughters, and at least a thousand prime horses."

"She snuggled up to me and said tartly, "I thought you would
never ask, especially since I've already told my father that I was
going to marry you." But, she added most primly, "Twelve children!
Matthew Michael O'Shannon, I'll have you know, I am not one of
your brood mares. If I have the first six; you can have the next six,
and we'll train at least two-thousand prime riding horses."

Barney snorted and said, "I sure hope those six grow up to be
more mature than Matt and Jon have been. An uncle can only be
expected to handle so much."

Jack jumped to his feet, and looked up expectantly. Teresa
petted him and said, "I have a real surprise for you, Jack. I have the
most beautiful female shepherd. She has one blue eye and her name
is Jill."

I laughed and replied, "We must read the same books. Does
that mean that we are compatible?"

Barney grinned his lopsided grin and said, "It just means I'll have to go along to prove to the priest that you two are sufficiently mentally competent to get married."

Buffalo spoke up, "Uncle no worry. Kickapoo brothers go with Man Who Flies Like a Bird, Man With Arms of Steel, and Man Who Sees Tomorrow. Buffalo, Who Kills Many White Men never kill white man until I see Shawn Nack—Man Who Flies Like a Bird. Now I have killed many bad white men—the visions of my Spirit Guide who gave me my name—all true. Cranshaw man fix gun that spits many bullets. We put it on wagon. Jon, Man With Eyes of an Eagle, has rifle with two eyes, We go—Geronimo come—we make him sorry."

Barney shook his head woefully, rolled his eyes to the heavens and said, "May God have mercy on Geronimo."

THE END OF THE BEGINNING